I0768563

Suggested Reading Music

(Scan with your phone camera)

Game On, Trouble

JAMES TAYLOR

story by JAMES TAYLOR & MARCO SPARKS

For villains and bastards

Table of Contents

Dramatis Personae

The Decedent

The Heirs

The Rest

Lai Saechao .... Second Baseman
JeRay Crawford .... First Baseman
Hamilton Webb ....Executor of RJ's Will
Victoria "Tori" Valentine .... Val's Daughter
Jimmy Figg ....Nerd
Nathaniel Davis .... Bigger Nerd
Asha Chowdhury ....Pixeldrome Employee
Rob Haines .... Pixeldrome Proprietor
Hector Villanova .... Mayor
Lambert ....Private Detective

The Stranger ....A Tall, Dark, and Strangesome Menace (Beware!)

TROUBLE AWAITS...

Chapter One

The Secret Heirloom

BY COURT ORDER, A LEGAL NOTICE WAS POSTED ON THE BACK PAGE of the *Blackbird Times* and ran for two weeks in the waning days of August.

Jenny Valentine never saw it. They don't deliver newspapers in jail.

Heavy footfalls thudded in the hall, getting closer. Keys jangled, and a satisfying metal *clank!* signaled the opening of her cell door. Jenny lay on the cell's lone amenity, a steel slab, and stared at the ceiling, refusing to acknowledge her visitor. Sheriff Lockhart had already tricked her twice before.

A package dropped onto her stomach, forcing all the air out of her lungs.

She gasped. "Asshole!"

"Get dressed," said the sheriff.

Jenny glanced down at the form-fitting orange coverall she'd been stuck in for the past two weeks. A custom order, extra small, just for her. The package in her lap was a plastic bag, stuffed with the outfit she'd been wearing when he arrested her at San Francisco International Airport.

"For real?" she asked.

He tossed a second item into her lap: a copy of the *Blackbird Times*, with a want ad circled on the back page. Jenny read the text, skimming back and forth over the words, evaluating every angle of Mr. Webb's notice. She glanced at her bare wrist, scowled, and finally turned to the sheriff.

"What time is it?" she asked.

"You've got 20 minutes," said Lockhart.

Jenny scrambled to her feet, taking the newspaper and evidence bag, and let Lockhart guide her to a stall with a privacy curtain where she could change. The bastards hadn't even folded her clothes. Her blue jeans looked like they were ironed with a rock.

"Charges dropped?" she asked, pulling on her favorite black top with the three-quarter-length sleeves.

"I wanted obstruction, for planting that bogus murder weapon on Valerie Valentine." Lockhart's voice came from the other side of the curtain.

"But you can't prove it," said Jenny. "Because I was locked up in here when it would have happened."

"I'm more interested in how you got your hands on some of RJ's blood," said Lockhart. "Maybe the same way you beat that BAC test?"

Jenny stepped out of the stall in her rumpled clothes, ignoring his questions. "That haunts you, doesn't it? Good. So the charges are dropped."

"Nope. The JCO's got you for criminal mischief—for setting Val up to get arrested at the storage facility."

"Oh, come on! That wasn't even me, that was Penny and Drew!"

"Your buddy Drew dropped a dime on you," said Lockhart. "Can't imagine why. To make a tedious legal story short, you're on house arrest with an ankle monitor for 60 days. After this thing in Town Square, you can only leave home to go to school. And you gotta pay a $3,000 fine."

At any other time in the past year, three grand would have been couch cushion money for Jenny, who had inherited her father RJ Valentine's $272 million publishing fortune for solving his murder. Except now, with the case against Val tossed, ownership of RJ's estate reverted to escrow, making Jenny a broke-ass teenager again. Mr. Webb had always said that there was a secret contingency in the will if the solution to RJ's murder was voided. This meeting in Town Square must be the contingency.

Lockhart handed her a smaller bag containing her locket, her red diamond ring—*you're not selling that!*—$50 in Euros, her watch, her iPhone, and a stolen poker chip from Schloss Schwarzwald.

"Is Shelly here?" Jenny asked. "Is she pissed?"

Lockhart nodded "yes" to both and pointed toward the station's lobby, where her aunt waited beyond the heavy glass door blocking her exit.

"It was a nice try, Lockhart!" said Jenny, raising her voice. "But they haven't built a cage that could hold Trouble yet!"

She sauntered out, slipping on her locket from the evidence bag— and tripped over her shoelace. She stumbled and slammed headlong into the glass door. "Ow, fuck!"

"Lemme get that," said Lockhart.

He reached under the counter. The door unlocked with a loud *BZZZ!* Jenny exited into the lobby and leveled a glare at her aunt. She'd hardly noticed Shelly's new look at the airport. Fashionable blonde highlights, sun-kissed bronze skin, lipstick in a lustier shade of red than the old Shelly would ever dare wear—oh, it was clear *some people* were enjoying the end of summer vacation.

"Two weeks!" Jenny shouted. "What the hell!?"

"It ought to be longer," said Shelly. "I'm not sensing a lot of contrition here. You were supposed to be ruminating on what you've done."

"Ruminate my balls!"

"You're gonna be 18 before you know it, Valentine," said Lockhart. "And then all of this"—he gestured with the ankle monitor device he was holding to encompass the entire police station—"gets a whole lot less like your dad's goofy books. So you might want to try developing a sense of personal responsibility. A lot of people are dead because of you."

"That's not true!" said Jenny. "I didn't kill Lance or Mr. White. Arty Porter did!"

The sheriff tensed. Shelly grimaced at Jenny.

"What?"

"You're behind the times," said Lockhart. "Arturo Porter is dead."

"Oh. Damn."

You as good as killed Mr. Porter by catching him, said her inner Jenny voice.

I didn't! her inner Trouble voice shouted back.

"How did he die?"

"Officially? Suicide," said Lockhart. "Stabbed himself in the chest up at the hot springs."

"Why 'officially'?"

"It's an election year," he replied. "Mayor Villanova is of the opinion that people don't want to hear about the Stranger anymore. So Arty Porter was the Stranger, and the Stranger is dead. Case closed. Hold still."

He crouched at her feet, fastening the slim device to Jenny's ankle. She pitched her gaze to the ceiling, trying her hardest to stay calm.

"Yes, hang your bell on Trouble. Guess I'll be missing Homecoming *again!*"

At her feet, an electronic beep chimed from her new ankle accessory. Lockhart stood up, his hand casually finding the small of Shelly's back.

"Where's my... uh, cousin?" Jenny asked.

"Kazumi's made a friend in town," said Shelly, using the name her sister Eliza adopted for her disguise as a distant cousin from Okinawa. "Tomorrow's the first day of school, and I didn't think she needed to be here for this."

"I'm not sure that's really for you to decide," said Jenny carefully, keeping her voice low as Lockhart opened the door to the station for them.

"She didn't want to come," Shelly muttered through her teeth. "And I don't blame her, after what you put her through."

"Okay, but you've only heard her side—"

"Chop chop, kiddo," said Lockhart. "Let's go find out how your dad's gonna make all our lives worse."

Jenny followed in a daze, rubbing the Ace of Clubs tattoo on her wrist. *Eliza didn't want to come?* But the game was still afoot. Weren't they in this together?

THE AIR OUTSIDE WAS SWELTERING, EVEN UNDER THE CANOPY OF oak trees which kept the park in Town Square shielded from the sun. Smoke from a wildfire in the foothills had turned the sky a sickly shade of orange-brown, and Jenny's throat was already feeling scratchy. Lockhart finally fucked off to usher some onlookers away, giving Jenny a moment alone with her aunt. They sat on the wooden bench Jenny donated last Valentine's Day.

"How is Drew?" Jenny asked.

"Not great, Jenny," said Shelly. "I suspect he regrets the day you ever darkened his door."

Jenny ran her thumb over the smooth grooves in the wood where fans had carved their initials.

DP

Is that you, Drew?

AAA

ML

DEB + TV

PG

LKO + RJV

"I have been ruminating, you know," said Jenny. "A lot. Don't tell, it'll ruin my reputation."

Shelly tilted her head to challenge the very notion. "And what, pray tell, has passed between those ears?"

"She's always 11 in the books," Jenny said.

Her voice caught—must be the toxic air. Jenny covered her mouth in a coughing fit.

By *she*, they both knew Jenny meant her fictional counterpart. Trouble, the World's Greatest Girl Detective. Star of a dozen junior readers mystery novels that made their author, RJ Valentine, a household name, then a multi-millionaire, then a murder victim. Trouble was Dad's tribute to the daughter he couldn't be there for. A precocious little scamp of a girl who never had to grow up, eternally solving mysteries in the idyllic yet stupidly crime-ridden Blackbird Springs of RJ's imagination.

"Dad wrote *Trouble Eight Days a Week* when I was 11, and nothing since," she said. "Like, that was my guide to life, and I was about to age past her. Maybe he was trying to figure out who an older Trouble would be."

"I can't even begin to articulate the many horrifying things in what you just said," said Shelly.

"That's 'cause you're a hater. The point is, I think she'd be smarter," said Jenny. "Well, not just smarter, but like… steadier. The recklessness would be for show, and she'd always be two steps ahead.

"And people would appreciate her…"

She coughed again, choking on the foul air—and her lingering bitterness.

"That's a nice thought," said Shelly. "Has it ever occurred to you that you don't *have* to model your life after a fictional character your deadbeat dad created to make himself feel better?"

"See? Hater," said Jenny. "But it doesn't matter anymore. I've aged out. I'm a senior now. This is gonna be my year, just watch."

Across the street, little Alicia Aaron—one of the six surviving heirs in Dad's mystery game—was limping up to join them. She didn't look half bad, in an undead sex crime victim sort of way, with her pentagram choker, crimson-red hair, and prosthetic leg. Alicia waved to Sheriff Lockhart.

What is it with those two?

"Shouldn't this criminal be in jail?" shouted Val behind them. "Do

I need to call the judge again, Blake?"

They turned to see Valerie Valentine, the dreaded widow, power-strutting over the park grass in four-inch heels, an evil iced latte dripping condensation in her hand. At her side was that new guy from the class trip, Nilay Nagra.

"Wassup Trouble!" said Nilay.

"She's still a minor, Val," said Lockhart. "I can't keep her in jail forever."

"But she framed me!"

"Prove it!" said Jenny. "Better yet, watch your ass, Val, because—"

"Jenny, keep your damn mouth shut!" Aunt Shelly bit out in Japanese as her phone began to ring.

"Oh, excuse me?" said Val. "English only, please. What's that supposed to mean?"

"I told her to keep her damn mouth shut," said Shelly. "And that goes for you, too, Valerie."

Her aunt and Val exchanged sneering glares before Shelly stepped away to answer her phone.

"Why are *you* here, Nails?" Jenny asked Nilay.

"Mrs. Valentine heard about my little deduction with those thieves at the castle," said Nilay, flashing a shit-eating grin. "If RJ's game is back on, you can't go wrong with a Boy Detective on the payroll."

"*Your* little deduction?!" Jenny said. "I was way ahead of you! If I hadn't disabled their guns—"

"Who says I wasn't accounting for that?" Nilay replied. "The way I see it—"

"Cork it, Nilay," said Val. "What's the deal, Blake? Didn't the original will say we only had a hundred days to solve the mystery? Shouldn't the money automatically go to the Valentine Foundation now?"

"There's some kind of contingency, Mrs. Valentine," said Alicia. "Mr. Webb won't say what, though. At least not to me."

"Even my lawyers couldn't get that part of the will unsealed," said Val. "It's nearly sundown, where the hell is Hamilton? He's late!"

"I still have three minutes," said Hamilton Webb.

"Jesus, you gave me a heart attack!" said Jenny, jumping half out of her seat.

Mr. Webb had a talent for materializing where you least expected him. The tall man with a hawkish nose was the executor of RJ Valentine's will. Just like at the first will reading, he was carrying a bulky leather briefcase.

"Are you *sure* you can't be my lawyer anymore, Mr. Webb?" Jenny whined.

"I'm not even sure if I can be *my* lawyer anymore," said Mr. Webb. "I already had to recuse myself from the charity you wanted to start and—well, your aunt can explain it. Suffice it to say, the estate is whole, the Trouble Foundation is kaput, you're broke, and Lance Ashcroft's parents added a few zeros to their bank account balance in place of a son. But let's leave that to the litigators, we're here to talk about the game."

He grinned tightly behind horn-rimmed glasses, his perfect incisors gleaming golden in the sunset.

"—no, Ma, it's not the same WiFi network anymore!" said Shelly, her voice rising as she dealt with her phone call. "No, it's called 'Onishi House'! The password is 'Peggy Olson'! No spaces or caps… You don't see 'Onishi House'!?" She covered the receiver with her palm and let out an aggrieved sigh. "Blake, I need to deal with this. Can you get her home?"

"You didn't want me to just lock her up again?" said Lockhart.

"Don't tempt me," said Shelly, giving the sheriff an indecent smirk. *Disgusting.*

As Shelly left the park, she passed another arriving heir: statuesque Yvonne Griffin, whose *Blackbird Times* office was right down the street.

"You *do* all read the paper!" She grinned. "I'm touched."

"Let's see," said Mr. Webb. "We're just missing—"

The rev of an engine and screeching tires interrupted him. They all turned to witness an open-top jeep making a tight right off of Broadway and parking in a disabled spot, right in front of the old town hall.

"Ah, there we are," said Mr. Webb.

The driver was the only guy in Blackbird Springs with the gall to illegally park right in front of the sheriff: his muscle-bound son Mason Lockhart. And swinging out of the passenger seat was Jenny's half-brother, Jack Valentine. Tall like his father RJ, and brooding like only a spoiled, handsome teenager could be. Jack scowled at the sight of them all and moved around to the back seat to help someone out.

"Junior, I told you not to bring her!" cried Val. "And letting *him* drive her?!"

Stepping gingerly out with a hand from Jack was Val's identical twin—or, rather, the younger, meaner, alcoholic version of her. Val's daughter from her first marriage, Victoria Valentine.

"She's very persistent, you know," said Jack, faking an insouciant yawn. "Not sure where she could have gotten that from, Mother."

"You need to be resting, Tori," said Val, a hint of real emotion slipping past her cunty facade. "The doctor said so."

Tori regarded her mother behind dark sunglasses, leaning on Jack as they walked to the park bench. Her skin was wan and sickly, and her gait unsteady. She wore a surgical mask to protect herself from the foul air.

It was the first time Jenny had seen Tori since she'd awoken from the coma the Stranger put her in on Valentine's Day. Since she'd awoken, changed her testimony, and helped destroy Jenny's frame job on Val.

"Shouldn't you be in jail?" asked Mason, walking over to Jenny. "I pictured you trading cigarettes for tampons with some 400-pound lesbian named Bertha."

"Shouldn't you be in college?" Jenny replied. "I pictured you getting paddled in a frat house basement by some date rapist named Chet."

"We're on the quarter system," he replied. "And Chet's a good guy, that girl's a liar."

He winked, and Jenny smiled for the first time in two weeks. Mason was an absolute clod and a tool, but he was one of the few people in the world who knew about her secret twin sister, and he'd shown shocking loyalty so far by not telling anyone. Even now, when they couldn't pay him for his silence any longer.

"No Kazumi today?" Jack asked.

Speaking of Danger. Jack almost seemed disappointed. Since when did he care about her fake cousin? Someone's watch beeped. To the west, in the smoky haze, the sun dipped below the horizon.

"Wonderbar!" said Mr. Webb, clapping his hands. "Let's get started."

He set the briefcase on the bench and popped the clasps. It was empty, except for an envelope and a digital recorder. With a twitch of his fingers, a letter opener appeared in Webb's hand. He sliced through the envelope seal, slid something small and golden from it into his palm, and took out a single page of creamy Valentine Manor stationery.

"Addendum!" Mr. Webb announced, reading the letter. "I, Jonathan Valentine, being of sound mind and body, etcetera etcetera, include these additional instructions, to be followed if the first accepted solution to my murder should prove false. Mr. Webb shall now play the audio from the included recorder."

He tossed the letter back into his briefcase and took up the digital recorder.

"You may want to scoot in," said Mr. Webb. "I'm not sure how loud this thing can get."

The other heirs leaned closer, surrounding Jenny and the lawyer. Tori coughed. Blake wiped beads of sweat from his brow and flicked his hand. Mr. Webb pressed a button on the device, and RJ Valentine spoke from beyond the grave once more.

"Greetings, mystery lovers! I'm recording this on the off chance— off, though hardly unlikely—that the first person to solve my murder gets it wrong. Hey, it happens. No good mystery is complete without a red herring or two. Heheh. If you solved it on the first try, frankly, I'd be a little disappointed. Since one of you struck out, it's time I splashed the pot. I'm naming one more heir: my killer! Obviously!

"To the man who styles himself the Stranger. To the one whose increasingly threatening notes have haunted me these past months, I leave this arcade token, and invite you to insert coin and join the game!"

Mr. Webb revealed the golden object he'd palmed: it was, indeed, an arcade token, about the size of a quarter. Everyone leaned even closer. Something brushed Jenny's hip. The token was embossed with the pixelated outline of a video game coin on one side. Mr. Webb flipped it over to show the words: **No Cash Value** stamped on the other.

"How are you supposed to give it to his killer?" asked Yvonne.

"Webb, take the game token and set it on the rim of the birdbath in the southwest corner of Town Square," said RJ on the recorder.

Everyone looked to Jenny's right. Only a handful of paces away, the old copper birdbath sat to one side of the cobblestone path that circled the park. Mr. Webb walked over and placed the coin on the edge of the basin. The burnished rim glowed golden brown in the sunset. Webb turned back and smiled expectantly, leaning on the birdbath with his left hand, daring anyone to approach.

"Not bad, eh?" said RJ. "I love you all, and I'm so sorry I can't be there to see how it all comes out. These are my final words on the matter. I swear! Maybe! Happy hunting, detectives!"

Everyone stared at the game token, faces full of consternation and befuddlement. Would anyone dare try to pick it up?

"Now what?" asked Alicia Aaron.

Somewhere overhead, Jenny thought she heard a sharp metal *clink!*

"Game on, Trouble," RJ added.

Jenny looked up just in time to catch a golden blur plunging straight down. Her heart skipped a beat—the thing looked ever so much like a giant game token! It struck Mr. Webb right in the head with a stomach-churning crunch!

Hamilton Webb stumbled forward. The golden disk fell to the side and thudded onto the grass. A wash of red gushed from a dent in the lawyer's skull, staining the cobblestones deep crimson. He was dead before he hit the ground.

Alicia shrieked and fainted.

Game on, indeed.

Chapter Two
No Cash Value

THERE WERE PILLARS IN JENNY'S LIFE THAT HELD UP THE firmament. Unmovable, unshakeable columns that defined the boundaries of her reality. People she trusted implicitly. Trouble? For sure. Shelly? Absolutely. Her aunt might be a stick in the mud, but she was utterly reliable. And Eliza she trusted with her life—even if her sister refused to come this evening. It hadn't occurred to her until now that Hamilton Webb was one of those pillars. Or that those pillars could be toppled over.

As she watched the paramedics do a perfunctory check for Mr. Webb's non-existent vitals before pronouncing him dead, an intrusive thought slipped through the ramparts that guarded her mind, hacking at her defenses, trying to plant a seed.

Are you sure you can trust RJ Valentine?

"This will sound stupid," said Jack. "But, like, I honestly didn't think Mr. Webb could die."

"Same," Jenny croaked out, her throat gone dry.

He squeezed her hand and drifted away.

Deputy Calderon arrived to cordon off this quadrant of the park with police tape. The paramedics, having finished whatever bureaucratic ritual was required to transmute a living patient under their care into a dead body for the coroner to collect, turned their attention to Alicia

Aaron, checking her for a concussion. Was it Jenny's imagination, or did one of those paramedics look familiar? He was a gaunt man with a soul patch who could have been 30 or 60. As if feeling her eyes on him, he looked up and squinted at Jenny. She swiftly averted her gaze.

"Must have rigged it to drop by remote," Nilay said, craning his neck back and pointing up into the oak tree canopy. "I think I see the mechanism."

"Radio controlled," said Lockhart, glancing around the park. "Could have been triggered from any line of sight."

"Or a cell phone, from anywhere," said Jack.

"Are we gonna talk about the elephant in the room?" Jenny asked. "Or should I say, the giant game token?"

The thing that killed Mr. Webb was a flat metal disk, maybe two feet in diameter. Jenny recognized it now as a 45-pound barbell weight, like the kind Jack put on the bench press at the Crow's Nest gym. Someone—please, not *someone*, the Stranger—had spray-painted it gold to look like a giant arcade token, and written in blocky, black letters:

NO CASH VALUE

"Tails never fails," muttered Mason.

"Could there be something on the other side?" asked Yvonne.

"Yeah, heads," said Jenny.

"Oof. Nice," said Nilay.

Lockhart grunted beside her, scowling at the giant "coin."

"Miggy, can you do the honors?" Lockhart asked his deputy.

Calderon came over, slipping on a latex glove, and lifted the weight plate.

Sketched in black on the opposite side, just as she'd expected, was the little peeking man in a hat.

13

"You gonna call this a suicide, too?" Jenny asked Lockhart.

He cracked his knuckles, and then all the joints in his neck.

"One could make the argument," said a new voice.

He was a tall man in a tailored navy suit. His slicked-back hair revealed a sharp widow's peak, and he moved with brusque confidence, unfazed by the tragedy. From the way he asked for—demanded, more like—a word with Lockhart, he could only be the aforementioned mayor.

As Lockhart walked off to have a chat with his boss, Jenny raised her gaze, finally taking in the view beyond the crime scene. A few rubberneckers were gathering at the police line to watch, amongst them Mason's girlfriend/baby mama Meghan May, and Jenny's estranged ex, Dinah Black. Dinah had abandoned the messy bangs and cardigans of summer for a wavy platinum bob that gleamed in the klieg lights. Jenny tried waving to her. Dinah gave her an icy hair flip, spun on her white tennis shoes, and walked away.

Yikes!

"Alicia, you okay to walk?" Lockhart asked the little redhead. She nodded, rubbing the back of her head. "All right, listen up, folks. If you were here when it happened, follow me over to the stage. Except for you, Mason. You can leave. Tori, you too."

"Later, bro," said Mason, slapping Jack on the back.

Jack winced—his wound from Austria was still healing—and gave Mason a hearty backslap in return before the younger Lockhart departed. Tori said nothing, following the rest of the heirs to the small amphitheater where a local theater troupe did Shakespeare in the Park once a month. When they had all gathered at the back of the stage where prying eyes and nosey ears couldn't intrude, Mayor Villanova stepped forward and addressed the heirs.

"We're gonna tell everyone this was an accident," the mayor said.

"How are you gonna call that an accident?" asked Jenny.

"This kinda shit happens every day," said the mayor. "Someone comes up with a goofy stunt for a birthday party, or a proposal, or a gender reveal, and they don't think it through, and next thing you know, your poor, overworked first responders are left to clean up the blood and baby blue chalk."

Oh yeah, the paramedic!

Jenny looked back at the crime scene, but the medics had already left.

"So you're gonna say Mr. Webb hung that giant coin in the oak tree, but somehow screwed it up, and it fell on him by mistake?" asked Yvonne.

"Sure!" said the mayor.

"But we all know that's not true," said Jenny. "Mr. Webb wouldn't have done the Killroy drawing on the coin. That was the Stranger."

She glared at Lockhart. Why wouldn't he say something?

"Election year, kiddo," Lockhart muttered.

"The police will, of course, investigate to determine if there was any criminal negligence," said the mayor. "Which means that this"—he held up the game token he must have retrieved from the birdbath—"is going into an evidence bag and never coming out. At least not until your… game is over. Are we agreed?"

A chorus of "yeahs" replied, making Jenny the only "no."

"It's a bad idea," she said as they all glared at her. "The Stranger won't like it. Dad left the token to him, and him alone. He's very strict about these things."

"The Stranger, or RJ?" asked Yvonne.

Are you sure there's a difference?

"Shut up!" Jenny said aloud what she'd intended to keep to herself. "Sorry, uh, but he killed Declan for trying to sell his heirloom, remember?"

"He didn't kill me for selling my key to you," said Alicia.

"No, but he took it from me immediately, and almost killed Jack and Tori," said Jenny.

"True. Somehow, it's never *you* who bears the brunt of his discontent, Trouble," said Jack.

"Jack's not wrong," said Lockhart. "There's a lot of bodies dropping around you, Valentine."

"What was it, thirteen in Austria?" asked Yvonne.

"Fourteen if you count Mr. Porter," said Nilay, looking up from his phone.

"Fifteen, if you count Declan," said Val. "Sixteen for Hamilton, and then there was Mr. Carnegie and his son-in-law…"

"Jorge Lopez, Lily Geist, Campbell Klein…" said Jack

"Not that *she* cares," Val added.

"STOP!" shouted Jenny. Her eyes were tearing up, but she didn't care. "I'm not the one doing this! So stop blaming me for shit I can't control! I saved your life, you ungrateful cow!" She jabbed a finger at Lockhart and the mayor. "And if *you* hadn't been so eager to put me in a cage for two weeks, I might have saved Mr. Webb, too!"

The lot of them suddenly found the ground or the horizon very interesting and worthy of closer study, too embarrassed to make eye contact. Except for the mayor, who returned her rage with a condescending smile.

"Douche chill," whispered Jack.

"Oh, whatever!" said Jenny. "Assume the worst of me. I don't care! But I'm the only one of you fuckers who has an alibi for Mr. Webb, so kiss my ass."

"Is it always like this with her?" the mayor asked Lockhart.

"You have no idea," said Lockhart.

"Consider me charmed," said the mayor. "But it's still five yeas to one nay, little miss. The yeas carry the motion."

Lockhart handed him a ziplock bag. Mayor Villanova slipped the game token into it and handed it back.

"You seem rather eager to bury that clue, mister," Jenny said.

The mayor flashed her another high-wattage, dickhead smile, and left the stage. Jenny whirled on Lockhart and unloaded.

"Damn, and I thought Shelly kept your balls in her purse!" she said.

"Shit rolls downhill, Trouble," said Lockhart. "And you're standing at the very bottom, so put a cork in it, or I'll call your JCO."

"Mixed metaphor," Alicia mumbled.

"If I may," said Nilay, stepping forward, "I think I can solve this one. The game token is from an arcade called Pixeldrome."

"And how would you know that?" Jenny asked.

"It's called Google Lens, Trouble," said Nilay. "You should think about modernizing your detective toolset, it's 2020." He glanced at his phone. "The arcade is 1.8 miles south of us. RJ Valentine filed a lawsuit against the owner of Pixeldrome, Rob Haines, in 2011. But it looks like he eventually dropped it and the records were sealed. Probably because they settled. So there's your suspect, and your motive, but…! Rob Haines was at the Valentine Foundation Gala on August 10th, the night of RJ's attack. Here's a photo of him from Insta with Mrs. Valentine, 20 minutes before Jack discovered an unconscious RJ in the study. He couldn't have been the killer!"

He turned his phone around to show them a photo of "Mrs. Valentine," standing next to a slight man in a rumpled suit. Both wore masks because the gala had a masquerade theme.

"Case closed! And in record time, I might add," said Nilay, very pleased with himself.

"That's not Val, that's Tori," said Jenny, studying the picture. "And you should stay out of this. You're not an heir, and the Stranger doesn't like interlopers."

"Funny enough, Dad would never take us to Pixeldrome," said Jack, glancing at Tori. "I asked for a birthday pizza party there once, when I was eight, and he drove everyone to Scandia in Santa Rosa instead."

"He and Rob weren't getting along, then," said Val. "Something about an unauthorized *Trouble* video game at his arcade."

"Really??" Jenny asked. "Have you played it?"

"No, you walnut," said Val. "Johnny and Rob sniped at each other for years over that stupid game. The lawsuit was Hamilton's idea, and it would have been a huge pain in the ass for us all if it ever went to discovery, so Rob just got rid of the damned game. But that was ages ago, and they've long since buried the hatchet. Christ, Pixeldrome sponsored one of Jack's Little League teams."

Or maybe RJ screwed this guy over, and he's been playing the long game to get his revenge ever since.

Jenny clenched her eyes shut, struggling to will away the doubt that was creeping into her world. No matter which way she analyzed the facts, she kept arriving at the same conclusion. *Game on, Trouble*, Dad had said on the recording, right before Mr. Webb died. *Game on…* The Stranger used those same words in the note he left Jenny, after murdering Declan Dillion in front of her…

"Okay, so why would Dad make the game token the Stranger's heirloom, then?" said Jack.

"Maybe it was just a guess. He's been wrong before, like with my heirloom," said Yvonne.

"Oh?" asked Jenny. "Do you want to share?"

Yvonne's heirloom, a hardcover copy of some obscure old pulp mystery novel called *The Stranger of Sausalito*, had eluded Jenny's investigative skills entirely. Ms. Griffin had, up till now, refused to spill even the most minor of details about it.

"You gonna share why you burned *your* heirloom clue to obsess over ours instead?" Yvonne replied.

Jenny's clue, a photo of her mother with RJ, was a sly hint at the existence of her twin sister. If the very pregnant Laura Onishi holding up two fingers (for two babies) in the photo didn't give it away, the map drawn on the back of the photo did. The map led to a treehouse on the Valentine property, where a whole dossier on Eliza was waiting for her. Jenny theorized that RJ had only recently discovered Eliza was still alive when he made the will. He must have figured she was either a prime suspect for his elusive stalker or a huge ally that Jenny desperately needed to meet. As it turned out, they'd already met without his help on the roof of an LA hospital—by crazy coincidence, on the very night Dad was attacked in his study 400 miles to the north. And no, Jenny wasn't about to share any of that! Or the fact that she never actually burned her heirloom, only pretended to.

"Touché," said Jenny. "But you're all missing the point. Forget about this Rob fucker and consider that giant gold coin over there."

"That's for me to worry about, not you," said Lockhart. "We'll check all the security cameras facing the park. Those weights aren't so common that we might be able to trace the sale. You know, real police work."

"Yes yes, but *why* would the Stranger have used a giant coin on Mr. Webb in the first place?" asked Jenny.

Unconsciously, she had begun to pace, fretting her hour upon the stage. Everyone had some kind of talent. Drew could hit fastballs. Charlie Zaleska was a wizard with makeup. Penny Griffin could crush anyone at trivia. And Jenny Valentine solved mysteries, no matter if she liked where the clues pointed or not.

"Good point," said Val. "The bastard should have dropped it on *your* head instead of poor Hamilton's."

"The Stranger doesn't want Trouble dead," said Jenny. "At least, not yet. He wants to play. 'Insert coin and join the game.'"

The other heirs chewed that one over. Each doing the math and deciding that, yes, somehow, this was still all Jenny's fault.

"Maybe *we* should kill her," said Alicia.

"What jury would convict?" said Val.

"A perfect murder," said Jack, winking at her.

They still weren't getting it.

"Think about it," said Jenny. "The Stranger couldn't have set up that coin trap without knowing what was in the will beforehand. And none of you did, right?"

They all shook their heads, confused.

"Only one person would have known what the secret heirloom was," said Jenny. "Would have known to rig up a murder weapon painted to look just like it. Would have known exactly where to drop that coin!"

"Mr. Webb?" Jack guessed.

"No, dummy," said Jenny. She swallowed hard, and the name burned like acid as it escaped her lips. "RJ Valentine."

Several mouths sprang open, ready to protest the allegation. One by one, each heir bit their tongue. They had to consider it.

Trouble's fictional father being the Stranger was a popular reader theory. One Jenny loathed. The thinking went: Book RJ was setting up all the mysteries as a way to connect with his daughter. It was the only way he knew how, after her mother died young. If it were true in the books, wouldn't it be true in real life, too? How could anyone *really* anticipate their own murder in their last will and testament, and set up a whole game of heirloom clues to catch the killer? Wasn't this the only sensible solution? Hadn't Mr. White insisted RJ was alive, right before he was killed at the castle?

Ugh! Please be wrong!

"That's not t-true," said a hoarse, stuttering voice from the back of the amphitheater stage.

Everyone had forgotten about her. Even Jenny.

"I knew what was in the will," said Tori Valentine.

"I knew it!" said Jenny.

"Fuck you, J-J-Jenny. You had no idea," said Tori.

How interesting. Was Tori's new stutter the result of her brain damage? Or was this a strategic pity play, after she'd just admitted to a motive and means to kill?

"If you knew about the secret heirloom, then…" Lockhart let the implication hang in the air.

"Victoria, sweetie, you're still healing," said Val. "You're confused and you shouldn't be speaking. The doctors said—"

"It d-d-doesn't matter n-now," said Tori. She pulled off the surgical mask, her jaw flexing as she forced herself to control her speech. "Webb is dead. So is Declan. Jack almost died t-too. You all need to hear this."

Yes!! Fuck that theory! I'm sorry I ever doubted you, Dad!

Jenny ceded the stage, thrilled to be wrong about her father, and let Tori unfold her tale.

"It all started with that d-damned game token," Tori began.

Chapter Three

Detective Daughter

T*ORI VALENTINE AWOKE WITH A START, CLUTCHING AT HER TUMMY. THE nightmare was already slithering out of reach, back into the fog of her* subconscious.

Hands tied. A looming silhouette. The bed of a pickup truck.

She groped for the butterflies in her stomach. It was her vibrating phone. Her father was calling at 9:07 AM on a Thursday. She was due to present her final oral arguments in Kirkwood Moot Court at Stanford in less than two hours.

"Daddy?" she said into the receiver.

Her free hand absently roved the other side of the bed. Cold and empty. Hazily, she recalled an argument with Darcy and a slammed door.

"Did you send this?" asked RJ Valentine.

Tori could detect from the hollow echo of his voice that he had her on speaker. He'd be in his study, then. Early for him.

"Send what?"

She wiped the sleep from her eyes, willing her head to stop pounding. Always the bed of a pickup. Oh, Casey...

"The game token," said RJ.

Tori frowned. Was this a code? She sat up and immediately regretted it.

"Shit! Hold on!" said Tori.

She barely made it to the sink in her little studio flat before vomiting up last night's Red Bull and Hennessy.

"You're not drinking again, are you, Tori?" asked RJ on the phone.

"No! No," said Tori, wiping her mouth. "I think I ate some bad pad thai last night. There's this new place, right off campus, I thought I'd try. Big mistake. This is definitely going in my Yelp review."

She rummaged in the minifridge for a Sierra Nevada pale ale and stealthily popped the cap. RJ was letting the silence hang between them. Judging her.

"Hmm," he finally said. "How does Trouble know someone's lying, when she can't see them?"

"Dad…"

"Tori."

She groaned and rubbed her numb face.

"They give too much information," she said, resigned to the lecture. "The guilty explain more than they need to. Give 'em time, and they'll always tell on themselves."

"Mmhmm," said RJ.

"I had a bad night," said Tori. "That fucking Fortune Teller! Forget it. What's this about a game token?"

"You're saying you didn't send it, then?" asked RJ.

"I'm saying I have no idea what you're talking about," said Tori.

"Not exactly a denial," said RJ.

"No! I didn't send you a fucking game token!" said Tori. "It's nine o'clock in the morning, Dad. What's going on!?"

"Not on the phone," he said. "I'll explain tomorrow. You're coming over for Jack's party, right?"

"His super sweet 16?" Tori chuckled. "Wouldn't miss it."

"That cocksucker Lockhart bought his kid some chintzy muscle car for his 16th," said RJ. "Do you think Jack's expecting one too?"

"Daddy, we don't say 'cocksucker' anymore, it's gauche," said Tori. "And Jack doesn't want a car. Rich kids don't drive themselves anymore, they Uber."

"That's so lame. What does he want, then?"

The access code to Dinah Black's pants.

"I don't know, get him a hooker."

"Well, that's gauche, Victoria," said RJ.

"Ooh, how about a dog?"

"No! Val just had the carpets cleaned," said RJ. "Hey, do you still have your fingerprint dusting kit?"

"Of course."

"Bring it tomorrow," said RJ. "And Tori?"

"Yeah?"

"I need you at your best on this."

She looked at the beer bottle in her hand.

"So… you're not coming to moot court?" Tori asked. "It's the finals."

"Sorry, but with this game token thing…" said RJ. "Don't worry, they put it on YouTube now. I'll be watching. You're gonna kill it."

She tried not to be annoyed. It would be a distraction if Dad came, wouldn't it? She downed half the bottle, washing away the taste of vomit, and with it, her fading memory of the nightmare. Only the feeling remained.

"I'm Tori fucking Valentine," she said. "I always kill it."

"That's the spirit! Give 'em hell, Trouble!"

*"D*ADDY*? A*RE YOU IN HERE*?" T*ORI ASKED*. S*HE PUSHED THE DOOR OPEN AND peeked inside.*

The chair at his desk was turned away, facing the courtyard through the bay windows. No one responded, so she moved into his study to get a better look. Maybe he was writing.

"Um, he's not here," said Dinah Black.

Jack's girlfriend was sitting in one of the Louis XIV chairs by the fireplace, reading a Thomas Pynchon novel. Dinah had recently started bleaching her hair and dyeing the tendrils that framed her face some gaudy shade of neon. She looked like one of those eGirls Jack watched play video games online. Tori found it unbecoming. Dinah was a Blackthorn; blue hair was beneath her. But Big Six breeding or not, she shouldn't be in Dad's study.

"What are you doing in here?" Tori asked.

"Jack sent me here," said Dinah, chewing on a tendril of neon hair. "He said I was distracting him from his homework. I finished mine faster than he could."

"I see," said Tori. "Well, I'm going to be meeting with my father in here in a moment, so… fuck off. Please."

"Absolutely!" said Dinah, snapping the book closed and rising to her feet. "I can read in the Map Room. How'd moot court go?"

What a cunt.

Like she didn't already know. Like Law School Twitter hadn't been trading memes all day about the nepo kid who melted down in the Kirkwood Finals and had to excuse herself. "Not great, Dinah!"

The study door, engineered to look like part of the wall, swung open, and her father entered.

"Hi Mr. Valentine," said Dinah, as she slid past him into the hall.

Dad raised an eyebrow at Tori, closing the door.

"Why was she in here?" he asked.

"Reading, apparently," said Tori.

He locked her with a hard stare, his irises wide with empathy.

"Do you want to talk about it?" he asked.

'It' meaning her moot court disasterpiece. But behind his mask of concern, she sensed his true mood. Anxious. Jittery. Had he slept last night?

"No, how boring," said Tori. "Tell me about this game token."

"Right," he said, snapping his fingers and pointing to his desk. "Someone sent this to me—or rather, they put it in our mailbox. There's no postage on it."

We're both so good at compartmentalizing.

He slid into his chair. Tori took her customary seat on the other side of the desk, absentmindedly wiping away a patch of dust from his glass bishop paperweight. She glanced at his blotter and saw that he'd drawn a star on today's date, the 15th. An old detective novel covered up the other half of the calendar.

"Check this out," RJ said.

From his desk drawer, he withdrew an A7-size manila envelope.

"Dusting for fingerprints won't do much good if you've already touched it," said Tori.

"I know," said RJ. "That's why I was careful not to touch it."

She got her little fingerprinting kit out of her handbag. You could buy officially licensed Trouble: Girl Detective Utility Gear with magnifying glass, plastic handcuffs, and fingerprinting kit at Target for $39.99. Those were toys, though; Tori's kit was the real thing. Dad talked Blake Lockhart into swiping one from Forensics and giving it to Tori for her own super sweet 16. RJ put the detective book away in the drawer, tilted the manila envelope, and let a little golden arcade token slid out onto his blotter.

"Pixeldrome?" she asked, recognizing the logo. "That place reeks of teenage boy and processed cheese. Why would you think I sent this to you?"

"I thought you might've… well, never mind," said RJ.

Tori tugged on latex gloves, and, with practiced efficiency, began to dust the game token with latent powder.

"So you want to tell me why this thing has gotten you so freaked?" she asked.

"Let's just say it's symbolic," said RJ. When Tori blanched at his non-answer, he went on. "Someone wants me to know that they know something about me. About my past."

"Oh really?" said Tori. "Is this the stalker?"

She carefully applied a strip of tape to the print she'd spotted on the token. RJ bit his cheek and gave a curt shake of his head.

"I don't think so," said RJ. "She'd just send her dirty panties or something—and she used the postal service. This doesn't feel like her."

"Well, you need to learn to be more careful," said Tori, squinting at the print. "There's only one fingerprint on this, and it's yours."

"You sure?"

"Right thumb," said Tori. "I practiced pulling this print a million times when you got me this kit. I know it by heart."

He sighed and leaned back.

"Oh well, it was worth a shot," he said.

He rapped his thumb on the desk blotter, more agitated than he was letting on. With the detective book out of the way, Tori noticed that her father had drawn another star on the calendar blotter, on March 10th.

"What happened on March 10th?" she asked, pointing to the blotter.

A shadow of sadness passed like a cloud over his face. In a heartbeat, the sun returned, and he was steely-eyed, implacable Daddy again.

"Tori. I called Dr. Brownwood."

She fumbled the powder putting it back in her kit. It spilled all over. "I don't want to go back there," she said.

"I know. That's why I made him give me the number of a better place. It's in Windsor. Great facility. Looks very chill."

"I can still take the bar," said Tori. "I don't even need moot court to graduate."

"Of course," said RJ. "You will, and you'll pass. This will be a great place to study. No distractions, no asshole classmates giving you shit. Look, I can't force you to go, but I think we both know you should. April 3rd is coming up. Do you really want to be at school for that? After what happened yesterday?"

Tori's heart froze to the core. April 3rd: the day Casey vanished. She gripped the edge of Dad's desk to steady herself.

"See, there you go," he added.

"Please don't be mean," she said between gasps for air.

"Easy, deep breaths. Count to ten," he said. "If I could take it all away from you, I would, Tori. God, I would,"

"What does Val think?" she asked when her breathing was under control.

"She wanted to 5150 you."

Figured. Tori sagged back in her chair. Rehab. Again. Son of a bitch. "What about all this?" she pointed to the game token.

"Don't worry about it," he said. "I'll handle it."

Dad swiped the game token back into the envelope and returned it to his desk drawer. He helped her clean up the powder and poured her a glass of scotch from the minibar. They clinked glasses, and he grinned at her.

"This is a 25-year MacCutcheon," he said. "You're going out on top."

Tori savored the smoky flavor burning in her throat. Why did never again *have to taste so damn good?*

to sober up, do a health cleanse, and get past April 3rd.

Five months later, she was still there.

Sober the whole time, thank you very much. Dad had been right; this was a great place to finish up her law degree. She had a private room, a decent therapist, and much-needed peace of mind. The facility was also home to a mellow golden retriever named Mindy, and Tori took her on walks all over the grounds. She could leave whenever she wanted to, but the time never felt right. Maybe November. Before the holidays, for sure. And then, one day in early August, RJ Valentine rang and told her it would need to be sooner.

"Thanks for coming, you look great," he said, settling into his desk chair. "Picture of health. Val and I are both proud."

Dad's study looked the same as always, but the vibe was all wrong. The drapes were closed, for one, and at this time of day, the courtyard would be gorgeous under the setting sunlight. His glass bishop paperweight, normally dulled under a layer of dust, was sparkly clean and gleaming. The faint smell of vanilla and Pine-Sol hung in the stuffy air.

"Something's different," she said, sniffing again.

There was a particular smell she associated with her father. Some combination of his aftershave, deodorant, natural body scent, and whatever else. Leather and mahogany and sandalwood. Daddy's smell. It was always strongest in this room, and it made her feel safe. But today it was gone.

"Just had the place steam-cleaned," he said. "We hired a new housekeeper, Mrs. Rivas. She's great."

"Carnegie let her go?" *Tori raised an eyebrow.*

"Yeah, Horace fucked up."

He bit his lip and glanced behind him at the closed drapes. It wasn't just the smell. RJ was different. In five months, he'd aged five years. Thinner. Paler. Jumpy and distracted. Jack's yearbook and an old brass key lay on top of his desk blotter. If his calendar was correct, he'd met with Mr. Webb this morning, and there was a reminder to call Blake.

"So," *said Tori.* "Who wants you dead? And how can I help?"

He chuckled. Dad loved gallows humor. "Well deduced, Tori," *he said, glancing over his shoulder again. "Yes, I fear someone is hunting this old fox. I'm taking precautions, but should the worst come to pass, Webb and I are preparing something special for my remainders."*

"Your what?"

"My heirs."

Right on cue, her old friend Anxiety returned. The racing heart, tingling spine, black vignettes at the corners of her vision...

She took a deep, calming breath and said, "You know I don't want anything."

"Good, because you're not getting anything," said RJ with a mischievous grin. "Except for new responsibilities, that is."

"I don't understand," Tori said.

Her curiosity was piqued, though. Nothing like a mystery to chase anxious thoughts away.

"Now that I Dream of Trouble *is finished, I'm working on a new kind of murder mystery," he said. "My own."*

RJ told her a story, and the sun went down behind the drapes. As he spoke, his mood lifted. It always did, when he had a good yarn to unspool. He'd designed a sort of mystery game. Seven heirloom clues, and a secret eighth, just in case the mystery was solved incorrectly. A bottle of Ressort Rouge, *a brass key, his blackbird statue, an old photo of him with some Asian woman, a book, a tarot card—and a noose.*

Tori shivered when he revealed that last item. "Is that...?"

He nodded grimly.

Oh, Casey.

"It's not for you," he said. "Don't worry."

The secret heirloom was the game token he'd asked her to dust for fingerprints back in March. He refused to tell her about the other heirs or explain the heirlooms, to maintain her objectivity.

"Admittedly, I haven't studied Estate Law," said Tori. "But I'm pretty sure this isn't legal"

"Webb's on it, that's not why I need you," said RJ. "You're insurance. I need you to keep an eye on the game. An invisible referee, just in case something goes fucky with Webb, or someone tries to cheat. I lied before, I moved $11 million into a trust under your name. Manage that well, and

you'll never need to work again, but that's up to you. My only request is that you take care of Mary Manuel and be ready to fill in for Mr. Webb if the need arises."

His phone buzzed. Tori thought his eyes brightened when he glanced at the screen. He snatched it up and fired off a text. Tori couldn't make out the message or recipient, but she could tell he wasn't using the Messages app.

"Why are you using Signal?" she asked, referring to the app known for secure, self-destructing communication. "Wait—who is that? Are you cheating on Val?"

He snickered.

"No, this is just a… collaborator. Though, now that you mention it, I'm pretty sure Val is cheating on me. That's a whole other game I need to talk to you about. She's going to ask you to come to her charity gala, and I need you to say yes."

"Wonderful. Are you sure you don't want me to help you solve these clues?" she asked.

"Absolutely not," he said. "Tori, this is real. This isn't your old man putting together a scavenger hunt. The heirs I've selected—well, let's just say I've picked them for a reason." He glanced down at the heirlooms and chuckled before he remembered he was trying to be serious. "Anyone who plays this game is in danger. Maybe is danger. And I don't want that for you."

MAYBE IS DANGER… CHEEKY, DAD. HE HAD AN UNCANNY KNACK for winking at her and Eliza from beyond the grave, but Jenny was growing less amused. Couldn't he have contacted her directly? Even once? She had so many questions he could no longer answer.

"So he thought we were all suspects," said Lockhart, chewing the inside of his cheek. "Except for Tori."

"Johnny always felt guilty about how Tori turned out, but he never stopped trusting her," Val said.

While everyone else politely ignored Tori's silent agony at Val's vicious comment, the oddest epiphany struck Jenny.

The way Tori said Dad frowned when she asked him about March 10th… That was Jenny's birthday. If Dad felt guilty about missing Jenny's childhood, how was Jenny supposed to feel?

"Tell me again why you never mentioned this whole 'test to see if Val was cheating' thing before?" Jenny asked Tori. "A year ago you acted completely shocked that Val had snuck off to the mansion alone."

"Well, I w-was upset with her," said Tori. "She never visited m-me in rehab. Plus, I knew she was on Dad's suspect list. I d-d-didn't know what to believe."

"Bullshit! What are you hiding!?" Jenny replied, perhaps a bit too sharply.

"I'm t-telling the truth!" said Tori.

"Not all of it!"

"Chill, Jenny," said Jack. "Why are you so pressed?"

"I'm not pressed!" Jenny shouted.

She was pressed. Anger was frothing in her heart, and she didn't know why. Afraid to speak, she stuffed her hands in her jeans pockets and was surprised to find a piece of paper in her left pocket that hadn't been there when she changed at the police station.

Hello, what's this?

It was stiff, like card stock, smaller than a playing card.

"She's mad that her frame job on me fell apart," said Val. "Not quite the brilliant Girl Detective you thought you were, eh?"

"I'm the greatest Girl Detective the world has ever seen," Jenny said acidly, casually palming the card in her pocket. "And we've been over this. I was in jail that whole weekend. It would have been impossible for me to plant the murder weapon on you."

Unless I had a secret identical twin going to jail for me…

"And yet, somehow you did," said Val.

Jenny pretended to run a hand through her hair, glancing at the card in her palm as it passed across her eyeline. It was one of Mr. Webb's business cards. He must have planted it on her when they were all leaning close to listen to RJ's recording. Written in rushed and messy letters were two words:

High Score

She couldn't be sure, but it looked like RJ's handwriting. Had he instructed Mr. Webb to give Jenny this extra hint? High score of what? The bootleg *Trouble* game Val mentioned? She wouldn't be able to check it out for at least two months because of her bullshit "criminal mischief" charge.

"Fuck!" said Jenny.

"What?" asked Tori.

"Nothing," said Jenny.

She rubbed her eyes, feeling suddenly exhausted, and slipped the card back into her pocket. Another fucking wink. Like the map on the back of her heirloom photo, or the clue he'd passed along through that blacksmith about Casey Klein's case. It was a dangerous game, and RJ Valentine had consistently put a thumb on the scale to help Trouble play it. It was sweet, but did he have to be *so* subtle? And to bring fucking Tori behind the curtain, not her…

"That was a very nice and touching story, Victoria," Jenny said, stilling her roiling emotions. *Be smarter. Be steadier.* "Really, the way you subtly blamed my father for your relapse? So choice. But there wasn't anything in there to make you any less of a prime suspect. If it's not RJ, then you're still the only other person who knew what was in the will."

Tori threw her hands in the air.

"How can the 'greatest Girl Detective the world has ever seen' be so d-dumb?" she said. "Weren't you listening? H-he said he had a c-c-collaborator."

"Exactly!" said Nilay.

"Oh," said Jenny. "You could have played that up a little more."

"Yeah, I didn't get that either," said Jack.

"RJ never loved working with a co-author," said Yvonne.

"I saw him three more times b-before the attack," said Tori. "He was messaging someone on Signal each t-time. I mean—Jack, Mom, you know that look he'd get? When he was writing? Or thinking about writing?"

Jack nodded.

"Oh, I'm well familiar," said Val, a sad smile on her lips.

"Th-that's what he always looked like when he got those texts," said Tori. "Whomever it was, they were in on the g-game, I'm sure of it."

"Then that would mean he was working with his killer," said Yvonne.

"Maybe he didn't know," said Alicia. "Signal is anonymous by design. The Stranger could have tricked him. Like in—"

"*Dial T for Trouble*," said Jenny and Lockhart in unison.

"*Dial T for Trouble*!" Nilay repeated a second later.

"Dorks," said Yvonne.

"For a while, I thought the p-person Dad was texting was you, Jennifer," said Tori. She gave Jenny an odd look. "K-kinda still do."

"If only," said Jenny.

"So we're saying the Stranger knew what was in the will the whole time?" said Nilay. "And now he's fucking with the heirs? Like he wants you guys to know it? What for?"

Another wink? Jenny had hoped Tori's story would remove RJ from the suspects list. All it did was raise more questions.

"Maybe he didn't like the cops giving all the credit to Arty Porter," said Jenny. "Maybe he was punishing Mr. Webb for accepting the wrong solution to the mystery. Maybe he's just a fucking psychopath. It doesn't matter. Same game, new lawyer." She looked at Tori. "Am I still eligible?"

"Yes, all of y-you are," said Tori. "Even the Stranger now, though D-Dad never explained to me why his killer would require a clue to solve a m-murder they, themselves, committed. You'll have to present your solution t-to me, this time. And the g-game is extended for 1 year. After that, the m-money goes to the Valentine Foundation."

"What if we all just refuse to play?" asked Yvonne. "What happens then?"

An unspoken thought passed between them, their eyes all drifting inexorably to the crime scene, where Mr. Webb's body was being loaded into the coroner's van.

"Game over," said Jenny.

Chapter Four

The New Girl

Eliza Valentine squinted at the mother-of-pearl hand mirror and wiped away the layer of water vapor from the shower. Her whole body shivered at the girl staring back at her. The ghost, the shadow, the night wraith she could never fully escape.

Danger.

Right on cue, her phone started buzzing, and wouldn't you guess who was on the line? The World's Bitchiest Girl Detective, her no-good sister, her evil twin: Trouble.

Eliza groaned, put her on speaker, and answered in her practiced British accent. "'Ello, cousin."

"Hi *Kazumi*," said Jenny. "What's that noise?"

"That's the shower, luv."

"Why are you talking like…? Never mind. This is going to sound like a dumb question, but, um, where do I live?"

This bitch.

"Grandparents' house, like before," Eliza said. "They'll be in bed by now."

"Do they… know about you and me?"

"Right. Yeah. Don't worry, they won't tell. For my sake."

"Okay, cool. Can you come let me in, then? I don't have a key, and I'd like to avoid Shelly if I can. Plus, I don't know if you heard, but some crazy shit went down tonight. We need to talk."

"Uhhh. See, the thing is…"

The shower faucet squeaked as it shut off, and Charlie Zaleska stepped out, dabbing droplets of moisture off her bare skin. She had the most peculiar scar on her collarbone. One Eliza couldn't help staring at every time Charlie gave her a peek. It was crying out for a nibble.

"She's busy, Jenny," said Charlie.

"See, I'm not actually at home right now," said Eliza.

"What!?" shrieked Jenny. "On a school night!? You ho!"

"There's a key under the little frog statue by the chrysanthemums."

She tapped **End Call** and got to work on Charlie's neck.

SHELLY WAS SURPRISINGLY COOL ABOUT LETTING ELIZA STAY OVER AT Charlie's place. Eliza may have neglected to tell her aunt that Charlie lived in a cute little condo all by herself. And that she was emancipated from her family. And that they were sleeping together. But come on! Why should Jenny be the only one allowed to have any fun?

It's not like she wasn't putting in the work. Tomorrow was the first day of school, which meant Eliza had to get up at 4:30 AM to become her new, better self: Kazumi Onishi.

First, there was Charlie's strict skin care regiment. Extra virgin olive oil as a base—no seriously, it worked!—followed by moisturizer and sunscreen. Then, contouring to make Eliza's cheeks and nose rounder. Clever highlights made her eyes appear farther apart than they were, and she liked to add a subtle cat eye to make herself look sophisticated. It took heavy pancake concealer to hide the Ace of Clubs tattoo on her wrist.

After makeup came wig fitting and wardrobe. She'd already planned out a whole sartorial arc for Kazumi's journey from goody two-shoes foreign exchange student to rebellious riot girl. Today, she was starting simple with a modest cardigan and pencil skirt.

The pre-dawn routine was imperative so that Eliza and Charlie could arrive at Basque Boulangerie Cafe before six and secure the best table on the patio. Rumor had it that after the disastrous senior class trip, Shani Wolf's parents were pulling her out of BSA and sending her to a private school in the City. Which meant there was an opening in the Bitchy Brigade. An opening for Kazumi, if she could meet their stringent requirements of being hot while having chill vibes.

"Oh no, Lizzy," Charlie said, nudging her and pointing to the headline of today's *Blackbird Times*.

Lawyer Killed in Heirloom Mishap

Underneath was a picture of Mr. Webb. A jolt of fear and grief seized her heart. No! Not Mr. Webb! Was that what her sister meant by "crazy shit went down"? *The fuck, Jenny??*

"'Mishap' my arse," said Eliza. "That was at the will reading for the Stranger. Dear god, what now?"

Before she could even process it, Meghan May arrived with Thanh Trân and Penny Griffin.

"Over here, ladies," said Charlie. "Kazu saved us seats."

"Aren't you Jenny's cousin?" Meghan asked, appraising Eliza with dubious concern. Then she spotted the newspaper. "Ew! No way! Mason was there last night. It was awful!" She snatched up the paper and tossed it into the street. "We are *not* bringing that energy into senior year, girls!"

Leave it to Jenny to ruin Kazumi's social status before she'd said a single word.

"Kazumi is nothing like Jenny," said Charlie. "She's a friend."

"Sorry about my cousin, she's wretched," said Eliza in her new accent. "Your top is lovely."

"Oh, are you British?" Meghan asked. "I spent a whole semester in Paris, you know."

It was a total lie. Meghan spent a semester hiding in a cabin on the outskirts of town, pregnant with a secret baby she'd still never revealed to anyone—even (especially?) her conservative parents. But that was all right. Their mutual lies added up to an understanding that appearances were all that mattered.

"I can *so* see you there," said Eliza. "You have that European quality.

Call me Kazu."

She'd originally gone with a high-pitched, chirpy voice for her alter ego as Kazumi. But shortly after adopting the new persona, Eliza realized she'd blow her brains out if she had to go around talking like some fresh-off-the-boat ditz all school year, so she modified her backstory to include several years abroad at a British boarding school.

"Jenny's not so bad, once you get to know her," said Penny. "But you're right, Meghan. New year, new energy. It's nice to meet you, Kazu."

They all willfully ignored the crime scene tape across the street in Town Square and filled Kazu in on the important gossip. In junior high, Eliza Valentine had been a total dork. But at Blackbird Springs Academy, Kazumi Onishi could be whoever she wanted to be. Kazu smoked cloves she bummed from Alicia Aaron and shared a tablet of Adderall with Thanh Trân. Kazu was cute, but lacked the kind of overt sex appeal that would make Meghan May feel threatened. Kazu spoke like a transfer from Hogwarts by way of Japan—and could get Penny the password for her superior British streaming service with all the best anime and BBC crime dramas. Kazu was a great hang who bought the table a round of scones and croissants as a welcome gift.

She was rocketing her way to It Girl status. The only one who wasn't enjoying herself was the one Eliza cared about most. Charlie spoke less and less as the sun rose. When the conversation turned to the senior class boys, Eliza squeezed Charlie's leg under the table and whispered.

"What's wrong?"

Charlie forced a smile.

"Sorry. Um… would you think me terribly cowardly if I wanted to keep us a secret?" Her face had gone pale; she wasn't joking. "Because of Mr. Webb. Just in case."

"No. No, that's fine. I get it," Eliza whispered, ignoring the disappointment that gnawed at her.

"I just don't want to be an avenue for someone to hurt you, or your sister."

Charlie returned the leg squeeze, and they forced their hands into their own laps. It could simply never be a normal life for Kazumi.

Danger was always lurking.

"Looks like fresh meat is back on the menu, gents," said Jack Valentine, walking up. He swung a toned, Levi's-clad leg over the back of the chair next to Eliza and took a seat. "I don't think we've been properly introduced. Johnny Valentine, but my friends call me Jack."

At the table across from them, Alicia Aaron lowered her book to watch, frowning.

"Kazumi," she said. "And you're barking up the wrong tree, mate."

All the girls tittered, but the rejection rolled right off Jack's back.

"Don't be too hasty, Kaz," he said. "We've got a whole year to figure that out. Love the accent!"

Jack's "gents" were Nilay, JeRay, and Lai. The latter two sleepily dapped up Jack and went inside to buy energy drinks. Nilay, on the other hand, was wide awake in a crisp suit and tie.

"Going by that accent, I'm guessing Hyde Park, am I right?" Nilay asked her. "I've got some friends there. Can I interest anyone in a cappuccino? Kazumi? Jack?"

"Brought my own go-juice," said Jack, tapping a high-tech thermos, which he began disassembling to pour himself a cup. "This stuff is swill," he said, gesturing at Eliza's latte. "If you're not roasting your own beans, you've never tasted real coffee. Want some?"

Charlie fell out of her chair, giggling like an idiot.

"What's so funny, Zaleska?" Jack asked.

"Nothing! Nothing!" Charlie said, beaming. "Go on, Kazu, try some!"

At least she was smiling again. Eliza would make her pay later.

"If you insist. Cheers," Eliza said, accepting Jack's little thermos cup and taking a sip.

Holy shit.

It tasted incredible.

"Not bad," Eliza lied. She pulled a five-dollar bill from her purse. "I bought the ladies some biscuits. Go get yourself a pastry, and eat a mint while you're at it."

The girls all tittered again as Jack smugly accepted the bill and headed inside the cafe.

"Bloody hell," she said.

"You could do a lot worse, Kazu!" said Meghan. "He's basically the hottest guy left on the market. He's rich and polite, and Penny says he's only kind of a head case."

"That's so gross! He's my sis—uh, second cousin's brother!" Eliza said.

"On her dad's side, though, right?" said Penny. "You're not blood-related, it's totes allowed—and honestly, kind of hot. Like Bridgerton!"

The rest of the Bitchy Brigade nodded sagely.

"Maybe Kazu isn't into boys," said Charlie.

Eliza blushed fiercely.

"Ohh??" cried Thanh.

"I've got appetite enough for both," Eliza said coolly.

"Maybe she likes them with more brains than brawn," said a nasal voice.

It was Jimmy Figg, the school prodigy who'd skipped two grades. He was holding his mocha and a blueberry muffin, hoping for a seat at their table.

"Talking of, where's that burly chap I saw at the airport?" Eliza said.

"Drew Porter?!" said Meghan.

"Do not go there!" said Thanh, and she was no longer grinning. "His dad's a fucking murderer!"

Meghan threw a protective arm around Thanh. Penny glared at them but bit her tongue, and the Queen Bee shot a warning glance at Eliza. Major party foul to bring up Drew! To make matters worse, Aunt Shelly chose that time to pull up to the curb and eject a sleepwalking Jenny from her car.

"Don't be late, and keep an eye on your cousin!" Shelly said, before zipping away.

"The Angel of Death approaches!" cried Jimmy Figg, still doggedly trying to be one of the cool kids. "Hey Jenny, is it true your dad got his lawyer killed in another one of his heirloom stunts?"

"No, that was the Stranger," Jenny said through gritted teeth.

"Arty Porter is dead," said Nilay. "There is no more Stranger, right?"

He said it in an odd tone, and he, Jack, Alicia, and Jenny all exchanged knowing glances.

What do they know?

Eliza might have piped up here to find out. But Kazu didn't want anything to do with Trouble business.

"Hamilton Webb will be pleased to hear that," Jenny said under her breath.

She snatched the blueberry muffin from Jimmy's hand and stuffed it in her mouth, uttering something unintelligible and probably filthy between bites.

"You were nicer last year," he said, pouting.

"Kazu! Making new friends already, I see?" Jenny said, swallowing her bite and ignoring Jimmy.

"Right, yes. Everyone has been quite welcoming," Eliza said. "Without you here."

"The pleasure is ours," said Nilay, darting into the last open seat before Jenny could take it. "We Unfridgeables could use some new blood to lighten things up, you know?"

"Unfridgeables?" asked Penny.

"That's what I'm calling us," said Nilay. "The ones who made it out of Austria alive. Catchy, right? We should get matching tattoos."

Meghan crinkled her nose, and Thanh glared laser beams at Nilay.

"The mood is lighter already, Nails," said Jack, grinning. He scooted closer to Eliza. "Sorry, New Girl, but everyone's gonna want a piece of you. My advice: lock down a good boyfriend soon, while your stock is high."

"Junior, I swear to god!" said Jenny, grabbing him by the ear. "You are not allowed!"

"OW! I'm just saying!" he said, wincing away from her. "Didn't say I was offering."

She let him go, with a stern glare that made her look just like Aunt Shelly.

"Didn't say he wasn't, either," said Lai, giving Jack a fist bump.

Jesus Christ.

"Run this by me again, Kazu," said Jenny. "You're from Okinawa, not England, *right?*"

"Mum and Dad work in Finance," Eliza said. She switched to Japanese and asked, "Can you *not?*"

"I guess you're still mad at me?" Jenny replied in their second language.

"Hey, come on, ladies," said Meghan. "Spill the hot goss in English."

Lai and Thanh shared what must have been a private joke in Vietnamese, both smirking.

"Yes! You're killing the vibe," Eliza said in Japanese. "You don't have to hang out with me, you know? In fact, it's better if you don't. Leave me alone!"

Jenny laughed loudly, which is how Eliza knew she'd struck deep.

"Whatever," she said, returning to English. "See you bitches later."

Jenny stalked off, and the whole table visibly relaxed.

"Thank god," said Thanh.

"Talk about not reading the room," said Meghan. "Why the hell did Dinah ever date that psycho?"

"I think she was just trying to piss me off," said Jack.

"It's not always about you," said Penny.

"I wouldn't be too fussed about her," said Eliza. "The bobbies slapped a transmitter on her pin. She has to leg it home right after lecture, or else it's back to the nick."

"I don't know what any of that means, Kazumi," said Thanh. "But if it translates to 'Fuck Jenny Valentine,' then pip pip cheerio, guv'nor! Get her ass!"

Everyone laughed. Including Eliza. She knew she should feel bad for treating Jenny poorly, but maybe it would do her sister well to suffer a little consequence for her actions. The rest of them certainly had.

FROM THEN ON, ELIZA HAD HER SPACE. SHE HAD COFFEE AT THE Basque in the mornings, and took her lunch in the cafeteria, always with the Unfridgeables. After school, she mostly hung out with

Charlie and the girls (though Jack had an annoying habit of inviting himself along), only coming home for mandatory dinners with the grandparents.

A journalism teacher had been hired to replace Mr. White, but Penny wasn't interested in working on the school newspaper or yearbook without her late mentor. Neither was Drew. Eliza rarely saw him these days; they didn't have any classes together, and he took his lunches alone under the sycamores by the school entrance. According to the latest gossip, the Winchester restaurant fired his mother Mirai after many wine suppliers refused to work with her. Eliza wished there was something she could do, but Drew was toxic to be seen with these days, and he wasn't friends with Kazumi anyway.

The only person besides Charlie at school who knew Eliza's true identity was Dinah. Fortunately, they rarely crossed paths. Dinah was taking a couple of AP classes at Calistoga College, (a hail mary to catch up to Penny in the valedictorian race) and when she wasn't, she wanted nothing to do with Eliza or Charlie, her ex.

Still, the Danger part of her brain liked to keep an eye out for the tall, blonde ice queen. Sometimes she'd spot Dinah out the window during English class, arriving late, gliding across the quad in her Hudson jeans and red scarf, looking more like a visiting college student than a teenager these days. It was as though, mentally, Dinah had already graduated and moved on. If so, good. The sooner Blondie was gone from Eliza's life, the better.

It was unclear where You-Know-Who went during lunch. The only class they shared was International Relations, first thing in the morning. They sat on opposite sides, and Jenny was usually late or falling asleep in her chair. They rarely spoke, even at home.

Autumn arrived. Nilay defeated Thanh in the Student Council election. His stupid "No Homework" campaign actually worked. Eliza finally ditched the wig and let her natural hair down. It was long enough now to pretend she'd gotten a chop. Aunt Shelly took her to a stylist to get a blowout. She switched from blouses and cardigans to rock band tees and hoodies. Not to be vain, but she looked so chic!

All the seniors took the SATs. Eliza tried to act like her score would matter, even though her entire academic record was stolen from some dead chick who went to St. Mary's in Cambridge. It was enough to get her into BSA, but she doubted it would pass muster at a college admissions office.

And then what?

Thinking about next year always put her in a dark mood.

It rained for two days straight, and all the wildfires went out. Finally, some fresh air. Nature was healing. Before Eliza knew it, it was already October.

"Kazu! Kohari! You're going to be late!" Aunt Shelly shouted from downstairs.

"In a minute!" Eliza yelled back, trying to concentrate.

Jack had bought her a jumper with a fur-lined hood and cat ears from Nordstrom last night—*I'm allowed to accept gifts! It doesn't mean anything!!*—and she'd bollocksed up the contouring on her nose trying to get her eyeshadow to match the sweater's shade of pink. She looked hideous!

"It's not working! I need to start over," she said.

"That'll take forever, Lizzy," said Charlie on FaceTime, providing moral and technical support. "Just blend it in with more foundation and try again."

"AAIIIGGHHH!!!!"

Charlie's eyes widened on the phone screen.

"Shit, that's my aunt," Eliza said. "I'd better go check."

Eliza hung up and hauled ass downstairs to see what Shelly was screaming about. It was Jenny, of course. She'd shaved the sides of her head, giving herself a dreadful mohawk. With the **I**  **MURDER** tank top and her purple Burberry trench coat hanging off one shoulder, she looked like Furiosa Trouble from the Darkest Timeline.

"It's school pictures today!" Shelly screamed.

"Duh, that's why I did it!" Jenny beamed. She glanced at Eliza and added, "Your nose needs work, Lizzy."

"Your grandmother is going to have a heart attack when she sees it," said Shelly. "And she's gonna take it out on me. Come on!"

Shelly grabbed her keys and beckoned them to the door. Jenny hung back a moment, so Eliza did too.

"I like it," Eliza told Jenny. "Now there's no way I can stand in as you."

"You could if you wanted to," said Jenny, her smile faltering. "I need your help. There's this arcade—"

"Not interested," said Eliza. "That's a Trouble problem, not a Kazu problem. Leave me the hell out of it."

"I've given you a month," said Jenny. "When are you going to stop punishing me?"

Eliza set her jaw, hardening her heart.

"I'll let you know."

Despite her conviction, Jenny's comments put Eliza in a sour mood, and then they were out of oat milk at the Basque! And she was pretty sure she was about to have her period! Disaster!

Eliza sulked through breakfast despite Charlie's best efforts to cheer her up by doing an absolutely filthy impression of Fleur Delacour discovering Bill Weasley's new predilection for raw meat. When the intercom came on during first period for morning announcements, Eliza barely paid attention to Vice Principal Carter announcing the nominees for Homecoming King until he said the name 'Jimmy Figg.'

Half the class audibly gasped. Everyone understood that Jimmy's nomination was a joke. Great. Now all the Unfridgeables would have to congratulate Jimmy and root for him sincerely, and maybe even let him sit at their table at the Basque, or else they'd look like arseholes.

Mr. Carter let the silence hang in the air long enough to let the seniors know he was judging them, before moving on to the other nominees: Lai, JeRay, and, of course, Jack. Then he got to the real shit: Homecoming Queen.

"Dinah Black."

Obviously. Eliza looked over to see Jenny's reaction, but her sister had her head on her desk, sleeping soundly.

"Meghan May."

Of course.

"Kazumi Onishi."

WHAT!?!?

She could feel herself smiling so wide her face hurt, dimly aware that Thanh Trân had been nominated too. That was nice for her.

But holy shit! Holy shit!! Homecoming Queen!!!!

She was walking on air at lunch, thinking about dresses and dancing with Charlie, when someone called out, "Hey Kazu?"

Eliza looked up to see Jimmy Figg standing before her with a funny look on his face. Without waiting for a reply, the little nerd reached down and yanked his shirt over his head. The girls all gasped at his pasty, bare torso, and the words written in black Sharpie across his scrawny chest.

Home
coming?

Jimmy stepped forward to go down on one knee and said, "Might this Homecoming King take thy Queen to the dance?"

"Oh! Blimey, Jimmy, I..." Eliza stammered, feeling her face glowing crimson.

After the joke nomination, wouldn't she look like the biggest git if she rejected him now?

"I mean, if you're not already going with anyone," Jimmy said.

That's your only out, D! Take it!

But with who? There was Charlie, but she'd promised to keep that a secret. Nilay was planning to ask Penny, and Lai and JeRay had dates already. Which left only...

"Aye, and there'd be the rub, Jimmy," Eliza said. Oh no, her accent was drifting into Irish! She swallowed and steadied herself. "I'm afraid I told Jack I would go with him, dear."

"You did?" asked Charlie.

At least Jack had the wit to play it cool, accepting fist bumps from Lai and Nilay.

"Sorry, Jimmy," Eliza said.

"Don't be sorry," Jimmy said hotly.

He turned and speed-walked away as fast as his scrawny legs could take him. He made it halfway to the cafeteria door before he remembered his shirt. Eliza fetched it from the floor and held it out for him, wincing. He snatched it up without a word and turned on his heel to stomp off again. Eliza cringed as her peers broke into a tizzy of laughter before he was even out of earshot.

"You know, it's like that old proverb," said Jack, grinning. "If you wait by the river long enough, the bodies of the girls who rejected you will eventually drift by."

"It's just as mates, Junior!" she yelled at him.

Jack raised a salacious eyebrow, and all the girls snickered. Eliza hid her mortified face in her hands. It was all so fucked up. Whatever. *Homecoming Queen!* She wasn't going to let Jimmy's awkward proposal ruin this for her. She glided through the rest of her classes on a euphoric high, and the first thing she said when she saw Jenny at dinner was: "Guess who got nominated for Homecoming Queen?!"

Jenny brightened. "Me?"

"Not with that haircut!" said their grandmother from the kitchen.

"No. Everyone hates you," Eliza said. "It's Me! I did! Can you believe it?!"

She wanted Jenny to be jealous. Instead, she gave Eliza a big hug and said, "I'm so happy for you, Lizzy. Do you want me to rig it so you'll win?"

"Absolutely not!" said Aunt Shelly.

Before she could say more, Baba called Shelly over to the stove to criticize her dumpling crimping technique.

"Thanks, but I don't think we vote till the dance," Eliza said to Jenny.

An argument broke out between Shelly and their grandmother in rapid-fire Japanese, too fast for the twins to follow, though Eliza thought she heard Mom's name in there a few times.

"Michelle, stop riling your mother up and get in here!" shouted Jiji from his study. "The goddamn WiFi is broken again!"

Shelly clenched her fists and marched out of the room, leaving Eliza alone with her sister. Jenny laughed and nudged her.

"You should go celebrate, they won't even notice you're gone," she said.

So Eliza did.

And thus, her troubles began.

Chapter Five

Mystery Flavors

Eliza texted Charlie, who texted Meghan. Somehow Jack wormed his way into the group chat, and before they knew it, all the Unfridgeables were meeting at the Red Grape to celebrate the Homecoming nominees. All of them, that was, except for Alicia Aaron, who declined, and Jimmy Figg.

Kazumi: We'll look like right bellends if we're all off having a pint without Jimmy.

JeRay: Pish posh!

Jack: What do you take me for, Kaz? Of course I reached out to Jimmy. 😀

Charlie: Stop emoji flirting with Kazu in the group chat, Valentine.

Jack: He said he was busy playing some video game tournament.

Lai: The passion.

Dinah: That is so sad. But good.

Thanh: There's still time to accept his proposal, Kazu 👑👑👑

Kazumi: SHUT UP!

WHILE ELIZA FUSSED OVER HER MAKEUP IN THE BATHROOM, JENNY had her own back-channel texting to attend to.

Penny: I feel like I shouldn't tell you.
Jenny: Come on! Why not?
Penny: You know why not, TROUBLE.
Jenny: I'm on house arrest!
Penny: Fine, we're going to the Red Grape.
Jenny: Hah! I knew it. Jack's favorite.
Penny: It's supposed to be celebrating the Homecoming nominees, but he's really celebrating Kazu finally agreeing to date him.
Jenny: Wait wat?
Penny: lol you weren't there, hold on.

Two minutes later, Penny's response came in the form of a long voice message explaining the Jimmy Figg incident at lunch. Jenny just about died laughing. Eliza being cornered into dating her own brother was too delicious! Almost enough to cure her depression. Almost.

Jenny: I'm dead. 💀
Penny: It was so awkward.
Jenny: You have no idea.
Jenny: But okay, the Red Grape. That's right down the street from a place I'm researching. Can you do me a favor when you're there?
Penny: Uhhhh what?

Her fingers flew over the virtual keyboard as she typed out her request.

THE RED GRAPE WAS A FANCY ITALIAN JOINT ON THE SOUTH SIDE OF TOWN. Their party was large enough to take over the whole outdoor area in the back of the restaurant. The ambiance on the veranda was killer. Strings of incandescent yellow bulbs crisscrossed above their heads, the tables had those charming red-and-white gingham tablecloths, and the back wall—original brick from the Mission days and covered in climbing ivy—made a perfect backdrop for their Instagram pics. Whoever ran the place was playing totally excellent music.

Jack ordered pizzas with buffalo mozzarella for the table. A fifth of Southern Comfort materialized from Meghan's purse, and they all took turns spiking their lemonades with it. According to Nilay, this drink was called an Alex Drake. While the others held a spirited debate about what song to pick for the Homecoming TikTok Dance Challenge, Eliza sipped her Alex Drake until she had a nice, mellow buzz going, and bopped her head along to Gwen Stefani's "Danger Zone" on the jukebox.

"We're not doing one of your boomer songs," Meghan sniped at Nilay. "It needs to be Cardi B or Megan Thee Stallion."

"But the theme is 'Totally Awesome '80s!'" said Nilay.

"You picked the theme!" said Meghan.

"Why do we have to do a TikTok Dance Challenge?" asked Eliza.

It was news to her that all the nominees were supposed to do some dance on stage during Homecoming. How mortifying! Not least because Eliza wasn't much of a dancer—even when she wasn't wearing platforms or high heels to make Kazumi look taller than Jenny.

"What's the matter, Kaz, your hips been telling lies?" said Jack.

"Mr. Carter says the mayor wants 'positive viral moments' for Blackbird Springs," said Nilay. "You know, stuff that doesn't involve murder and misery and You-Know-Who." Everyone's eyes flicked to Eliza. "Not to mention the Jimmy situation. You assholes couldn't have just nominated me?"

"This is what it's really about," said Penny. "He's feeling left out."

"And now you'll floss to 'Material Girl,' you pricks," said Nilay.

Conversation turned to dresses and dates, and who was likely to win the Homecoming crowns.

"I just don't want you guys to get your hopes up," said Jack. "It's hard to beat an incumbent. Though, with Kazu at my side, someone might have a chance of finally toppling Dinah."

Everyone "oohed" at the challenge, and turned to Dinah, who'd been quiet the whole evening. She finished her bite of Caesar salad and daintily wiped the corners of her mouth.

"It's fine," she said. "I'd be happy for Kazumi."

"Psh, please! Little Miss My Shit Don't Stink has won every single year since junior high," said Meghan.

"Times change," said Dinah. "Honestly, I don't care. Someone else can have a turn."

"This false modesty is all part of her campaign strategy," said Charlie.

Dinah winked and blew Charlie a kiss. Eliza went temporarily blind with rage, only blunted when Charlie squeezed her knee under the table.

"Why the scowl, Kazu?" asked Penny.

"She's just sore because the only one who *actually* asked her to Homecoming was Jimmy effing Figg," said Jack. "You're welcome, Onishi."

Eliza didn't need a mirror to know she was flushing crimson red.

"Eat shit!" she yelled at him.

She hadn't meant to shout, but something in Jack's comment slipped beneath her armor and struck home. Before she could process her emotions, she realized everyone was getting up to leave and debating about dessert.

"Pie Oh My never fails," said Nilay.

"Too many calories," said Meghan. "Let's go to Mystery Flavors!"

They boxed up the leftover pizza, paid the bill, and bounced. As they walked to Mystery Flavors, Eliza stewed on the Homecoming question. Going to the dance with her brother was embarrassing, sure. But what really bothered her was that Charlie never asked. Or maybe Eliza should have asked her? Not that they could go for real if they wanted to keep their relationship a secret, but it would have been a nice gesture.

"Wait, I thought we were going to Mystery Flavors," Charlie said.

The boys had taken a detour into an arcade on this side of the street.

"Nilay has to prove to Penny that he can beat Jack at a game of *Street Fighter*," said JeRay, ecstatic at the challenge. "It's so fucking on!"

Penny shrugged at the boys. "All I said was that Jack is pretty good at it," she said, smirking. "Maybe they have air hockey."

The girls glanced up at the place, scowling. The arcade was a squat, windowless building with a single entrance and a neon sign above, styled to look like an 8-bit, pixelated coin.

"It's giving strip club for babies," said Dinah.

"Fuck it, I'm cold," said Thanh.

She yanked the door open and a cacophony of video game bells and chimes spilled out. The other girls followed her inside. Eliza was instantly hit with the strong scents of melted cheese, hot dog grease, and male body odor. Memories of going to Chuck E. Cheese with Nurse Bennett flashed in her mind. Her reward for being the only one in second grade to pass every times table, even division. The giant mouse guy had terrified her, so she hid in the ball pit, crying.

Danger would never.

Black lights from hidden recesses turned everyone's skin blotchy shades of violet. An '80s song with lots of synthesizers and drum machines was blasting on the sound system—no wonder Nilay wanted to come here. Most of the games lining the walls were either decades old, or jumbo-sized mobile phone apps.

"A dollar to play *Angry Birds*?" said Dinah. "As if!"

"Isn't that Alicia Aaron?" said Meghan May, pointing to a girl playing an old-school *Ninja Turtles* game in the corner. Her hair looked black in this lighting, but Alicia's prosthetic leg was unmistakable. She was consumed in the game, giving them no notice. "Too busy to hang with us, but she comes here? Couldn't be me."

The arcade was mostly empty, save for Alicia and a crowd of dudes gathered around a giant LCD screen that took up the whole eastern wall. They were cheering on two contestants playing *Street Fighter* on the huge screen. Eliza frowned, stretching higher on her tiptoes to get a look at them.

Is that…?

She maneuvered around to the side and her suspicion was confirmed: Jimmy Figg was one of the players. Sensing her gaze, he stole a glance her way and instantly blushed, fumbled with his joystick, and lost the round. The crowd hollered abuse at him.

Eliza ducked out of his eyeline, just as humiliated.

"Guys, Kazu is *so* turned on right now!" said Thanh, who had gleefully watched the scene unfold.

"Why don't *you* go to Homecoming with him, Thanh?" Eliza yelled at her.

Thanh's face fell and she turned away. Damn, right—Lance. Eliza hadn't meant it like that. She left that corner of the arcade and spotted Penny wandering around with her phone out, turning left and right like she was searching for something. Jack was speaking privately to Alicia, then he turned away, oblivious to Alicia's soft smile for him, and walked over to the main counter. A girl their age waited, slumped on one elbow, sneering at them.

"What's that about!?" he asked her, pointing to the crowd. He had to shout over the music and cheering.

"Tournament," said the girl.

"Is that the only *Street Fighter* machine you have?" he asked.

"Technically, no," she said with a heavy sigh.

For an arcade clerk, she seemed weirdly hostile to these basic questions. Eliza squinted for a better look. It was hard to tell in this light, but she might be South Asian. She had thick glasses and flat, dark hair, pulled to the side in a severe plait. Her acid-washed jean jacket had the sleeves pushed up to her elbows, showing off several jelly bracelets on her wrists that glowed neon in the lighting.

"Uh, where's the other one?" Jack asked. "We want to play."

"You can't," said the girl. "It's in the VIP section."

She nodded to a velvet rope on her right, stretched across the opening to a stairwell that descended below the main arcade floor. A sign in front read:

Lvl 50+ Only

Jack shook his head, pulling out his wallet.

"Fine, how much?" he asked.

The girl shook her head right back, mocking him.

"There's no buying your way in, rich boy, you have to earn it," she said.

"Look we're just trying to settle a debate," said Nilay, joining Jack at the counter. "Can't you just let us get a game in? Just one."

"Try Skeeball," she said.

"Let's just go," said Nilay.

"What else is down there?" Jack asked the girl, pointing to the VIP stairwell.

"Level up and find out," she replied, twitching an eyebrow.

"This place is fucking lame!" Meghan yelled loudly. "That *Mario Kart* game ate my dollar!"

"You have to use tokens," said the clerk.

"Jack! Penny! We're going to Mystery Flavors!" Dinah called over to them.

Her brother gave the sour girl behind the counter one last smoldering frown of displeasure, before letting Nilay pull him away, muttering about "Harbor High kids" under his breath.

It was a relief to get back outside, away from the noise and smells and flashing lights. Charlie waved to her, leaning against a light post.

"Were you out here all this time?" she asked.

"Those UV black lights are a no-go," Charlie said, pointing to her chin where, Eliza knew, scars from bad acne were hidden below layers of makeup.

"Sorry, I would have stayed with you," she said. "What an awful place. You didn't miss anything."

"I'm fucking freezing!" Thanh said.

She was hinting to the boys that she'd accept a jacket, but not one of those idiots was feeling chivalrous that evening, so Eliza lent Thanh her hooded cat-eared jumper.

"You sure about that?" Nilay asked Jack, deep in conversation about something dance-related. "I was gonna hire Clark Thompson to DJ."

"Ew, not him!" said Thanh.

Clark Thompson was a sophomore with his own DJ equipment, whom Vice Principal Carter was always letting run the sound at school events. He wore silk shirts and sunglasses indoors and played entirely too much "Brass Monkey" by the Beastie Boys. Everyone hated him except for Nilay.

"See, Thanh's on board," said Jack. "We're gonna get Mason's band to play. They do lots of '80s songs."

"Wait, including—" Penny was cut off by a ringing bell that was mounted above the front door of Mystery Flavors Frozen Yogurt.

Just like the lobby door in Schloss Schwarzwald...

"Speak of the devil," said Jack. "Bro, hope you've still got your bass, you're playing the dance. No arguing."

Drew Porter stepped out, holding a small cup of frozen yogurt smothered in butterscotch syrup. The boys dapped Drew up while Thanh watched in barely concealed disgust.

"I think I left my AirPods at the Red Grape," Thanh said, then sprinted back down the street.

"Dude, we haven't played together in months," Drew told Jack. "And Alicia and I broke up, remember?"

"Too bad, it's time to stop hiding and get back on that horse," said Jack.

"I wouldn't call it hiding," said Drew, his jaw set, speaking through his teeth. He stepped aside to let them pass and enter Mystery Flavors. "It's more like I know when I'm not welcome."

"That's over now," said Jack. "And anyone who's got a problem with it can take it up with me."

Drew looked like he might have a problem himself, but Jack had a wild glint in his eye, daring anyone to challenge him.

"Chill, Jack. It's all good in the hood," said Nilay, "BRB. I'm gonna run and get some pie."

Nilay jogged off down a side street. The rest of them filed inside the frozen yogurt shop. Eliza was pleased to see Drew lingering. He still looked anxious, but at least he wasn't hiding anymore.

"That was very kind of you," Eliza said to Jack. "I didn't realize you and Drew were friends."

He shrugged. "I don't exactly have friends, but Drew's a good guy. He's been in the penalty box long enough, hasn't he? Hey, will you let me buy your ice cream, at least?"

"Load up, mates; Jack's buying!" Eliza said.

"You're lucky you're cute," said Jack. He flashed a smirk and grabbed a little sample cup. "Do they even have fro-yo in England? Even if they do, Mystery Flavors is something else. They always have one batch with no food coloring, just pure white. If you can guess the flavor, they give you a discount." He filled his little cup with plain-looking soft serve and sampled it with his tongue. "Interesting…"

Eliza slipped away to find Drew by the door. She held out her hand. "I don't think we've been properly introduced. I'm Kazumi."

"I know," he said, narrowing his eyes. "Trouble's cousin."

"As everyone loves to remind me," said Eliza. "I guess that makes you that murderer's kid?"

His eyes flashed.

Not expecting that kind of pushback, were you, Drew?

"Touché," he said and shook her hand. "You're not for real dating Jack, are you?"

"Goodness, no!" She rolled her eyes. "I have to pretend, to avoid going to Homecoming with that little cunt Jimmy Figg."

That cracked a smile on Drew's flinty exterior. "No one swears like the British."

Charlie materialized to her right, weaving her arm around Eliza's. "Back off, Porter, I'm trying to convert her."

Eliza waved to Drew and allowed herself to be led away.

"What happened to keeping things a secret?" Eliza murmured.

"I reserve the right to be a jealous bitch," said Charlie. "I should have asked you to the dance."

Relief—and something else warm and comforting—bloomed in her heart.

"And I should have asked you," said Eliza.

She squeezed Charlie's arm and broke apart as Jack approached.

"Everybody get a taste?" he asked as he passed Eliza a sample.

Eliza darted her tongue at the soft serve and tasted something sweet with a hint of spice. Maybe nutmeg? She suggested eggnog. Jack went with caramel. Meghan and Dinah both guessed dulce de leche. JeRay was convinced it was butter pecan.

"It's cinnamon," Charlie muttered.

"She's right!" said the clerk, pointing to Charlie.

"You didn't even try a sample!" said Penny.

"I'm allergic," said Charlie. "I know the smell—though this is artificial."

"That's cheating. She's a super taster," said Dinah.

"Not to be that bitch, but who are *you two* taking to the dance?" Meghan asked, pointing to Charlie and Dinah. "Am I sensing a reconciliation?"

The two exes both glared at Meghan. *Good.*

"There's always Jimmy," said Penny. "He still needs a date."

"Talking of Jimmy, where is Thanh?" Eliza asked hastily, desperate to change the subject. She glanced out the window of the shop, frowning. "That was poor form, letting her run off alone."

"She'll be back as soon as…you know," said Penny.

Drew indicated that he should leave.

"Don't. She shouldn't take it out on you when my sis—*stupid* cousin…" Eliza trailed off. Was it her imagination, or did she just see someone dressed all in black duck into an alley across the street? "Let me go talk to her."

Eliza slipped out into the night, passing Nilay in the doorway as he returned, out of breath, with lemon meringue pie for himself and Penny. A bank of fog had crept in from the hot springs north of town, muffling the street sounds and turning her skin clammy. She was missing that jumper now, so she lit up a dart to keep her lungs warm. As she crossed to the far sidewalk, she absentmindedly found herself taking care that her platform Vans hardly made a sound on the asphalt. One hand rummaged in her purse, digging for her old kunai dagger. When her fingers brushed the carbon fiber handle, a rush of sensation shot up her arm. She was becoming *her* again.

Danger.

Eliza blinked, shaking off the sensation, and found herself at the opening of a dark, deserted alley. There were enough cardboard boxes in her path for a whole host of Strangers to be hiding behind. She took a drag from her clove cigarette, psyching herself up to enter the alley, when a strong hand gripped her shoulder.

He was lucky the knife got stuck in her purse.

"Oi! You startled me!" Eliza shrieked at Drew, pulling her purse back as casually as possible. "What d'ya want?"

"Call me paranoid, but no one connected to your cousin should be wandering off alone into dark alleys," he said.

She blew smoke in his face to hide her bashful smile.

My sweet Drewboo.

"Right, then. Tag along."

She waved him after her, and they ventured into the alleyway. Adrenaline thumped in her heart every time they rounded a big box or dumpster, but that tall, dark, and strangesome menace never materialized. The alley dumped them out at the other end onto Fifth Street, where a vagrant sat on top of a *Blackbird Times* vending machine, eating some scavenged pizza. He nodded hello to them.

"'Sup, man?" said Drew, and turned to Eliza. "What are we looking for?"

"I don't know," Eliza said. "I thought—"

A piercing scream behind them cut her off. Without another word, they both sprinted back the way they'd come. There was a commotion in front of the Red Grape. Meghan was there, and Jack and the boys were running over to her from Mystery Flavors.

"What is it?!" Eliza asked.

"It's Thanh!" said Meghan, her eyes wet.

"Dead?"

"No! Jeez, Kaz! She—come and see."

They followed Meghan around the side of the Red Grape, to the veranda where they'd just dined. Thanh Trân was slouched over one of the cute bistro tables, her hands covering her face, sobbing. All around her—on the gingham tablecloth, Eliza's pink jumper, the stone floor—were strands of shiny black hair. Thanh's hair.

Someone had shaved her bald.

Chapter Six

Alibis

L ATE THAT NIGHT, JENNY SAT CROSS-LEGGED ON HER BED, PRACTICING ON a particularly challenging grade-1 deadbolt with her lockpick kit. With her headphones in, she didn't even hear her sister come in until Eliza flung herself onto the mattress, yanking the cable out of her laptop, and filling her bedroom with the sounds of a cute Chinese girl whispering about Magneto in a valley girl accent.

Whatever had crawled up Lizzy's ass was forgotten for a moment as Eliza raised an eyebrow and glanced at the YouTube video, titled **ASMR — Jubilee Heals Your Wounds After Fighting the Brotherhood of Evil Mutants**.

"Seriously?"

"It helps me focus!" said Jenny, reddening. She lunged past Eliza to slam the laptop lid shut and mute the video. "I'm looking for costume ideas for Halloween!"

Eliza gave her the most condescending eye roll of all time before shooting lasers at her, hand on hip, just like Aunt Shelly always did.

"I'm going to ask you a question, and I want you to be honest," Eliza said. "Did you shave Thanh's head?"

"Someone shaved Thanh's head?" Jenny asked, frowning.

"Was it you?"

"Of course not," said Jenny. She pointed to her ankle monitor. "I'm on house arrest."

"I don't believe you."

"Yes, but I believe me," said Jenny. "And unlike you, I know how to spot a liar."

"What? That doesn't even make sense."

"Why would I shave Thanh's head?" asked Jenny.

"Didn't you just say at dinner that you would rig the Homecoming vote?" said Eliza.

"I was joking!" Jenny laughed. "And that's not how I would do it. Come on, tell me everything."

"Later, I'm tired."

"Please?" Jenny asked. "I need this! I've been cooped up for a month!"

"You've no one but yourself to blame for that," said Eliza.

Jenny's spirits fell. File it away as another fun senior year adventure she'd missed out on. It only really hurt to think about when someone reminded her of it.

"Fine," said Eliza, heaving a dramatic sigh. *Gosh, how magnanimous of you, Lizzy.* "This all started with your dumb idea that I go celebrate…"

Eliza recounted all the details from her eventful night: from dinner at the Red Grape to popping into the Pixeldrome arcade to getting frozen yogurt, right up to the part where Thanh got chloroformed back at the Red Grape veranda and woke up with all her hair shorn off.

Jenny listened intently, perking up when Lizzy got to the arcade. Penny had already texted her the video she took of the place, but hadn't seen anything that looked like a *Trouble* video game in it. Maybe it was just her imagination, but wasn't her sister laying it on extra thick with all the details about her social life, just to rub Jenny's lack of one in her face? Was it really necessary to mention that Drew still despised her? When Eliza finally finished humblebragging about her daring trip into the alley, only to run back and find Thanh bald, Jenny picked up the grade-1 deadbolt and fiddled with her tension bar, that old Trouble hamster wheel spinning up inside her skull.

"You didn't happen to see… a *Trouble* video game at the arcade, did you?" she asked.

"I don't think so." Eliza frowned. "It was a bunch of old games, and phone apps like *Cut the Rope*. Arcades are weird now. I didn't know there was a *Trouble* game. Why? Does it have to do with Thanh?"

"Maybe. Probably not. When Mr. Webb died—"

"Nope! Nope!" Eliza cut her off. "I don't want to know! I'm done with that shit. I asked you about Thanh."

"I mean, it's obvious," Jenny said, suddenly feeling very over Lizzy and her cool kid bullshit. "You've been Kazumi for too long if you can't see it."

"See what?" Eliza asked.

"You're supposed to be the smart one, Lizzy!" Jenny groaned. "Now you're a fucking airhead."

"Fuck you! I don't know why I talk to you," Eliza said.

"Because we watch out for each other," said Jenny. "It's what Dad wanted."

A ripple of strong emotion marred Eliza's over-contoured face. Jenny braced herself for a particularly nasty insult, but it never came.

"What?" Jenny asked.

Was it something about Dad?

"Nothing," said Eliza, swallowing whatever she'd wanted to say. "Forget it. It's Thanh's problem, not mine. I don't even care."

She hopped off the bed.

"Well you should care," said Jenny. "He was trying to shave your head, not Thanh's."

"Who?" Eliza asked.

"Jimmy Figg," said Jenny. "Duh!"

On Sunday morning, Blake came over for breakfast—which Eliza knew meant he'd slept over, gotten up early, snuck out, and returned with coffee, pretending he and Shelly hadn't been violating Baba's "no boys in the house" rule. She sighed, observing as Shelly watched Blake cook eggs and bacon in the kitchen. Jenny could scoff, but Eliza thought they were adorable.

"It's sweet!" Eliza whispered.

"Says the girl who's going to Homecoming with her brother," Jenny muttered, giving Eliza a spiteful smile. She'd been delighted by that news, mentioning several times over the weekend, without prompting, how embarrassing it must be for Eliza.

Blake carried a sizzling skillet over to the table, serving them over-easy eggs and bacon—foods Eliza didn't even care for, but she liked the idea of being cooked for by a lover.

"Mr. Lockhart, sir, did you hear what happened on Friday at the Red Grape?" Eliza asked innocently in her Kazumi voice, smothering her eggs in furikake seasoning.

"I did," said Blake, scowling. "We're looking into it. The poor girl's parents are furious. It was probably some punk kid from Harbor High."

"I see. Um, my cousin had an idea about it," Eliza said.

Silverware clinked on Baba's china, and Blake paused mid-chew to fix Jenny with an authoritative stare.

"Did she now?" he said, flicking his eyes back to Eliza. "If you want my advice, Kazumi, I wouldn't listen to any ideas your cousin has."

"I solved your cold case!" Jenny snapped at him. "Campbell Klein would still be making sculptures out of little girls if not for me!"

"Campbell Klein almost killed you," said Blake. "It was only dumb luck that kept you from becoming her next piece of corporate art."

"Batori," Eliza said under her breath.

"The point is, I know who attacked Thanh," said Jenny.

"How would you know?" asked Shelly. "You've been on house arrest?"

"Just tell him the story, Kazu," said Jenny. "The way you told me."

Eliza launched into an abbreviated retelling, leaving out the teen drinking and her cigarette. Blake stayed quiet, eating his breakfast. When she finished, he smeared a napkin over his mouth and gave Jenny a queer look.

"I see," he said.

"How interesting that Alicia was at the arcade," said Jenny, leveling an equally odd look back at the sheriff.

What is it about this arcade?

"I suppose you're going to tell me that Alicia attacked Thanh, thinking it was Kazumi?" Blake said. "Because she's jealous that Kazumi is dating Jack?"

"She is?" Shelly exclaimed.

"We are not dating!" said Eliza. "He's just taking me to Homecoming!"

"He's what?!" asked Shelly, her expression somewhere between deranged amusement and concern.

"Close, but not quite," said Jenny. "Thanh was attacked because she was wearing Kazu's sweater, but it wasn't Alicia, it was Jimmy Figg. He was humiliated when Kazu rejected his Homecoming proposal. It's like that saying, you know: 'Boys are afraid of being laughed at, girls are afraid of being murdered by boys they laughed at.'"

Blake pursed his lips, thinking it over. "It sounds nice, but where's your proof?"

"Have you met Jimmy?" asked Jenny. "Total incel vibes."

"Yes, I'm sure that will convince a judge. 'Your Honor, the vibes were straight cringe. For real, for real! No cap!'"

"You're so dumb!"

"To be fair, Blake, this is the kid I was telling you about," said Shelly. "He's the reason I stopped wearing anything with a hint of curves at school. Little pervert."

"He was right there, at the arcade, and he saw Kazu," said Jenny. "He's got motive, means, and opportunity."

"Maybe motive and opportunity," said Blake. "You think he carries around hair clippers and chloroform, just on the off chance a girl he's psychosexually obsessed with happens by?"

"You *don't?*"

That earned her sister a rare, genuine chuckle from Blake.

"He did know we were going to the Red Grape," said Eliza. "We invited him, but he had that tournament to play in."

Blake cracked his neck and looked at Eliza.

"Which he *was* playing in, with lots of witnesses. I'll keep it in mind. But despite what your cousin thinks, we do real police work in Blackbird Springs."

Jenny blew a gigantic raspberry, summing up her opinion of the Blackbird Springs Police Department. As much as she didn't like taking her sister's side, Eliza had to admit she had a point.

THANH DIDN'T COME TO THE BASQUE THE NEXT DAY, OR TO SCHOOL, either. No one would say it aloud, but Eliza, Dinah, and Meghan all understood that their odds of becoming Homecoming Queen increased substantially in her absence. Eliza wanted to share the Jimmy Figg theory with them, but every time she turned around, the little nerd was lingering nearby, close enough to eavesdrop. She could feel his eyes on her all through AP Calc, though if she ever looked his way, his head was always buried in his graphing calculator. At lunch, he took a seat at the table next to the Unfridgeables, still trying to horn in on their scene. Eliza was about to text the group chat about him when it all went fuck up.

"Oh shit," said Charlie.

"Hey Jimmy, whatcha got in here?" asked Jenny.

Eliza had barely registered Jenny's entrance into the cafeteria—so strange to see her in here, where she rarely ventured—and now her sister was unzipping Jimmy backpack while it was still on his back.

"Hey!" shouted Jimmy, his hands groping behind him. "Stop it!"

"Any clippers in here? Trying to finish the job?" Jenny asked. She spilled the contents of his bag onto the cafeteria floor. There were binders, an iPad, a video game controller, and—*seriously, Jimmy?*—a box of magnum condoms.

"My man!" said Lai, grabbing the box. "Thanks for picking these up for me, Jimbo. I was running low."

Jimmy tried to laugh along with the rest of the cafeteria, even as they were laughing at him.

"Oh, what's this?" Jenny said, pulling an envelope out of the side pocket. "Addressed to Kazumi!?"

Eliza's face went beet red, and so did Jimmy's. He lunged for the envelope and missed, falling out of his chair onto the floor. Jenny held it up in triumph, but before she could open it, Vice Principal Carter marched up behind her and snatched it out of her hand.

"Miss Valentine! Really!" said Mr. Carter.

"He's the one who shaved Thanh's head!" said Jenny, jabbing a finger at the humiliated Jimmy. "Search his locker, I'm sure he's got the clippers hidden somewhere."

"I didn't!" said Jimmy. "Give it back!"

"Tsk tsk, you're losing your touch, Trouble," said Nilay. He stood and held out his hand to the vice principal. "If I may, Richard. As Senior Class President, Jimmy's one of my constituents."

Mr. Carter handed over the envelope, and Nilay returned it to Jimmy with a paternal pat on the shoulder.

"The police checked the camera footage at Pixeldrome last night," said Nilay. "Jimmy was inside the whole time when Thanh was attacked."

"How would *you* know!?" Jenny shouted.

"Valerie has an understanding with the department," said Nilay. "I called in a favor."

Valerie??

"So you see, it couldn't have been Jimmy," said Nilay. "Leave him alone."

"Perhaps we need to have a chat with your juvenile court officer, Jennifer," said Vice Principal Carter.

It was Jenny's turn to blush now. Her eyes cast about, beseeching the others for help, and landed on Drew. All she got back from him was a stony brick wall. *Good boy, Drew.* Vice Principal Carter led her away. JeRay tried to help Jimmy re-pack his bag, but the little nerd was terminally mortified. He grabbed his things and hurried to the exit, leaving his half-eaten chicken nuggets behind.

"Douche chill!" said Jack, earning a giggle from Alicia.

"Great, now he's gonna come back with an AR-15 and shoot us all," remarked Penny.

Eliza grimaced. She'd be target no. 2, right after her sister.

Some fucking theory, Jenny.

THE UNFRIDGEABLES TABLE AT THE BASQUE WAS FROSTY THE NEXT morning, and it wasn't just the early October cold spell.

"No offense, Kazu, but you can't just go telling your cousin about stuff like Thanh's attack," said Penny. "Her brain is always gonna run wild—especially when she's been cooped up on house arrest for a month."

"Penny's too kind," said Drew. "Everything she touches turns to shit."

Eliza was forced to bite her tongue. With Drew on the Trouble hate train and Charlie out sick, there was no one else present to take her side. Her girlfriend had texted at sunrise saying she felt ill and wouldn't be attending school.

"Lesson bloody learned," Eliza said, and lit up a clove cigarette.

"If Jimmy gets a sympathy vote for this, I'm gonna be so pissed," said Jack. "Fucking Trouble."

"Shut up, Jack," said Dinah. She had deigned to join them this morning, perched on the railing enclosing the outdoor seating, nibbling on a vegan energy bar. "You and Kazu have the crowns all sewn up. People love voting for a couple."

"We are not a couple," said Eliza. "If it helps, I stole my cousin's best wig for Thanh." She pulled the custom chestnut wig Jenny had commissioned out of her school bag. "It cost her like $12,000."

"Thanh will die before she wears that," said Meghan.

"So don't tell her where it came from," said Dinah. She took the wig from Eliza and tried it on.

"All right, awkward question," said Jack. "If not Jimmy, then who *did* attack Thanh?" He glanced at Dinah. "Gross, you look like Tori."

"Imagine being attracted to your own sister," Dinah said, flashing a nasty smile at Eliza.

"I'm not supposed to say, so don't tell," said Meghan. "But Mason told me the cops arrested some homeless guy for it. He had, like, Thanh's AirPods on him, so they're pretty sure he did it."

"Bollocks! It wasn't him!" said Eliza, forgetting her place. "Drew and I saw him, he was a block away when you found Thanh."

"Maybe he ran over there after he did it?" suggested Nilay. "Trying to set up an alibi."

"The point is, we don't need to worry about this shit anymore, *Kazu*," Meghan said. The warning tone in her voice did not go unheeded. "We should be focusing on our dresses and the TikTok Dance Challenge, and who we can score some molly from, for the after party."

Listen to her, Kazu!

Eliza mentally kicked herself. Kazu didn't care about mysteries or a little injustice. Kazu cared about winning Homecoming Queen. It was only a few days away, and she hadn't even begun to practice for the TikTok Dance Challenge.

For the rest of breakfast, she forced herself to make idle chit-chat, wishing Charlie were there to pinch her under the table. When the time came to start walking to school, Jack hung back, shooting Eliza a look that requested she stay back too.

"Yes?" she asked, once they were alone.

Jack reached out and took the clove cigarette from her lips.

"My sister's a bad influence on you, Kaz," he said and stubbed it out in his palm. "What color is your dress going to be?"

"What's it to you?"

"We need to match," he said. "I'm no philistine."

"Hah!" She shouldered her purse and walked with him. "It's pink. Thanks for asking."

"Millennial, or Barbie?"

"Flamingo."

AFTER SCHOOL, ELIZA PICKED OUT A TIKTOK ROUTINE THAT DIDN'T look too difficult, and set about practicing in her mirror. Every time she ran through it, her reflection looked like she was trying to solve a math equation through interpretive dance while holding in a fart.

"The thing is," said Eliza, her cheeks flushing, "I've never actually been to a school dance."

"Never? Like ever??" asked Charlie. She was FaceTiming from her condo, where she was still down bad after eating some bad Korean takeout.

"It always seemed scary in junior high, and then Nurse Bennett got sick, and we moved, and I was homeschooled…"

"I seem to recall you shaking your little booty at that club in Paris," said Charlie.

Eliza grinned and twerked a little for the camera. "That was after a lot of screwdrivers and Jenny's Adderall. There's also… well, when I'm playing Jenny instead of being myself, it sort of brings out another side of me. I don't know, it's like, I can do whatever I want because it's not *my* reputation being tarnished. But this time, Kazu's rep is on the line, not hers, you know?"

"You two are so fucking twisted, swear to god," said Charlie.

"But I'm the good twin!"

"Sure you are. Well, I'm not going to tell you to take more of your sister's study pills," said Charlie. "But a little liquid courage couldn't hurt. I'll bring my flask."

"So you're going, then?" Eliza asked. "You won't still be sick?"

"I think I'll be better by tomorrow," said Charlie. "Just need to be extra clear on the 'no garlic' thing with the Korean place next time. Of course I'm going! Are you crazy? You're going to be my Homecoming Queen! Go on, try it again."

Eliza bit her lip and tried to concentrate. Just a sweep of the arm, stomp her feet one-two, swing her hips—

"This is dire," said Charlie. "Maybe we should say that they don't have school dances in jolly old England. Or TikTok. Or rhythm."

Eliza stuck her tongue out. At least with Jimmy Figg at Homecoming, she was guaranteed not to be the worst dancer there.

THE REST OF THE WEEK PASSED WITHOUT MAJOR INCIDENT, THOUGH Eliza still felt Jimmy's stare every day in AP Calc and at Lunch. Creep. Shelly made Jenny eat lunch in her classroom, so she couldn't cause any more drama in the cafeteria. Thanh still hadn't returned to class and was threatening to skip the dance, too. Unfortunately, she hated how she looked in the chestnut wig Eliza lent her. On Thursday, Nilay and Penny went Instagram official, though everyone knew they'd been sneaking around making out in the All Gender restroom for weeks. On Friday afternoon, Jack surprised Eliza with a special request.

"My mother wants to meet you, and do pictures at the penthouse," Jack told her over the phone. Homecoming was only hours away. "No complaining."

"Bloody hell," said Eliza.

"I'll send the car over in an hour."

"You're not coming yourself? What if my aunt wants pictures?"

An empty threat, Eliza would die before she let Jenny and Shelly see her like this with her brother.

"We'll send her some," he said. "I still need to do my hair."

Eliza scowled and threw her phone down. Jack had like three inches of hair, max. He could roll out of bed and you wouldn't know the difference. Eliza, meanwhile, was struggling to give her hair a layered, wavy look, which she didn't quite have the length to pull off.

There was a knock at the door, and Jenny poked her head in. She appraised Eliza's look—a strapless pink silk dress with flamingo feather earrings to match—and sneered.

"A lot of effort for your half-brother," she said, snickering.

"It's for Charlie," said Eliza. She sighed and tried to flatten the ends of her hair that kept sticking out. "Ugh. I look like Alice from *Twilight*, so I guess she'll be happy. What do you want?"

"I don't think you should go tonight," said Jenny, her expression going serious.

"Don't be ridiculous. Of course I'm going."

"Okay, well then I…" Jenny creased her brow. "I should go in your place."

"Fat chance!"

"Look. I don't know how he did it, but I'm sure it was Jimmy who attacked Thanh, and he's going to try again," said Jenny. "I need to be there, and I can't be with this fucking beeper on my ankle!"

"That's your fault, not mine!" said Eliza. "Besides, we couldn't switch places even if I wanted to because of that."

"If we did it quick, and you stayed here, I'll bet it would work."

"I know what this is," said Eliza. "You're trying to sabotage me."

"I swear I'm not, Lizzy. I'm telling you I've got a bad feeling about Jimmy."

"You were already proven wrong once, and it's not like you've got any new evidence. You've been stuck here on house arrest."

"But I *do* have new evidence," said Jenny.

"Which is? Let's see it."

"It's not anything I can show you," Jenny said. She grabbed a brush and stepped behind Eliza to work on her waves. "It's Jimmy's body language. There's a... looseness to it since Nilay cleared him. Like he knows he got away with it. But yesterday, he was tensing up again. He's plotting something."

Eliza rolled her eyes and gave her hair up as a bad job. She allowed Jenny to follow her into her bedroom. "I've never been to Homecoming before, you know?"

"Neither have I," said Jenny.

"I'm sorry, but no. I'm probably going to be elected Queen tonight. I'm not missing that—and you can't do my accent anyway. It'll be fine." Eliza lifted her foot onto her bed and pulled the daringly high dress slit aside to expose her leg. "It's not like I'm some shrinking violet."

She strapped her kunai knife to her upper thigh and let the edge of her mouth curl into a familiar smile. "Danger is still my middle name."

Chapter Seven

Dancing Queen

THE CROW'S NEST ELEVATOR CHIMED AND THE DOORS SLID OPEN. Eliza had never been inside Jack's penthouse, only Jenny had. She braced herself for the coming awkwardness, stepped into the hallway, and knocked on the door. Quite rudely, it swung open immediately.

Val wore a fabulous white Canada Goose coat and black leggings, with her chestnut hair brushed to one side like a classic film star.

"The girl I've heard so much about," Val said, in an almost friendly voice. She snatched a crystal dish from the end table in the foyer and thrust it at Eliza. "You look lovely, except for the feathers. Have a mint."

Eliza meekly accepted and popped the buttercream mint into her mouth.

But I liked my feathers. Do I have bad breath?

She waited for Val to turn around and discreetly breathed into her hand.

No? Fuck you, Val!

"Junior will be out shortly," Val said. "Take a seat."

Eliza glanced around, feeling weirdly panicked. The penthouse suite had a broad living room area full of couches and chairs to lounge on. Val was playing Celine Dion on the sound system. On a long end table, all 12 collector's editions of the *Trouble* books were displayed in a row. Eliza took a seat in the nearest armchair so she wouldn't have to look at them.

"Can I get you something to drink, dear?" Val asked.

It was incredibly strange to be in the company of Valerie Valentine without getting full-blast hostility from her. She felt at a loss for how to respond, which her host interpreted as confusion.

"Oh, right. KAZUMI, WOULD YOU LIKE SOMETHING TO DRINK?" Val practically shouted at her, speaking slowly and pantomiming like Eliza barely understood English.

In Japanese, Eliza said, "If I can ever prove you had a hand in my mother's death, I'll kill you."

Val blinked, uncomprehending, and gave Eliza a wide, condescending smile. Jack saved her, walking out from his bedroom in white slacks and an unbuttoned shirt in the shade of pink that exactly matched Eliza's dress. He stood on his bare tiptoes, holding up two pairs of fancy, designer shoes.

"What do you think?" he asked.

Eliza opened her mouth to answer, but Val immediately cut in.

"The Pradas," said Val. "And that white blazer I got you for Christmas. No tie, it's only Homecoming."

"Right," he said. "Thanks, mom."

"Would your friend like something to drink?" Val asked him.

"Maybe something light, like a rosé," said Jack.

He retreated to his room to finish dressing. Val busied herself in the kitchen, searching for a bottle in their dedicated wine fridge. Eliza stuffed her hands into the cushions of the armchair—and her finger brushed a cold, metallic object. Curious, she pulled it out to look. It was a pin, like the kind you wore on a coat lapel. Circular, with blocky numbers in silver overlaying a gold disk: **+99**

That blocky font tapped gently on the door of her subconscious, reminding her of something… someplace—

"Here you are, dear," said Val.

Eliza stuffed the pin back into the armchair cushions and accepted a healthy glass of rosé.

"This is a Woodhall '20," Val said. "A good year, for wine."

Eliza forced a smile that didn't reach her eyes. Val took a seat on the couch opposite her, curling those killer legs underneath her like a particularly pampered cat. She regarded Eliza like a tasty canary and sipped her wine.

"You're quite pretty," Val said. "But you're not the one for him."

Eliza took a sip, which turned into a gulp, which turned into downing the whole glass in one go.

"I know, Valerie," she replied in perfect Queen's English. "We're just friends."

She wanted to see the surprise on Val's face. Shock. Indignation, at least. What she got instead was a sly grin.

Jack returned, fully dressed, bearing a pink carnation corsage for Eliza. In his white blazer and slacks, he looked like a Miami drug dealer. "Ready?"

"Desperately," said Eliza.

"Pictures first!" Val insisted.

She produced a DSLR camera with a big, fancy flash, and Eliza and Jack were forced to pose for what felt like a thousand photos.

"Don't forget to take photos at the dance too," said Val when she'd filled up the camera's memory card. "We'll order you a copy, Kazumi."

"Oh, that's all right, you don't have to," said Eliza.

"It's nothing," said Val. "My family owns the portrait studio the school uses, so they're practically free. Have fun, you two. But not too much fun."

It was hard to believe this was the same cafeteria she ate lunch in yesterday. The Student Council Event Committee must have used a firehose to decorate, covering every surface in hot pink and neon blue. Streamers hung from the scoreboard, and floor-to-ceiling black velvet curtains hid the bleachers on either side of the auditorium. Fog machines kept the floor blanketed in thick mist up to Eliza's knees. A Bangles song pulsed on the sound system.

Penny Griffin, looking stunning in a bright yellow cocktail dress, was chastising Nilay by the voting table about the fog.

"It's too much like Schloss Schwarzwald!" Penny said, making the fog swirl as she kicked at it. "Bad vibes! And no one can see our shoes!"

Drew agreed, helping Alicia set up her drum set on stage.

"The last time I was in fog this thick, I found a body in it," said Drew. He had come in a simple day-glow purple dress shirt and black slacks. Still looked yummy. "Two bodies, if you count Mr. White."

Penny made a horrified face. Jack shot Nilay a frown and made a "cut it off" gesture with his right hand—the one that wasn't gripping Eliza's like a lifeline. She couldn't tell if it was his hand or hers that was sweating. If she could just extricate herself from him for two seconds to properly appreciate Charlie's darling little black dress with its white Peter Pan collar and flared hem…

"We need drinks!" Eliza said, sending Jack to the refreshments table.

She could feel Alicia's green eyes drilling through the back of her skull from the stage.

"Feeling better?" she asked Charlie.

"Homegirl rallied from her bad garlic chicken to put us all to shame in that LBD," said Penny.

"This old thing?" Charlie said with a sanguine grin. "It was hiding in the back of my closet. Was supposed to be my confirmation dress, believe it or not." They hugged, and Charlie gave her a secret squeeze where no one could see. "You and Jack make *such* a cute couple!"

"Shut up!" said Eliza. "Has anyone heard from Thanh?"

Penny shook her head.

"Bollocks. What a shame," she said. "I suppose we're down to three."

"Make it two," said Dinah, materializing from the fog in a high-collared Princess Di dress, all white with red polka dots and big shoulder pads.

"What do you mean?" asked Eliza.

"Ask Mason," Dinah said, frowning at the back of the cafeteria, where Mason Lockhart had just entered in a baby blue tux.

"Is Meghan not coming?" Charlie asked him.

Mason grimaced, joining Drew to help set up the band's equipment.

"Nah." He surprised them all by blushing. "We got caught."

"What do you mean?" asked Penny.

"You know. *Caught*," said Mason.

Recognition dawned and all the girls shrieked. Even Eliza.

"How!!??" they all demanded.

"Her mom was supposed to be shopping in Santa Rosa, but for some reason, she came home early," said Mason.

"Rookie mistake!" Eliza scolded him.

Idiot! Why risk it at Meghan's house when they had their cabin to bone in?

"Dude, I could have rented you a room at the Crow's Nest," said Jack, returning with red solo cups for him and Eliza. He pressed one into her hand; it was overflowing with white smoke. "Dry ice. It's just fruit punch."

She took a sip and allowed Jack to slip his arm around her elbow.

"There's vodka in this," she said.

"Whazzup!!" said Lai, flashing a bottle of Tito's from under his sports coat.

"I know, I know!" said Mason. "It's a good thing her dad wasn't there. He wants to murder me now. He made Meg swear on a stack of bibles when she was 10 that she'd wait till marriage."

"Fuck him!" said a squeaky voice behind Mason. Little Alicia Aaron, gripping her drumsticks, white-knuckled. Her look was straight fire. A sleeveless gown made of layered crimson and black lace, with a slanted hem falling to her ankle on the left, only to soar upward to the right and expose her whole thigh and prosthetic leg. It was daring and transgressive, and Eliza was kinda jealous. "He doesn't control her fucking body!" Alicia yelled. "Son of a son of a bitch cocksucker!"

She said it just as "Tainted Love" by Soft Cell ended, leaving them all in an awkward silence until a new track came on the P.A.

"Uh. Word!" said Penny to the general agreement of all.

Who knew the little redhead held such strong opinions about overbearing dads?

"Well, Kazu," said Dinah. "It is down to you, and it is down to me."

"Unless we get write-ins," said Nilay. "You can still write me in, you know!"

"I'm already demanding a recount," said JeRay.

"Fuck it," said Mason. "Let's shred."

He tapped a pedal at his feet and played a reverberating chord on his guitar, the noise seeming to fold back in on itself as it echoed back and forth across the auditorium. Drew and Alicia joined in on bass and drums, and Eliza recognized the song as something by The Smiths. She took another sip of her spiked punch, letting the vodka soak into her bloodstream, and wiggled her way onto the dance floor. Jack could follow if he wanted to.

Back at home, Jenny paced around her bedroom with mounting anxiety, trying to think about anything other than Homecoming. It might have helped if she hadn't spitefully dressed in what she would have worn to the dance: a corset top, leather pants, and chunky Doc Martens boots.

She rubbed her face. Fuck! Her whole body was tingling, like spiders might start crawling out of her skin at any moment. She grabbed her phone for the thousandth time and checked her socials again. Ooh! Lai was streaming!

Jenny watched the grainy video with rapt attention as Lai's phone camera pointed this way and that way on the murky dance floor. Drew's band was playing, with Mason crooning some '80s song. The audio was terrible, but she could make out Penny's laugh nearby as Lai narrated. He was making all the girls model their fits. There was Eliza, looking prissy and plastic in her elegant pink dress. And then Dinah!

Oh, girl, what are those shoulder pads?

Her hair was so cute, though.

No! Wait! Dammit, Lai, go back!

He'd turned his phone to the stage again, where Nilay had joined the band, doing a goofy little boogie as he wove between Mason and Drew and Alicia's drum kit. Lai flipped his phone around on himself, singing along to "Material Girl" for his viewers. But Jenny wasn't paying attention to him anymore.

Did I just see what I think I saw?

She scrolled back in the video to watch the camera move again. It took several tries to get the stream to pause at the perfect spot, and when it finally did, her heart froze to the core. Right when Lai flipped his phone, the camera panned up over the stage. Hiding on the lighting rig above was an unmistakable silhouette. A tall, dark, and strangesome menace.

Lizzy, beware!

"Shelly!"

Jenny raced downstairs. Shelly was lounging on the couch, grading papers. She looked up at Jenny's panicked face and frowned.

"Oh boy, what now?"

"You need to see this!" Jenny said, holding out her phone.

But when she tried to show her aunt, the stream wouldn't load. An alert appeared on the screen: **No Connection**.

"Shit! Not now!"

"Dang it, the WiFi's been doing that for weeks," Shelly said. "Just reset the modem. It'll come back in 10 minutes or so."

Eliza might not have 10 minutes. Jenny cursed under her breath.

"What?" Shelly asked. "Is it important?"

Jenny ran through her options in her head and did some quick Trouble math. As usual, lying was the best course of action.

"Fine. No," Jenny said, faking a grin. "I just wanted to show you a funny video where this guy totally owns his Econ teacher about inflation."

"Of all the things that didn't happen, I'm sure that didn't happen the most," said Shelly.

Jenny forced a smile and retreated upstairs. Once she snuck out the window and left the property, the police would get an alert from her ankle monitor. They'd be after her in no time. She'd just have to be faster.

LIVE MUSIC WAS SO MUCH FUN! EVERY THUNDEROUS BEAT OF ALICIA'S kick drum reverberated in the hollow of Eliza's chest, knocking loose her inhibitions and sending pleasing vibrations to every extremity. Eliza danced with Jack, danced with Charlie, danced with JeRay, danced with Penny—even danced with Drew when she boldly got up on stage after a second cup of spiked fruit punch. Kazu was a party girl, and to be with her was to be having fun.

All the while, her fellow nominees took their turns in the TikTok Dance Challenge. Nilay relented and picked a song by the Weeknd that *sounded* like it was from the '80s but wasn't old enough to have a mortgage. Jack went first, performing a technically proficient but passionless floss. Dinah's was better, nailing a lot of old-school moves like a real '80s girl. Then JeRay announced he would show them all how it was done, in what he claimed afterward was a classic Michael Jackson routine.

"Did he really grab his balls that much?" Jack asked.

"He really did!" JeRay insisted. "He invented it!"

All the while, Lai roamed amongst them with his phone, broadcasting the whole thing on a live-streaming app, should any viral content occur.

Jimmy went next. He was dressed in a whole-ass tuxedo, which might have been adorable if he wasn't still wearing his backpack over it. And if he weren't such a little turd. He just kind of swayed around and tried to make fart noises with his armpits. Jack needn't have worried about any sympathy vote for him. By the end of the Weeknd song, people were booing him off the stage.

"Jimmy! You owe me a dance, big stud!" Eliza shouted as he ran away to sulk.

A bit nasty of her, maybe. She really would have, though, if he'd been man enough to come back. Instead, she danced with Charlie again while Alicia took over vocals for a cover of the song ScarJo sang in *Lost in Translation*. And then, way too soon, it was Kazumi's turn.

Oh shit! Here we go!

Eliza took Mason's hand, letting him pull her up onto the raised stage. Discreetly, she popped one of Jenny's study pills and downed another sip of punch.

"Give it up for Kazu Onishi!" Mason said into his mic. "Y'all sick of this song yet?"

The same Weeknd song began to play again. Eliza let muscle memory take over, stepping in rhythm, swaying her hips, swinging her arms, smiling for the crowd—

"STOP! LOOK OUT!!"

Oh no. Eliza knew that voice. It was hers, after all.

"Jenny Valentine, everyone!" Mason said on the mic. "Get up here and shake your moneymaker, you little psycho!"

A commotion stirred in the back of the cafeteria. The crowd parted to admit a half-Japanese girl with a mohawk wearing leather pants and a purple corset top.

"No! Up! Up!" Jenny shouted, pointing at Eliza.

Eliza had given up her routine by now, furious at her awful sister who had to ruin every fucking shred of a good time she might be having. Jenny grabbed a soda can from the refreshments table and hurled it at the stage. Or, rather, above it.

The soda can impacted with something. A big, black shape fell from the lighting rig in the rafters, landing right at the foot of Alicia's drum kit. Everyone screamed.

"Got him!" Jenny shouted in triumph, running up to the stage. "Don't let him get away! Who is it!"

Mason and Drew were already kneeling over the prone form. Eliza saw now that it was a man in a dark coat, wearing a black mask and a black fedora. The Stranger??

"Dude! Kazu?!" said Jack.

He was staring at her with concern. Eliza's kunai dagger was gripped in her fist. She didn't even remember drawing it.

"I saw him on Lai's stream!" Jenny said, leaping onto the stage. "He was about to attack Kazu!"

Drew unleashed a stream of filthy curse words in English and Spanish. Mason laughed and kicked the body over with his shoe.

"You've been had, girl," he said into the mic. "This ain't the Stranger, it's Vice Principal Carter's date!"

It wasn't a body. It was a blow-up doll, dressed up like the Stranger for Halloween. Dressed, no doubt, for the exact purpose of drawing her stupid sister out of her house arrest.

"Oh poop," said Jenny.

"MASON!!" shouted someone in the audience. The crowd parted to reveal a middle-aged man with a ruddy face, holding a Louisville Slugger bat.

"Mr. May! What a pleasant surprise!" said Mason, trying and failing to hide his shit-eating grin.

He was cut off by a loud electronic *squelch!* from the cafeteria entrance.

"Jennifer Valentine, you're under arrest!" said Deputy Calderon, his voice amplified by the megaphone in his grip.

He'd brought officers Peña and Mack with him. Mason conferred with his bandmates and unstrapped his guitar, keeping the mic.

"One! Two! Three! Four!" screamed Alicia, launching into a propulsive new beat.

Eliza whirled on Jenny as the cops pushed through the crowd. "One fucking night! You can't give me one fucking night to myself!?"

Jenny had the gall to look wounded. "I was trying to protect you."

Drew laid down some synths and bass. Eliza recognized the song now—it was that one from the old music video where the girl goes into a black-and-white comic book.

"Get down here and fight me, boy!" Meghan's dad yelled at Mason.

"Why don't you come up here and smell my finger, George," Mason replied.

Several things happened at once. Meghan's dad charged the stage; Calderon lunged to cut him off and missed; Mason retreated with his wireless mic, crooning the first bars of the song; and—no bullshit— half a dozen feral hogs stampeded into the cafeteria from the side exit.

Chaos. Students ran pell-mell in every direction to avoid the rampaging hogs. Calderon's megaphone was making awful electronic feedback, forcing Mason to sing louder. Dinah shrieked and climbed up on the refreshments table. Nilay screamed, "Not like this!!" while Lai gleefully filmed it all. Only Drew and Alicia kept it together, banging out the song while madness raged around them.

Jenny yanked Eliza out of the way of a charging Mr. May and

screamed in her ear, pointing. Eliza turned to see a figure dressed all in black retreating to the exit. Jenny gave chase, only to be tackled by Deputy Calderon before she made it halfway.

Cursing, Eliza dove into the mayhem. Maybe she could reach the other exit and cut them off. The smell of the hogs was overwhelming. Was JeRay trying to fight one? A scrum of freshmen forced Eliza further away from the exit. She leaped up, using a hog as a stepping stone, and vaulted over them. Her head spun as she steadied herself. *Don't puke! Don't puke!* She found herself face-to-face with Mason as he came out of the breakdown to nail the falsetto bridge.

There! Behind him! Through the other exit, she saw the dark figure fleeing across the quad.

Mason reached out and pulled her aside, just in time to dodge a home run swing from Meghan's dad. The men danced and jabbed at each other, with Eliza caught between them.

Fuck this!

Eliza punched Mr. May in the throat and grabbed the bat. She spun around Mason, freeing herself from the fight. Where was that exit now? She took a step toward the door, Mason ducked with his mic, and Mr. May's fist swung past him at the edge of her peripheral vision—

POP!

Stars exploded in her vision, and she knew no more.

If there was a silver lining to it, George May wouldn't be policing Meghan's sex life any time soon. Eliza hadn't been conscious to witness it, but Penny and Dinah assured her that Deputy Calderon's takedown of him was brutal and well-deserved. While it wasn't the viral moment Nilay and Mr. Carter had hoped for, Kazumi getting leveled by an angry parent was doing great numbers on Lai's TikTok. And Jenny's house arrest was getting extended another two weeks, meaning they were all saved from her ruining Halloween too.

On the other side of the ledger, Eliza had a shiner so bad even Charlie's magic makeup skills wouldn't be able to cover it up. And whoever was behind the Stranger decoy and feral hogs—not the real Stranger, Jenny now confidently declared—had gotten away.

Mr. Carter corralled all the interested parties onto the stage, refusing to let them leave until he had the answers he wanted. Eliza lay slumped in Charlie's lap, holding an ice pack to her face.

"You're sure you saw someone else release the hogs?" Vice Principal Carter asked Alicia Aaron. "It wasn't Jennifer?"

He desperately wanted to put it on Jenny. They all did. But the facts wouldn't cooperate.

"I'm sure, Principal Carter," said Alicia. "Drew and I both saw them run out the side exit." She turned to Jenny, who was handcuffed to the kick drum. Her sister's lip was bleeding from Calderon's rough tackle, but her expression was oddly calm. She was off in Troubleland, no doubt. Alicia went on. "She didn't release the pigs, but I *would* like to know why she's wearing my corset top! Give it back, Trouble!!"

Jenny blinked and grinned like a madwoman.

"We've got a problem, guys," said Nilay. He was frowning at a clipboard. "The Homecoming vote's messed up."

"Mr. Nagra, I could not possibly care less about that right now," said Mr. Carter.

"With respect, Richard," said Nilay, "Homecoming can't end until winners are declared. It's right there in the new charter I wrote."

The vice principal fumed, glancing at Calderon to back him up. The deputy shrugged.

"Fine! What's the problem?" Mr. Carter asked. "Did they get lost in the chaos?"

"No, they're all there," said Penny. "Perfectly preserved in the lockbox. But it seems we've had a surprise write-in campaign."

"She tampered with the lockbox," said Nilay. "She must have!"

"Just spit it out, Nails," said Jack.

"By unanimous write-in vote," said Nilay, "This year's Homecoming King is…" He sighed and glanced at his clipboard again as if the result might have changed. "Junior Valentine, which I assume means you, Jack."

All the dudes slapped Jack on the back and dapped him up.

"And the Queen?" asked Dinah.

"Jennifer effing Valentine," said Nilay.

All heads turned to the worst sister a girl could ask for.

"Ohmygod! You didn't!" Jenny screamed in a girly lilt. "I'm so honored!! Do I get to do my TikTok dance? I've been practicing!"

Chapter Eight

Trick or Treat

Be like Mr. Duck. That's what Jenny's new court-ordered therapist told her. Let all the hate and negativity wash over her, like water off a duck's back. She couldn't control what other people thought of her, or the way they reacted to her stunning Homecoming Queen victory, but she could control how she responded to them.

Jenny was trying to be like Mr. Duck, but she didn't have beautiful, mottled, waterproof feathers. And this wasn't water dripping down the front of her Halloween costume.

"I SEE YOU, YOU LITTLE SHIT!" Jenny screamed at the tow-headed 10-year-old who had just thrown a raw egg at her. "I KNOW WHERE YOU LIVE!!"

"So what?! Loser!" he shouted back.

He stepped out from behind Shelly's Volvo and made stupid boy faces at her, daring Jenny to violate her house arrest again. One of his little buddies was hiding behind the car, giggling his stupid ass off.

"What are you gonna do about it, huh!?" he said.

"I'll fuck your father and give him a son he can love!"

Later, as Jenny tried to scrub the egg off her brand-new, yellow vinyl trench coat, Shelly gave her the inevitable lecture about not making the neighborhood boy cry.

"He started it!" Jenny said. "Ugh, this coat is ruined. I was going to return this tomorrow!"

"Better the jacket than Lala's clothes," said Shelly.

Her aunt had loaned Jenny some of her mother Laura's old clothes after finding a box of them in the garage. Mom had some seriously bitching retro clothes, which Jenny cobbled together into her costume as Jubilee from the X-Men, with help from the yellow trench coat she ordered off Amazon. She didn't exactly have the money to pay for it, and once Shelly noticed the charge on her credit card, Jenny would be screwed. But that was a problem for Tomorrow Trouble.

The doorbell chimed.

"Can you get that?" Shelly asked.

Jenny gestured incredulously at the grimy stain on her coat.

"Blake's taking me to the French Laundry," Shelly said, protectively crossing her arms over her elegant evening dress. "I can't be getting egged on your account."

Jenny let out a symphony of scoffs and groans to make her displeasure known before scampering to the foyer. This time, she was smart about it and stood to the side as she threw the front door open.

No projectiles sailed by, but no one said "trick or treat" either.

After a pregnant pause, Sheriff Blake Lockhart, wearing a perfectly tailored black suit, ducked his head inside, giving Jenny a questioning brow raise.

"Looks like you got a 'trick,'" he said, with his usual cop condescension.

Jenny tried lighting him on fire with her mutant powers, but once again, no dice. She held out a plastic pumpkin full of candy. Lockhart fished through it and pulled out the last Charleston Chew—her favorite.

Be like Mr. Duck.

"Have her home by nine," Jenny said sweetly.

"Nine AM? I can do that," he said. The cad. "Michelle can trust you to behave while she's out, can't she? It took months to get this reservation."

"Two more weeks, Lockhart," Jenny said, lifting her leg that still sported the ankle monitor. "Two more weeks until this thing comes off, and then it's over for all you hos."

After the requisite gross smooching and complimenting of Shelly's fabulous dress, the two lovebirds skedaddled with one last warning to stay out of—well, you know.

"I'm going to call the house every hour, so you'd better be here to pick up," Shelly said.

"You don't have to do that," Jenny said.

"Oh, but I do," said Shelly. She wiped a stray piece of eggshell from Jenny's hair and smiled sadly. "You look so much like her."

"Jubilee?"

"Your mother. Don't eat too much candy."

Jenny closed the door on them and groaned. This sucked so hard.

Jiji and Baba had gone to Santa Barbara all weekend for a jazz festival, and Eliza was at the Harvest Festival with the Bitchy Brigade, leaving Jenny stuck at home by herself on her favorite night of the year. Dejected, she ate several fun-size Twix and debated whether to order a pizza from the Red Grape. Maybe she could get them to put it on Jack's tab.

The doorbell chimed again.

Jenny groused and got up. Maybe it would be a little girl dressed as Trouble. That always cheered her up. She swung the door open, not even bothering to keep clear this time, and held out the bowl of treats.

It wasn't a little girl in a Trouble outfit. It wasn't even a little kid at all, but a massive guy wearing an LA Rams jersey over a furry wolf-man costume. Jenny tensed, ready for anything—except what happened next. Teen Wolf pulled off his gnarly wolf mask, and Jenny gasped.

"I need your help," said Drew.

"I'M SORRY, I DIDN'T THINK I WAS WORTHY OF HELPING YOU," SAID Jenny. "I thought 'Everything I touch dies.' What changed, *Drewboo?*"

After two months of shunning, she wasn't going to make it easy for him. He made a pinched face and unzipped his costume halfway, pulling out a padded shipping envelope he'd tucked inside. From it, he withdrew a nondescript smartphone with a cracked screen and held it up for her to read. Though garbled now, the screen functioned enough for Jenny to make out a 6-digit passcode prompt, and a warning above it.

Incorrect Passcode
Try again in 5 minutes. You have 3 tries left

Jenny squinted at the display. Tech was more Danger's area of expertise, not that she cared to help these days. Drew offered no further explanation; he was forcing her to figure it out. It wasn't his phone, clearly. There was no 49ers case, for one. Drew didn't have an Android, and he wouldn't forget his passcode, which was always **555789** (Trouble's suitcase combination in *Trouble in Paris*).

Jenny winced. There could only be one answer to the riddle: it was Arturo Porter's phone. "How did you get it?"

"It just showed up one day in my mailbox," Drew said. "A couple weeks after they found him."

He let her examine the envelope. There was no postage or return address, only Drew's first and last name written in big block letters in black Sharpie.

ANDREW PORTER

"Looks like the Stranger," she said.

"I considered that, but I'm pretty sure that's my dad's handwriting," said Drew. "He would label the dry goods in the pantry in all caps like that, on masking tape."

"He didn't include the passcode?"

"In the note, he said he wasn't including it, just in case the police got it. He said I'd figure it out."

Every word out of his mouth dripped with bitter recrimination.

"I'm sorry, Drew," Jenny said.

"I didn't come here for an apology," he said. "I'll pay you $5,000 if you can crack this for me."

"That's very generous, but I don't see how I can if you can't," said Jenny. "I'm no hacker, and surely you knew him better than me."

"Thought I did," he said sharply. "As you can see, I have three tries left."

Jenny studied Drew's face. The anger was still there, along with mourning and loss. But there was something else, too: excitement. Could it be, after months of hating, that her former sidekick had started to miss the game? Miss her?

"$10,000," she said. "Tax-free, and under the table."

"Deal," said Drew.

THEY'D HAVE TO DO THEIR SLEUTHING FROM HOME SINCE JENNY couldn't go anywhere. Drew ordered that pizza from the Red Grape and gave her the rundown on what he'd already tried: his birthday, Arty's birthday, Mirai's birthday, their wedding day, Y2K, the night before Y2K, and Arty's ATM PIN, which was **4949**, with Drew adding an extra **49** at a guess. They had three tries left.

"What else did the note say?" Jenny asked.

In reply, he handed her a scrap of Schloss Schwarzwald stationery, on which a note had been scribbled in tidy handwriting.

> Drew,
>
> I'm sorry it worked out this way. I wrote you a longer letter in the app. Can't include the passcode, in case this gets intercepted. I'm confident you'll figure it out.
>
> I love you,
>
> Dad

"He really poured out his heart there," Drew said after she read the note.

"Your father struck me as a man of exactitude," Jenny offered. Drew snorted. "What I mean is, I think he was the most precise about the things he cared about the most."

"That's an excellent excuse for being a withholding prick, I'm gonna use that," said Drew. "Well, ideas?"

"There are six sentences here if we count the salutation and the sign-off," said Jenny. "Six numbers in the passcode. Maybe if we convert the first letter in each sentence to a number, like in *Trouble*

Eight Days a Week..."

She grabbed a pen and worked it out on the back of the note.

    D = 4
    I = 9
    I = 9
    C = 3
    I = 9
    I = 9

For **499399**.

"Shall we try it?" Jenny asked.

"Sure."

Jenny punched in the code on the cracked screen. A little wheel spun, and an alert appeared.

Incorrect Passcode
Try again in 1 hour. You have 2 tries left

"Damn," said Jenny.

Drew shook his head. "Hidden codes don't seem like Dad. It would be simple, I think."

"Okay, no worries, we've got two more tries," said Jenny, trying to remain upbeat. "And an hour to kill. So, how've you been?"

He glared, still trying to maintain his wounded tough guy facade.

"Don't act like you're the only one whose life sucks," said Jenny. "The whole damn school hates me now—even my best friend."

"I don't *hate* you," said Drew. "You just..."

"I just bring pain and misery everywhere I go. I know," she said. "At Schloss Schwarzwald, in the maze, you told me it wasn't my fault. That it was the Stranger doing all this. Did you mean it?"

"I guess it was easier to mean it when wasn't affecting me personally." Drew got up and paced the living room, which would have been more dramatic if he weren't wearing a wolf-man outfit. "If I hadn't shown you the hair dye. If you had just let him go."

"If I had, and the Stranger was still forcing him to murder people, is that better?" asked Jenny.

He flopped back down onto the couch. "That's what makes me so angry. Not at you, but at the whole stupid world."

"It's not the world, it's the Stranger," said Jenny. "Don't forget that. He's not some supernatural force. He's just a man."

"You're sure he's a man?"

Jenny bit the inside of her cheek. "Sometimes. At the castle, for sure. But then, that *was* a man."

"Arty Porter. Big man."

The doorbell rang. Jenny made no move to answer. Drew raised an eyebrow.

"Fuck 'em," said Jenny.

"What if it's the pizza?"

"Oh, right."

Jenny got up to get the door. She came back with another egg dripping down her face, and no pizza.

"Next time, you're getting it!" she snapped at Drew, then went to the sink to clean her pink mirrored shades.

Out of the corner of her eye, she saw him crack a smile. Good. At least she hadn't smashed an egg on her face for nothing.

When the pizza did arrive, it was accompanied by a Postmates order Drew put in for a case of Mountain Dew Code Red and a big box of Mike and Ikes candy. They ate on the couch and watched *Scream* while waiting for the passcode timeout to expire. Jenny had no clue what to try next.

On the TV, it was the scene where Billy and Stu accost Randy at the video store. It was so obvious, in retrospect, who the killers were. Though two killers had always kind of felt like cheating to Jenny. Could there be two Strangers? Or did the Stranger achieve the same misdirection by forcing people like Arty Porter to do his dirty work until they were no longer useful to him?

Randy was talking about motives and the millennium on screen.

"I've never understood this line," Drew said with a mouthful of pizza.

He was housing two slices at a time, one on top of the other, the way only hungry teenage boys can.

"I think it's because they thought everyone would die in Y2K or something," said Jenny.

"I guess it's just like… without a motive, there's no mystery," he said. "And that's boring."

"What was Arty's motive?" Jenny asked.

"Wow, vibe killer."

"It's ten grand, I'm trying to think."

"I mean, protecting my mom and I, right?" he said. "That's the noble version. He might have been more concerned about catching a murder charge from the shit that happened there 20 years ago."

Her watch vibrated. It was time to try another code. She picked up the phone and wracked her brain.

"Wait," said Drew. "He put a lock on that bridge when we were in Paris! Oh, but it was a key lock, not a combination one."

"Do you know your mom's measurements?" Jenny asked.

"No."

"Does she hate me?"

"She's never mentioned it," said Drew.

So, yes. Ugh. Mirai Porter was possibly the coolest lady Jenny had ever met. And she'd lost her husband for it, thanks to Jenny befriending her son.

"It's gotta be some number that comes easily to you," she said. "Any number you're always thinking about?"

Drew bit his lip, thinking, until a sad smile peeked out.

"We always used to joke about that scene in *Spaceballs* where his combination is 1-2-3-4-5," Drew said. "He loved that movie, which was weird for him because he was usually such a tight ass."

Jenny shrugged and punched it in.

1•2•3•4•5•6

No dice.

Incorrect Passcode
Try again in 2 hours. You have 1 try left

"Sorry," said Jenny.

Drew's smile melted away. He shrugged and turned up the volume on the TV. What would he do if she guessed wrong again?

THEY WERE ON TO *SCREAM 2*, AND DREW WAS REGRETTING EATING all those Mike and Ikes. Jenny, meanwhile, had anxiously put away seven Code Reds and was having to pee every 10 minutes. The caffeine rush felt almost as good as Adderall. She had no clue what to do with their last guess.

On the TV, Sydney's boyfriend was singing to her, standing on the dining hall table.

"Do girls like this?" Drew asked.

"If anyone ever did that to me, I'd transfer schools," she said.

"What if Dinah did it?"

"…I mean, I don't think she would."

"Mmhmm," said Drew.

"You know, Drew," Jenny said, popping another can of soda. "I've been patiently waiting for you to explain this costume of yours."

"I lost a bet," he said.

"You're going to have to do better than that, mister."

He sat up and turned to her. "So I was at the Harvest Festival, and everyone was there, and I had to wear this stupid Teen Wolf costume because JeRay outhit me in batting practice, and Meghan May was passing around a flask—which was pretty bold since she just got off restriction—and they were gonna skip me in the rotation, but then your cousin Kazumi made sure to give me a sip, which was very sweet, I like her, and the next five years flashed before my eyes. Lots of booze and parties and trying to get laid—and believe me, I'd very much like to do all that, but I'm gonna be 18 in few weeks, and I'm dealing with fucking probate lawyers, and Mom's got a new job now, and I thought, why am I in such a hurry? I'd rather be eating junk food and overdosing on caffeine and watching horror movies and…"

He glanced away, too shy to say it.

"Solving mysteries?" Jenny guessed.

Drew tried and failed to fight his grin. "Is it true Mr. Webb got decapitated?"

"Hah! I knew it! You *did* miss me!"

"It's a total cope," said Drew. "Can we just pretend, for one night, that Schloss Schwarzwald didn't happen yet? Aside from, you know, cracking this stupid phone?"

"Of course," said Jenny. "But let's circle back to you liking my cousin."

"I just meant she was cool," he said, though his red-tipped ears suggested otherwise. "I think she's with Charlie; they're together a lot. It's fucked up, though, right?"

"Charlie? She's fine, I guess. Not much of a kisser, in my opinion."

"No, I mean me!" said Drew. "Mom will cry herself to sleep some nights, and there's still this small part of me that's like: I wonder what clue Jenny's working on now? When someone shaved Thanh Trân's head, I got *excited*. I wanted it to be the Stranger. Am I just a horrible person?"

"Catching the Stranger is the best and maybe only way to bring justice for Mirai—and Arty," said Jenny. "So I say no. But as for me? I've been on house arrest for two months, so I haven't been able to do shit, except research old video games."

Drew was confused, so Jenny gave him a recap of the events in Town Square: the secret heirloom, Mr. Webb's murder, Pixeldrome, and Tori's tale. Just as she suspected, he ate it all up like an addict jonesing for his fix. By the time she'd caught him up, the movie was over and they were almost due to try a final code. She examined the shipping envelope the phone came in. No postage, no return address…

"How was this even delivered?" she asked. "It was just in your mailbox one day?"

"Yeah," he nodded. "I tried—we have one of those doorbell cameras now, and the mailbox is just in frame, but by the time I thought to check it, all the videos from that day had rolled off the buffer. The cat—we got a cat. Mom needed…something. And Dad was always allergic. Anyway, she's always setting off the motion detector, so if you don't check within a day, you're usually SOL."

"You know," Jenny said, smiling, "If this were a *Trouble* book, this would be one of those seemingly insignificant details that's actually the key to the whole mystery."

"Right?" Drew grinned. "He would have gotten some trusted childhood friend or ex-lover to deliver it, and they'd know some crucial thing when Trouble tracked them down."

"Like the fuckin' code!" said Jenny.

"Pssh. Yeah," said Drew. "But really, it was probably just some college kid my dad hired off one of those gig websites or something. Whatever one was the cheapest."

Her watch vibrated again. Time for one last try at the code.

"Fuck it," Drew grabbed the phone. "I don't even care anymore. You're too late, Dad. You had your chance and you blew it."

He mashed the **0** button on the keypad to burn their last try.

To their mutual shock, the code was accepted.

"Oh shit! Did it work?" Jenny yelped.

Drew stared at the phone in disbelief.

"How the fuck was I supposed to guess that?! Asshole!"

He wanted to be angry, Jenny could tell. But his lower lip was already starting to quiver.

"Hey, why don't we call it a night? You can read it on your own," she said.

"You sure?"

"It's fine. Just let me know if he left any clues," Jenny said.

She walked him to the door and was debating whether or not she should give him a hug, when he dug into his wolf-man suit.

"Almost forgot," he said and pulled out a stack of hundred-dollar bills.

"I didn't solve it, though," said Jenny. "You did."

He shrugged. "Close enough."

And then he left. No hug. That was okay, at least he didn't *totally* hate her anymore. At least she could afford her ruined yellow trench coat now.

Jenny tidied up their pizza boxes and soda cans, even though she doubted she'd see Aunt Shelly tonight, who'd never even called once. After a long shower, Jenny changed into PJs and carefully folded

Mom's old clothes. It was hard to picture her mother ever wearing a glittery, midriff-baring crop top. Jenny knew she'd died young, but in her imagination, she was always older. Mom-aged.

After watching two *Scream* movies, going into the dark garage was almost enough to get her adrenaline pumping. Jenny snorted.

Reduced to psyching yourself out in your own garage, Trouble. Wasn't this supposed to be our year?

She located the old box marked **Laura — Closet** and returned the clothes she'd borrowed.

"Thanks, Mom," she said.

Just as she was closing up the box, something caught her eye. There was a blue t-shirt, half-buried below other tops, with a familiar logo on it. Jenny frowned, pulling the shirt out. When she unfolded it and held it up under her phone's flashlight, she gasped. Real adrenaline coursed in her veins this time.

A pixelated gold coin was stitched onto the sleeve, and across the front, in big retro lettering was a name.

Pixeldrome

Chapter Nine

Pixeldrome

"**L**AURA ONISHI PIXELDROME" DIDN'T RETURN ANY SEARCH RESULTS, but Jenny wasn't sure Google was even a thing yet when Mom died. Trouble used the *Encyclopedia Britannica* a lot in the books, and it always seemed to have the right answer for her. Unfortunately, Jiji didn't have one in his study. Just legal thrillers and a bunch of old *Ellery Queen* issues.

While she waited for her house arrest to end, Jenny meticulously cataloged everything in the **Laura — Closet** box. Weirdly baggy jeans, animal prints, short skirts, flannel, denim jackets, some wraparound sunglasses straight out of *The Matrix*, and a sequined underarm purse with a very short strap. Honestly, not Jenny's style at all. Eliza might like the skirts, though. And lastly, the Pixeldrome shirt: size small, 100 percent polyester.

What did it mean? Had RJ known there was some connection between Mom and the arcade? He must have. Jenny had to go there in person. The short video of Pixeldrome that Penny had sent her was unfortunately of no use at all. She needed to see the place with her own eyes. Jenny glared at her stupid ankle bracelet. Three more days…

The hours passed at a glacial pace. Drew was sitting with the cool seniors again at lunch (who called themselves the Unfridgeables—how lame!), and Jenny didn't want to mess that up, so they would only talk after school via text. He promised he was working on an epic Big Board in the meantime.

When the day of her freedom finally arrived, she asked Shelly about Mom's Pixeldrome shirt. She'd been reluctant to. Surely, Lockhart would have told her aunt about the game token and Mr. Webb, right? But Shelly didn't react at all.

How interesting. Still keeping secrets, Sheriff?

"Oh yeah, I remember this," Shelly said, holding up the shirt. "Lala used to work there."

"Seriously!? At Pixeldrome??"

Shelly raised an eyebrow at Jenny's interest in the place. "Yeah, over the summer, before she went to college." She let out a snicker. "Funny you should ask. Your Jiji and Baba always blamed UC Davis for changing her. Their perfect little angel got a taste of college life and started smoking cloves, dating guys in bands, and complaining about the patriarchy. But it started that summer, working at Pixeldrome."

An icy shiver rippled down her spine. Jenny could feel her heart pounding in her chest, threatening to burst through her ribcage.

"What do you mean?" Jenny whispered.

"She worked nights and didn't get home till late," said Shelly. "And every time she did, she was a little more cynical, a little more rebellious. More... worldly, you could say. A couple of older guys worked there..." Shelly hesitated and fixed Jenny with a furrowed brow. "I know it's different for you, and probably way too late, but we've never really had *the talk*, have we?"

"Oh god, why?"

"Jennifer. There's going to come a time in your life when it will feel like you've invented sex. That nobody's having it like you're having it, and everyone who isn't is still living in a little kiddie world where they couldn't possibly fathom experiencing life the way you do. And in some sense, that may be true. But losing your virginity doesn't make you a different person, and you should be wary of anyone who tries to convince you otherwise—even if you really like them."

Jenny contemplated crawling inside the box labeled **Laura — Clothes** and boxing herself up for all eternity. "Are. You. Trying. To.

Kill. Me?"

"I am trying to start treating you as the young woman you'll soon be," said Shelly. "Jiji and Baba never did with us, and it sure as hell backfired on them with Lala. I don't think I need to worry about that with you, but this is all a prelude to say…"

She pulled out a boxy device and knelt, pressing it against Jenny's ankle. With a beep, the ankle monitor's red light switched off, and the lock disengaged. Jenny's time was served; she was finally free!

Shelly rose, waving the monitor in her face. "Don't. Break. Any. More. Laws. You'll be a legal adult in four months. You're just about out of second chances."

FREEDOM. FINALLY. PIXELDROME WAS THE PRIORITY, BUT SHE'D promised to stop by Drew's place first. Drew had said on the phone, "Penny's coming over too if that's all right." Of course it was all right! It took her back to junior year and making plaster casts in the Haunted Vineyard with the two of them. Good times.

When she arrived, she discovered that Drew hadn't just made a new Big Board, he'd remodeled the entire detached garage into some kind of dude's paradise.

"Holy shit!" said Jenny. "This is a whole-ass masturbatorium!"

"Hah! I said the same thing!" said Penny

"Stop calling it that!" Drew insisted.

The formerly spare garage now featured thick luxury carpet and leather couches, a gigantic widescreen TV, lots of video games, LED lighting, and some sort of high-tech mini batting cage. Arty's workbench was still there, awkwardly shoved into the corner behind the batting cage. Maybe that was the part of his dad Drew wasn't willing to part with.

"Be honest. How much did this cost?" Penny asked.

"Not to be a douchebag, but I honestly have no idea," said Drew. "I kinda lost my mind a little after Austria, and I'd just made a killing off the Bitcoin crash, so I had money to burn."

Penny did a Superman dive onto one of the couches and sank into the cushions. "Oh my god, I need one."

"You can't go through your midlife crisis yet, Drewboo," said Jenny. "You haven't even had your first ex-wife."

"Yeah, yeah. Check this out. Hey Siri, Big Board!" Drew grinned and waited. Nothing happened. "Shit, hold on."

"Womp womp," said Penny.

He tapped on his phone for what felt like a solid minute before the new Big Board finally unfurled from the ceiling on electronic motors.

"I got an upgraded projector screen," Drew said. "Smart home integration's a little iffy, though."

Jenny wanted to tease, but it was pretty sick. All their photos and clues and red yarn connections were taped to the white screen. He'd added a drawing of the new eighth clue: the Pixeldrome game token, and a red strand of yarn connecting it to the big question mark in the middle.

"Would you mind if…" Penny bit her lip. "It's stupid, but can you put Nilay on the board?"

"Uhh, why? Do you know something we don't?" asked Drew.

"Nilay can't be the Stranger," said Jenny. "He wasn't even here junior year."

"I know, but I don't want him to feel left out," said Penny. "He's more sensitive about it than he lets on!"

"I mean, sure," said Jenny, rolling her eyes. "Find him a spot, Drew. But you can't tell him about any of our leads, Penny. Not if he's still helping Val."

"It's such nonsense," said Penny. "I think he's hoping she'll hook him up with an internship at the Foundation."

Jenny glanced at Drew and asked, "Anything in your dad's letter?"

"A lot of life advice, like 'Don't sleep with a woman you wouldn't want to raise kids with,' and 'Save 10 percent of your salary for retirement, no matter how little you're making,'" said Drew. "He said we should dig up RJ's corpse, just to be sure."

"He's in a marble crypt, we'd need heavy machinery," said Penny.

"Sorry, but I refuse to believe he's the Stranger," said Jenny.

She wasn't sure who was less convinced: Drew and Penny, or herself.

"Anyway," said Jenny. "Let's run it down. The wine bottle, photo, tarot card, noose, and blackbird statue are all solved, leaving us the key, the book, and the game token. Penny, can you tell us anything about your mom's heirloom?"

"Nada," said Penny. "I don't even know where she hid the book, but she insists it's a dead end, and not to worry about it."

"Okay, so that leaves us the key and the token," said Jenny. "The Stranger's got the key, which means our only shot left is the game token."

"Hmm. Maybe we could re-create the key," said Penny. "I'm taking a maker class this quarter to fill my schedule. Mr. Stephenson has a 3D printer. Did you take photos of it?"

Jenny grimaced and shook her head.

"Rookie mistake, Trouble," said Drew. "Alicia might have some…"

"Let's back-burner that," said Jenny. "The game token feels hot right now. I just learned my mom worked there after high school. That can't be a coincidence. I think my dad wants me there."

She didn't mention the **High Score** note she'd received. Like Eliza, that had to remain an ace up her sleeve.

"So, shall we go?" Jenny asked.

"Where?" said Penny.

"To Pixeldrome! Right now! I'm dying to see what a hundred dollars in quarters looks like," Jenny said.

Drew winced. "I wish I could, but I have to be at the airport in an hour. My mom and I are doing a college tour of Arizona State and SDSU."

"ASU??" Penny looked like she might puke. "Drew, I'm sure you're envisioning a bunch of blonde babes with big boobs, but you would hate going to a party school."

"Wait, what school is this?" Jenny asked.

"And sorry, Jenny, but I'm supposed to meet Nilay for lunch," said Penny.

Jenny sighed, trying to hide her disappointment. The cat nudged her leg, demanding a pet.

"Okay, well, maybe it's better I go alone, to get a feel for the place," she said, leaning down to give the kitty some scritches.

I could use some scritches…

"I wouldn't get your hopes up," said Drew. "I've been there before. Bunch of Harbor High losers—and the owner's a creep."

BOY, DREW WASN'T KIDDING. JENNY HADN'T BEEN INSIDE OF Pixeldrome for 10 seconds and already some big, oafish asshole was accosting her.

"What's up, normie?" said the big lunk. "Can I borrow a dollar? I'm willing to pay you back in sexual favors—"

"Get the fuck away from me!" Jenny said, snapping out her collapsible riot baton.

Remember what Shelly said! Don't get arrested!

It was hard to focus with her senses overloaded by the hyperactive synth music, neon lighting, and staccato beeps and boops from dozens of arcade games. It smelled like the birthday pizza parties she'd never been invited to as a child. Vaguely, she became aware of someone cackling at them. Jenny peeked around the oaf's massive frame to see Jimmy Figg watching from a *Ninja Turtles* arcade cabinet, laughing his ass off.

"Dude, you fracking liar!" said the big guy.

"Wait, did he tell you I'd be into that?" Jenny asked, pointing her baton at Jimmy.

"No, he told you me you'd pepper spray me," said the boy. "We had a bet."

"What— Why…? What is wrong with you?"

"Nathaniel thinks he can take a shot of mace to the face," said Jimmy, coming over.

As diminutive as Jimmy Figg was, this Nathaniel idiot was the reverse. Easily over six feet, with enough girth to play offensive tackle. He might have passed for an adult if his moony baby face hadn't given him away. Jenny hated him instantly.

"Mace and pepper spray aren't the same thing," said Jenny, collapsing the baton against her palm. "And you'd go down like a stuck pig. Where's this *Trouble* game that's supposedly here?"

"Not for you!" said Jimmy in a sing-song voice.

"Great, another one," said Nathaniel. "You're gonna have to level up like that retard over there."

He pointed over to the tables in the food court area, where Alicia Aaron was reading a book, a rubbery slice of pizza untouched at her elbow.

"Dude! Fuck you! You don't fucking say that about her! Or anyone!" Jenny snapped the baton open again.

Don't get arrested!

"Relax, she didn't hear me," said Nathaniel.

"*I* heard you!"

"Oh! I'm sorry, are you a retard, too?" Nathaniel asked with mock concern.

Don't get arrested!!!

"Does he know who I am?" Jenny asked Jimmy Figg. "Because it sounds like he has a death wish."

"Your powers are useless here," said Jimmy. "We out-level you."

"I don't know what kind of nerd shit you're talking about," said Jenny. "But it's no excuse for being offensive. You're being ableist, and misogynist and… probably racist, too."

"Like she's the arbiter of good manners," Nathaniel said to Jimmy. "If we're so offensive, then why are we both friends with a based, lesbian woman of color?"

"Hah!" said Jimmy, and they both crossed their arms like they'd made a clever point.

"Are these idiots bothering you?" asked a girl, walking over.

At first glance, Jenny thought she was another customer. One who was super committed to the whole '80s aesthetic of this place. Looking closer, she could see the girl had on a Pixeldrome polo shirt underneath her jean jacket. Her complexion was a rich olive. She wore thick, black frame glasses, and a sneer that wasn't doing her face any favors. Still, there was an undeniable vibe Jenny was picking up. Was this the aforementioned "based, lesbian woman of color"?

I'll bet she gives some scritches…

"Yes. These incels are being quite rude," said Jenny. "Can't you, like, kick them out?"

The girl rolled her eyes and turned to the boys. "Jimmy, Nathaniel, stop scaring the hos."

"For your information, I am not an incel," said Nathaniel, all haughty now. "I lost my virginity when I was twelve."

"Getting dome from your pedo aunt doesn't count," said the girl.

"Yes it does!" he snapped back.

Jenny could feel her brain leaking out of her ears. What kind of sick hellhole had she just stumbled into? *Fucking Harbor High!*

The girl must have noticed her blue-screened expression. She grinned and pulled Jenny aside. "You must be a level zero," she said. "Welcome to Pixeldrome. Outside, it's the 2020s, but inside, you're in the '80s, girl, and you can say whatever you want. It's kinda refreshing, once you get used to it. Unless you're a loser."

"And you are?" Jenny asked.

"Asha. Tell me you're not about to ask to speak to the manager like some Karen?"

Jenny was, but now she'd feel lame if she did. "No Karens in the '80s, Asha," Jenny said instead.

"Touché."

"I heard there was a *Trouble* video game here," said Jenny. She put on her most winning smile. "I'd like to play it, please."

Asha snickered. "Sorry, babe. Pussy pass denied."

Condescension dripped off her every utterance. Jenny was used to it from adults, and sometimes Jack, but when girls her age acted like this, it activated all her buried insecurities and sent her right back to sophomore year, when She Who Must Not Be Named teased her in front of all the cool girls for being obsessed with her.

"Oh, don't pout!" said Asha. "It's not—"

"Not available to level zeros," said an older man with a reedy voice. "You gotta be a VIP to play any of my custom games. But surely you already knew that, Jenny Valentine?"

Jenny forced her attention away from the mean arcade clerk—whom she sort of wanted to make out with—to this new prick. He was around Lockhart's age, Jenny guessed, with none of the sheriff's good looks or physical fitness. Lank and skinny, with hollow cheeks and dark circles under his eyes that spoke to his poor nutrition. His shaggy mullet of hair was shoe-polish black (obviously dyed), and he wore a faded Van Halen t-shirt over acid-washed jeans.

"You must be Rob Haines," said Jenny.

"The Girl Detective, everyone!" Rob said, giving her sarcastic applause. "I was warned about you. 'Someday, a crazy, wild-eyed girl in a purple trench coat may show up asking about the game. And if that ever happens…' Heheh."

Asha laughed too. Jenny didn't get the joke.

"*Back to the Future 2??*" Rob said in disgust.

"Um, sure. How do I become a VIP, then?" Jenny asked.

"By earning XP and leveling up," said Rob. He flipped a coin at her with his thumb. Jenny caught it and glanced at her palm. It was another Pixeldrome game token, with the embossed pixel-drawn coin design, just like the one RJ bequeathed to the Stranger. "First game's on me."

"She doesn't look like much of a gamer," said Nathaniel. "Probably one of those fake eGirls who pretends to play so she can sell her bathwater to simps."

Jenny closed her eyes, blocking him out. How the hell did Mom ever work here? Surely it wasn't always like this. "I play games, I earn XP, I level up, I become VIP?" she asked.

"When you hit level 50," said Asha.

"What level are you?"

"69," said Asha with a wink.

"Nice," said Jimmy.

"Nice," said Rob.

"And how long did that take you?" Jenny asked.

Asha shrugged, considering. "Maybe a year? I just spawned in one day and never left."

Jenny grimaced and turned back to Rob. "May I speak with you privately?"

Asha snickered again, but a look from Rob sent her and the incels back to minding their own damn business.

Rob crossed his arms. "Look, we don't want any Trouble here. Pun intended."

"I just need to see the game, then I'll be out of your hair," said Jenny.

"No can do," said Rob. "Not unless you make level 50. Wouldn't be fair to the others." He nodded to the food court, and Jenny caught Alicia Aaron looking away and pretending to read her book again. "How would you feel if I let her down there for free?"

For someone who sold her heirloom, Alicia Aaron sure didn't act like she was out of the game.

"Can you give me a list of all the VIP members?" she asked.

"No."

"Why not?"

"You think I want you harassing my best customers?" he said.

"One of them could be a killer."

"I sincerely doubt that."

"Okay, can you tell me who has the high score on the *Trouble* game?" Jenny tried.

"I do," he said, which made Jenny narrow her eyes. "I have the high score on all of them."

She glanced behind him, at the big arcade version of *Angry Birds*. Sure enough, the top score was credited to **ROB**.

"You earn all these high scores? You don't just rig the machines?"

"Of course," he said, affronted by the idea. "There's nothing more boring than cheating at your own game."

The hair on the back of her neck stood up just then, though she couldn't say exactly why. *Cheating at your own game...*

"As you say."

"I'm disappointed in you, Girl Detective," said Rob. "I keep waiting for you to ask an interesting question."

Well, she couldn't leave this has-been disappointed, could she? "You bought this place in the '90s?" Jenny asked.

"Yep."

"What year?"

"94," he said.

Mom was Class of '97, meaning…

"Then you must have known Laura Onishi," she said.

"There we go!" He snapped his fingers, grinning. "Let me show you something. Just a taste."

Rob gestured for Jenny to follow and led her past the counter where Asha was slouched. Behind her was a giant LED leaderboard. The top spot, at **LVL 99+,** was occupied by **ROB**.

"You cuck! You're not seriously letting her down there, are you?" asked Asha.

"Suck a dick, Ash!" said Rob.

"You wish!"

"Isn't she a minor?" Jenny asked.

"There's grass on the field," said Rob. "Play ball!"

He laughed at his crass humor and pulled aside a velvet rope blocking access to the basement. The stairwell was bathed in blue and orange neon, illuminating dozens, maybe hundreds of photos that lined the walls.

"Everyone who beats *Double Dragon 2* on one quarter gets their picture on the wall of fame," he said. "And a big XP boost."

"Why that game?"

"It's my favorite," said Rob. "Let's see, here she is."

He pointed to a photo, about halfway down the stairwell. Jenny leaned closer and gasped. It was her mother, no older than Jenny was now, posing in front of the arcade cabinet. Unlike all the photos Jenny had seen of Mom, Laura had styled her hair in bouncy curls here. She wore daisy duke jean shorts and that same Pixeldrome shirt that Jenny found in the garage. There was a golden pin on her lapel.

"Dogs out for free," said Rob, pointing to Mom's bare feet. "She was a goer, that Laurie." He pulled the print off the wall and handed it to her. "Keep it, I've got copies."

Something about the way he said it made Jenny want to retch. She looked away, to the door at the bottom of the stairs. There was no handle on it. "Is that the VIP room?" she asked.

"Yep."

"How do you get in?"

"By earning XP and reaching level 50," Rob said and ushered her back up the stairs. "You can stick around, but try to behave yourself. And don't bother trying to break in. You won't succeed, and it will just make a big hassle for all of us."

"Can't I just pay you?" she asked. "I have ten grand."

"You can't buy your way into the VIP room, Trouble," said Rob. "It's the principle of the thing, you know? You're going to have to earn it."

He headed off to what must be a back office area, taking a moment to give Nathaniel a wet willie on the way.

Great. If she wanted to see this stupid *Trouble* game, she'd have to spend hours around these assholes, grinding video games that were obsolete before she was even born.

"I gotta level with you, sweetie," said Asha, still smirking behind the counter. "I don't think you have it in you. But I won't complain about watching you go."

There were a lot of insults she could have hurled back, but at that moment, anything and everything that popped into her head felt toothless and lame. These people were level 69 shitheads, and Trouble was intended for junior readers. Eternally 11 years old… She was out of her element, and she wasn't sure she wanted to be in theirs.

Jenny tossed the game token back to Asha and walked out of the arcade.

Chapter Ten

Career Day

THERE WAS NO BETTER TIME OF YEAR THAN A MID-AUTUMN weekend in Calistoga County, Eliza decided. Perfect weather for a cardigan sweater, leaves browning before they fall, and pumpkin spice lattes for all. There was something about the position of celestial bodies, the angle of the sun, and their northern hemisphere latitude that made the light scatter differently. She took a lazy Sunday drive with Charlie, cresting rolling hill after hill, chasing endless rows of verdant vineyards, limned in golden hues like the Elf-realms of her favorite fantasy books.

Was this what RJ meant in his diary? About knowing I'm in the good times before they're gone?

All too soon, the weekend was over. The forecast threatened rain, her sister was in a crabby mood, and the Unfridgeables' usual Monday lunch in the cafeteria was invaded by a swarm of local employers, soul-sucking corporate chains, and three branches of the United States Armed Forces. It was Career Day. The BSA seniors, imminently staring down the barrel of impending adulthood, got to ditch third and fourth period to network with prospective employers, judge them by the extravagance of their booths, and sign up for mailing lists they would never, ever, stop getting spam from.

All the other seniors treated it like a joke, only interested in hunting down the corporations with the best swag giveaways. For Eliza, it *was* a joke—Kazumi wasn't even real—and yet, that anxiety of adulthood hit her harder with each Fortune 500 booth she passed. The golden joy she'd felt a day ago was already fading to black and white.

"Supposedly, one of those guys was on Seal Team 6," said Jack, pointing to the US Navy booth.

The boys rushed over to check it out.

"Uh, Kazu, catch up with us later?" said Meghan.

She and Penny didn't wait for a reply before hurrying to join the boys. Eliza was left alone with Charlie—normally a pleasant development, but today it rankled. Ever since Homecoming, she'd been sensing the subtlest of cold shoulders from her friends. Even Jack had stopped flirting with her.

Which is a good thing! But still, what gives?

She rubbed her temples, fighting a headache, and tried to give the booth for Santa Rosa Memorial Hospital her attention. Once upon a time, she wanted to be a nurse…

"Okay, they have a L'Oréal booth!" said Charlie, bouncing excitedly on the balls of her feet. "I read they have some cool Intern Abroad programs."

"You're going abroad?" Eliza asked, with more concern than she'd intended.

"Not yet!" Charlie said. "Maybe sometime next year. If I even get in. Come on, we agreed not to worry about that, remember?"

"I know, I know," said Eliza. "We are carpe-ing the diem."

"I'm gonna carpe some samples."

"You go ahead," said Eliza.

Charlie pouted. "You sure?"

"It's fine, I want to check out the photography booth," said Eliza. "I'll find you later."

She squeezed Charlie's hand and set off across the cafeteria, where a portrait studio was advertising careers in the exciting world of dealing with annoying kids who wouldn't smile for the camera.

Actually, no she wasn't. She was getting out of here. Eliza changed course and made for the exit.

ELIZA LEFT CAREER DAY ALONE, WITH AN ODD LOOK OF determination on her face. Jenny watched her sister go, suspicious.

What is she up to?

Eliza had hardly spoken a word to her since the chaos at Homecoming. Jenny thought she knew why. Baba had lectured her afterward that it was rude for Jenny to rig the vote for herself when her sister had earned a nomination. Not that anyone could prove Jenny rigged it…

She paused, feeling someone's eyes on her, and turned to see Jimmy Figg staring from the Healthcare Careers corner. He flashed her a jocular smile like they were secret Pixeldrome buddies now. As if!

"Miss Valentine, have you considered a career in private investigation?" said an oddly-accented voice.

Jenny turned with a start to see she'd just passed a tiny booth advertising careers in **Inquiry Services**. An older man in a shabby knit vest sat on a folding chair behind the table, wearing a newsboy cap.

"Motherfucking Lambert!" Jenny said, delighted to see him.

The P.I. held a finger to his lips.

"Let us not bring attention to ourselves," he said. "I arranged to meet you this way, as I understand you are being watched more closely than usual."

I am?

"Wait, do you mean this isn't a real booth?" Jenny asked, snatching one of the fliers on his table. The outer cover showed a picture of a man looking through binoculars, but inside, the brochure was blank white paper. "Nice. How did they let you in?"

"You would be amazed how far you can get, by pretending you belong," said Lambert. "I have something for you." He slid a manila envelope across the table to Jenny. "The photo samples you requested."

"Thank you," said Jenny, stuffing the envelope in her backpack. "Unfortunately, I'm a little tapped out these days. Do I have any more credit with you?"

"That depends on the ask," said Lambert.

"There's this guy, Rob Haines," said Jenny. "I'd like to know more about him."

"I can assemble a standard dossier," Lambert said. "Anything else would require a further retainer."

"Gotcha, let's do that, then. Thanks again," said Jenny. She zipped her backpack up and glanced at the fake flyer for careers in detective work. "Any advice on becoming a P.I.?"

He chortled. "For starters, Miss Valentine, you must be licensed by the state to operate as a detective. Which means you'll need a clean criminal record. Not to worry," he said when Jenny's face fell. "Your juvenile crimes will be sealed when you turn 18. But once you do, it all counts."

Jenny smiled for his sake and left the cafeteria. Great, even fucking Lambert was giving her the "you'll be an adult soon," speech. Like she wasn't in danger of a madman trying to kill her every waking moment. But sure, be careful you don't fucking jaywalk once the calendar hits March 10th.

AFTER SCHOOL, JENNY RODE HER BIKE UP HIGHWAY 12 UNDER overcast skies and made a right at Cellar Drive. She passed the turnoffs for the mansion and the vineyards and pedaled to where the road dead-ended in a berm, with undeveloped land beyond. Leaving the bike behind, she followed a gurgling creek through a grove of oak trees until she reached a broad oak with two-by-four rungs nailed to the trunk. Up amongst the sturdy branches sat the treehouse her father had once built for Jack.

Eliza lived here in the early days before they'd won the game and the mansion. Now the treehouse served as Jenny's last-ditch safe house. She was pretty sure the Stranger didn't know about it. If he did, he would have stolen her photo heirloom she kept stashed here. Ascending the uneven footholds was always her least favorite part; heights were Danger's thing, not Trouble's. She reached the trap door fighting nausea and pulled herself into the little cabin. Then she lay on the floor awhile, allowing her equilibrium to settle down. The familiar confines of the treehouse had a calming effect. It still smelled, faintly, of her twin sister.

After a spell, Jenny rose to her feet and turned the dial that engaged the electricity in the cabin for an hour. The bare lightbulb hanging from the ceiling flickered on, giving much-needed light on a gray afternoon. In the corner by the camp bed, a lava lamp began to burble. It was an Eliza addition, scrounged from a thrift store in Santa Rosa. The portable radio in the kitchenette crackled to life, and the ominous piano chords of Beethoven's "Moonlight Sonata" filled the tiny space.

Nah, wrong vibe, Jenny.

She fiddled with the dial, dodging static and talk radio until an '80s song came through. That was more like it. From under the camp bed, she retrieved the brick of cash she got from Drew and a folder with her heirloom photo inside. Along with the heirloom photo was a surveillance photo that Eliza had recovered from the briefcase RJ left in his abandoned hotel room at the Crow's Nest. Using her phone as a magnifying glass, Jenny got to work.

In the heirloom photo, which showed her mom and dad in front of the old Poison Pen, there was a little black dot and a squiggle in the lower left corner. The other photo, taken of the two as they entered a room at the Crow's Nest hotel, had the same black dot and squiggle: a photographic fingerprint from a dirty or scratched lens. Going by the fullness of her mom's pregnant belly, the two photos had been taken months apart, meaning plenty of others could have been taken in between with that same fingerprint.

She'd asked Lambert to collect old photo samples from all the private investigators who worked in the North Bay 17 years ago. Fingers crossed one of their samples would have that photographic fingerprint. If it did, she'd know which P.I. was spying on her parents. Find the P.I. and they might just find the bastard who ran Laura Onishi off the road on that fateful rainy day. And if they found him and could prove Val hired him, they'd finally tie that evil bitch to Mom's murder, too.

That was a lot of "ifs," and as Jenny studied each photo sample, their likelihood moved ever further out of reach.

She checked the photos twice. Then again. And another time too.

None of them had the black dot. Or the squiggle. Dammit! They were all clean.

Wait! What about that photo of Mom from the arcade?!

Jenny retrieved it from her bag and hovered her phone's camera over it, studying every inch of the halftone print.

No dice. All that work, plus a bottle of *Ressort Rouge* for Lambert—and she'd hit another goddamned dead end.

"Excuse me, who's up there?" called a woman's voice from below. "Sh-show yourself, won't you?!"

She'd recognize that phony mid-Atlantic accent anywhere. It was Tori Valentine. Daughter of a bitch! Jenny froze. Maybe if she stayed silent, Tori would go away.

"This is private property! You're t-trespassing! If you d-don't open up, I'm calling the p-police!"

Don't get arrested!

"What do you want? I'm busy!" Jenny yelled back.

"Goddamnit, J-Jenny! You can't be up there!" Tori said.

Jenny threw open the hatch and shouted down at her. "Why not?!"

She'd moved too fast. Her vision wasn't ready for her to be staring straight down. With a sudden rush in her head, she gagged and threw up. The puke fell right through the hatch, and Tori made frightened squirrel noises and stumbled out of the way.

"Eww! Are you drunk?!" Tori yelled.

Jenny rolled away from the hatch and wiped her mouth, fighting the reflex to vomit again. How miserable! And the afternoon had started so well with Lambert's surprise appearance…

"No!" she said.

"Sick? I can't be near sick people!"

"I'm not sick."

"…Pregnant?"

"Fuck you! I'm gold star!" said Jenny. "I'm just not good with heights."

"All the more reason to get down from there!" said Tori. "You're an insurance nightmare."

Jenny wasn't going anywhere until the ceiling stopped spinning.

"Hey Tori, you're forgetting to do your stutter," Jenny called down.

"It c-comes and g-goes," said Tori. "Dear god, w-w-what did you eat for lunch?"

"Dr Pepper and Sour Patch Kids?"

From below, she could hear feet and hands clambering on the footholds. Moments later, Tori's head appeared in the hatchway next to Jenny. She climbed inside and closed the hatch.

"From one gold star to another, we need to have a conversation about your nutrition," said Tori. "What are you doing up here?"

Her eyes darted around at the surveillance photos, at the brick of cash, at Jenny's heirloom. Tori smirked and grabbed it.

"Hey!" yelled Jenny.

"Relax, I'm not a contestant," Tori said, peering at the picture of Jenny's parents. Her mom looked fantastic in a halter top and was holding up two fingers at RJ. Most would read it as a peace sign, but Jenny knew it meant two babies: twins. "She gave me a peanut butter sandwich once," said Tori.

Jenny bolted upright, the nausea gone.

"You met her?"

"Once," said Tori. "A long time ago, when Dad couldn't find a babysitter and had to bring me to class."

"What do you remember about her?" Jenny asked.

"Just the peanut butter sandwich," said Tori. She tossed the heirloom photo back onto the camp bed. "Look, you can't be up here."

"Can't you just ignore me?"

Tori shook her head. "I expanded the security at Valentine Manor. Every time you come here, you trip the alarm. The guards can't be dealing with breaches all the time. You're going to have to find somewhere else to do your research. Besides, if I let you stay, I'd have to allow all the others to come use the property too. No special favors, especially not for the massive p-pain in my ass who already cheated in the game once."

Jenny groaned and began gathering up her things.

"I'm going to be back here someday, you know?" she said. "When I win, this will all be mine again. And I'll stock it full of Dr Pepper and Sour Patch Kids and Vyvanse."

"When are you going to g-grow up, Jennifer?" asked Tori.

Jenny considered Tori—still frail from the coma, haunted by traumatic loss, looking older than her years from alcoholism—and was certain that growing up was for suckers.

"When are you gonna tell me all the stuff you left out of that story you told us in the park?" Jenny replied. "I know there's more to that conversation with RJ about the contest that you're not telling. Something about Val, am I right?"

Tori offered Jenny an unreadable smile that didn't meet her eyes. She looked so much like her mother Val just then that Jenny had to remind herself not to slap the smile right off her face.

"Will you be able to get down, or do I need to call the fire department?" she asked.

"I'm not a cat!" Jenny growled and zipped up her pack.

THE CLOUDS HAD DARKENED DURING HER TIME IN THE TREEHOUSE, and a metallic tang tickled her nostrils; it would rain soon. Jenny tried texting Eliza, but as usual, her sister was ignoring her. Probably with Charlie. Fine! If Lizzy was going to be a bitch about it, Jenny would have to make this awkward. She rode back into town, heading for the new condos a block from Town Square where Charlie lived.

The lobby required key card access, so Jenny loitered by the entrance until a delivery guy from Calistoga Plasma exited the building. She slipped inside before the door closed and took the stairs up to the third floor. Charlie's unit was at the east end of the hallway. Jenny skipped the doorbell and pounded hard on the knocker.

Footsteps inside, and a soft snarl.

Did she just growl at me?

"She's not here, Jenny," said Charlie from within.

"Bullshit! I need to talk to her, so get her out here," Jenny said.

Charlie sighed and opened the door. She was in her pajamas, with her hair pulled up in a messy ponytail. Her pupils flickered red in the glow of the emergency exit light behind Jenny as she sipped on some kind of bougie Capri Sun drink. She was less than thrilled to find Jenny darkening her doorway.

"I'm not lying. You can tell that, right?" asked Charlie.

"As a matter of fact, on you, I can't," said Jenny. "I need to talk to her. Badly."

"I'm sure you do, but she's still not here."

"Fuck it, I'll wait," said Jenny.

"I'd rather you not," said Charlie. "Something tells me that Eliza won't be back till you're gone. And she doesn't want to talk to you, anyway."

"Is she still pissed about Homecoming?"

"You humiliated her," said Charlie. "And people saw her pull that knife at the dance; she freaks them out now."

"That's stupid, she's hiding the best part of herself," said Jenny.

"Oh, she'd love to hear that," Charlie said. "Best be getting along now."

"Hold on," Jenny said.

She pulled her backpack off her shoulder and took out the big dossier envelope Lambert had given her. The other photos of Mom were in it too, save the heirloom one. With a purple pen, she left Eliza a note.

> **Lambert's photo samples. Might be a dead end :(**
> **Plus a new photo of Mom. Might be more, but not**
> **telling until you're willing to talk.**
> **XOXO**
> **— Trouble**

"Can you give her this? When she gets back?" Jenny asked.

"Sure," said Charlie.

She was about to close the door when Jenny stopped her. "Hey, Charlie?"

"Yes?"

"You do makeovers, right?" Jenny asked. "Do you think you

could help me with one? I need to change my style up to fit in better somewhere."

"I say this with no malice intended, Jenny, but I'd rather not do something like that with you," said Charlie. "Not while the Stranger is still out there. Just you coming here puts Kazu and me in danger. For both our sakes, I need to ask you not to stop by again."

Her expression was full of pity, and Jenny didn't want any of it.

"Whatever, coward," she said, and threw open the emergency exit stairwell. "Just give her that note, and tell her to call me!"

She sprinted down the stairs and out into the darkening dusk. Forgetting she'd ridden her bike there, she walked without purpose until she found herself by the pond in Town Square. Mr. Duck was sitting on one of the park benches. Jenny sighed and shuffled over.

"Hey, Mr. Duck," she said, plopping on the bench next to him. "Some day, huh?"

HONK! HONK! HONK!

Mr. Duck quacked up a storm, flapping his wings at her, and hopped back into the pond.

HONK! HONK! HONK!

He was still telling her off as he swam away to the far side. A thick wet drop struck her cheek. Either she was crying, or it had finally begun to rain.

Chapter Eleven

Little Lies

Nurse Bennett used to say, "You're a California girl, Elizabeth. Your feet should touch the ocean at least once a year." In Eliza's childhood, that meant a summer trip renting boogie boards at La Jolla, rollerblading by the Oceanside Pier, or making sand candles in the shadow of the Golden Gate. How long had it been? She wracked her brain. At least three—no, five years since she'd performed the ritual. On short notice, the rocky sandbar the locals called Goat Rock Beach would have to do.

Eliza dug her toes into the wet sand, letting the wash of the latest breaker reach her bare ankles. The narrow strip of sand and rocks ran across the mouth of the Russian River. It would be underwater again within an hour. Heavy winds chopped up the surf and her hair was already wet from the spray. Dark clouds would dump rain all over the coast any minute now. She closed her eyes and breathed in the salty air. Nurse Bennett was right. Eliza needed this.

"Miss! Miss!" called a park ranger, fighting through the wind to reach her. "You can't be out here! High tide in a storm is dangerous!"

"That's okay, mister!" she shouted at the surf. "Danger is my middle name!"

"Huh?! I'm serious, you could be swept away! Come on!" He signaled for her to walk with him.

Eliza dutifully followed. She'd never possessed her sister's capacity for rebellion. When she reached higher ground, she peeled off toward the parking lot. One of Valentine Vineyards' jeeps was waiting for her. Months ago, back when Jenny ran away, Eliza had disabled the LoJack on it so she couldn't be tracked. With all the upheaval around RJ's estate, Tori Valentine might never notice it was missing. She hopped inside, glad she'd put the soft top on for winter, and checked her phone. There was a message from Jenny, which she deleted, and another from Charlie.

Charlie: You Know Who came by looking for you. Where are you?

Kazu: Needed some P&Q to study. Be over in an hour.

Well, maybe an hour and fifteen. She wanted In-N-Out first.

By the time her curfew approached that evening, Eliza's belly was full, and all her wants were sated.

The In-N-Out was fantastic. And the burger wasn't half bad either, heheheh.

"What are you smiling about?" her girlfriend asked.

Charlie batted her eyelashes, looking over from her vanity where she was trying out a new mascara sample she'd scored from the L'Oréal booth.

"It's undignified," said Eliza. "A total Jenny line."

"I feel sort of bad now, turning her away," Charlie said. "Did you look through the stuff she left you?"

Eliza sighed, buttoning up her blouse, and snagged the manila envelope off the table.

New pic of Mom huh?

She dumped the contents out on Charlie's little dinette and shuffled through the photos. They were all random surveillance samples from Lambert. 8 x 10 glossy photos of men ushering women into motel rooms. Men performing feats of physical strength when they were supposed to be injured. Men purchasing illicit substances in dark alleys. Just as Jenny said, none of the prints appeared to bear the little photographic fingerprint from the heirloom photo. Damn. Could Val have taken the ones of Mom and Dad herself? Maybe Kazu could talk Jack into showing her an old photo album…

Her pinky finger brushed the last photo sample aside to uncover the new one of Mom that Jenny's note mentioned. Laura Onishi, hardly older than Eliza herself in it, was standing next to an arcade cabinet. Was that the same stupid arcade that Jack and Nilay dragged them to last month? She looked closer. Mom was wearing a t-shirt from the arcade, with some wild curls in her hair.

"Should I curl my hair?" she asked Charlie.

"Only if you let me dye it blonde."

"No, I want it black," she said. "Wait a minute, I've seen this before!"

She brought the photo over to Charlie, using the vanity lighting to get a better look.

"What a babe! That's your mom, right?" said Charlie.

"Yeah, see this pin?" Eliza said, pointing to a gold pin on the lapel of her mom's shirt. "It says '99+' on it. I've seen that before…" She wracked her brain for the location, absentmindedly rubbing off the concealer on her tattoo. "Something to do with Jack, I think—Oh! Homecoming! The penthouse! This was in the couch cushion!"

"That same pin?" Charlie asked.

"Or one just like it."

"Why would it be in the couch cushion at the Crow's Nest penthouse?"

"I don't know…" Eliza said, trailing off. Could Val have somehow taken Mom's pin… and then lost it in the couch cushions 18 years later? "But it's too weird of a coincidence. That woman wanted my mom dead, and now she just happens to have a pin Mom used to wear in her possession?"

"Sounds like a mystery for your sister," said Charlie. "She did seem very eager to speak with you."

Eliza scowled. "I'm not talking to her." She studied the grainy pin in the photo. "Maybe it's like a trophy to Val. She wears it in secret, and it came off one night…"

"Or it's for the Class of '99, and some random other millennial dropped it there before Val moved in," said Charlie.

"Mom wasn't Class of '99. This is gonna bug me. Shit, I gotta go."

"Always a pleasure," Charlie said, giving her a kiss goodnight. "You want my advice? Either forget about it or talk to Jenny."

Eliza would do neither. The game, the heirlooms, the Stranger, RJ—that was Jenny's business. Before Eliza ever knew or cared about the fate of her famous, wealthy father, she knew from Nurse Bennett's journals that her mom spent her final days paranoid and terrified. Someone named Valerie Valentine was trying to kill her. Then Laura Onishi wrapped her car around a redwood tree, despite her clean driving record. It had been Danger's mission, ever since she learned her true name, to take revenge.

And here, finally, was a piece of evidence that connected her mom to Val.

"Something's different about you today, Jack," Eliza said.

Jack blushed, all modesty. "New haircut," he said, grinning. "You noticed?"

They were at the Basque before school, as usual. Eliza had been working all week to thaw the weird tension between Kazu and her friends. She'd talked Thanh into ditching the bad wigs and rocking her hair short. "Guys go crazy for the pixie look, isn't that true, Jack?" A swift kick under the table earned his enthusiastic endorsement.

"For real," said Lai. "When they look a little like a dude, but they're a girl… hell yeah."

Meghan was easier. Eliza scored tickets to Taylor Swift's new tour, then claimed she couldn't go because her parents were visiting that weekend. Meghan wasn't about to turn down free Taylor tickets. To win Nilay back on her side, she merely needed to ask him about the recent election and let Nilay pontificate for hours about the American bicameral system. Penny was harder to read, but she was probably just preoccupied with the valedictorian race. Dinah Black was attempting a furious comeback, using elective courses at Calistoga College to boost her GPA, and Penny was in danger of pulling a B+ in Consumer Finance.

"It's the dumbest class!" Penny vented one day after receiving a mediocre grade on a quiz where they calculated their estimated tax rate. "Nobody does their taxes by hand anymore! We have computers! Ms. Williamson can't even use the internet without googling Google.com first!"

Everyone was starting to forget about that time at Homecoming when the foreign exchange student pulled out a knife like her awful cousin and got in a fight with Meghan's dad. Now, if she could just get her brother to ask her out on a date.

I know, I know.

"I like it," Eliza said, pushing aside the swoop of hair that Jack let fall over his left eye and ignoring the glares from Charlie—and from Alicia Aaron at the next table over. "You know, I never thanked your mum for sending the dance photos over."

The package from Stratford Photography went straight into the bin.

"How's she keeping up these days?"

"Mom?" Jack shrugged. "I don't know. She's really into these 'women's retreats' of hers lately."

"Dude! No parents around? Party at the penthouse!" said Nilay. "You down?"

"That would be fabulous! Can we, Jack?" Eliza asked breathlessly.

"She doesn't like having people over," said Jack, frowning. "Especially when she's not home."

The boys loudly booed Jack, suggesting they'd have to start hanging out at Drew's place instead. He did, after all, have the better television now. This fact turned Jack's ears red.

When it was time to make the trek to school, Eliza hung back, pretending to rummage in her purse. "Oh you must hate me, Jack, I didn't mean to put you on the spot like that," Eliza said. "I'm sure your mum would be cross if she caught you throwing a rager with half the senior class showing up."

"Don't worry about it, Kaz," said Jack. "It's not much of a place for parties like the mansion was."

"That's true, it felt more intimate, you know?" said Eliza. "Probably better for small groups, or maybe just a friend. Let's catch up to the others."

Because boys were stupid in these matters, it took Jack until the following afternoon to intercept Eliza leaving school and ask if she was free on Sunday. "Mom usually goes out on Sunday evenings, and I was thinking we could go over the AP Government homework together. Half the stuff Nilay's been telling you is way off."

"Brilliant!" said Eliza, giving him a playful pat on the shoulder. "Now Jack, just so we're clear, this isn't a date."

Then she winked at him.

I'm going to hell for this.

"Of course not," said Jack, smiling broadly like he was in on the joke. "Perish the thought, Kaz."

"It's settled, then. See you Sunday!"

Workers in the Crow's Nest lobby were putting up Christmas decorations when Eliza arrived on Sunday evening. *Damn, already?* Thanksgiving was still days away! She made a quick stop at the pop-up See's Candies to buy chocolate lollipops for Penny, who loved them. That ought to ease the tension with Pen, if there even was any. And fine, a butterscotch one for Trouble, too.

Unfortunately, Charlie didn't have a sweet tooth for Eliza to indulge. She was in the doghouse for going on a date with Jack, especially after Charlie got a look at the form-fitting red dress and black ribbon choker Eliza would be wearing. Candy wouldn't cut it; she could only get back in her secret girlfriend's good graces by letting Charlie take that dress off later tonight, hopefully after a successful fact-finding mission at Jack's penthouse—*and nothing more!*

On the elevator ride up, she popped a breath mint and artfully tousled her hair. Maybe she should've curled it… On the top floor, she knocked softly—and Valerie Valentine immediately answered.

"Kazu, darling!" said Val.

Eliza cursed in Japanese.

"Mom, I said I'd get it!" she heard Jack down the hall.

Val pulled her in for the sort of hug where it felt like they barely touched each other, and then shoved the crystal dish of mints at her. "Love this," said Val, brushing a finger over Eliza's choker. "Keeps your head on, does it?"

"Sorry," Jack said, grabbing Eliza's hand and pulling her away from his mother. "I thought she'd be gone by now."

Quite the opposite. Val took a seat with a glass of red wine in the very armchair that Eliza needed to search. Drat!

"Don't mind me," said Val, tapping her phone. "Just waiting to hear back from someone."

Eliza smiled through gritted teeth and retreated with Jack into the suite's little dining room, where his AP Government book was already cracked open. He threw an annoyed glare at his mother and gestured to his schoolbook. "Study now, eat later?"

"Brilliant! I brought some practice test questions."

They dutifully quizzed each other, checking answers in the textbook, and Jack discoursed on all the ways Nilay had misunderstood how power actually worked in Washington. "Communism sounds great in theory, but if you want to get anything done, you need a Pericles to cut through the bullshit..."

While he blathered on, Eliza kept one eye on the living room, where Val sipped her wine and refused to leave the damn penthouse.

"I think I'm going to order in," Val announced an hour later, finally rising from the chair. "Your friend Nilay is coming over with some new information. You hungry?"

Nilay's coming over? What information??

Eliza caught Jack's eye. He grimaced and shrugged. *What are you gonna do?* The fact that Nilay was on his way over didn't seem to faze him. How baffling.

"Please," Eliza replied. "Maybe something light, like a salad."

Val nodded approvingly and paced around the kitchen, calling in to place their order. The armchair was wide open. Would it be weird if Eliza went over and sat in it?

"Yes, and a wedge salad," Val said into her phone. She ran a critical eye over Eliza's figure. "No croutons."

Can't I just take my revenge now? Mom would understand!

Eliza rose, voicing her need to stretch, and drifted into the living room. The armchair was only paces away when Val brushed past her and plopped back down in it.

"Any plans for Thanksgiving, Kazumi?" she asked. Without waiting for an answer, she went on, "I'm taking Jack to Vegas. The Venetian. I've got tickets to see New Order."

Eliza smiled blankly, leaning on the couch armrest across from her. *Get out of that fucking chair!*

"Mom, she doesn't know anything about New Order," said Jack from the kitchen.

"Oh come on!" said Val. "'Blue Monday'? Alexa, play New Order."

An upbeat song with lots of synth and electric drums played over the penthouse's many hidden speakers. Eliza had heard this song before, and recently. She bit her lip, thinking.

"See, she knows it!" said Val.

"I think this was playing at that video arcade you dragged us to, Jack," said Eliza. "Why was it you wanted to go there?"

Val shot an odd look at Jack as he took a seat on the couch. "Oh, you went to Pixeldrome, did you?" she asked him.

"We were in the area," said Jack. He patted the couch cushion next to him, but Eliza remained standing. "Took the girls to Mystery Flavors and Nilay wanted to check it out."

Val furrowed her brow, sucking in her cheek like she was biting her tongue. Eliza was no Girl Detective, but this felt like an important detail.

"Yes, that's what it was called, Pixeldrome," Eliza said innocently. "A rather queer name, isn't it? That cousin of mine mentioned going there the other day, too." Some sort of unspoken understanding passed between the other two. Eliza pressed further. "My aunt showed me a photo of her late sister there. At Pixeldrome, that is," said Eliza. "Was it popular back when you were young too, Mrs. Valentine?"

Val's eyes flashed laser beams at her. Eliza had just committed, like, a triple faux pas, but it's not as though Kazumi was expected to know any better.

"I wouldn't know. I don't like you going there, Junior," said Val. "Those Harbor High kids are bad company, and there are too many vagrants on the south side."

The conversation ended awkwardly, and they were all forced to sit and listen to the old pop song.

"Shall we play Scrabble?" Val suggested.

Jack leaned his head back, apologizing to Eliza with his eyes. The night was a bust, though not for the reasons he was thinking. The Stranger himself wasn't getting Val's ass out of that chair, it seemed. A new plan took shape in her mind.

"I'd be delighted, but I fear my aunt is expecting me home soon," Eliza said. She drifted casually to the glass sliding door that opened onto the penthouse balcony. "Thank you for having me, Mrs. Valentine. The view up here is magnificent."

Using her body to screen the act, she flicked the sliding door's lock open.

"You're always welcome," said Val, with a smile that said the opposite.

"Have fun in Las Vegas," she said to them. "I suppose I shan't see you till next week, then. Walk me out, Jack?"

IT WAS A CLOSE THING, BUT ELIZA MANAGED TO GET AWAY FROM HER brother with only a hug instead of a goodnight kiss. God, were they dating, now? Oh dear.

"Want anything from Vegas?" Jack asked.

"Oh stop, you don't have to get me anything."

"I know," he said, smiling sweetly at her.

"Send me a selfie in front of the fake Eiffel Tower," Eliza said. "On Thanksgiving, when I'll be stuck at dinner with my cousin."

That way she'd know for sure the penthouse was empty.

"Sure thing," said Jack. "Hey, that thing you mentioned about a photo of Jenny's mom at Pixeldrome… was that real? Or were you just messing with my mother?"

"I would never!" Eliza said, holding a hand to her mouth in fake surprise. "At least I assumed it was from that arcade. She was standing next to a video game."

"Interesting."

"Is it?"

Is it?

"Just something between Jenny and I," Jack said. "See you around, Kaz."

THANKSGIVING IN THE ONISHI HOUSEHOLD WAS A PLEASANT AFFAIR, aside from Jenny sulking all day. Eliza got permission to invite Charlie, and Blake came over early with Mason and Meghan May. Those two kept making excuses to go on shopping runs, disappearing for an hour or two, and blaming long lines at the store. The adults snickered, thinking they were onto the young couple. Eliza knew they were really visiting their secret child, little Lilah, at the Lockhart cabin in the woods north of town.

"She wants to wait till school is over," Mason said after Eliza asked him privately during halftime why they were still hiding Lilah's existence. "She doesn't want her family involved with Lilah at all. Like never."

Understandable. She knew Shelly would have preferred the same arrangement where RJ was concerned. What would Jenny have thought, if she ever *had* met him? Would she still have appreciated his trademark mischievous smile when it was directed at her, full of knowing and not telling?

Blake brought over a crockpot of Swedish meatballs, which he and Jiji scarfed down while watching the Cowboys get embarrassed at home. Aunt Shelly and Baba busied themselves in the kitchen, and Charlie turned out to be a wizard at cleaning and stuffing a turkey. Eliza was in charge of napkins and flatware, and Jenny was on beverage duty—though she spent most of the day buried in their Nintendo Switch, playing old video games, and glaring whenever Blake cheered a touchdown or high-fived Jiji.

"Kohari! Beer me!" their grandfather called in Japanese.

Blake repeated the phrase, having learned it from Jiji, and both men laughed.

"Listen to that phony kiss-ass," Jenny muttered, pouring herself another glass of Martinelli's sparkling cider.

"You're just jealous because Jiji likes him," said Eliza.

Charlie shoved two Sierra Nevadas over at Jenny, dispatching her before a proper argument could start. Eliza winked and gave her a pinch under the counter. She'd never done the traditional Thanksgiving Dinner thing before, and she wasn't going to let Trouble spoil her mood. Nurse Bennett had always ordered takeout, which seemed so cool at the time, but now Eliza understood what she was missing. There was a warmth in the house beyond the heat from Baba's oven working overtime.

At five in the afternoon, they all joined hands around the table to say some words about the food. It was a motley group to call a family, but it felt as valid as any. Granted, her grandmother didn't know that Shelly had been hiding THC oil in Baba's bottle of ipecac syrup. Meghan didn't know Charlie and Kazu were secretly dating. Blake didn't know he had a granddaughter. Eliza didn't know what all this fuss over that arcade was about. And Jenny didn't know—well, it was best she never found out about *that*. But all families had secrets, didn't they?

Most importantly, when Eliza announced after dinner that she was in a food coma and going to bed early, none of them knew that she'd carefully avoided eating even a single slice of turkey, that she'd crushed an Adderall into her sparkling cider, and that she'd reserved a room on the sixth floor of the Crow's Nest the day before under false name.

Kazumi retired to her bedroom to sleep, Eliza washed off her makeup and hid her hair under a black beanie, and Danger snuck out the window.

Chapter Twelve

I Think We're Alone Now

IF THE SECURITY GUARD PATROLLING THE SIDEWALK IN FRONT OF THE Crow's Nest happened to look straight up, he would have noticed an insane teenage girl, dressed all in black, scaling the side of the hotel on a nylon rope. But he didn't look up. Why would he? Weren't there easier ways of breaking in? What kind of psycho would even dare?

Me!

The freezing wind on Eliza's face was just as refreshing as the spray of the ocean at Goat Rock Beach. What Nurse Bennett had never thought to tell her was that when Danger was your middle name, you needed to feel a hundred feet of empty air beneath your toes once in a while, too.

She'd lucked out, getting a room just below the penthouse on this side of the hotel. It was almost too easy to hook a line on the balcony railing above and climb up. Now, the moment of truth: had Val or Jack noticed the sliding door was unlocked in the four days since Eliza visited?

They had not!

The door slid open, whisper-quiet, and Eliza slipped inside. First things first, she checked her phone. An alert had come in while she was dangling off the side of a building: a message from Jack. As requested, he sent a selfie, standing in front of the fake Eiffel Tower in

Vegas, wearing a tuxedo. Perfect. She'd have the place all to herself.

Kazu: Very nice! Put $20 on black 13 for me 007!

She hit send, but the message failed. Damn, reception sucked in here. She returned to the balcony, holding her phone out over the long drop. After a moment, the *bloop!* of a sent message sounded.

Now, to work. Eliza walked to the armchair in the living room and dug her hands into the cushions. Cold metal met her left hand and something jabbed her in the index finger.

Ow!

She pulled her hand out, sucking on her finger, and looked at the object she'd stuck herself to obtain. It was the gold pin. There was a **99+** device on it, styled in a blocky font—to simulate pixels, like an old, low-resolution video game, she now realized. Eliza compared it to the photo of Mom she brought with her. It was the same pin, or one just like it.

But why would Val have the pin in her chair cushions? She didn't read as the trophy-taking type. Eliza needed more; the pin wasn't enough. There was precious little in the way of personal touches in the penthouse suite. There was the row of *Trouble* books on the end table. Jack's SAT scores on the refrigerator door—*he got a 1600?!!* A book bag from a Valentine Foundation charity drive. She peeked inside and found a galley copy of *Hands of Adamant*, Alicia Aaron's smutty portal fiction novel she'd leveraged Jenny into publishing. Was Jack reading this, or Val?

Eliza moved to the master bedroom. The closet was filled with Val's glamorous wardrobe, and a shoe collection to make Eliza stop and gawk. On the vanity mirror, Val had stuck a recent ticket for *Hamilton* in the City, and a birthday card from Jack. Seeing this relaxed, human side of Valerie Valentine made Eliza's blood boil. All the birthday cards Jenny and Eliza could have given Mom, if not for this woman.

In the nightstand drawer, she found a Gideon bible, a bottle of ibuprofen, and Val's vibrator. Eliza removed the batteries from it and peered at the framed photo under the bedside lamp: a family portrait of Val, RJ, Jack, and Tori. Jack couldn't have been more than 12 years old. Dad had that same grin he always had on. Even in family pictures, he was performing his wily author character.

Eliza picked up the photo frame and gently shook it. The glass front clacked against the wooden sides. Was there something else there? She pried the back of the frame loose and checked behind it. Nope, no secret clues, just a logo for Stratford Photography. She reassembled the frame and put the photo back as she'd found it, exhaling a frustrated sigh.

Was this it? Just the pin? Maybe she ought to put it back where she found it. It might prove more useful as a big reveal.

Unbidden, an intrusive thought whispered, *Jenny would know what to do next.*

"No! Absolutely not!" Eliza told the empty penthouse. "She gave me a concussion and a broken wrist! She almost killed me with fent-laced painkillers!"

As if in response, a female voice erupted in laughter close by. She heard a key card beep and the door to the penthouse swung open.

"He had no idea!" said Val, laughing again. A male voice laughed with her.

FUUUUUUCCCKKKKKK!!! How!?!? She was supposed to be in Vegas!!

A glance confirmed that there was no balcony off the master bedroom. To reach an exit—either the front door or her rope on the balcony—she would have to leave the bedroom and cross into the living room. Eliza was trapped!

"Have a seat on the couch," said Val. "I need to take these off, my feet are killing me."

"All right if I mix myself a nightcap, Mrs. Valentine?" asked Nilay Nagra.

Nilay? What are you doing here?

"Help yourself," said Val.

Her voice got louder as she spoke; she was coming this way! Eliza dropped to the floor and rolled under the bed. The doorknob turned, and quiet footfalls padded into the room. Eliza held her breath. The footsteps were halfway to the closet when they abruptly halted. Val inhaled sharply.

"Kazumi?" she called softly.

Eliza's heart skipped a beat.

From the living area, Nilay raised his voice. "Alexa, play some '80s music!"

A bubblegum mall pop song thumped through the suite's speakers. Val stalked to her closet. She was searching. If Eliza stayed where she was, she'd surely be found. Fuck it. She scrambled to the other side of the bed and made for the door. Maybe Nilay would be distracted and she could slip out. She reached for the doorknob, opening it a crack—

"Not so fast," Val whispered, covering Eliza's mouth with her palm and pressing cold metal against her neck.

Eliza raised her hands, acutely aware of the knife at her throat, and made to turn around. Val let her, keeping the knife tip an inch from Eliza's chest. She wore a red evening dress and had her hair up in an intricate bun.

"You again," Val said quietly. "Unless you've got a very—and I mean *very*—compelling reason for breaking into my home, you're going back to jail for a long time, Jennifer."

Eliza blinked.

Oh, right, she didn't have her Kazumi makeup on. Eliza opened her mouth, grasping for an excuse, and found her brain completely void of a single lie worthy of her sister's effortless bullshit.

"Val…" she said.

"Hey! Hey! Stop right there!" Nilay shouted from the living room.

Val dropped the knife and reached for the door. It was Eliza's turn to grab her. She smothered Val's mouth and hissed, "Quiet! He's not talking to us!"

They both stared through the crack in the doorway. Nilay was standing by the armchair, staring toward the balcony. A moment later, a silhouette stepped into view. A tall, dark, and strangesome menace. Beware!

"Well, well, well, we meet at last," said Nilay. "Was I getting too close? Feeling the heat?"

The Stranger's response was to draw a big fucking Bowie knife.

"Come on, man! Where's the sport in that? You blackguard, you rogue!" said Nilay.

It was all still a game to him. Nilay pushed up the sleeves of his white blazer and raised his fists. The Stranger tilted his head, considering. Meanwhile, '80s pop bounced happily on the stereo, belying the very real threat. Shrugging, the Stranger stabbed his knife into the coffee table, removed his black fedora, and placed it atop the knife handle. He tapped his foot, adjusted the black latex gloves he was wearing, and assumed a similar boxing pose.

"That's more like it!" said Nilay. "Let's do the man dance!"

"He's insane!" Val whispered.

Eliza shushed her, and the fight began. Nilay rushed forward, delivering a flurry of quick jabs that overwhelmed the Stranger. Krav Maga, Eliza recognized from her self-defense training. Nilay landed several open-hand punches to the Stranger's torso before using his legs to execute a perfect takedown.

Holy shit! Could he do this? Could he win?

The Stranger rolled away, regaining his footing, and shoved Nilay back with his superior strength.

"That's right, bitch! I trained with someone who trained with someone from MARCOS!" said Nilay.

He pushed his blazer sleeves up again and held out his right hand, beckoning for the Stranger to come at him. The Stranger rose wearily, planted his back foot, and rubbed his wrists. He danced forward and back, feinting punches before kicking out with a long leg to knock Nilay back.

"Wait a minute!" shouted Nilay. "I know who you are!"

In a blink, the Stranger darted to the side and plucked his knife from the table. Nilay lunged to counter. The Stranger pirouetted away, redirecting his momentum, and plunged the knife into Nilay's ear, all the way to the hilt.

The cocky grin froze on Nilay's face. Val stifled a gasp into Eliza's hand. The Stranger yanked the knife out and pushed Nilay back into the armchair behind him. Dark red spilled from his ear onto his white sports coat.

Nilay "Nails" Nagra, the new guy who once joked he'd 'make it to Act III, at least' slumped his head forward, and died.

Val whimpered, and Eliza winced, hoping the Stranger wouldn't hear. Suddenly, the music stopped, and the lights in the living room went out. It was hard to tell in the moonlight, but it looked like the Stranger was prodding at Nilay's body. Searching for something. How had he gotten in? Did he know Val was here too? Eliza locked eyes with Val and held a finger to her lips.

Val nodded and knelt to retrieve her knife. Eliza pointed to the closet. Val shook her head and pointed to the bathroom. Eliza glared and jabbed her finger at the closet again. Val made a stink face but followed. They crept slowly, fretting every whisper of noise on the carpet, until they reached the walk-in closet.

With sound-dampening dresses and gowns hanging all around them, Eliza pulled Val's head close and muttered softly in her ear, "The bathroom is too loud. Hard surfaces. Echoes."

"Right," whispered Val. "Smart."

Eliza smiled ruefully. It would have been nice to claim she'd thought of it on account of being the smart one, but it was a plot point in *Nothing But Trouble*. She would have to be Danger *and* Trouble tonight if they were to have any chance of getting out of here alive. She checked her phone, and of course, she had no reception.

"Do you have a signal?" Eliza asked Val.

"My purse is in the living room," said Val. "What about the hotel phone?"

Eliza raised a finger for Val to wait and tiptoed back into the bedroom to check the phone by the nightstand. There was no dial tone. The Stranger must have taken the kitchen line off the hook. She returned to the closet, shaking her head.

"What is he doing?" Val asked.

They could hear shuffling through the closet wall. Random thumps and scraping noises. If Eliza's spatial reckoning was correct, the kitchen would be on the other side of this wall.

"He's looking for something," said Eliza. "Sooner or later, he's going to make his way in here." She glanced at the "knife" in Val's hand. With the surge of adrenaline fading, she saw now that it was a nail file. Eliza had her little kunai dagger tucked into her waistband, but it felt woefully inadequate against the Stranger. "Do you have any weapons in this penthouse?"

Val's eyes widened, as if struck with an idea. She pointed past Eliza, to the back of the closet where her small fortune in shoes were artfully arranged in a grid of cubby holes. Creeping carefully, Val set two pairs of Jimmy Choo pumps aside and reached deeper into the cubby hole. Whatever she pulled out scraped across the cubby surface, sending Eliza's heart into her throat.

They both froze, white-faced, and listened.

In the kitchen, the soft rummaging continued, uninterrupted.

Eliza glared murder at Val, who merely shrugged back and set a little black case on the carpet. It was about the size of a thick hardcover book. *Order of the Phoenix*-length, with an electronic keypad on top. Val punched in a series of numbers, trying to hide the access code by using her ring finger while pretending to press with her index finger.

Nice try.

The code was **031503**.

The day Mom died. But also the day Jack was born.

The case beeped and its clasps popped open—thunderously loud in the silence. They both cringed again, waiting for the Stranger to notice. This time, they didn't hear a thing.

Val opened the case and gasped. Inside, it was full of black foam, with a section cut away in the shape of a nasty little pistol. But instead of a gun, the foam cavity was empty, save for a little card with a handwritten note on it.

No guns, Viv
— XOXO Johnny

Eliza and Val stared at each other, united beyond fate or grand design at that moment in their mutual loathing of the man who'd called himself RJ Valentine.

"Well," said Eliza.

"Junior has a sword," Val whispered. "We got it for him for

Christmas one year."

LOL dork. "What kind?"

"A Turkish scimitar. It's a replica from a book he was obsessed with," said Val.

A loud creaking sounded nearby like wood dragging on stone. Eliza padded over to the bedroom door and peeked out through the crack. Across the living room, she could just make out the wide foyer that led to the suite's front door. The Stranger had dragged the end table across the foyer opening, barricading the door. He knew they were here.

Eliza hurried back to Val. "He blocked the exit, so here's what we'll do," she whispered.

She got her phone out and set a timer for one minute. This had worked once on Eliza. Hopefully it would work on the Stranger, too.

"You hide in the bathroom, and when the alarm goes off, he'll come looking for it," said Eliza. "Don't run! Let him get all the way into the closet, then sneak out and hide in the kitchen. He already checked it, he won't think to look there again. I'll get the sword from Jack's room, and then we'll see how willing to fight he is."

"He'll kill you!" Val hissed. "We need to run for it!"

"This isn't a debate," said Eliza, and started the timer. Val's microbladed eyebrows shot to the ceiling. "Come on."

She tucked the phone deep into the shoe cubby and scuttled on tiptoes to the bathroom on the other side of the suite. Val had no choice but to follow. Once they were both inside, Eliza closed the bathroom door to a crack.

BEEP! BEEP! BEEP! BEEP!

The timer! Their minute had already passed, terrifyingly fast. In the space of a moment, the bedroom door eased open. The Stranger hadn't come blustering in like a brute; he was being cautious. After pausing to take in the room, he moved toward the source of the beeping in long, purposeful strides.

Eliza nudged Val and eased the bathroom door open. With the Stranger's back to them, they crept out, silently crossing to the bedroom exit.

"Kitchen," Eliza whispered, and hurried across the living area, trying not to look at Nilay's corpse as she passed by. His lifeless eyes were still agape, as if he were bewildered that he had died. She reached Jack's room, casting about for this Turkish scimitar. It wasn't hard to find, seeing as he'd mounted it over his bed. Eliza felt momentarily affronted. Worldly Kazumi would never date a guy who slept under a toy sword. *As if!*

"Not really the time, babe," she said to herself and reached up to take the scimitar down from its mount.

From behind her in the living area, a yelp escaped Val's lips. Eliza spun, yanking the scimitar from its scabbard. There was a crash outside—another scream of terror. She threw the scabbard aside, grabbed the dagger from her waistband, and rushed into the living room.

The Stranger had caught Val as she tried to crawl under the end table to the exit. She was too terrified, in the end, to keep hiding in the kitchen. One black-gloved fist was pinning her by the neck, while the Stranger's other arm was raised high, his glimmering knife poised to make its fatal plunge.

Eliza's mind wrenched her back to an argument she'd had with Jenny a year ago, after Jenny stopped the wine forgers from poisoning Val at Declan Dillion's memorial service.

It was past 2:00 AM, and Eliza's fingers were going numb gripping the window sill. Inside, Jenny's cheeks were still streaked with mascara from her meltdown at the Winchester.

"It was my decision, and I don't regret it," Jenny whispered through a crack in the window.

"I do!" Eliza whispered back.

She'd clambered up on top of Jiji's barbecue to reach the bottom of the window outside Aunt Shelly's old bedroom, engaged in a perverse balcony scene with her star-crossed twin sister.

"What about Mom?" asked Eliza. "And Dad? You said yourself there's a good chance Val killed him, too. Didn't we swear an oath of revenge? How many opportunities like that are we gonna get?"

"You're saying I should have killed her?" Jenny asked. "Without any proof?"

"I'm saying you didn't have to do anything!" Eliza hissed. *"We have Nurse Bennett's journals. We* know *she's guilty. Whomever these poisoners are, they were doing us a favor, and you choked!"*

"'To know, and not act, is still to act,'" Jenny said. *"That's straight from the books. Trouble would never—"*

"Oh, Jesus Christ."

"Fuck you, Lizzy! You weren't the one who'd have to live with that on your conscience!" Jenny said. *"Just… just go. I'll talk to you later."*

"When?!" Eliza asked. *"You're on house arrest for a month! What am I supposed to do until then?"*

"I don't know," said Jenny. *"Follow Val around? Maybe those guys will try again and you'll get your wish."*

The whole memory flashed in her mind in the space of a heartbeat. It had taken a year, but the Stranger was about to grant Eliza's wish. All she had to do was nothing at all.

"Hey!" she shouted.

With the flick of her wrist, she sent her kunai dagger spinning at the Stranger's back.

He wheeled and the knife caught him dead in the chest—

Or, it would have, if the Stranger hadn't grabbed a copy of *The Smell of Trouble* and held it up as a shield. Danger's kunai was buried in the collector's edition's hardcover, right between the illustrated eyes of everyone's (least) favorite Girl Detective.

The Stranger looked down at the knife he'd stopped inches from his heart and cocked his head. Eliza had the odd impression that he was smiling under the black mask.

"Yeah, that's right!" Eliza yelled. Left-handed, she twirled Jack's sword in a double moulinet and advanced on the Stranger. "Forgot about me, didn't you? Well, the police are on their way, Killroy!"

The Stranger didn't speak. When he released Val's throat and leveled his long knife at Eliza, the message was clear.

"You might win. In fact, you probably will. You've always been bigger and stronger. But do you think you're getting out of here without leaving any DNA behind?" Eliza raised the sword higher, distantly impressed that her hand wasn't shaking. "I promise you, it won't be clean. I'm not Nilay, I fight dirty! And then the police will know who you are, and they'll catch you, even if I can't."

Seconds ticked by. Val sobbed on the carpet. Eliza didn't dare breathe. The knife in the Stranger's hand wavered as he considered the scenario. Slowly, he reached inside his dark trench coat with his free hand and pulled out a spray bottle of Clorox.

Eliza's brain was still trying to parse this development when he turned the bottle on Val and hit her with several blasts of bleach. She squealed as he doused her in cleaning fluid.

Oh, he's covering up! He really is *spooked about his DNA!*

Before Eliza could lunge with the scimitar to spill said DNA, the Stranger bolted across the living room, opened the sliding door, and leaped off the balcony!

"Wait!" Eliza cried out and rushed after him.

Did he just...?? No, he'd swung on Eliza's rope and was sliding down to the balcony below.

Eliza hacked at the nylon cord, but she was a second too late. The rope fell harmlessly to the sidewalk, with the Stranger safely on the floor below. He leaned out to take one last glance up at her, waved, and fled.

"Toodaloo, you fucking coward!" Eliza shouted down at him.

"Thank god! Thank god! Thank god!" Val kept repeating behind her.

Eliza sagged against the balcony railing, suddenly processing how close they'd come to dying.

"Oh Nilay, you poor thing!" Val said, finally registering his corpse, seated so calmly in that chair.

Eliza crossed to the armchair and pulled Nilay's eyelids down.

"I'm sorry," she said. "You didn't deserve this."

Val stared at the balcony, still in shock. "Do you think the police will catch him? He can't have gotten far."

"Doubt it," said Eliza. "I lied, I didn't call them yet." She snatched Val's purse off the coffee table before she could go for her phone. "And before I do, I've got a few questions for you, Valerie."

Chapter Thirteen

Homewrecker

THE DRESS VAL WORE WAS MORPHING FROM RED TO WHITE. Pinprick dots of bleached fabric were spreading all over her body where the Stranger sprayed her with Clorox. It made for a twisted mirror image of Nilay's corpse, with his white sports coat soaked in deep crimson. Say what you will about the woman, she knew how to accessorize.

Eliza gave Val a tissue to dab her smeared eyeliner, and watched in fascination as Val transformed from the horrified woman she'd been a minute ago back into the frigid, evil stepmother.

Or maybe Val isn't doing any of that—you are.

"Why did RJ call you 'Viv'?" Eliza asked.

"Really? That's what you want to know?" said Val.

"We're working up to the big questions," Eliza said. "How do you get *Viv* from Valerie?"

"Valerie Isabel Valentine," said Val, sniffling and wiping the bleach from her face. "Johnny was very particular about the names he used. My first husband called me Val, so to Johnny, I was Viv. 'There's power in names,' he liked to say."

"Lady, you don't need to tell me."

Val let out a chuckle that was half a sob. Eliza withdrew the golden **99+** pin from her pocket and held it up for Val to see.

"Where did you get this pin?"

Val squinted at it and shrugged. "I've never seen that before in my life."

"Bullshit. It was in your chair cushions."

"Maybe the maid dropped it?" Val offered. "I don't know what to tell you, it's not mine."

"Do you know whose it is? What it is?" Eliza asked.

Val held out her hand. Eliza was wary, but she was getting nowhere, so she let Val hold the pin.

"First of all, Jennifer, I would never wear something like this," Val said. "My clothes are not the kind you poke holes in. The Valentine Foundation orders pins for events sometimes, and ours always have magnetic clasps, not this cheap garbage. You said you found it in my chair cushion? Why were you even here? Was it for that?"

"This is my interrogation, not yours," said Eliza. "Who did you hire to take photos of RJ and my mother, back when she was pregnant?"

Val's eyebrow twitched. She tried to cover it by rolling her eyes, but Eliza was sure the question had caught her off guard. "I didn't hire anyone," said Val. "And that was years ago, what does it matter?"

"It matters."

"Enough to break into my house?"

"Why were *you* even here?" Eliza replied. "I thought you and Jack were going to Vegas!?"

"It was a gift for his SAT score," Val said. "He thought we were both going, but I surprised him and let him go on his own. I stayed and had Thanksgiving at Rosie's with friends. When I was coming back from dinner I ran into Nilay. He said he had new information about Johnny's game and wanted to talk in private." She glanced at the body of the late Boy Detective and swallowed another sob. When her eyes returned to Eliza's, an angry fire burned within them. "If you don't call the police right this second, I'm going to scream until the whole hotel hears. I'll say anything to put you in jail for the rest of your miserable life."

Eliza bit her lip. This attempt at an interrogation had gotten her nowhere, and she had no doubt Val would do exactly as she threatened.

She held up a finger and walked to the balcony to text.

D: I need you to text Blake and tell him there's been a murder at the Crow's Nest penthouse. And then I need you to hide. You can't be seen while Trouble is at the crime scene.

D: I'll explain later.

Eliza made to put her phone away when a reply came in.

T: Not Jack?

D: Nilay

T: Damn

T: Poor Penny

T: Done, talk later

"All right," Eliza said. "I texted Blake."

"How do I know you're not lying again?" Val asked.

In answer, Val's phone rang. It was Blake. Eliza didn't hear his side of the conversation but could parse that Blake was checking to see if Jenny was lying to him—and was stunned to learn she was not.

"Do we need to get our stories straight?" Eliza asked.

"No one will believe you were here by my permission," said Val.

"We'll say Jack told me I could come over and use the place while you guys were gone," said Eliza. When Val hesitated, she added, "Don't forget I saved your life. Again. I didn't have to."

Val nodded vaguely, already bored with the conversation.

"Humor me and answer one more question while we wait."

"Fine. What?"

Eliza knelt in front of Val and looked her straight in the eyes, watching for the tells Jenny had tried to teach her. "The night my mother gave birth to me, she told the attending nurse that Valerie Valentine was trying to kill her. Why do you think that is, Val?" she asked.

There was still some color left in Val's cheeks for the question to drain away. Her lips compressed into a grim rictus. "Because she deserved it," said Val. "Let me tell you a story about Laura Onishi."

If Junior didn't get here soon, Val was going to lose her mind. Her back ached, she got winded just crossing the room, and she had to pee constantly. It couldn't have been this bad with Victoria, could it? God, to be 21 again. What a body she'd had then. Indestructible.

"Two weeks!" she told her belly, taking careful steps to the end table where the housekeeper dropped off the day's mail. "Or I'll make them cut you out!"

He kicked!

"Oh you heard that, did you?" she cooed at her stomach. "You're going to be a smart one, just like your sister."

"Who are you talking to?" Victoria's little voice called from down the hall.

"Your brother," said Val, sifting through the mail.

A few bills, half a dozen junk mailers from charities she'd donated to, and a thick manila envelope with her name on it. But no postage?

"What if he's broken?" Victoria asked.

Her daughter toddled around the corner with Casey, the little blonde girl from the neighborhood she'd befriended.

"He's not broken!" Val snapped. "Where's your father? I thought he was watching you two?"

"Coming!" Johnny said, catching up to the girls. "Sorry, got distracted by the news. I think we're really going to war soon. Great timing to put a book out, jeez." He frowned at the envelope in her hand. "What's that?"

"I'll let you know." She grimaced and rubbed her back. "I need to pee. Can you?"

Val tucked the thick envelope under her arm, shoved the rest of the mail into her husband's hands, and nodded to the girls.

He collected them and led them back to the living room. "You guys want to hear about a story I wrote?" he asked them. "It's about a cop!"

"No!" said Victoria.

"Is there a dog in the story?" asked Casey.

"Yes, there should be a dog!" said Victoria.

"Well, there are K9 dogs, they're like dog police..." RJ said, trailing off

as he shut the door.

Val smiled and sighed. If he weren't so good with Victoria, she probably would have divorced him a long time ago. That and the fact that little Junior was on the way. She shuffled to the powder room to make water and returned to the chaise in her day room to lie down. Now, what was this envelope about? More charity bait?

She sliced the envelope open with a manicured nail and reached inside.
Oh hell.

Val didn't even need to look to know. Thick premium glossy stock? An envelope with no postage and no return address? These had to be photographs. Of the incriminating sort. Sad to say, it wasn't her first encounter with that kind of material. Being a Stratford, heir to a vineyard, two restaurants, the Cellars, a Shell station, and a portrait studio, one simply had to expect that sooner or later another bottom feeder would come along, trying to shame her into a handout.

Feeling inside the envelope, her fingers found a scrap of common paper and pulled out the typed note.

> **Mrs. Valentine,**
> **If you don't want this embarrassment all over town, you'd**
> **do well to follow these instructions.**
> **Down to the cent!**

And then the usual. A seven-digit ask—exorbitant, but theoretically doable. An account number for a bank in the Cayman Islands or wherever the blackmailer thought they couldn't be traced. A promise to return the negatives upon payment, etcetera, etcetera.

Junior kicked again.

"I know," Val said, rubbing her tummy. "I won't let them take what's yours."

With great reluctance, she dumped out the envelope into her lap, and forced herself to go through the pictures to see what this latest "embarrassment" was about. All it took was one photo to get her blood boiling.

"JOHNNY!!!" she screamed. "GET IN HERE!!!"

THE PART THAT STUCK WITH VAL LATER WAS THAT HE DIDN'T EVEN APOLOGIZE. This was his revenge, for her little lapse with an old college friend in the second year of their marriage. God knew she regretted it, but at least she hadn't gone and done this!

"Oh, so you're spying on me now?" Johnny asked when she showed him the photos. "That's ironic."

"I didn't ask for these, you careless moron!" said Val, trying to remain calm. "Someone must have noticed you gallivanting all over town with some whore who wasn't your wife!"

She shoved the blackmail note in his face.

"Laura doesn't deserve that, Viv. She's good people."

"She's pregnant!" Val shrieked at him. "And you're still seeing her!? What does she think is going to happen when she has that baby?"

"I don't know," Johnny said. "You and I were in a bad place when Laura gave me the news."

"Well, it couldn't have been that *bad of a place!" Val jabbed both index fingers at her swollen belly.*

"We both know what that was about," said Johnny. "You were feeling guilty and you wanted absolution."

"I don't seem to recall you complaining."

"I did, actually! You just didn't listen. And then you were meeting him behind my back in the City again a month later!"

"To tell him it was over for good!" Val said, wincing as Junior kicked. "I thought you'd be doing the same!"

"What did you want me to do, tell her to get rid of it?" Johnny ran a hand through his hair like this was all his struggle to bear. "Her parents disowned her, she doesn't have anyone else."

"YOU have someone else!"

She tossed the surveillance photos in his face, each showing her idiot husband going to shops, going to dinner, and checking into hotels with his very pregnant mistress.

"Oh, who cares? Pay 'em off. You can afford it," he said, crumpling up the note. "Not like you haven't dipped into the Stratford coffers before to cover up your indiscretions."

"This is your *indiscretion, not mine," said Val. "What if they ask for*

more?"

Johnny bit his lip, thinking.

"So, how about this: you pay half, and say the bank only allows a transfer that big once a week," Johnny said. "Then while they wait, we have your Dad's accountant trace the funds like he did last time. And we blackmail them right back! Mexican standoff. They return your money, and we all pretend this never happened."

She could see him already writing the outcome in his mind. A perfect ending to his problem, if only the rest of the world would cooperate.

"We got very lucky last time," said Val. "I doubt we would again."

"Then call their bluff. I'm the one being embarrassed here, not you."

"What a typical fucking man you are." Even as she said it, the germ of an idea tickled the edge of her consciousness.

"It's true! I'll look like an asshole, everyone will take your side, your Dad will probably knee me in the balls the next time he sees me, and I can… work something out with Laura."

"You told her you were leaving me, didn't you?" Val said. It wasn't a question.

"Six months ago, you wanted me to leave!" Johnny protested.

And what has he been telling her lately?

Val rubbed her temples. Junior was kicking up a storm and she needed to pee again.

"Please get out of my sight," Val said through her hands. "If I see one more second of your smirking face I'm going to murder you—and I actually don't want to do that. I'm carrying your child, for Christ's sake!"

"Yeah, sure," Johnny said. "What are we going to do about…?"

"Don't worry about it," said Val. "I'll take care of it. Just watch Victoria, I need some time alone."

He beat a swift retreat, and Val considered the evidence. Most blackmailers would have sent the photos to Johnny. Tried to get him to pay them off with some of Val's money. Only a woman would have assumed it'd be Valerie who'd want to keep things quiet. Only a woman would understand that kind of embarrassment and shame. And what woman did Val know of, disowned by her family and desperate for cash after learning her baby's father would never actually leave his wife?

She flipped open her cell phone and dialed the Crow's Nest hotel.

"Yes, thank you," she said when the concierge picked up. "I'll be swinging by to visit soon. Can you tell me what room Laura Onishi is in?"

"Ah, ma'am, we don't normally give our guests' room numbers out without—"

"This is Valerie Valentine speaking."

"Of course," said the concierge. "Looks like she's in room 525."

THE LITTLE TRAMP SQUEALED LIKE A CAUGHT RAT WHEN VAL UNLOCKED THE hotel door and stormed in.

"How did you—what are you doing!?" Laura asked, backing up until her calves hit the bed and she fell back onto it.

She was as big as a house! Jesus H, Johnny. Did he even shower between crawling out of her bed and into ours?

"I thought we should speak in person," Val said, walking around the suite like she owned the place. She essentially did, seeing as Johnny was paying for this room with her credit card. "I know you know who I am, and I wanted to make it clear, face to face, with absolutely no ambiguity, that your little scheme won't work."

It was there in her eyes, the way her brown irises shrank. Guilty!

"What the fuck are you talking about?" Laura said and pushed Val away. "Get out of my room! You can't be here!"

Val pushed her right back, pressing her neck into the mattress. Junior kicked again. Or maybe it was hers; their bellies were pressed against each other.

"I can be wherever I please in this town," Val said. "So believe me when I tell you that if you ever try a stunt like this on my family again, it will be the last stunt you ever pull."

There it was, not only guilt but fear, too. Good. She released Laura's neck and straightened her maternity dress.

"Are you threatening me, Valerie?" the idiot asked.

"I'm warning you," said Val. She probably needed to walk a careful line here, just in case. "I'm already a widow once over, Laura. So you can trust that I will do what needs doing if you ever mess with me again."

"He hates you, you know!" said Laura. "RJ can't wait to leave you!"

Val frowned. RJ? Oh, right, Johnny.

"You sad, delusional girl." She considered Laura's belly. "I hope you're ready to be a single mother."

"Why won't you just let him go?" she asked.

"That's not how marriage works," Val said. She needed to pee again, so it was time to wrap things up. She tossed the crumpled-up blackmail note in Laura's lap. "Your mistake was overvaluing your worth. Five million dollars? Please. Be reasonable."

Val rummaged in her purse and got her checkbook out. She clicked the pen and licked the tip.

"How's $40,000 sound?" she asked. Laura made a gargled squawk of rage. "I can go lower," Val added.

The woman glared hatefully at Val, but the fight had left her. Laura's gaze fell, and the angry scowl collapsed into a self-loathing grimace.

"Fifty," said Laura.

"Mother to mother, I can get to fifty." Val scribbled on the check and signed it. "On the condition that you leave this town and never return. I've heard your parents want nothing to do with you, so there's no reason for you to stick around anyway, right?"

She tore out the check and set it on the nightstand, as one pays a whore.

"We'll always be a part of his life, Valerie," Laura said quietly. "Nothing, not even the entire Stratford fortune, will ever change that."

Val opened the hotel room door and looked back.

"If you're not out of this hotel by nightfall, I'll know," she said. "You don't want me to know."

She stalked off to find the nearest ladies' room, rubbing her stomach and cooing softly to Junior about all the many facets of life she couldn't wait to show him. He already had a big sister; he didn't need any more.

STROBING RED AND BLUE LIGHTS FLICKERED THROUGH THE BALCONY window. Emergency vehicles had arrived down below. Eliza tried to calm her trembling fists.

"You're lying."

"Am I?" Val asked, savoring Eliza's fury with a cruel smile.

Eliza studied every inch of Val's face, searching for a hint of deception, but she just couldn't tell. It was a mistake to come here tonight. This had turned into Trouble business after all.

"If what you've said is true, you basically just admitted to putting out a hit on my mother," Eliza said, scratching the tattoo on her wrist.

"Please, I had nothing to do with her accident."

"What about you threatening her? Saying you were already a widow once?" Eliza asked.

Val rolled her eyes and sighed. "My first husband died of a drug overdose. Some people wanted to see drama where there wasn't any and made lots of insinuations. One of them tried to extort me like your mother, but my father's accountant caught them red-handed. It was an empty threat, I only said it because I wanted to scare her, and clearly it didn't work. If your mother hadn't been so desperate to see Johnny that she went speeding down Highway 12 in a rainstorm, she'd probably still be alive."

"If you hadn't scared her away in the first place—"

Eliza was cut off by a knock at the door. It was the paramedics—not that there was anything they could do for Nilay now. Blake and Officer Peña followed soon after with a forensics guy.

"I thought you went to your room to play video games?" Blake said to her.

Eliza gave him Trouble's best impish smile while the forensics guy roved about, taking photographs.

"I needed a break from all the Thanksgiving shit, you know?" Eliza lied. "Jack said the penthouse was empty if I wanted a place to chill. And then You-Know-Who showed up. Well, Val and Nilay got here first, but the Stranger arrived right after."

Blake turned to Val, raising an eyebrow. "That so?"

"More or less," said Val. "I'm going to need to have a chat with my son about whom he allows over."

"Why does it smell like bleach?" the forensics guy asked.

Eliza tried to explain the Stranger spraying it around, and his fear of leaving DNA, but she was distracted. One of the paramedics, the one with a soul patch, had been mean-mugging her since she got here. She was about to say something when Tori showed up at the door.

"Sweetie, you can't be here," said Officer Peña. "It's a crime scene."

"Can't you j-just ask? It's my mom," said Tori.

Peña grimaced and called over to Blake. "We got room for one more, boss?"

"I thought we were trying to get a DNA hit here," said the forensics guy, scowling at Tori. "She could foul up the sample."

"I'm over here all the time, you'll f-find mine regardless," said Tori.

Was she? Jack never mentioned it. Then again, he hadn't mentioned her new stutter, either.

"It's fine, Bill," said Blake. "Get over here. I think we might have a print."

Eliza moved closer to get a look. Blake had put a blue post-it note on the sliding glass door to the balcony, where a bloody thumbprint was easily visible against the glass.

"That's the way he escaped," said Eliza. "Down a rope tied to the railing."

"See, I keep telling you, kiddo," said Blake, peering closer at the print. "Actual police work is gonna be what gets this guy. You need to clean up your act and cross that blue line if you want to do real detective work."

"ACAB."

"Th-that's impossible," Tori said in her ear. Far from comforting Val, she'd sidled up behind Eliza to get a look at the thumbprint. "You're s-s-sure the Stranger left that print?"

I didn't see him leave it, but whose else would it be? Nilay's?" Eliza asked. She was expecting a stuttering retort, but Tori had gone pale when Eliza glanced back to get a look at her. "What?"

"The thumbprint..." said Tori. Her jaw hung slack, and her gaze lingered out over the balcony, staring at nothing. "I'd recognize it anywhere."

Blake and the forensics guy turned away from the print, questions hanging on their brows.

"It's Daddy's," said Tori.

Chapter Fourteen

XP

The tomb of RJ Valentine was sealed closed with a two-ton slab of white marble. There was simply no way a human being could escape it on his own, even if he'd been playing dead in the casket the whole time. And Jenny had checked for his breath with her phone screen, hadn't she? Jack saw it too.

RJ Valentine was dead.

Except odd things kept happening. The convenient notes Jenny received from her dad on occasion—which he theoretically could have written before his passing, but still. And Hamilton Webb's clockwork demise, practically walked to his death by the instructions in RJ's will. Then there was Mr. White, who told Jenny with all sincerity that RJ was still alive, right before he died. The way the Stranger seemed to lash out violently whenever anyone threatened to violate the spirit of the game. And now, RJ's own thumbprint, literally left in Nilay's blood, at the scene of his murder.

Sorry, Nails. I should have warned you harder not to play.

Once again, Jenny's least favorite *Trouble* theory was staring her in the face, daring her to come up with some alternate explanation. At present, she didn't have one. But she didn't see how RJ could still be alive, either.

"What if he grew a clone body in a lab?" said Mason. "He's rich.

They do that, you know? To harvest for organs. Like in *Never Let Me Go*."

They were standing around RJ's tomb at Black Rock Cemetery on a crisp Sunday morning. Tyrone the city worker was here, operating a hydraulic lift, along with Lockhart, Deputy Mack, and a forensics guy. Mason tagged along with his father, and Val was here as they needed her permission to exhume the body. Nobody needed Alicia Aaron around, but she came anyway, perhaps because Jack was here too, fresh from the airport after his trip to Vegas.

Eliza had told Jenny all that occurred in the Crow's Nest penthouse on Thanksgiving night—the **99+** pin, Nilay's murder, Val's story about the blackmail, the weird paramedic eyeballing her—but declined to come along as Kazumi.

"What did the Stranger do, right before Nilay said he knew who it was?" Jenny had asked her later that night.

"I don't know, got to his feet and kicked Nilay?" Eliza said. "Maybe he recognized his shoe?"

"Damn! You should've been recording it on your phone…"

"I had my hands a little full, Trouble!"

Far from rekindling the fire in her sister to solve mysteries, Nilay's murder had Eliza retreating ever further into her Kazumi identity. She'd even begun holding elaborate fake conversations in Japanese with her "parents" on the phone from Okinawa whenever schoolmates were around.

"I think we might still be a ways off from human cloning technology," Jack said.

Jenny studied her brother, searching for an emotion, but he was locked down behind dark sunglasses. He'd liked Nilay, hadn't he? They shared a certain distinguished aesthetic. Both saw themselves as leaders of their peers. Nilay wasn't on the baseball team, but he helped throw batting practice for them. What was Jack thinking now?

Over by the tomb, Tyrone shouted an alert and started up the hydraulic lift. There was a grinding scrape of stone on stone, and the white marble slab rose, inch after inch, above RJ's final resting place.

"This is cool, but I gotta jet," Mason said. He gave Jack a hearty slap on the back. "My money's still on a clone. Take it easy, bro."

"Are we even sure it was his fingerprint?" Jenny asked aloud. "What if Tori's lying?"

"Believe it or not, we don't just take people's word for it," said Deputy Mack. "We checked."

"And you just happened to have RJ's fingerprints on file?"

"He went and got fingerprinted years ago," said the deputy. "To coach Little League. The Valentine Foundation insisted on it for all the coaches, if I recall."

The slab had completely cleared the tomb now. The hydraulic crane stopped lifting and Tyrone carefully swung it to the side, cautioning everyone to stay out from beneath it no matter how secure it appeared.

"Moment of truth, folks," said Lockhart.

He and the forensics guy pulled on latex gloves and covered their faces in surgical masks.

"Will it smell?" Val asked.

Lockhart nodded grimly, prompting Val to back up further. Alicia pulled out a notepad and scribbled in it. She was wearing a Pixeldrome shirt today, which filled Jenny with rage, and beneath it, an existential despair. She knew she needed to go back to that damned arcade, but she didn't want to. For the first time in her life, she'd encountered a mystery she wasn't eager to solve. She hated the people at Pixeldrome and hated even more the idea that her mother could have been one of them. Dad must have known Jenny would connect her mother to the game token clue. What was he hoping she'd learn about Mom?

"Final guess?" asked Jack.

"Twins," said Alicia.

"Still dead, fingerprint faked by the Stranger," said Jenny.

"Hmm," said Jack. His face was still a mask, but his hands were clenched into fists.

"You want him to still be alive," Jenny said.

"You don't?" he asked.

"Not this way."

Lockhart lifted the casket lid and waved his hand, banishing the putrescent air. Jenny was thankful she was too short to see inside the coffin.

"Huh," said Lockhart with a chuckle. "You're all wrong, but Jenny's closest." He reached into the casket and raised the shrunken, decaying right arm of RJ Valentine. "Wave to your kids, RJ," said Lockhart.

"Blake! Really!" shrieked Val.

Jenny would have been just as outraged if her mind wasn't busy processing two new details. The first, and most obvious, was that RJ Valentine was missing a thumb. The second was that when Lockhart told RJ's corpse to wave to his "kids," he'd been looking at Jenny and Jack—and Alicia too!

"We'll take DNA swabs to be sure," said the forensics guy.

Lockhart nodded. "Jack, Jenny, if you don't mind?"

"We should get everyone's DNA on file, don't you think?" said Jenny. "Starting with Alicia, if we're going alphabetically."

Alicia squawked and backed away from Jenny, stumbling over the uneven terrain with her prosthetic leg. "I don't consent!"

"Oh yeah? Something to hide?"

"Leave her alone, Jenny," Lockhart said in a commanding voice. He turned to the forensics guy. "Assuming this *is* RJ, would a thumb keep for a year?"

"In theory, if you preserved it properly," the guy said. "Or they could have made a mold of it to use instead."

Jack turned to Jenny. "The thumb was there when we viewed him at the funeral, wasn't it?" he asked.

Jenny bit her lip, thinking back. "Yes. You patted his hand after I kissed him on the cheek, and then I got worried and asked the Undertaker if that was safe... Wait! The Undertaker!" She turned to Lockhart. "He was a trophy collector! He took little vials of blood from the people he embalmed if they interested him. Including RJ's!"

"Did he?" Lockhart said, an odd smile creeping over his face. "So *that's* where the blood came from."

Jenny's ears turned pink. They'd used that blood to doctor a fake murder weapon, which she planted in Val's purse while Eliza was in jail at the police station posing as Jenny.

"Allegedly!" She grinned.

"Regardless, the Undertaker is dead," said Lockhart. "Someone else must have snuck in after you and Jack left, and cut the thumb off."

"But why would this bastard leave the thumbprint on my sliding glass door?" Val asked.

Jenny had been thinking about this all weekend and could come to only one conclusion.

"So we'd be here, doing this," she said. "I think the Stranger meant for us to exhume Dad after Mr. Webb and the game token murder. We would have if Tori hadn't revealed that RJ had a secret collaborator."

"To what end?" Val asked.

"Because he hates the 'RJ is the Stranger' theory too," Jenny said, smiling. "He doesn't want us giving RJ credit for his masterpiece. He needs us to know, beyond a shadow of a doubt, that RJ is dead."

"Where does that leave us, then?" Jack asked.

"Same place as always," said Jenny, scowling.

The forensics guy approached, bearing a big Q-tip. Alicia said goodbye to Jack and bolted. He and Jenny stuck around to give DNA samples, and then had the awkward timing to run into Penny as she arrived at the cemetery for Nilay's funeral.

Oh, damn. Poor Penny!

"Hey, Pen," said Jack. "How are you holding up?"

Penny opened her mouth, but no words came out. She shook her head behind dark sunglasses of her own.

"Should we stay?" Jack asked.

"I don't think that would be a good idea," Penny said, her voice strained with emotion. She turned to Jenny. "Especially not you, no offense. I'm sorry, Jenny, but I don't think I can play these reindeer games anymore. Please, just leave me out of this. And if you care about Drew, you'll stay away from him, too. It's not safe."

They let her pass. Jenny couldn't even protest; what Penny said was totally fair. But she and Jack didn't have a choice in the matter. They were heirs, and this was their game to play. Like it or not, she needed to start playing it again.

"Hey, *Kazu*, where'd you put that 99+ pin?" Jenny asked her sister when she got home.

Eliza reached over and retrieved it from her nightstand drawer. She tossed it to Jenny and went back to reading her book—a galley copy of Alicia's *Hands of Adamant*. Jenny considered the pin, frowning. Could this have been their mother's? Could their mother really have asked Val for a payoff?

"You don't believe that stuff Val said about Mom, right?" she asked.

Eliza lowered her book.

"Maybe there were sides to Mom that we wouldn't understand," she said. "She was desperate, and alone, and days away from giving birth. Who can say what either of us would have done in her shoes?"

The flicker of an idea sparked in her mind.

In her shoes…

She'd asked Charlie to help her find a new style to fit in at Pixeldrome. Maybe what she needed was an old style. Laura Onishi's style.

"Great idea, Lizzy," Jenny said and hurried down to the garage.

The box labeled **Laura — Closet** was right where Jenny left it when Shelly gave her The Talk. *There's going to come a time in your life when it will feel like you've invented sex.* Had Shelly been thinking of Mom when she imparted that bit of wisdom?

"Were you a blackmailing badass, Mom?" Jenny asked aloud.

She picked out a pair of high-waisted acid-washed jeans, a scoop neck Wu-Tang t-shirt, some Chuck Taylors, and Mom's old puffy windbreaker jacket. From the drugstore, she purchased a home perm kit. The jeans fit perfectly, which is how Jenny knew she was on the right track. She brushed her now wavy mohawk to one side and admired her look in the mirror: a white Wu-Tang shirt with the Red Sun of Japan tucked into her jeans, and Mom's jacket over it, with the sleeves pushed back to her elbows. As a final touch, she affixed the 99+ pin that Eliza found to her collar.

Oh yeah, I could invent sex with this look.

A dozen Harbor High kids were milling around Pixeldrome when Jenny strolled in the following day after class. There was a thing for Nilay at the school, but Jenny figured it was best if she didn't attend. Alicia Aaron must have felt the same; she was here too, playing *Frogger*. Jimmy Figg and Nathaniel gathered around the *Street Fighter* game with some other nerds. And of course, there was that Asha girl, looking bored and sullen—until she spotted Jenny, and her mouth spread into a shit-eating grin.

"You came back!" Asha said, looking Jenny up and down. "Are you supposed to be a gamer now? *My culture is not a costume*, Trouble."

"Bite me, Asha," said Jenny, and pointed to the pin on her collar. "I made level 99, can I see the VIP room now?"

"Psh, real 99s don't need to ask," said Asha. "Who'd you steal that from?"

"My mom," Jenny said.

"Oh yeah, Rob said she was cool." Asha paused, favoring Jenny with a sympathetic pout. "That usually means he fucked her, no offense."

Well, that didn't take long. Jenny already wanted to murder her. "Why are you so horrible?"

Asha's eyes flashed, and she nodded to all the dorks playing with Jimmy and Nathaniel. "Notice anything different about me, compared to them?"

Jenny scanned the crowd, not that she needed to, to grasp Asha's point.

"A bunch of mostly white, almost entirely male gamers, compared to a queer girl with thick glasses and olive skin? Yeah, sure."

"Not queer, lesbian," Asha corrected her. "And I know I don't need to tell you that people say horrible things to me all the time. Except they say it in a way where they have plausible deniability. Or they say it by not saying it, and letting me decipher the implication. And I can either keep my mouth shut and feel like shit, complain about it, and feel even shittier when they gaslight me, or give it back so hard that it doesn't hurt anymore. You should try it sometime. It feels fucking awesome to stop being a victim."

It wasn't a philosophy Jenny agreed with, but she couldn't help pitying Asha. She'd spent three months getting shunned and ignored by all her classmates, and it sucked.

"All right," said Jenny. "Well I'm not fucking that crusty old burnout who owns this place, and I'm guessing that fucking you wouldn't get me anything—except herpes—so how else do I become a VIP?"

"You could always compete in the Pixeldrome Open," said Asha. At Jenny's questioning eyebrow, she went on, "It's a tournament Rob holds every year on New Year's Day. First place is a thousand bucks, and automatic level 50 for VIP access—but you gotta be level 10 to join."

"Shit, why didn't you say so?" said Jenny. "I can do level 10."

"You also need to be, you know, good."

"Trouble can do anything she sets her mind to. Where do I sign up?"

Asha sighed. "Come on."

They moved to a little kiosk at the end of the counter, and Asha walked her through the process of creating an account to track her XP. Asha activated a membership card with a device like they used at the Crow's Nest for room keys and handed it over. It was midnight black, with that pixelated coin in gold on one side, and Jenny's account info printed on the other.

"All you need to do is swipe your card on a game's reader thing before you play, and you'll start earning XP," said Asha. "Let me show you."

Asha slid herself over the counter and grabbed Jenny's hand. The touch sent a pleasant spark up her arm as Asha guided her to the coin machine. Jenny turned her $20 bill into a bunch of golden Pixeldrome game tokens, and Asha showed her how to swipe her card on the NFC reader affixed to the side of the *Super Mario Kart* game. It was one of those driving games where you sat in a pretend car seat with a steering wheel and gas pedals. Jenny took the left seat, and Asha dropped into the seat on the right.

"Cover me?" Asha asked, swiping in and pointing to the coin slots. "I'm good for it."

"I'll bet you are."

Jenny deposited two dollars in tokens into the machine, so they both could play.

"I don't have herpes," said Asha. "Just, for the record."

"Oh, so that's just your face?" Jenny said, smirking. "Hope you don't mind getting your ego bruised, 'cause I rule at *Mario Kart*."

It wasn't just bravado, Jenny always beat Penny and Drew in *Mario Kart*. They picked their characters, and the race began.

Two minutes later, Asha let out a nasty laugh and blew on her hands, pretending to cool them off. "I thought you were good at this?" she said.

Jenny bit her tongue, feeling her face redden. Asha had destroyed her. She came in seventh to Asha's first place. "I'm not used to the steering controls," Jenny said lamely.

"Skill issue," said Asha. "That's why you need to practice here, instead of sulking at home because that fat loser called your cripple friend a retard."

"Dude," said Jenny.

"Relax, I know Alicia from way back," said Asha. "She used to go to Harbor Elementary before she got herself transferred to your fancy charter school. If you really want to offend her, ask her whose dick her mom sucked to make that happen."

Jenny winced, glancing over to the *Frogger* game where Alicia was playing. She was staring intently at the screen, but Jenny thought her cheeks looked more flushed than usual. Like she might have heard them.

"Anyway, you play the game, you earn XP," said Asha. She pointed to the phone-sized monochrome screen that had been installed on the dashboard, where Jenny's progress was tracked. Jenny's screen showed:

JTV | LVL 1 | +15XP | 15XP TOT

On her right, Asha's screen displayed:

ASH | LVL 69 | +256XP | 2419395XP TOT

"How much XP per level?" Jenny asked.

"It starts at a thousand, and goes up a thousand each level," said Asha. "Let me show you the leaderboard."

She pulled Jenny out of the driver's seat and walked her back to the counter. Behind, on the big LED board, was **ROB** at the very top with 10 digits worth of XP. Asha slid over the counter again and typed on her keyboard.

"Here's me," she said. The leaderboard scrolled down a short way to highlight her score. "And here's you."

This time, the board scrolled for a very long time to find Jenny's stats, all the way at the bottom. Asha showed her Jimmy Figg and Nathaniel's ratings too. They were both in the mid-30s. Alicia Aaron had already climbed to level 12.

"That's smart, actually," said Jenny. "It makes people keep playing, and spending money here, to level up."

"It's called 'gamification,'" said Asha. "It's how you sucker morons into doing what you want them to, and make them think they're enjoying it."

"Would my mom be on here?" Jenny asked, pointing to the leaderboard.

Asha shook her head. "You get retired after a year if you don't play. But the level 99 GOATs all get a plaque down in the VIP room."

"Can't you just, like, go down there and take some pictures for me?" Jenny asked.

"Nope. Gotta play like everyone else," said Asha. She leaned closer, lowering her voice. "There *are* other ways of earning XP if you're the right kind of free thinker."

"Is this where you ask me to deal drugs or something?" Jenny asked.

"Oh my god, you're so sheltered, it's adorable," said Asha.

"I am not sheltered! I…I fucked a con artist and helped her steal a priceless red diamond!"

"That sounds like something you made up." Asha leaned closer still. "I'm not trying to sell you on anything. I'm talking about RAM. Random Acts of Misanthropy."

"What's that?"

"It's not doing what society tells you to do. Rob believes in transformative change through small feats of rebellion."

"And how many of these 'acts of misanthropy' involve sucking him off?" Jenny asked.

"Not as many as you'd think," Asha said tartly.

"You didn't…?"

"No, god! Take a joke, Trouble. Rob's got his whole philosophy, but for me, I just like to stir shit."

"I've noticed." Jenny flexed her jaw, considering. "I'm gonna pass, though. I'm on probation, and my JCO would love to put me back on house arrest. Trouble's gotta be on her best behavior."

"Lame."

Asha made to turn back to her busy job of being a sourpuss, so Jenny reached out and redirected her gaze, holding her fingers on Asha's cheek just long enough to give her something to think about.

"I'm not done with you yet, Asha," Jenny said. Asha's eyes widened, and Jenny nodded back to Alicia across the room. "You said you go way back with Alicia? What else can you tell me about her?"

"She smells poor," said Asha. "Or at least she used to."

"Okay, but beyond that? Who's her dad?"

"I don't know, some white trash redneck?" said Asha. "I don't think he's around anymore."

"Could he have been her stepdad?" Jenny asked.

"Maybe?" Asha shrugged. "Why?"

Jenny bit her lip. "Just a theory. I think her real dad might be… someone else. But I'd need a DNA test to prove it."

"Oooh! Why didn't you say so?" asked Asha. She opened a drawer behind the counter and pulled out a pair of scissors. "I'll give you 1000XP if you can go snip yourself a hair sample without Alicia noticing. 2000XP if she does."

This bitch isn't kidding about stirring shit.

Jenny scowled and took the scissors, casually making her way over to Alicia. Nathaniel waved from behind the snack bar counter, where he apparently worked, slinging corn dogs and pizza. She made a mental note to never eat here.

"What do you want? Don't distract me!" Alicia chirped, seeing Jenny approach in the video screen's reflection.

"Just watching," said Jenny. She moved directly behind Alicia, where her reflection wouldn't show, and reached into her jacket for the scissors. "Are you a big fan of this one?" she asked.

"You get more XP for older games," Alicia said. "The owner is some kind of weird loser who's stuck in the past. No offense."

"I'm not stuck in the past!"

Alicia laughed. Jenny snipped off half an inch of her crimson-red hair. She caught the falling hair in her left hand and tucked the scissors back into her jacket just as Alicia turned around.

"What are you doing?" asked Alicia.

"Nothing, just watching!" said Jenny.

Alicia stepped away, wary, and gave her throwback outfit a double take. "Not stuck in the past, huh?" she asked.

"Trouble never misses an opportunity for a good disguise." Jenny turned Alicia back around. "Don't screw up your game."

Jenny returned to Asha at the counter, triumphantly displaying the red hairs in her palm.

"I'm only giving you 1000XP for that," Asha said. She typed into her console. "Congrats! You made level 2!"

"Not bad for a day's work," said Jenny. "It's been real, but I need to deal with this." She clutched the hair in her fist, careful not to lose any strands.

"What are you gonna do, clone an army of cripples?" Asha asked.

"Yes, that's exactly what I'm going to do, Asha."

"I prefer Ash," said Asha. She sighed deeply. "Gawd. I guess I'll be seeing you, then?"

She tried to sound uninterested, but Jenny had the feeling Asha was excited at the prospect. With a little effort, Jenny might yet flirt her way into the VIP room.

"Count on it."

Chapter Fifteen

Wallflower Girl

LAMBERT KNEW OF A LAB THAT COULD RUN DNA TESTS, BUT IT would take weeks for Jenny to get the results on Alicia Aaron's sample. She included a sample of her own, for the lab to compare against. In the meantime, she tried to distract herself from the thought of being sisters with Alicia by grinding XP at Pixeldrome or hanging out with Drew in his masturbatorium.

After Penny's plea/warning, Drew continued to behave at school as though he wanted nothing to do with Jenny. Then she would sneak over in secret, on days when he didn't have baseball practice, and they'd discuss theories and play old video games.

"Gawd, can you even imagine?" Jenny groaned. They'd returned to the topic of Alicia's parentage again—or rather, Jenny had, as she couldn't get it out of her mind. "It would make her crush on Jack so much funnier, though."

"Honestly, I doubt you're related," said Drew. He was practicing his swing with his high-tech baseball tee while Jenny played *Final Fight* on an old Super Nintendo that Drew bought off eBay. "Alicia has a February birthday. I mean, that's a lot of jam for one dude to be slinging."

"Please never use that term in front of me again."

"Baby batter? Daddy sauce? RJ Relish?"

Jenny grabbed the nearest tool within reach from Arty's old workbench and hurled it at him.

He yelped, laughing, and managed to catch it. "Careful! You can hurt people with these!" he said.

"Don't be a pussy, it's just a screwdriver."

"It's a center punch. According to YouTube, these are perfect for breaking car windows, if Trouble ever needs to." He underhand tossed it back to her.

"I'll break *your* car window!" Jenny glared, but there was no heat behind it. "Why else would RJ put Alicia in the will, though? 'No mystery is complete without the following.' Without a secret daughter? He already had one: me!"

"Is that why it bothers you so much, Jenny?" Drew asked.

Maybe? Jenny could tell herself that Mom was Dad's true love, and he was held captive by Val's prenup. But if Dad was having a *second* affair at the same time?

"What can I say, I'm an only child," Jenny said, grinning.

Heheheh.

"Only children represent!" Drew gave her a fist bump.

"You're probably right," Jenny sighed. "I mean, Alicia doesn't even look like me."

But as the calendar turned to December, Alicia's features began to look more and more familiar. She didn't *not* have cheekbones. Jenny found herself studying the few pictures of RJ she possessed, comparing the shape of his nose, his narrow chin, the blue eyes they both shared…

Her brain was starting to do funny things with Alicia's face whenever they saw each other. She might have truly lost it if a new distraction hadn't arrived for Jenny to fret over: college.

Their 12th-grade English teacher, Mr. Cage, designated a wall for students to show off what schools they got accepted to. He kept construction paper and art supplies handy so they could make little signs to advertise their haul. Jenny's desk sat right along that wall, and on a Monday in early December, she took a seat after lunch to discover a big sheet of yellow paper proclaiming that Dinah Black had gotten into Brown University.

Dinah had applied Early Decision, which meant she was for sure going there, Eliza was delighted to explain. Jenny didn't know exactly where Brown was, but had a strong suspicion it was on the East Coast.

"It's where rich girls go to get their MRS degree," said Shelly.

"What's that?"

"Oh, Jenny."

"Not always. Hermione—I mean Emma Watson—went there, and she's still single," Eliza said. Her face fell. "I'm gonna be the only senior without a college on the wall."

"Just make something up. Tell them you're joining Dauntless."

Lizzy gave her the finger.

"Neither of you is going to have a college on the wall if you don't apply somewhere, Jenny," said Shelly. "Your Jiji will be very disappointed if you don't at least try to get into UC Berkeley."

"Sure, maybe the Stranger can follow me there," said Jenny.

"Those seasons always suck," said Eliza.

Penny joined Mr. Cage's wall the next day with an acceptance to Pepperdine, where she was now committed to attending after a brief flirtation with Howard. Drew, Jenny knew, was fielding scholarship offers from ASU and San Diego State. He was in deep discussion with Jack, Lai, and JeRay over which college had the hottest co-eds.

Someone, probably Penny, put up a banner in Nilay's name. For Harvard. He was the first BSA graduate to attend. Or, he would have been.

On Friday, there was another addition to the wall. Not for a college, but an advance promo for Alicia Aaron's book, *Hands of Adamant*. There was an author photo in black and white—where her makeup and lighting were way too soft, in Charlie's semi-professional opinion—and a bio blurb.

> Alicia Aaron is a talented emerging voice in the New Adult genre from Blackbird Springs, California. After a train accident left her with a prosthetic limb, Alicia was inspired

to write romantic fiction with positive representation for differently-abled readers. When she's not attending class or working on her next novel, Alicia can be found hiking the golden hills of Calistoga County or playing with her cat. *Hands of Adamant* is her debut novel.

"Couldn't be me saying it, but I ain't ever seen that chick on a hiking trail," said Meghan, who sat nearby.

"Alicia lost her leg in a train accident?" Jenny asked aloud.

"Yeah, you didn't know that?" said Meghan.

"It always seemed rude to ask," said Jenny. "Like, the train ran over her leg?"

"I guess so." Meghan shrugged.

A shiver ran down Jenny's spine. It took a moment for her brain to catch up and identify the cause: empathy. She *knew*, somehow, in a way that made all the odd pieces of the Alicia puzzle snap together. This wasn't some old movie. Girls didn't just get hit by trains in the 21st century. Alicia had been out on those tracks for a reason. The same reason Jenny went to the roof of the hospital that night, before she met Eliza. She'd tried to kill herself.

ASKING ALICIA ABOUT IT WAS OUT OF THE QUESTION. JENNY KNEW how she'd feel if anyone other than Eliza or maybe Shelly broached the subject with her. But she needed to know more. Was this the hidden detail that somehow connected her to RJ's will? She thought about trying Tori, but that bitch would never tell her anything useful. Which left Jack.

Of all the Unfridgeables, Jack probably hated her the least. Unfortunately, he hung out with Kazumi and the Bitchy Brigade constantly, making it hard for Jenny to get a moment alone with him. She'd have to try him at the Crow's Nest. He usually worked out in the evening, so Jenny took a break from hate-flirting with Asha and dumping game tokens into *1943* to swing by the hotel.

She made it almost halfway across the lobby before security stopped her.

"What do you mean, '86ed'?" Jenny asked the maître d' as the rent-a-cops escorted her out.

"It means you're banned from the premises," said the snooty little asshole.

"I know what '86' means, dickweed. I'm asking why?"

"The last time you were here, a guest was murdered," said the maître d'. "The Crow's Nest would like to cordially extend you a middle finger, and ask you to never patronize our establishment again. Good day, Miss Valentine!"

Security shoved her over the threshold and out onto the sidewalk. Great! So much for that idea. How the hell was Eliza always over here, on her fake dates with her brother?

Oh, right! Kazumi…

Lizzy would kill her. But Lizzy was over at Charlie's place, obsessively listening to the new Taylor Swift album. Jenny only needed to talk to Jack for a few minutes. Her sister would never even know she was here.

"Pip pip cheerio, I'm Kazumi Onishi! I went to Hogwarts or something, innit? Even though I'm from Okinawa. I'll fancy anything you say because I want you to like me, *mate*. My cousin Jenny is the worst! Torch! Lift! Our cars don't have trunks, they have boots!"

Jenny appraised her makeup job in the bathroom mirror. It might not be quite as good as when Charlie did Eliza's disguise, but it was close enough. And after listening to her sister speak as Kazumi for months, she had the accent down pat. She wore a thick scrunchie over her wrist to hide the Ace of Clubs tattoo. After pulling on a wig that matched Eliza's style, she was back at the hotel only 90 minutes after getting thrown out.

The 4-inch heels forced her to walk slowly and play it casual. No one stopped her as she reached the elevator and stepped inside, pressing the button for the second floor. The glass door to the gym required a key card to open, but as luck would have it, Jack was leaving just as she approached.

"What are you doing here?" he asked, smiling.

It was so galling the way people smiled at Kazumi.

"Was in the area and thought I'd pop in," she said in her best British accent. "You busy?"

"Just finished my workout," he said, and tucked his head, smelling his shirt. "Sorry, I probably reek right now. You mind if I shower real quick?"

Kazumi didn't mind. Jack led her to the elevator and swiped his card to send them up to the penthouse.

"Is your mum home?" she asked.

"Nah, she doesn't like being here anymore," Jack said. "Doesn't feel safe."

Sure enough, when they reached the penthouse, the place looked spare and sterile. The hotel had removed the chair where Nilay died, and all traces of the Valentine family had vanished with it.

"We're moving out soon, as a matter of fact," Jack said. "Tori's letting us lease Valentine Manor for now."

"Oh is she?" Jenny asked. Maybe a little too snidely.

"But I've got the place all to myself for the weekend," he said, shooting her a furtive grin.

Oh come on, Jack.

"Right. About that, Jack."

"Hold that thought. Lemme shower first," he said, already peeling off his tight workout shirt.

There was a thin white scar on his shoulder blade, courtesy of Big Karl at Schloss Schwarzwald. Now they both had permanent marks back there. Almost twinning.

Ordinarily, Jenny would have snooped while she waited, but there wasn't anything left in the penthouse to inspect. The master bedroom was empty. Jenny helped herself to a can of Sofia sparkling wine from the fridge, took a seat in the new armchair, and texted Eliza.

> **T:** You still at Charlie's?
>
> **D:** Yeah, why?
>
> **T:** No reason, Shelly asked

Excellent. Jack returned from his bedroom, freshly bathed and smelling of men's cologne. "You wanted to talk about this weekend?" he asked.

"Right. Isn't it time you started dating again?" Jenny asked.

He furrowed his brow; the question had caught him flat-footed. "*You*, not *we*?" he replied.

"Honestly, Jack. Not that our will-they-won't-they hasn't kept our mates entertained, but are you so daft that you're unaware of the wallflower girl who *actually* fancies you?"

It took him a moment to get it, and then he rolled his eyes. "That's nice of you to shoot her shot, but I can't date Alicia, Kaz."

"Why not?" Jenny asked. "She's a looker, isn't she? You hardly notice the leg, and she's well fit."

Jack sighed. "Hold on. I need a beverage for this." He rummaged in the fridge. "I don't know how to say it without sounding like a conceited asshole."

"You?! Never!"

Jack didn't laugh at her joke, so Jenny laughed for both of them. He took a seat across from her on the couch holding a glass of white wine. "She wants it too much," Jack said. "It wouldn't work. Don't get me wrong, it's not about the leg or anything. She's cute. Would def hit. But you can't date someone who's built up this whole impossible image of you. I did that with my ex, Dinah, always putting her on a pedestal, and I feel like all that did was make her like me less."

"Okay. She was also a lesbian, though, right?" Jenny asked.

"Apparently," said Jack. "It doesn't matter, though. It's paradoxical, but I'd need Alicia to be sick of me before we could ever hook up."

"I suppose you're being thoughtful," Jenny said. "I do worry about the little one. She used to be rather depressed, didn't she? Before her accident, I've heard. Is that true?"

"Uh, I guess?" Jack shrugged. "I didn't know her too well then, but she used to live in Alkali Estates. That's got to be depressing enough. I think Mason said once that her dad was a real piece of shit."

"Was he? Interesting," said Jenny. "How so?"

"You'd have to ask Mason," said Jack. "Ironically enough, I think your cousin moving here was great for her. Alicia's maybe the only one in town who can say her life got better when Trouble came to Blackbird Springs."

"That was because of the estate money, right? My aunt explained it vaguely, something about your father's will? Did he know Alicia?"

Jack shook his head—and then seemed to catch himself, a crease forming on his brow. "Well, that's all part of the mystery, isn't it?" He sipped his pinot grigio and peered at her with fresh eyes. "It's a 'no,' then, huh? You and I? Damn, I was about to invite you to my Christmas party? What a power couple we would have made under the mistletoe."

"We really would have," said Jenny. "You're like a brother to me, you know? I hope we can still be friends."

"What every guy loves to hear," Jack said, smiling as a little part of him died in the depths of his eyes.

"I wouldn't say no to that party invitation, though," Jenny said. "But only if—er, my aunt will want my cousin to come along." Her brother raised an eyebrow. "Sorry, but Shelly has been asking me to spend more time with her. She's not so bad, once you get to know her. I think she's been having a rough go of it."

"Thanh will throw a fit."

"Thanh can get over it. Please? For me?"

Jack grimaced, running a hand through his wet hair. "I'll think about it," he said. "Let me talk to her. I've been meaning to have a chat with her anyway."

"Thanks, Jack. I'd better be going." Jenny downed the rest of the sparkling wine and stood up. "Oh, and make sure you invite Alicia too."

Jack blanched at the suggestion.

"Just be normal about it," Jenny said. "You're still putting her on a pedestal, same as with Dinah, just in a different way. Happy Christmas!"

THE INTERVIEW HADN'T BEEN A ROUSING SUCCESS, BUT AT LEAST she'd solved Eliza's Jack issue for her. Maybe there was something about Alicia's dad? Some connection between him and RJ? Provided, of course, that RJ wasn't her dad, too. Jenny shuddered at the thought. She slipped out of the hotel lobby and paused on the sidewalk, considering her options. It wasn't too late; Pixeldrome would still be open for a while—

A cry rang out.

Jenny looked up in time to see a mountain bike skid to a stop in the street, not five yards away. The bike bore a small man, dressed all in black, wearing a ski mask. He pointed something at Jenny that bucked with recoil as it made a series of loud, hissing bursts.

A paintball gun, Jenny realized belatedly. It was firing at her. The bike rider emptied his whole canister, slung the gun over his shoulder, and pedaled away into the night. Jenny blinked and looked down. Near as she could tell, not a single paint pellet had struck her. She patted herself down to be sure and glanced behind her to see the lobby doors of the Crow's Nest peppered with splashes of neon orange, save for a Trouble-sized gap in the middle.

One of the doors opened and Drew burst out, a bewildered grin on his face and a bag from See's Candies in his hand. "What the hell was that?" he asked, gawking at all the paint splotches.

"Common Trouble fan L," said Jenny.

Drew looked her up and down, furrowing his brow. "No hits. Maybe they were trying to scare you."

"I think he just had terrible aim," said Jenny. "What are you doing here?"

"Christmas Shopping," he said, brightening and holding up the See's bag.

"Ooh, gimme! Please?"

He rummaged in the bag and tossed her a butterscotch lollipop.

"I'm supposed to go visit Dad's folks with Mom tonight," Drew said. "You know, family holiday party. It's gonna be so fucking awkward. What are you up to?"

"Talking to Jack," Jenny said. "If I can get him to sweep Alicia off her feet, maybe she'll lose interest in Pixeldrome and that'll be one less competitor in that New Year's tournament."

Drew smiled tightly.

"Cool, yeah, good luck getting Jack to blow my ex's back out," said Drew. "I'll just cheer him on from the cuck chair over here."

"Oh stop, you're gonna be swimming in it at San Diego State or wherever you end up going," said Jenny. "Hey, question, though: what do you know about Alicia's dad?"

Drew's eyes glanced up and to the left, "Not much. I think he split before we started dating."

"Did Alicia ever talk about him?" Jenny asked.

"Not really," Drew said, his eyes darting to stare at the paint-splattered doors again. "Anyway, I gotta run. Wish me luck."

"You'll get through it," Jenny said and hugged him.

Drew headed off down the street. Jenny stared after him, itching her wig, troubled in a way she'd least expected to be. He lied to her just then. Or if not, he didn't reveal the whole truth. Drew never did that. What was it about Alicia Aaron that he didn't want her to know?

Chapter Sixteen

Under the Mistletoe

WINTER CAME TO BLACKBIRD SPRINGS LIKE A THIEF IN THE night, covering the rolling hills in an early frost that had the local wineries scrambling to save their prized grapevines from ruin. Jiji was up before dawn, out in the vineyards with the viticulturists, offering what advice he could. When Eliza shuffled downstairs with Jenny, their grandfather surprised them by cooking breakfast.

"They should have been prepared for this," he said to them while tending to the eggs with a soft touch of the spatula. "You have to run the sprinklers every night. Dad ran them from Thanksgiving to Easter, but they don't like to do that anymore. The water isn't so cheap because we send it all down to those bastards in LA."

Their great-grandparents, Kenji and Reiko, had been viticulturists for the Big Six vineyards. Jenny always referred to this fact bitterly, like they'd been cheated out of the vineyards' wealth after all their hard work. And maybe there was some truth to it, but Kenji and Reiko had a happy home and a family, and sent Jiji to law school so he didn't have to work in the fields, and Eliza thought that wasn't so bad a life. She and Charlie should be so lucky.

Charlie.

Eliza frowned, trying not to overthink things with her secret girlfriend. They'd been together all weekend, and yet somehow, it felt like they were further apart than they used to be. Ever since Charlie mentioned studying abroad, Eliza sensed her pulling away in small, subtle ways. They never really talked about the future anymore; that was verboten. Everything was living in the now, and YOLO, and enjoying every last drop of senior year, even as an invisible rift formed beneath their feet.

When she got the text in the group chat that the Basque was canceled—it was too cold to sit outside, and everyone was going to Starbucks instead—another pang of concern touched her heart. Change, that fickle beast, wasn't going to let Eliza encase her life in amber.

Sitting inside the chain coffee shop, with a never-ending stream of anxious morning commuters hovering around them while they waited for their mobile orders… it just wasn't the same.

"I must say, I'm rather cheesed of this place," Eliza said to no one in particular.

"Agreed, the vibes are chalked," said Jack. "Be right back."

She watched him slip outside, where he was joined by her sister.

What's she doing here?

Eliza barely saw her sister these days outside of family functions and International Relations in first period. Jenny had adopted this weird retro look and, as far as Eliza could tell, spent all her free time at that arcade on the south side. It was somehow related to RJ's game, which meant Eliza would never set foot in there again.

The conversation between the two was a short one. Jenny smiled at their brother and left without coming inside to order. Jack returned, sighing, and poured some of his special brew into a mug he brought with him.

"What was that about?" Eliza asked.

"Uh, I was telling your cousin we got the DNA results back," Jack said.

"From the crime scene?" Eliza asked.

"That, and from my dad," he said, frowning. "The cops didn't find anything at the penthouse. And, um, they confirmed it's him in the tomb."

Damn, guess that means we really are his kids.

She'd been secretly hoping the DNA test would come back and show they weren't related. That would have been so funny. She did not share this hope with Jenny.

"I'm sorry, Jack." Eliza touched his shoulder, sympathetic. Jack stared at her hand like it confused him, so she pulled it away.

"Also, I told your cousin she could come to the party," Jack added. "She promises to be on her best behavior."

Thanh groaned and uttered some choice words about what Jenny's promises were worth.

There's a party?

"There's a party?" asked Jimmy Figg, who was lingering near their table, like usual. How did he know they were going to Starbucks?

"Uh, yeah, this Friday after school gets out, at the mansion," said Jack. "I guess you can come too, Jimmy. But wear something nice, it's a black tie dress code. You too, Alicia. Not the black tie, I mean, but you should come."

Everyone glared at Jack for inviting Jimmy—except for Alicia, who was delighted.

"Are you sure this is a good idea?" Penny asked. "After Nilay?"

"We can't live in fear, Pen," said Jack. "Nilay wouldn't want that. Tori's going to beef up security, so there's no need to worry."

Yet worry Eliza did. All week, the vibes with Charlie were weird, and she kept catching Jack staring at her out of the corner of her eye. She'd turn his way to find him studying a book or his phone or whatever, but she'd know he'd been watching her. And not in the sappy lovestruck way, either. There was something ominous in his regard—like he was studying her.

That wasn't all. Her friends no longer looked her way first to laugh at their jokes or accompany them to the ladies' room. It was as though they'd suddenly remembered she was an exchange student, not long for Blackbird Springs, and adjusted their investment in her accordingly. Eliza found herself making excuses to study in the library during lunch, even though her grades were meaningless.

It was there that Charlie found her on Friday, re-reading the part in *Deathly Hallows* where Ron abandons the trio like a complete git.

"Hello Elizabeth," Charlie said, since no one was around to hear. She took a seat across from Eliza at the table and reached out to touch her hand. "I have some news."

"Bad news?" Eliza guessed.

"Bittersweet news," Charlie said. "I got accepted to that internship with L'Oréal. They like my YouTube channel, and they want to make it a whole marketing thing."

"Oh. Wow." Eliza tried to smile for her. "What's the bittersweet part."

"It's in Paris," Charlie said. "And it starts in January."

Eliza's stomach turned over. She suddenly felt off-kilter, like someone had just kicked out the stool beneath her feet. January! That was only a fortnight away!

"I'm sorry," said Charlie.

"No, don't be," Eliza said, swallowing her disappointment. Charlie didn't deserve to feel bad about a great opportunity. *Even if I'm dying inside?* "Honestly, I'm so proud of you, congratulations! You worked so hard to get this."

They stared at each other a while. Eliza thought about kissing her, but at the moment, it seemed wrong. Were they breaking up? Did Charlie want her to fight for this?

"I feel like I should be screaming and begging for you to stay," she said. "But that's selfish. You'd be a fool not to get out of here. This town is a death trap."

Another long silence passed between them.

"When do you go?" Eliza asked.

"New Year's Day," said Charlie. "I could always say no, or put it off till summer?"

The bell rang, saving Eliza from having to answer that question. She gathered her books and stood, then gave Charlie a long, deeply felt hug.

"We should be celebrating. Let's get trashed tonight. You're going to Jack's party, right?" Eliza asked. "Weird that he never really invited me."

"Like he needs to invite his favorite," Charlie said, and smiled.

Charlie had such a fabulous smile. The way dimples formed on her dewy cheeks when she was really happy. And her hazel eyes, always so lively, so knowing, so wise beyond her years. Honestly, it might be the best smile in the history of smiles, and it was just for Eliza. Until January.

"On the bright side, I'll finally be single to date my brother," Eliza said, before rushing out of the room so Charlie wouldn't see her cry.

JENNY PUT THE FINAL TOUCHES ON HER PURPLE EYESHADOW WINGS and pursed her lips in the mirror. Damn. Her dress was a form-fitting black number with a neckline that went all the way up to her chin. One shoulder was bare, and the other had a sleeve that ran down her whole arm, with a black glove to cover her hand, too. The slanted hem barely covered her ass, but no matter. She wore slinky purple leggings underneath, with her favorite Doc Martens to make herself feel tall. She was nearly Kazu's height when her sister peaked into the bathroom and announced she was leaving, if Jenny wanted a ride.

"You know this is a Christmas party, right?" Eliza asked. "You look like you're about to hack the Gibson."

"What's a Gibson?"

"You should know these things if you're pretending to be an eGirl," Eliza said.

Unlike Jenny, Eliza wore an elegant green satin cocktail dress with little dragons embroidered in red thread around the flared waist, and elbow-length green gloves to match. Her Kazumi makeup perfectly masked her puffy cheeks, though it couldn't hide her bloodshot retinas. Something was up between her and Charlie. Jenny chose not to bring it up, it being the holidays and all.

"I like your dress," she said instead. "Shall we?"

Eliza drove them in one of the Valentine Vineyards jeeps, which she'd never returned after the estate reverted to escrow. Good for her.

The broad, Mediterranean-style wings of Valentine Manor were lit up for the evening by floodlights embedded in the ground surrounding the mansion. Jenny caught glimpses of the golden stucco walls through gaps in the rows of grapevines, as Eliza turned off Cellar Drive onto the long driveway that led up to the house. A security guard stopped them at the gates and checked their names against a list before letting them pass, and another guard was there at the front door to usher them inside. Tori wasn't fucking around these days.

The great hall, with its double-staircase balustrade, was festooned with evergreen garlands and gold tinsel and smelled of pine and nutmeg. The right side of the entryway was cordoned off with velvet ropes, directing guests down the hall to the left.

"Merry Christmas, Onishi clan," said Jack. He wore a tuxedo, because of course he did, and cradled a brandy snifter full of eggnog in his hand. "Jenny, that is… a look."

He hugged her—and then didn't hug Eliza.

Wow, he's really over her. You're welcome, Lizzy.

"Kazu, smashing as always," Jack said, almost off-handedly. "Mi casa es su casa. Except su casa consists of the ballroom, living room, and guest bathrooms only." He waved to the velvet ropes. "Sorry, Tori insisted. She expressly wished me to communicate to you, Jenny, that 'tis *not* the season for Trouble."

"Well, that's just a lie."

"Who's here so far?" Eliza asked.

"Everyone except Meghan and Mason," Jack said. "He said he couldn't make it, and her dad is back on his bullshit. You two are fashionably late." He stopped at the double doors to the ballroom and held his arm out to Jenny. "Shall we make an entrance?"

Jenny shrugged and took his elbow, and he escorted them inside. Orchestral Christmas music tinkled from the ballroom speakers. An impressive charcuterie spread and beverage table anchored one side of the room. On the other was a roaring fire and a large flat-screen TV, on which an old black-and-white movie was playing.

"Here comes Trouble," Jack said, calling out to the crowd. "*Now* it's a party!"

A smattering of greetings and waves came their way. Penny and Charlie were warming themselves by the fireplace, Drew looked spiffy in a suit jacket, and Alicia Aaron was almost wholesome in a simple azure dress and cardigan. It was weird to see Jimmy Figg here, after spending so much time in his vicinity at Pixeldrome. They locked eyes but quickly looked away, some unspoken agreement passing between them that what happened at the arcade stayed at the arcade. And there in the corner, sipping champagne, was an angel all in white: Dinah Black.

"I'm gonna mingle," Jenny said, detaching herself from Jack.

Eliza followed suit, making a beeline for Charlie.

"Find me later, there's something I wanted to chat about," Jack said to Jenny, and strolled into the crowd, calling, "Mistletoe, Penny! Give us a kiss!"

Is he drunk?

Jenny headed for the snack table, stuffing her face with cured meats and brie, and helping herself to a goblet of holiday punch. Lai lingered nearby and offered a splash from his flask when she held out her drink.

"Merry Christmas, Lai," Jenny said.

"Take it easy on Thanh, tonight, eh?" he said.

"Oh, yeah. Sure. Cheers."

Jenny took a big sip and let the rum from Lai's flask relax her nerves. She emptied the glass and filled another, tapping Lai on the shoulder for another slug. Why hadn't she ever thrown a party like this when the mansion was hers? She moved amongst the crowd, looking for opportunities to join the conversation. Penny and Thanh were enjoying themselves playing Giant Jenga, but it was probably best to steer clear of them. No matter which direction Jenny wandered, Dinah seemed to drift in the opposite direction, like two moons in a binary orbit, never to cross paths.

After a while, she tried making small talk with Alicia about Pixeldrome, and the two shared a calorie-free discussion on the topic of Rob Haines and his weird, desperate obsession with his dorky youth. Eliza was making frequent trips to the eggnog bowl which, Alicia warned, had been spiked with a bottle of brandy.

"I can't help but notice my brother is standing all alone over there, under the mistletoe," Jenny remarked.

"Shut up," said Alicia, blushing.

As if sensing their eyes, Jack turned and headed their way. Alicia squeaked and vanished.

"Check it out," Jack said. "I think Jimmy's going for round two with Kaz."

He pointed to Eliza, lingering unaware under a sprig of mistletoe by the fire. Jimmy Figg set his glass of eggnog down on the hearth and said something to her, pointing up above them.

A crash sounded. Jenny glanced over her shoulder to see Thanh laughing, holding a Giant Jenga piece, the rest of the Jenga tower collapsed in front of her.

Her sister audibly scoffed, and Jenny turned back to see Eliza grabbing her glass of eggnog from the hearth and leaving Jimmy in the lurch.

"Ouch. Denied," said Jack.

Jimmy tried to grin and laugh it off, sipping his own eggnog. Jack gestured to the big TV, where Jimmy Stewart was currently trying to jump off a bridge.

"What's your favorite Christmas movie, Jenny?" he asked. "Sometimes I feel like I hardly know you."

"Not this one," Jenny said. "I always hated it."

"That's funny, so did Dad."

"I like the claymation one with Rudolph," said Jenny. "Where he sticks it to all the assholes who won't let him join in their reindeer games."

"That's not exactly how I remember that one going," Jack said. He put an arm around her shoulder and gave her a squeeze. "You just need a win, kiddo."

"You can't call me that, I'm older than you," Jenny said, shrugging out from under his arm.

"Yeah, but I'm taller," he said.

Another crash interrupted them. Jimmy Figg had dropped his glass of eggnog, the crystal shattering on the hardwood floor. He was doubled over, holding his stomach.

"Oh shit!" said Jimmy.

He tried to move, taking awkward steps. The smell hit her nose first before Jenny noticed the wet spot on the back of Jimmy's beige slacks.

Oh. Shit.

"Did he just?" Jenny asked.

"Goddamnit, Jimmy!" said Jack. He pointed to security. "Get him out of here."

"Ohhhhh ewww, he's leaving a t-trail!" Tori said, grimacing at the scene as the guard hustled Jimmy away. "Christ. I'll get a mop. I can't ask Mrs. Rivas to clean that up."

Jack tugged at Jenny's arm. "We need to talk," he said.

"I had nothing to do with that!" Jenny insisted. "Maybe it was the Brown Note?"

"Not about Jimmy! Come on."

Jack led her out of the ballroom, and back down the hall, to RJ's study.

"Have a seat," he said.

Jenny obliged by hurrying past him to take her chair behind the big desk.

"What's up?" Jenny asked.

"How well do you know your cousin?" he asked.

"Kazumi? Uh, pretty well, I guess?"

"But you hadn't met her before this summer, right?"

Jenny had to think about it. According to the story they'd put out, the answer would have to be "no." Her pulse began to rise, and the buzz from the holiday punch evaporated. "What are you getting at?" she asked.

Jack leaned forward, sucking on his inner cheek. "I don't think Kazumi is who she says she is."

No fucking way. "Are you drunk?"

"Think about it, Jenny," Jack said. "She shows up out of nowhere as this cousin you didn't even know you had. She has this weird international backstory that sounds made up, and an accent that comes and goes. She strings me along, almost like she needed an excuse to meet my mom."

"Now hold on, you were the one hitting on her, if I recall."

"Sure, but still. She's a little off, right? The knife at Homecoming. The way she sometimes doesn't respond the first time someone calls her name."

Jenny's heart froze to the core.

Jack stood up, pacing in front of the desk. She couldn't recall ever seeing her brother so wound up. "A week ago, I was talking to her, and she started asking about Alicia. About why she was in Dad's will."

Gaslight him. You have to.

"So? Who do you think she is? A fucking fed or something?"

"I think she's another reporter, like that Jeffrey Jordan guy my mom tried to hire," said Jack. "I think she's posing as your cousin to spy on us, for a story. It's why she teases, but won't actually date me."

Before Jenny could manage a suitable dismissive retort, the door to the study opened behind Jack—and Eliza stumbled in, prodded from behind by a stone-faced security guard.

"You said to keep an eye on this one?" the guard said. "Caught her trying to sneak into the conservatory."

"Oh, very interesting!" said Jack, shooting a triumphant glance at Jenny. "Leave her, and lock the door behind, my man."

Jenny didn't dare speak. Eliza's eyes bugged out, searching for answers. Once the security guy left, Jack gestured to an open chair in front of the desk.

"Have a seat, Kazumi. If that *is* your real name."

"It is," Eliza said. "Sorry, I just wanted to get some air. What the bloody hell is this?"

In Japanese, Jenny said, "He knows you're not my cousin."

"No! Does he…?"

"Hey hey, none of that, come on," said Jack.

"Not yet, but we have to tell him," Jenny continued, ignoring Jack's request for English.

"We don't! Make something up! Anything!" Eliza replied.

"Come on!"

"He's too close already. It'll be worse if he finds out on his own," said Jenny.

"Trouble," Eliza said, switching back to English, "don't you dare!"

Jenny buried her head in her hands. This was her fault. She'd been too nosy, posing as Kazu last week.

"Jack, I'm begging you to drop this," Jenny said. "It's not what you think, and you have nothing to fear from Kazumi."

He studied the two of them, all his Christmas cheer replaced by paranoid suspicion.

"I can't do that, Jenny," he said. "Do I need to call my mother in here? Or get your JCO involved?"

She looked at her sister, who was screaming "Don't!" with her pleading eyes.

Sorry, Lizzy. My bad.

Jenny rose, and walked to the nearest bookshelf, retrieving a copy of *Trouble Eight Days a Week*. "Swear on our father's immortal soul that what I'm about to tell you doesn't leave this room," she said, holding out the book. "No matter what you hear, you can't breathe a word of it to anyone. Do you promise?"

Jack hesitated, shrewdly thinking the request over. "Will you swear the same, to tell me the truth?" he asked.

"Trouble's honor," Jenny said.

She crossed her fingers behind her back, and Jack placed his hand on the book.

"You fucking suck, Jenny," said Eliza.

"I'll take it to the grave," said Jack.

Jenny sighed and flopped back into Dad's chair.

"How much do you know about the night I was born?" asked Jenny.

"What's that got to do with this?" he asked.

"Humor me. C'mon. How good's your Trouble lore?"

Jack blinked, steadying himself, and recited, "Jennifer Trouble Valentine was born at 12:04 AM on March 10, 2003, at Santa Rosa Memorial Hospital, to Laura Onishi. The attending physician was Dr. Rohan Singh."

Jenny whistled. "Pulled my birth certificate, did you?"

"Wouldn't you?" he replied.

"Fair. But there's something that wasn't on my birth certificate," said Jenny. She glanced at Eliza. Did she want to do the honors? Guess not. "At 12:09 AM, a second girl was born. My identical twin. Jack, meet Elizabeth Danger Valentine. Your half-sister."

Jack glanced left and right, incredulous, gawking at the two of them. "But—but she doesn't look anything like you."

"It's just makeup," said Eliza, dropping the accent. She yanked the glove off her right hand in disgust, revealing her matching Ace of Clubs tattoo. "Most of spring and summer, it was me you were seeing, not her."

"I was the one who asked you about Alicia last week," Jenny said. "I'm sorry, Lizzy. This is all my fault."

"You fucking bitch."

"But that means…" Jack turned to Eliza, his face going red.

"Yeah. Awkward," said Eliza.

It was sinking in, and Jack was no longer incredulous. He was furious. Any second now, steam was going to start shooting out his burning ears.

He clenched his jaw, speaking through his teeth. "Did either of you have anything to do with Dad's murder?"

"No," they replied as one.

He paced the room, stopped to pour himself a scotch from the minibar, and downed it in one go. "I made you a promise, and I'm good to my word," he said. "But I'd prefer you both get out of my sight. I don't want anything to do with either of you."

JACK STORMED OUT OF THE ROOM.

Eliza glared murderously at Jenny. "I asked you not to."

"I know. But it was too late," said Jenny.

"I deserved to tell him on my terms," said Eliza.

"You're absolutely right. I suck. I'm a total piece of shit. Just go ahead and hate me. Everyone else already does."

"Yes! They do!"

Eliza hopped out of her chair and made for the door. Jenny trailed behind, hoping she wasn't about to do something even more rash. In the ballroom, half her peers were playing Twister, clueless to the sturm und drang radiating in waves off of Jack and Eliza. Jack was jumping up, trying to reach a sprig of mistletoe. With a final leap, he snatched it and yanked it down.

Her brother smiled. A sort of manic, psychotic charm bloomed on his features. He straightened his tux jacket and walked over to Alicia Aaron by the fire, where she was doing her best to pretend that she hadn't been watching him.

"Hey Red, I don't know if you realized, but you're standing under the mistletoe." Jack raised his arm, holding the sprig above their heads. "Rules are rules."

Alicia's jaw dropped. She looked close to panic.

Jack settled her nerves by planting a kiss on her.

The Twister game was forgotten, and everyone whistled at this delicious new development. Drew threw a "thanks a lot" smirk at Jenny. Alicia came up for air, giggled shyly, and pulled Jack closer for more.

Eliza scoffed and marched over to Charlie. "Don't worry, I'll protect you till New Year's," she said and kissed Charlie with twice the passion her brother had managed.

That one earned a hearty cheer from the others.

"Dude!" said Lai.

"I knew it!" Thanh yelled.

The ballroom exploded in a buzz of conversation, which the two kissing couples were oblivious to. Jenny caught Dinah's attention and strolled over. For once, the orbit was broken, and her ex allowed her to approach.

"Hey there, stranger," said Jenny. She shrugged and nodded to Charlie and Eliza. "We can do better than that, can't we? 'Tis the season?"

Dinah gave her a brittle smile. "Not on your fucking life, Jenny," she said.

"I was kidding," said Jenny, as her insides disintegrated. No, she wasn't. "Merry Christmas, Dinah."

"Merry Christmas, Jennifer," Dinah said. Then she walked away to refresh her drink.

Afterward, Jenny couldn't recall how she got out of there. A Lyft ride, maybe? She sort of blacked out in misery and the next thing she knew, she was pounding on the locked door of Pixeldrome.

"Lemme in!" she slurred.

Had she borrowed Lai's flask? Or maybe stole it? Her watch buzzed: a call from Drew. She ignored it.

The door opened a crack.

"We're closed," said Asha. "Oh, it's you. Are you lost?"

She allowed the door to open wider, so Jenny slipped inside. The arcade was empty now, and Asha was blasting a K's Choice song on the sound system.

"Where is everyone?" Jenny asked.

"It's just me, I'm closing up," said Asha. "What's up with you, loser?"

Jenny clenched her fists, fire in her eyes. "I intensely dislike you!"

Asha laughed. "You're a shit liar, Trouble."

Jenny grabbed Asha's jean jacket by the collar and pulled her in for a hot, breathy kiss. Her lip gloss… was that bubblegum flavor? Jenny didn't hate it. She parted her lips and let Asha's tongue do the rest.

There was stumbling. There was fumbling. There was a break room with a couch. Asha pulled Jenny's dress over her head and admired the view.

"No bra? Slut," said Asha. "I'm giving myself 10,000XP for this."

"I'll give you something better, you dumb bitch," said Jenny, and went to work on Asha's belt fastener.

Chapter Seventeen

Video Games

GIVING UP DIDN'T HAVE TO FEEL LIKE A FAILURE. GIVING IN didn't have to feel like weakness. What Jenny was feeling the next morning, honestly, was relief. There was no pining, no nerves or worry about whether or not Asha *really* liked her, or just wanted to use her. Jenny wanted to sleep with her, so she did. And she'd do it again.

Provided, that is, they could find a suitable spot for continued activities. Asha was shoving her off the break room couch at 6:00 AM, demanding they dress and delete the security footage before Rob showed up.

"Will you get in trouble?" Jenny asked.

"No, I don't want that old pervert cranking it to us," said Asha, tossing Jenny her leggings before pointing to a darker patch of skin on her thigh. "You gave me a bruise."

"Good."

They dressed, and Jenny followed Asha into Rob's office, where she used his computer to fix the video footage.

"Won't he notice it's gone?" Jenny asked.

"I'll just replace it with Thursday's," said Asha. "Okay, let's go."

She led Jenny to the back exit, where an old, beat-up Honda Accord waited. Jenny had to toss three trash-filled Taco Bell bags onto the pavement to clear the passenger seat for herself. Where to? The treehouse was out, and Jenny didn't think she could sneak Asha into her grandparents' house…

Reading her mind, Asha said, "If we hurry, my roommate won't be up yet."

"Wait, I thought you were in high school?"

"I'm fucking insulted," Asha said

She started the engine. A hip-hop song bumped on the stereo. She made no effort to turn it down, and pulled out, heading west.

"How old are you?!" Jenny shouted over the music.

"18, relax!" said Asha. "What, you thought I was out and still living at home? Bitch, please! No dykes allowed under a Desi roof! I got a place by the college. My roommate has a girlfriend, so I'm pretty sure he won't try to rape me."

The place was a rundown apartment complex that catered to students of nearby Calistoga College. It stank of old beer and male body odor. Jenny barely got a look at the mismatched Goodwill furniture and flat-screen TV on the floor before Asha shoved her into her bedroom. She only had a twin-size bed, but they were small enough to fit. Asha locked the door with an actual padlock on a latch she'd installed.

Jenny bent to retrieve a little stuffed polar bear from the floor. "What's his name?"

"Clarence." Asha kicked off her shoes. "Now. Where were we?"

A week of winter break passed in a blur. Jenny and Asha spent hours in her tiny bedroom, making ample use of that twin-size bed. When Asha had a shift, Jenny went to Pixeldrome too, grinding her way to level 10 for the New Year's tournament. If Rob was out, they'd kill the cameras and lock the break room door during Asha's lunch for a quickie. Jenny gave in and ate the corn dogs and pizza, even if Nathaniel was working. They spent their free nights watching Asha's trashy bootleg anime. They fucked and listened to Lana Del Rey and played video games. They fucked while listening to Lana Del Rey's "Video Games."

On Christmas, she traded some Adderall with Asha for her stash of Norco and spent the day zonked out on prescription opiates, ignoring Eliza's bitter hostility while everyone smiled and opened presents. Their grandparents gave them matching tennis bracelets, and they had to pretend to like them and put them on. Lockhart, thankfully, was doing his own Christmas with Mason.

As dinner was winding down, she got a text from Drew.

Drew: Don't suppose you're free tonight? The big board could use an update.

Jenny: Sorry, got family shit. Maybe later?

The second Jiji and Baba went to bed, Jenny was back at the arcade.

That night, she beat *Mortal Kombat II* on a single quarter, a feat that finally pushed her over the threshold to level 10.

"Yeah! Suck it, Shao Kahn!" she shouted, slamming her palms on the cabinet dash.

"Check it out, loser," Asha said, pointing to the leaderboard over her head, where Jenny's stat line flashed.

JTV | LVL 10 | +550XP | 55375XP TOT

"Now you just need to destroy that little cripple next week," said Asha.

"Maybe she won't even play, now that she's with Jack."

"Do you think he takes her leg off when they do it?" Asha grinned. Even since Jenny told her about Jack and Alicia getting together, they had become her favorite topic of discussion. "Does he kiss the stump? Poor fucking girl. As soon as your brother gets tired of throwing humps into her ran-through ass, she's gonna find another train to finish what she started."

"Jesus, Ash!"

"Am I wrong? You see that lasting?"

"You're so gonna get me canceled one of these days," Jenny said.

"There's no such thing! I keep telling you, they can't cancel you if you don't give a fuck," Asha said. "The sooner you realize that nothing fucking matters, the more powerful you'll become."

"So you're into straight-up nihilism, then?" Jenny asked.

"Earnestly claiming an 'ism' is fake and gay. Come on, you need to practice *Time Killers*, it'll be in the tournament."

It was easy for Asha to say. She didn't have millions of followers on Instagram and a massive fanbase to set an example for. Still, it was a tempting idea—to be a Jenny that gave no fucks. *That* Jenny would never have gone to the roof of the hospital over some closet case bitch who was too afraid to be gay on main. Maybe someday they'd make a pill for it, a pill to stop caring. In the meantime, there was always alcohol. Rob wouldn't buy them any, but he'd taught Asha the best way to shoplift it. And as a bonus, he gave them 500XP each time they did it.

Six cases of Pabst Blue Ribbon and about two dozen orgasms later, it was New Year's Eve. Maybe Eliza was doing something with the Bitchy Brigade. Maybe she'd been ostracized after Jack turned on them both. Jenny didn't know, and a steady trickle of booze kept her from worrying about it. Shit happened.

I tried my best, Lizzy. At least your brother doesn't want to fuck you anymore.

She and Asha rang in 2021 with Taco Bell and a bottle of Malibu rum. They'd stolen Rob's golf clubs from his office and snuck into the far end of the GolfMax driving range, where they took turns hitting balls back at the yuppie pricks in the stalls. Jenny stroked one that missed some old fart by inches, and collapsed in a cackle on the grass.

"Did you see that? I'm locked in!"

"You better win tomorrow," said Asha. "Don't embarrass me."

"It wouldn't matter if you'd just let me into that stupid VIP room!" said Jenny.

"Dream on, bitch."

Jenny was sort of hoping that all this sex would be the key to getting Asha to sneak her into the VIP room, but her new… girlfriend? FWB? staunchly refused to acquiesce, no matter how well Jenny made her body quiver.

"There's nothing lamer than cheating at a game," Asha would always say. "You gotta earn it."

New Year's Day arrived with a wicked hangover. Jenny stumbled into the bathroom and puked, hoping Shelly didn't hear. That Cheesy Gordita Crunch looked—and tasted!—so much less appetizing on the way back up. She hopped in the shower and slammed a can of Pabst to wash the tang of vomit away. Staring at herself in the mirror after, still dripping on the bathroom rug, Jenny admired the purple hickey on her collarbone, courtesy of Asha. Was this what Shelly had been talking about? Something about inventing sex? It was hard to imagine her aunt ever getting a trashy love bite like this on her neck.

She stopped at McDonald's on the way for a hash brown: *the* perfect food to defeat a hangover. Fortified with a nice layer of grease in her belly, she arrived at the arcade, ready to kick some ass and hurt some feelings.

Most of the tournament contestants were ugly incels from Harbor High and a few sad older guys wearing faded Zelda shirts with holes under the armpits. Jenny would have been the only girl in the tourney if not for goddamn Alicia Aaron. The attentions of one Jack Valentine were apparently not enough to keep her away.

Jenny blew a winking kiss at Asha behind the counter and asked Alicia, "Why do you even bother? What's in this for you?"

"Why do you ask questions you already know the answer to, Trouble?" said Alicia. "Don't play dumb. The game is afoot."

"But you got the boy, you got your money, your book is coming out. Don't you realize all you're doing is putting yourself in the Stranger's crosshairs by playing RJ's game? Remember Nilay?"

"Of course I do. But were Lily or Lance or Mr. White playing your dad's game?" Alicia asked. "We both know the only way we're safe is by solving the mystery. You're just scared I'm gonna kick your ass."

"Wow, look at this newfound confidence!" Jenny sneered. "Jack must be *quite* the boyfriend."

"You can't rattle me, Trouble," said Alicia, even though her ears were flushing pink. "And Jack and I are none of your business."

Alicia turned up her nose and marched over to the signup table. "Psh! Well, Jack and you…"

She couldn't think of a good comeback. Whatever. Jenny had been mainlining this arcade for two weeks straight, and she hadn't seen Alicia in here once. There was no way she wouldn't be rusty.

"I put you in the bracket with Nathaniel," Asha said, coming over. "You better not lose to that fat fuck."

"The highlight of that idiot's life was getting touched in the bathing suit area by his aunt," Jenny said. "How good can he be?"

Pretty good, it turned out. The first stage of the Pixeldrome Open was a qualifying round where everyone played as far as they could make it on a single quarter in *Golden Axe*, a side scroller where you ran around hacking at monsters, and little bastard hobbits tried to steal your shit. Only the top four in each bracket qualified to move on. Luckily for Jenny, she'd practiced the game a ton, and cruised to a respectable placing. Nathaniel, though… he probably would have beaten the whole game if Rob hadn't stepped in and called the match after he qualified.

Unfortunately, Alicia did too. So much for rust. They'd all played at the same time—Rob had somehow gotten the game to play on a bunch of different cabinets, so they weren't stuck waiting their turn.

"It's called ROM-hacking," Asha said, in answer to Jenny's question about it. "Rob is a total sperg for shit like this."

Round 2 had Jenny facing off in a best-of-five matchup against that fucker Nathaniel in *Mario Kart*. She annihilated him in three straight races for the win. She'd been nervous before the first race, but once she got into a zone, she realized she outclassed him. Even a blue shell couldn't save his pathetic ass.

Round 3 matched Jenny against a little 12-year-old in *Street Fighter*. He was crushing her until she figured out she could just mash the Kick button. The kid was so busy trying to do special moves that he couldn't figure out how to defend such a simple attack, and lost, screaming and throwing a fit about Jenny being "so cheap!" He seriously started crying, and his mom had to hustle him out of there. Yikes!

The tournament paused for lunch, and Jenny followed Alicia out front to bum a clove cigarette.

"You're smoking again?" Alicia asked warily.

"Only on special occasions," Jenny said, forcing herself not to cough as she took a drag. Her lungs burned, and she covered her distress by gulping down a Mountain Dew she'd poured from the soda fountain. "You must recognize a lot of these dudes. I heard you used to go to Harbor Elementary."

"Yeah, so?" Alicia asked.

"I just thought it was interesting," Jenny said. "What made you switch schools?"

Alicia stared at her shoes, and her voice hardly rose above a mumble. "I had to. They have better disability services at Blackbird Springs Academy."

There was a part of Jenny, the part that still believed in happy endings and righteous justice, that felt for Alicia just then. Wanted to reach out and hug the girl. But Alicia was the competition, and if Jenny had to destroy her, keeping her distance was for Alicia's own good.

"Damn, and I thought I was ruthless," Jenny said. "Imagine throwing yourself in front of a train to get into the rich kid school. Was that your mom's idea, or your dad's?"

She didn't get an answer. Alicia stared at Jenny in shock for what felt like an hour before throwing her cigarette at Jenny's feet and limping back inside. Good. Maybe she'd be rattled for their next match.

They were in the semi-finals now, and the four players left were Alicia, Jenny, Jimmy Figg, and some old-ass dork with a bald spot. All she needed to do was crush Alicia in *Time Killers* and then beat whoever was left in the finals, and Jenny would finally be a VIP, finally get to see what the hell was up with this mysterious *Trouble* video game, and finally figure out why her father had sent her and the Stranger both to this accursed arcade.

Time Killers was a *Street Fighter* knock-off with the gimmick of being able to cut your opponent's arms and head off. If you were bad enough to get your head cut off, you would die instantly. Alicia joined her at the cabinet, cracked her knuckles, and said, "Don't be mad, Trouble. You earned this."

The game began. Jenny picked the girl character who had some kind of lightsaber sword. She danced in with a few jabs, testing Alicia's defenses—and then Alicia's character cut her head off with his chainsaw.

Fuck!

It was okay. Lucky shot. The match wasn't over yet, and they were playing best-of-five sets.

Ready? Fight!

Jenny made sure to remember to block this time. She leaped over Alicia's chainsaw guy and got some good hits in, lopping one of his arms off. Yes! Alicia did some kind of combo and suddenly Jenny's lightsaber girl was stunned. "No!"

Alicia calmly cut her head off again.

It didn't get much better from there. In one match, Jenny managed to cut off both of the chainsaw guy's arms, but he still head-butted her to death. And then Alicia decapitated her again in the next game. And again. And again.

And then it was over. Three straight sets and Jenny was out. Alicia walked away from the controls without a word.

Asha was no comfort. "You fucking sold," she said, shaking her head.

"I feel like she cheated!" Jenny said, her face feeling hot.

"She didn't cheat, you just sucked. Look on the bright side, more time to grind with me."

Honestly, that didn't sound like much of a bright side at the moment. Jenny was forced to watch in agony as Alicia dispatched Jimmy Figg in the finals and her score on the leaderboard shot up dozens of levels.

AAA | LVL 50 | +1185375XP | 1275000XP TOT

Not only had Jenny lost, Alicia now had access to the VIP room. She'd be free to investigate the *Trouble* game, and Jenny was helpless to stop her.

"There's probably some sort of moral you should learn from this, Trouble," Alicia said, coming over to rub it in.

"You know I needed that more than you!" Jenny said. "Why do you even care? You sold your heirloom! The game is for me, not you!"

Alicia laughed.

"Take it up with RJ," she said, and dug a finger under her collar, pulling out a thin gold chain. "And don't be so naive. Did you actually think I'd sell you my key without making a copy first?"

Dangling from the end of the gold chain was an old-fashioned skeleton key: Alicia's heirloom.

"You lying little—"

Jenny made a grab for the key, but Alicia ducked out of her reach. Before she could make another attempt, Rob interposed himself between them.

"None of that!" Rob yelled. "No fighting in the arcade—unless it's in a kiddie pool of chocolate pudding and you're both in bikinis."

"That's mine by right!" Jenny shouted.

"You never said I couldn't make a copy! And I gave you the original," Alicia said. "Not my fault you and Mr. Webb, may he rest in peace, didn't cover that in our contract."

"Hah! A Valentine getting shafted by a legal loophole?" said Rob with a harsh grin. "Something something hoisted by your own retard. Fucking delicious. Come on, fire crotch, we gotta get you set up for VIP access."

Chapter Eighteen

Twisted Sister

S FO's International Terminal A was as crowded and chaotic as ever on a Friday night, and the holiday wasn't helping. Navigating her way through traffic was stressful enough for Eliza without the looming heartache sitting next to her in the jeep's passenger seat.

She'd insisted on driving Charlie to the airport. These past two weeks had passed like a dream. Glorious and fantastical, and over too soon. All of a sudden, the sign for **Air France** was only a hundred yards ahead, here to take her girlfriend away, maybe forever. Eliza couldn't help but think back to Jenny's breakup with Dinah. At the time, she'd yearned for a relationship to cut her that deeply.

Who was that idiot, and what was she thinking??

"This is fine here," Charlie said.

Eliza parked and hopped out to help with the luggage. Exhaust fumes burned her nostrils, and a cacophony of whistles and horns and public address announcements left her feeling hurried and panicked. She pulled Charlie's heavy suitcase out of the back seat while a nearby cop yelled at another traveler to move it along.

"Jeez, what do you have in here?" Eliza asked.

"Mostly dirt—dirty laundry," Charlie stuttered, avoiding eye contact.

Was there anything else? No. Charlie had her purse and her carry-on. This was it.

Was this it?

"Okay," Charlie said.

She extended the handle on her big suitcase. They stared at each other.

Eliza couldn't hold it in anymore. "Don't go."

Hot tears streamed down her cheeks.

"I'm sorry," said Charlie.

"I'll wait for you," Eliza found herself saying. "I'll call you every day."

Charlie shook her head. "We agreed," she said. "It's not fair to you. You still have half a senior year left, I won't have you being miserable over me."

"I'll be miserable no matter what."

A car honked. "Let's go, girls!" the cop shouted.

"You won't be. You have your sister, and you have Jack now, too."

"He hates me, and I hate her!"

"Give it time, Lizzy. We'll do like we said: we live our lives till summer, and when we meet again, it'll be with love, and no expectations. If it's meant to be, it's meant to be."

Eliza couldn't even contemplate the "no expectations" part of their agreement right now. She pulled Charlie close for one last, desperate, passionate kiss, her lips and tongue screaming *remember me!* until that pig of a cop pulled them apart.

"Move the car! Now!" he yelled in her face.

Charlie grabbed her suitcase and turned away. Eliza knew she wouldn't look back. Charlie was strong that way. With the cop still shouting, she hustled back to the driver's side and got in. The ceaseless rush of traffic dragged Eliza away from her first love, and she drove alone into the cold, bitter night.

JENNY SHOULD HAVE KNOWN SHE COULDN'T TRUST ALICIA. THAT little snake! She'd "sold" her heirloom skeleton key to Jenny for a brick of cash and a guarantee that Trouble, Inc. would publish her stupid portal fantasy smut, *Hands of Adamant.* At the time, Jenny figured Alicia was happy to get some money and pretend to be a writer. Hadn't Alicia been the first one to turn her heirloom in, way back at that first will reading, when Mr. Webb offered them each a cut of RJ's fortune if they all agreed to forfeit the game? Or was it all a long con, rightly predicting that Jenny would never agree to turn her back on the mystery?

There was no way Alicia could be the Stranger, right? Too small, for one, and missing a leg; the Stranger was much too athletic. But what if Alicia was part of a team? Sell the heirloom, and then your bigger, stronger partner steals it right back? And now she had access to Pixeldrome's VIP room, too. There were some serious implications there, but at the moment, Jenny just wanted revenge.

"I've got it! Her leg!" said Asha.

It was after hours at Pixeldrome, and they'd turned the cameras off to have sex in the break room. With that mission complete, Jenny played big spoon and squeezed her handful of Asha, eager to hear more.

"What, we cut off the other one?" Jenny asked.

"No, you psycho," Asha said. "We steal the prosthetic!"

"Oh, because that's so much more sane!"

"I mean, I'm not saying you go full fucking Jigsaw on her, Trouble. You just snatch the thing and hold it hostage until she gives you that key you want back."

Jenny laughed, imagining Alicia hopping around on one leg, her face going as red as her stupid hair.

"We don't even know for sure if she ever takes the thing off."

"I'm sure she must," said Asha. "You wait until she's asleep, or in a compromised position, and then you sneak in and snatch it! How hard could it be? I'll bet your brother's giving her a deep dicking on the reg. Just do it while they're getting busy."

"Oh god, don't even give me that mental image!" Jenny said. "Even if she does take it off during sex, how would I get close enough to steal it?"

As she said it, an idea came to mind: hiding under her bed, just like she had in Schloss Schwarzwald. Drew had only weaseled a handjob out of Alicia then. Was she giving her dreamboat Jack full access?

"You're the Girl Detective. You figure it out."

"Have you heard from Charlie, Kazu?" Meghan asked. "I'm so jealous of her—not that I didn't have my semester abroad in Paris, but still!"

It was Monday morning, and the Unfridgeables were once again huddled inside Starbucks to escape the cold.

Unfridgeables... No one used that term anymore. Not since Nilay was killed.

"She's still getting settled in," Eliza replied through her teeth.

The girls nodded, sharing glances. Eliza was sure they were eager to gossip about her and Charlie, but couldn't do so with her present. So she made it easy for them.

"Blimey, I've got to run to the post before class," she said, rising and grabbing her bag. "See you at lunch?"

They said their goodbyes, and Eliza told herself she was just imagining the eruption of giggling from inside the coffee shop as soon as she was out the door. She took a deep breath and glanced around. Which way was the post office, anyway? Her eye fell on a small girl with a wavy mohawk and retro styling. Trouble.

She was walking south from Town Square, which made her think of Charlie's condo, which made her eyes water all over again.

"Is it as weird for you as it is for me?"

Eliza jumped with a start. She'd been so in her head that she didn't notice Drew standing next to her, peering into the Starbucks window. "Bloody hell? Is what weird?"

He pointed inside, at Jack and Alicia sitting together. "Both our exes dating each other," Drew said.

Eliza snorted. "Jack isn't my ex. He and I were never dating."

"Sure," said Drew. "Sometimes it feels like Alicia and I were never really dating either."

"That's not what Jenny told me," Eliza blurted out before she had the good sense not to.

His ears went red. "Your cousin's been telling stories outta school," he said. "How is she, these days? She hasn't returned my texts all winter break."

"Honestly, Drew, I put a lot of effort into not knowing how she is these days," said Eliza. "I know she was your friend, but from my perspective, any time someone involves themselves with Jenny Valentine, their life gets worse. Considerably"

"It's almost like Trouble is her middle name," said Drew. Eliza glared laser beams at him. "Look, you don't need to sell me on the dangers of befriending Jenny. She does mean well, though."

"These days I'm not terribly sure," said Eliza. "And no, it's not weird fathoming Alicia and Jack. I think it's sweet. She's allowed, innit?"

"I guess," said Drew with a sigh. "It was never gonna work out for us anyway. She's a Giants fan."

Eliza blew a raspberry and told him she needed to get to the post. As she walked away, most of her mind drifted back to that Christmas party, and that incredible kiss with Charlie under the mistletoe.

Oh, Charlie! How could you leave?

But another part of her mind—the secret, hidden, Danger part—was thinking: *Go A's.*

ALICIA HAD A CONDO IN THE SAME NEW BUILDING AS CHARLIE DID, on the floor below. Next to her door was a little hand-painted plaque that read:

The Aarons

Jenny rolled her eyes and pulled out her lockpick set—only to stuff it back into her coat when the door opened.

"Can I help you?" asked a woman.

She didn't need to be the World's Greatest Girl Detective to deduce that this was Alicia's mother. The same pale skin. The same red hair. Fuck, Jenny had forgotten all about her.

"Um, yeah. Mrs. Aaron, right?" Jenny said. "Just the woman I wanted to see."

Mrs. Aaron narrowed her eyes, an expression remarkably similar to the one her daughter often gave Jenny. They could be twins, except for the crow's feet, the softer shade of red locks, and, obviously, the intact right leg. From her scant research, Jenny knew this must be Alice.

"You're that Trouble girl, aren't you?" said Mrs. Aaron.

"That's me!" Jenny beamed. "Do you mind if I ask you a few questions?"

"Alicia was right, you've got some nerve," said Mrs. Aaron. "If you think I'm gonna spill dirt on my own daughter—"

"I wouldn't dream of it," Jenny said. "That's not why I'm here. This is a cute plaque, did you paint it yourself?"

She pointed to the **Aarons** sign. Alicia's mom had been ready to shut her down, but as Jenny knew from *The Smell of Trouble*, careful flattery was a great way to throw a reluctant source off their game.

"Uh, yes, I did," said Mrs. Aaron.

"I'm here to ask about your husband, Mrs. Aaron," said Jenny. "Alexander."

The thinnest of smiles that Jenny had elicited with her compliment abruptly vanished, replaced by what JeRay would have called a bad poker player's version of a poker face.

"What about him?"

"I understand he's missing, I thought I could help," said Jenny.

"What are you, a skip tracer now? Gonna get me some child support? He's not missing, the bastard ran out," said Mrs. Aaron.

"I see," said Jenny. "And you don't have any idea where he might have gone?"

"He was always talking about going back east. I'd wager he finally did, and good riddance."

"And you say he ran out. Do you recall when that was?"

Alice Aaron shifted from one foot to the other. A nervous tick. "Summer before last."

"Do you remember the month?" Jenny asked. "June? July? August?"

"August, maybe," said Mrs. Aaron. "I should get back to my work."

"Anything you remember about the last time you saw him?" Jenny asked.

"It's no mystery," she said. "The bastard ran out. He was always talking about going back east. We don't miss him. If Rodney or one of his work buddies put you up to this, you can tell them I'm sorry, but I don't have a new address. I don't think Alex was interested in keeping in touch. And I'd appreciate it if you didn't come around again. I've got the impression from Alicia that you haven't been very kind to her, so whatever it is you're up to, we're not interested."

Mrs. Aaron slammed the door in her face, leaving Jenny to ruminate on the interview. *The bastard ran out. He was always talking about going back east.* The way Alicia's mom had repeated those phrases… it was almost rote. Rehearsed.

"Well, she's a fucking liar," Jenny said to herself.

FOR THE NEXT FEW WEEKS, JENNY SPLIT HER TIME EQUALLY BETWEEN grinding XP, fooling around with Asha, planning vengeance on Alicia, and looking into the maybe mysterious disappearance of one Alexander Aaron. Okay, not equally. Mostly gaming and fucking. But she tried to find time for the weird business with Alicia's dad. She was also overdue to hang out with Drew, but he always seemed to text when she was in the middle of a tough level or knuckles deep in Asha. Sorry, Drewboo! Have better timing!

Stealing Alicia's leg from her condo looked like a no-go since Alice didn't appear to ever leave their condo. And now that Jack was back living at the mansion, surrounded by Tori's enhanced security, committing the theft there seemed impossible. If only she could get the two of them alone, at some other less secure location.

Jenny pondered her dilemma, walking to Pixeldrome one afternoon in the drizzling rain. When the ugly exterior of the arcade loomed before her, she was struck by two epiphanies. The first was that she fucking hated this place. Why was she always here?

The second was that maybe she was overthinking things with Alicia; there was always chloroform.

The rain suddenly ceased. Was this a sign? Was she on the right track? No, someone had extended an umbrella over her head.

"Miss Valentine," said Lambert in that odd accent of his. "I expected to find you here."

"Oh, hello there," Jenny said.

"I have two items that may interest you," Lambert said. "The first is my write-up on the owner of this establishment." He nodded to the arcade. "And the second is the results of the DNA test you asked me to facilitate. I consider us now even, though another bottle of *Ressort Rouge* would certainly buy you many future favors on my behalf."

He handed her a large manila envelope and a smaller letter.

"I'll let you know," Jenny said and hugged the old man. Her last bottles were hidden at the mansion, if Tori hadn't found them. Tricky to retrieve. "Thanks, Mr. Lambert!"

She hurried inside Pixeldrome and found a quiet corner in the snack bar area. As quiet as could be, that was, with all the bells and chimes and pounding synthwave of the arcade. First, she opened the thick manila envelope containing Lambert's long-awaited dossier on Rob Haines.

Motherfucker took long enough. When did I ask for this? November?

At least Lambert had gone beyond a basic background check. Rob's record was mostly clean. A DUI a decade ago. A few parking tickets. He was a registered Democrat, donated regularly to the mayor's campaign fund, and contributed lightly to a few local charities. Pixeldrome appeared to be little more than a break-even business; the bulk of Rob's income came from earned interest. He was pulling down over $10K a month from his investment portfolio, and he owned the arcade and his chic two-bedroom bungalow in West Blackbird Springs free and clear. On top of that, Lambert noted a regular quarterly deposit into Rob's account, usually in the neighborhood of $50K, from a source he couldn't track down.

Of more interest was the $9K cash deposit Rob made on September 3rd of last year. Just two days after the game token heirloom was revealed, and Mr. Webb was killed. Coincidence, or a payoff? But for what, VIP room access? She'd tried that and Rob turned her down over his supposed principles. Jenny grumbled and read on.

There were pages on all Rob's likely romantic partners over the years—always much younger than he—and Lambert had left comments on the ones Rob settled lawsuits with over sexual indiscretions. Classy guy. Rob Haines wasn't likely to win Blackbird Springs Man of the Year any time soon, but his alibi the night of Dad's attack checked out. Near as Jenny could tell, he was just another son of a bitch in a town full of them.

"*High score.* What were you trying to tell me, Dad?" Jenny said, paging through the dossier.

She'd just have to get into that VIP room and find out. She glanced over to the counter. Like always, the stairway to the basement was roped off in velvet. Jenny had snuck down there on a few occasions while Asha napped in the break room after a shift, but had been wholly unsuccessful at forcing her way inside. There wasn't even a doorknob or a lock to pick. However one entered the VIP room remained, frustratingly, a mystery.

Whatever was down there hadn't appeared to give Alicia Aaron any new leads, at least. Or maybe Alicia was just busy getting busy with Jack instead of working on the case.

Speak of the devil.

The smaller envelope was a letter from GenSys Paternity Solutions: the results of Alicia Aaron's DNA test. Finally, proof. At last! Her hands shook as she ripped the report from the envelope and skipped right to the bolded text at the bottom:

Probability of Siblingship: 0.00025%

Alicia didn't share any DNA with Jenny, and therefore, with RJ Valentine. She wasn't Dad's kid.

"Boom! I knew it!!"

"The hell are you crowing about?" asked Nathaniel.

"Shut the fuck up, Nathaniel."

Jenny read on. Who Alicia *did* share DNA with was much more interesting. According to the note from the lab, most people shared about half of their DNA with each parent. Alicia's chromosomes, though, shared more than half. Significantly more. They would need additional testing to confirm, but there was only one rational explanation for Alicia's abnormal genetic makeup.

Alicia's parents, Alice and Alexander Aaron, were brother and sister.

Fuck the leg, I own your fucking soul now, Alicia.

Chapter Nineteen

When She Was Bad

THAT WEEKEND, CHARLIE POSTED A NEW YOUTUBE VIDEO OF herself walking around Paris and doing a makeup tutorial at the L'Oréal offices. She hadn't called, she hadn't written, yet she looked as effervescent and sanguine as ever, whether she was showing off a new palette, joking with a pretty co-worker, or seamlessly switching between English and French with the local merchants. She looked happy. Eliza watched the video three times, and contemplated driving back to the coast and walking into the sea.

Instead, she drove to Dusty's Batting Cages. They had a new side area for axe throwing, and Eliza wanted very badly to hurl edged weapons at things until her arms gave out. She paid for a stall and collected her axes, plus a few throwing knives, then went to work on the pockmarked piece of plywood hung up for target practice. It was easy to imagine the faces of Campbell Batori and Burke Brunner on the plywood. Sometimes she saw RJ, and Jenny too. She told herself she was practicing missing them.

"Damn girl, what did they teach you at that boarding school?"

Eliza squeaked and missed her shot by a foot. Sorry, Dad. Once again, Drew Porter had caught her amidst a reverie, and now she was blushing fiercely. Her makeup might hide most of it, but not her ears!

"My father thought it was important that I learn to defend myself,"

Eliza said. "You know, from the Yakuza, the Japanese Mafia."

She couldn't resist it, and watching Drew's face war between skepticism and admiration was exactly what she needed to retake the upper hand.

"Wow, that's uh…"

"Drew, I'm just taking the piss!" Eliza said, giving him her best girlish giggle.

"Hahaha, of course, I figured," said Drew.

"I didn't fancy running into you here," said Eliza.

Lies! I planned this. I am a mastermind!

"I wanted some live balls to work on my swing," Drew said.

Eliza nodded to his equipment bag. "Just beginning, or just finished?" she asked.

"Beginning," Drew said. "I'm in no rush, though. You, uh, mind if we chat?"

The way he asked it, a little too casually… Eliza was duty-bound to make him work for it.

"About what?" Eliza asked, feeling devilish.

"Just had a question, no biggie."

She held out an axe to him. "You get one question for each target you can hit," she told him.

Drew grinned sheepishly and accepted the throwing axe. "For the record, my aim might not be so hot," he said. "I severed a nerve in my throwing shoulder last year."

No, I severed it.

"No excuses, it's not that hard," she teased.

He lined up his shot and threw the axe. It went straight down, bouncing on the concrete two yards in front of them.

"Hey, easy there!" warned an attendant at the end of the range.

Eliza cackled and Drew's cheeks went red.

"*It's not that hard,*" Drew repeated in his version of a British accent.

"I'll wager Jack could do it."

He smirked and tried again. The axe almost hit the plywood this time.

"Just gotta find my range."

Five more tosses earned them increasingly dirty looks from the staff. When Drew finally managed to stick an axe into the plywood, two feet below the target, Eliza called it a success.

"Close enough, what do you want to ask me, sir?"

"I was just thinking about what a bummer Valentine's Day always is when you're single, you know?" Drew ran a hand over his buzzcut. "And I know Charlie hasn't been gone for too long, and I don't mean to put you on the spot or anything, but I was thinking, you know, if we really wanted to stick it to the holiday and get through it without all the usual depressing shit and tables for one and all that, we could totally hang out."

"Sorry, was there a question in there?" Eliza said, grinning madly.

Why was she torturing him like this? But it was so much fun!

"Er, yeah, uh, Kazu, how do ya feel about getting a bite, Sunday after next?" he said. "Just the two of us, at the Red Grape?"

"Like a *date?*"

"Yeah, a date."

Eliza was practically *levitating!* She had to look down to check that her shoes were still touching the floor.

"That's quite charming of you to ask, Drew," Eliza said. She held a finger to her chin. That bitch Dinah was always doing this when she wanted to play the coquette. "But."

Poor Drew deflated. He nodded, his gaze falling, and sighed. "But. Right."

"I don't want to go to the Red Grape," said Eliza. Drew's eyes flicked up, new hope swelling. "I don't want to go anywhere in Blackbird Springs, for that matter. Meaning no offense, but I'd rather keep this between the two of us. I don't want Meghan May and the Bitchy Brigade getting their two pence in and piling on expectations before they're wanted."

"Yeah, totally, that makes sense," said Drew. He wore a big dumb grin on his face now. The hard part was over. "We can, uh, go somewhere in Santa Rosa."

"Brilliant, and would you mind if we didn't do Italian? Take me somewhere I'll only find in America."

An idea popped into Drew's head, and he smirked, saying, "All right, Americana. I know a place. But just remember, you asked for it."

"You devil!" She patted him playfully on the forearm. *Goddamn, to be held by those pythons…* "Now go practice your swing before they kick us out."

"Sure. Totally. I'll text you," Drew said.

He shuffled off, punch-drunk. Eliza waited until he was out of sight to pump her fist and hurl two knives at once at the target. Each struck to the left and right of the bullseye.

Still got it, Danger!

On Monday, Jenny approached Jack and Alicia in the cafeteria at lunch, and told the little inbreed that she had two weeks to return the skeleton key to Jenny's possession. If she didn't, Jenny would be forced to take drastic action. Alicia was unfazed, and Jack told her to fuck off.

Fine. They can't say she didn't warn Alicia.

Drew had witnessed the encounter, and texted her immediately afterward.

> **Drew:** What kind of drastic measures are we talking about?
>
> **Jenny:** It's a secret, but it's good!
>
> **Drew:** 🫤

Oh get over it, Drew. Alicia moved on, you should too.

As Alicia's deadline ticked closer, Jenny passed the time googling Alexander Aaron and grinding at Pixeldrome. She was up to level 25 now. Halfway there! But so much more XP to go.

When next Friday arrived, and Alicia hadn't made a scintilla of effort to get Jenny that key—even a look at it—Jenny figured she had no choice but to act. Valentine's Day was that Sunday, which meant the campus was redolent with pinks and reds. Thanh Trân, the Class President again after Nilay's death, talked Jimmy Figg into dressing up like Cupid to deliver valentines during lunch. Jimmy made sure to give one to Kazumi, winking at Jenny across the cafeteria as he did. The joke was on him: as soon as his back was turned, Eliza tossed the card on Meghan's tray as she was getting up to throw it in the garbage.

Jenny marched up to the cool seniors' table, where Jack and Alicia were sharing sushi he got delivered (deep-fried California rolls, a total gaijin order), and issued her final ultimatum.

"Alicia Anne Aaron, you have something of mine," Jenny said. "If you don't hand it over right this second, I'm going to ruin your life."

Alicia studied her, still more curious than concerned. It briefly crossed Jenny's mind to wonder if Alicia even knew. No, of course she did. That's why she didn't want her DNA checked.

"This isn't the way, Jenny," said Drew.

"There's nothing you can say about Alicia that's going to make us take your side over hers," Jack said.

"I wouldn't be too sure of that," Jenny said, grinning.

A chorus of disproval came in from the other cool kids.

"I don't know what you think you know, but I'm at peace with my choices in life," said Alicia.

"Were you at peace when you tried to throw yourself in front of that train?" Jenny said. "Yeah, that's right. You guys ever wonder how Alicia got nailed by a train? It wasn't an accident. What happened, you lose your nerve at the last second?"

The cafeteria went deathly silent. Eliza was staring at Jenny, mouth agape in shock.

"Dude," said Lai.

"Jenny, don't," said Drew.

Alicia laughed. "Seriously, was that it?" Alicia asked, smirking. "That was a long time ago, Trouble, and I was in a bad place. I'm a different person now, and I feel no shame over it."

How dare you laugh it off, you almost died!

Jenny felt flushed all over. A mania was taking control. She didn't want to go there, but Alicia was forcing her hand.

"Why don't you tell them *why* you were out there on the tracks?" said Jenny. Alicia frowned. "Or, oh, is there maybe still some shame?

Is that why you paid Mr. Hooke to keep your name out of his Ghostwriter posts last year? Last chance, Alicia. Hand it over."

Jack rose to his feet as if to shield his girlfriend from Jenny. "I think we're done here. Sincerely go fuck yourself, Jenny."

"Is there a problem?" Vice Principal Carter asked.

He must have noticed the tension, and as usual, was sticking his nose where it wasn't wanted.

Just give me the key, Alicia! I don't want to do this!

"No problem," said Jenny. She held out her hand. "The key, Alicia."

There was a buzzing in her ears. It was as though Jenny was witnessing the whole scene from outside her own body. Alicia shook her head slowly, her face as white as a sheet. Drew and Eliza gaped in horror. Jack loomed over Jenny, furious. Penny bit her fist, aghast. Vice Principal Carter cleared his throat, all paternal authority. At the center of it all was Jenny, fire burning in her eye sockets, ready to set herself ablaze. She could already smell the smoke.

"Why don't you come with me, Miss Valentine," said Vice Principal Carter.

You could have stopped me, Alicia! This is on you!

"Don't you think people have a right to know?" Jenny asked Alicia. "Especially Jack? I mean, I don't know what your plans are, Junior, but I'd caution against kids. Birth defects, you know?"

Alicia leaped to her feet in a fury. "Don't you dare, Trouble!" she screamed.

"What the fuck are you babbling about?" asked Jack.

"That's enough!" shouted Vice Principal Carter.

"Do you guys smell smoke?" asked Penny.

"I'm saying Alicia's mom is also her aunt! And her dad is also her uncle!" Jenny shouted as Vice Principal Carter restrained her. "I don't know how this connects to my father's murder yet, but I'm onto you, Alicia. You're a freak! An incest baby! Feeling ashamed yet?!"

Eliza gasped. Alicia let out a guttural shriek of rage and ran limping from the cafeteria as fast as her prosthetic leg would carry her. Jack went after her. Drew shook his head sadly.

"Dude, that's fucked up," said Lai.

"Oh shit! Fire!" Penny yelled.

She pointed across the cafeteria, where flames and thick black smoke were shooting out of a trash can. The fire alarm began to wail. Students scrambled to their feet to clear the area.

"Suspension, five days," said Vice Principal Carter. "And I'm scheduling a hearing for expulsion."

"Cool, see you next week," said Jenny, and stomped out of the cafeteria.

AUNT SHELLY WOULD SURELY GROUND HER WHEN SHE GOT HOME. Jenny was a step ahead, though. *Can't ground me if I don't* go *home!* She walked south to Pixeldrome (where else?) and dumped a bunch of tokens into *Lethal Enforcers*, a shooter game where you blasted away at the screen with a big fake gun.

"You know you're not supposed to shoot the innocent bystanders, right?" Rob asked.

Asha was in class, so Jenny would have to talk her own shit at him.

"Innocent? What the fuck is innocent?" Jenny said. "Nobody's innocent."

"That's what I've been trying to tell you kids," Rob said, grinning. "The sooner you guys realize the world is a bullshit sandwich with a side of misery, the better equipped you'll be to get ahead of the rest of the NPCs."

"Whatever you say, man," Jenny said, blowing the head off a lady who wandered into the middle of her shootout.

"See, your mom got it, Jenny," Rob said. "Nobody was sharper than her at pointing out all the crooks and liars."

"How'd she stomach being around you, then?"

He laughed. "Because I'm honest. I'm the only guy who would keep it real with her. Harsh truths, man. She respected that."

Jenny scoffed and murdered another innocent. "'Harsh truths?' I just told a harsh truth, and now I might get expelled."

Suddenly the whole story was spilling out of her. Jenny's fear that RJ might have fathered Alicia. The DNA test. Attempting to extort

Alicia for the skeleton key. Exposing her parentage to the whole school as her former friends looked on in horror. Why was she telling this loser?

Rob roared with laughter when she got to the incest part.

"That's fucking awesome!!" he said and held up his hand for a high five. Jenny felt a twinge of pride and an avalanche of shame as she slapped hands with his sweaty palm. "Seriously, epic shit, Valentine. You know what? Fuck it! 250,000XP for that. You earned it."

Whoa. That put her…well, her brain couldn't do the math for it, but way higher than she was!

"For real?" she asked Rob.

"Hell yeah, girl. Check it out." He jogged over to the terminal behind the counter and punched in her big gain. Behind him, the leaderboard chimed like a slot machine and flashed her new total.

JTV | LVL 33 | +250000XP | 577585XP TOT

"Goddamn," said Jenny. "That's like half my XP!"

"In this house, random acts of misanthropy do not go unrewarded," said Rob.

"I guess I'll need to do more," said Jenny.

"Hey, just keep me out of it if you get caught," Rob said, cackling. "But I mean, not to get all fate and destiny, but you were born for this, weren't you? A name like Trouble? Why did you ever think that meant being a hero? Honestly, I don't think RJ ever understood why Laura named you that."

He smiled like the devil himself. Jenny wanted to dispute the point, but what did she really know? She'd never even spoken to her mother. Like it or not, Rob Haines probably knew her better. Maybe Mom was more of a rebel than even Aunt Shelly knew.

"Holy shit, what'd I miss?" said Asha, coming in through the back office and gawking at the leaderboard.

"The game has changed, Ash," Jenny said. "You in the mood for Trouble?"

Icy wind whipped at her hair and burned her cheeks as Jenny ran from the scene of the crime. She and Asha had just broken a whole carton of eggs on the hood of Meghan May's father's BMW. They reached the end of the cul-de-sac and jogged around the corner, making sure they were well out of sight before stopping to catch their breath.

"Now I kinda want an omelet," said Jenny.

They burst into giggles and hurried back to Asha's car.

"There's always Denny's," said Asha.

"Hold on a sec," Jenny said. "I've been dying to try this."

She retrieved a hand tool from her purse: Drew's center punch thing, supposedly perfect for breaking car windows. Jenny walked past Asha's Honda to a Ford F-150 parked a few yards ahead in front of a million-dollar house.

"No, do the Tesla," Asha said, pointing to the electric vehicle in the driveway. "Fuck the environment."

Jenny grinned and moved over to the Tesla. In *Nothing But Trouble*, the titular Girl Detective found herself trapped in the back seat of a car that had been driven off a pier (by the Stranger, naturally) and was sinking fast into Calistoga Lake. Using her wits, she managed to reach the tire iron in the trunk and smash the rear window open, then swam to safety. Not bad for Book Trouble, but Real Trouble couldn't count on a conveniently located tire iron.

Let's see if Drew's right about this thing.

Gritting her teeth, she positioned the center punch in the middle of the driver's side window and pushed. The tip of the tool retracted into the handle with a *squeak* until some mechanism triggered and released the spring-loaded tension.

Crash!

In a blink, the entire window spiderwebbed with cracks and fell apart like magic.

"Holy shit, that was awesome!" she said.

"I wanna try!" said Asha.

Jenny handed it off so Asha could take her turn. Another *crash!* and another window disintegrated into shards of glass.

"Dude!" shouted Asha.

"Right?!" said Jenny.

They took turns doing the rest of the Tesla's windows. Something about the instantaneous shattering was extremely satisfying to Jenny, in her destructive state of mind. This tool was definitely going into Trouble's bag of tricks. *Good call, Drewboo.* But, speaking of windows, a light just turned on inside the Tesla owner's house.

"Shit, we better get out of this neighborhood," said Asha. "That's gotta be worth a few thousand XP, right?"

"Let's go do a lawn job," Jenny suggested as they hurried back to her car. If only they could do one on Valentine Manor's lawn. "No wait, I've got a better idea."

It was shockingly easy to get a can of gasoline. All you had to do was act like your car broke down. They were smart, though. They went to a different mini-mart to buy matches. Asha killed her headlights before turning right onto Cellar Drive. They cruised in silence, with only a slim sliver of waxing moon to guide their way, until they reached the berm at the end of the road. A heavy mist hung over the nearby trickling stream.

"I don't know how good security is, so we'll need to do this quick," Jenny said.

Asha grabbed the gas can and they hurried into the woods. When they reached the treehouse, her girlfriend stared up at the little cabin in the eaves, grinning, and took a swig from the fifth of tequila they'd swiped.

"You sure you don't want to christen the place first?" Asha asked, giving her a dirty leer.

"I wish, but I think an alarm goes off somewhere when the hatch opens." She took the tequila bottle from Asha and swallowed a gulp. Awful!

For some reason, she thought of Dinah.

"Fuck you, Tori," Jenny said and traded Asha the booze for the gas. "If I can't have this place, nobody can."

She poured gasoline all over the trunk of the big oak, sloshing it liberally on the steps leading up to the treehouse.

"I love the smell of gasoline," said Asha, and held up the matches. "You want to do the honors?"

Jenny answered by shoving her tongue down Asha's throat.

"You do it," she whispered, hot in Asha's ear.

One lit match held to a gasoline-soaked two-by-four and Asha had the trunk of the oak tree roaring. Within 30 seconds, the flames were licking the platform the treehouse rested on. After a minute, the whole tree was engulfed in fire.

Jenny captured it all on her phone, relishing the blaze even as she was forced to step back from the heat.

"Rob ought to give us 20,000XP for this, easy," she said.

They jogged back to the car with the gas can in tow. Asha flipped a bitch and they got the hell out of there, laughing the whole way back to her apartment.

When Jenny awoke the next morning, she was so hungover that the FaceID on her phone didn't recognize her. She groaned and punched in her passcode. Surprisingly, she only had a single message: from Aunt Shelly.

ShellsBells: I love you, Jenny. Please come home.

"So you can ground me and send me back to therapy? Fat chance, Shelly," Jenny said to herself.

The twin bed was empty beside her. She had a vague memory of Asha giving her a squeeze and saying something about working an early shift. Damn, it was already past 11:00 AM. No bother, Jenny could lie here all day if she wanted.

Except she had to pee!

Unfortunately, one glance at the toilet had her fighting to keep the vomit down. She desperately needed a hash brown. After relieving herself, she pulled on some clothes—then took them off when she realized her underwear was on backward—and slipped out of Asha's bedroom.

"Uh, are you all right?" a male voice asked.

Asha's roommate was frowning at her from the dilapidated couch, where he was lounging in sweatpants and watching *Dragonball Z* on TV.

"Yeah, why?"

He raised an eyebrow like she was some kind of failed science experiment. Jenny caught her reflection in the microwave door. Her mascara was smeared down her cheeks from fresh tears.

"Huh." Jenny blinked. "I'm good. I was just gonna pop out for a sec to get some McDonald's. You want anything?"

"No thanks," the boy said. "I'm going to be leaving soon. You know, and locking the door…"

Translation: Hit the bricks, girl.

"It's cool. Catch you later, man."

Jenny let herself out of the shithole apartment and hoofed it the half-mile to the nearest McD's. All she wanted was to fill her tummy with grease. The smell of it had her near drooling as she waited in line. It was about to be her turn to order when the well-dressed man in front of her glanced back and gave her a start.

"Oh!" he said, just as surprised. "Wasn't expecting to see you here, Miss Valentine. I don't think we've been properly introduced. Hector Villanova. I'm—"

"The mayor, yeah, I remember," said Jenny, declining his offered handshake.

They each regarded the other for a spell.

"How's the college search going?" the mayor asked.

"Eager to get me out of town?" Jenny replied.

"You bet your ass I am," he said. "Do you know how many homicides we had in our peaceful hamlet in 2016? None. 2017? Nada. 2018? Zilch. 2019? Oops! Three. 2020, if we include that class trip to Austria? 19! Guess what changed?"

"You break a mirror, maybe? And I think you're forgetting to count Campbell Klein's victims, or are you sweeping them under the rug again?" said Jenny. "And you left out 2021, which is back to zero."

"Well, it's only February."

"Is one of you ready to order?" asked the clerk.

"Forget it," said the mayor.

He took off, fully disgusted with her. The clerk raised an eyebrow. Jenny shrugged. Fuck the mayor. Her first bite of hash brown was pure ecstasy. She was definitely going to puke this up in half an hour.

Especially with the long walk to the arcade jostling her stomach. Jenny was so tempted to call a Lyft, but she'd plowed through most of the $10,000 Drew had given her grinding XP. She needed to start being more frugal.

And then, as if she had manifested him from thin air, Drew's big Tacoma pickup suddenly skidded to a stop right next to her and pulled forward onto the sidewalk to block her path. He rolled down the passenger side window.

"Need a lift?" he asked.

His tone was light, but Jenny sensed a lecture lurking.

"I was gonna walk."

"Where to?" he asked.

"Pixeldrome," she said.

"That's like three miles. Come on, I'll take you there," said Drew.

Fuck it, her feet hurt. She climbed into the cab and fastened her seatbelt.

"Thanks," she said.

He pulled back into traffic. That synth-wave Weeknd song from the Homecoming dance challenge was playing on his stereo.

"Are you practicing for TikTok, Drewboo?" Jenny asked.

"Nah, it reminds me of someone," he said, a little smile twitching at the corners of his mouth.

He merged into the suicide lane and pulled a sharp U-turn.

"Wait. Where are you going?" she frowned. "Pixeldrome is that way."

"Right," said Drew. "I lied. There's someone you need to talk to."

Chapter Twenty

Phantom Limb

JENNY WAS SO SURE DREW WAS DRIVING HER TO ALICIA. MENTALLY, she was already making strategies for how to get that skeleton key. Most of her plans involved tackling the little redhead and yanking the chain right off her neck. They didn't go to Alicia's house, though. They went to Drew's.

"You want me to talk to your mom?" Jenny guessed.

"No, she's working," said Drew. "Come on."

Jenny warily unbuckled and slid out of the cab. Drew waved her toward his detached garage. He'd made some improvements since her last visit. Shit, how long ago was that?

November? I've been busy with the XP grind, I guess.

The roof of the garage was now covered in solar panels, and two blue 50-gallon drums were sitting on the lawn out front.

"Apologies in advance. I saw this in a movie once."

Without warning, he palmed the back of her head with his massive hand and shoved her face into the first barrel. It was full of ice-cold water!

"Sppbbbth!" she sputtered when he let her up for air.

Then he shoved her right back into the other barrel, this one filled with warm water.

And back and forth, with barely a chance to breathe in between.

Am I being waterboarded?

Trying to fight back was pointless. Drew's grip was far too strong to escape. After the twelfth round of dunking, she slapped her hands on the sides of the barrel and he let up.

Jenny sucked in a huge breath, her lungs heaving. "Thanks, asshole."

Up came the hash brown, last night's tequila, and another Cheesy Gordita Crunch. Some still-functioning part of her brain made sure to aim for the grass instead of the barrels, in case Drew wasn't finished dunking her.

"I'm never eating Taco Bell again," she said, when her throat was finally her own again. "Or tequila!"

There it was again, that flash of Dinah in her mind's eye. In Dad's study. Vaguely sinister. Right, she'd made Jenny drink tequila when she dumped her, to give her a taste aversion to the shit.

You tried your best to warn me, babe.

"You good?" Drew asked. "Need a little more?"

"Maybe one more."

Drew dunked her again. At least her running mascara wasn't an issue anymore. Jenny stumbled away, wiping her face, and coughing up more phlegm.

"There's no one here for me to talk to, is there?" she said. "I've been bamboozled."

"There will be," said Drew.

He had his phone out, selecting a contact. He held it to his ear, waiting as it rang, and handed Jenny a towel he'd thoughtfully had near at hand.

"Hi, is this Mr. Lockhart? ... It's Drew Porter, sir. ... I'm fine, thank you. Listen, I need your help. And your discretion. Mason said I can trust you. Can you come over to my house right away?"

Scant minutes later, Sheriff Lockhart pulled up in front of the Porter house in his big police SUV. He wore his freshly-pressed tan uniform today, and mirrored shades from behind which he could stare inscrutably at Jenny.

"Figures. Your aunt's looking for you," Lockhart said. "Any reason why I shouldn't take you in?"

"Any reason why you're wearing sunglasses when it's overcast?" Jenny replied.

"I need you to clear something up with Jenny," said Drew. "A certain misunderstanding that has her headed down the wrong path."

"What kind of misunderstanding?" Lockhart asked, his scowl shifting to Drew.

"The current disposition of one Alexander Aaron, and what you and Alicia were up to the night RJ Valentine was attacked," said Drew.

Wait! What?!

The scowl froze on Lockhart's chiseled jaw. He was still as a statue for several seconds before reaching up to remove his sunglasses and rub his eyes. In the distance, a train whistled.

"Told you, did she?" Lockhart asked. "I thought I'd taught her better."

"What the fuck is going on?" Jenny asked.

"She didn't tell me," said Drew. "I was kinda guessing, honestly, based on some weird stuff she's said, certain topics she avoids, and the fact that she keeps your card in her wallet." He turned to Jenny. "You gotta leave Alicia alone, Jenny. She doesn't have anything to do with RJ's death, and the sheriff can prove it. Can't you?"

Was this the secret Drew'd been holding in, back when he lied to her at the Crow's Nest before Christmas? Why wait until now to tell her?

Blake squinted at the two of them, and Jenny watched him run through scenarios in his head. He could deny it. He could arrest Jenny. He could shoot them both and make it look like a murder-suicide.

"We won't tell. Trouble's honor," said Jenny.

Lockhart glanced at the sky, scowling some more, and nodded to the detached garage. "It'll rain soon," he said. "Let's talk inside."

EVERYONE KEPT TELLING HIM TO TAKE TIME OFF.

It's okay, we'll cover for you. Really, you didn't have to do this. Miggy can take your shift for a while. Take some time. Focus on yourself, Blake. Mason needs you right now. We know you must be hurting. The mayor understands. It's no trouble at all. Take some time. We'll be here for you when you're ready. We're so sorry. Fuck cancer. Take some time.

What good was time, now that Lilah was gone?

They didn't get it; the only thing holding Blake Lockhart together was the work. Free time was his arch-nemesis. He didn't need to drop shifts. He needed more of them. The less time spent at home in an eerily empty house, the better. Mason would be fine. He was at that age now where being together with his pops in a suddenly mom-free world would only make the grief twice as bad for them both.

This was how he found himself manning the station one night when the call came in: another domestic disturbance over at Alkali Estates. Neighbors heard some couple the next trailer over screaming bloody murder at each other. They did this every other Friday, but this time, it sounded bad. He might have hit her.

A train whistled in the distance.

Lockhart hopped into the cruiser with the rookie, Peña, and sped off. If he was lucky, he might get to hit someone tonight.

"No siren, boss?" the rookie asked.

"For this? Nah," he said. "Not unless there's imminent danger. Sirens make people jumpy. Don't want to escalate the situation if we can avoid it."

Halfway to the trailer park, dispatch radioed in another alert. There was a train accident, not far from the Estates. They wanted him to check it out first. Lockhart grimaced. He couldn't punch a train.

He turned to the rookie. "This might be tough to see," he said. "You wanna stay in the cruiser?"

The rookie shook her head. She had that can-do fire in her belly that all the recruits came out of the academy with. Eager to prove how tough they were. He ought to tell her there was no coming back from seeing human entrails smeared dozens of yards down the train tracks, but he was too dead inside to care. Might as well get it over with, if she was gonna last in this line of work.

Then they got to the scene, and it was Lockhart who found himself retching in horror. The little girl's right knee was mangled beyond belief, the leg barely hanging on by shattered bones and ligaments. She had red hair. Just like Lilah's.

THEY AIRLIFTED THE GIRL BY HELICOPTER. MEDICS SAID IF SHE WAS LUCKY, she'd only lose the leg. Best they could tell, the train had struck something on the track that shot away and clipped the girl in the leg. Why was she out near the tracks? The parents couldn't say. But when they gave Lockhart their address, the reason became obvious: they were the Domestic call he and the rookie had been headed to check out in the first place. Mom and Dad fighting, daughter can't take it and runs away. Bad luck running by the tracks.

If it weren't for the rookie hanging around, Alexander Aaron would need a new spleen. Lockhart settled for arresting the piece of shit, even if his wife refused to press charges. Let him rot at the station for a few days.

Thank god the girl made it.

Two weeks later, he swung by Blackbird Springs General. Not with flowers or a stuffed teddy bear; Lockhart brought his business card. Her name was Alicia. She was well enough to talk now, the doctors said, but don't push her too hard.

"If he ever so much as lays a finger on you or your mom, I want to know," he said, placing his card on the table next to her.

"Why?" she asked. "The cops never do anything."

"Don't call the cops, call me," said Lockhart. "I'll handle it."

She sniffled. "I was trying to handle it myself," she said.

At the time, he didn't take her meaning.

"Don't," said Lockhart. "If you ever need help, anything at all, you call me."

Poor thing. He hoped she'd call. But in case she didn't...

Alexander Aaron worked the vines at Woodhall Winery. Lockhart knew the type immediately. You always had to keep an eye on the white guys who worked those jobs. Rare to find one who didn't resent the shit out of having to earn an honest living next to a bunch of migrant folks. After his shift, Alexander could usually be found at the Bad Egg, telling anyone at the bar who would listen about how big a deal his family was back in Ireland. Stupid prick thought he was some kind of displaced nobility. What was it Fitzgerald said? "Temporarily embarrassed millionaires?" No shit.

Lockhart waited until the bastard was properly pissed one night, then picked him up walking to his car at closing time. He could have busted him for drunk driving, but that might make Alicia's life worse. Instead, he drove Alexander to the edge of town and beat the ever-loving piss out of him. Warned him to leave his wife and kid alone, or next time, Lockhart would bring a shovel.

It seemed to work. The calls from neighbors stopped. Lockhart would cruise by now and then, to let Alexander know he was watching. Alicia looked to be getting along the best she could with her new prosthetic leg. Tough limp on the kid.

"You shouldn't smoke," he told her during a visit.

She was in high school by then, a year behind Mason, and had started dressing like one of those goth girls. Well, the kids didn't call it goth anymore, but you get the idea.

"I've seen the actuarial tables for amputees," Alicia said, pointing to her leg. "Cancer is the least of my concerns."

He stiffened, a knife piercing his heart.

"Sorry," said Alicia. "I'll quit soon."

Lockhart took a deep breath like his shrink had coached him to. A train whistled in the distance.

"Mrs. Manuel says you've been spending a lot of time out by the tracks," Lockhart said. "Anything I need to worry about?"

Alicia shook her head. "It's like exposure therapy. Don't worry, I'm fine."

Indeed, she was fine. Right up until a summer night in August when she called him in the middle of the Valentine Foundation Charity Gala, begging for help.

Lockhart hated these things. Having to get dressed up in a monkey suit and glad-hand the landed gentry of Blackbird Springs—hell, he'd

arrested a dozen of these chumps for DUIs. If the Valentine Foundation wasn't such a big supporter of the local LEO charities, he'd never show his face around these people. But they were, a point that Mayor Villanova never got tired of reminding him, come gala time.

"They need to see their Sheriff Lockhart," the mayor would say. "He's an institution."

He didn't mean Blake. He meant the fictional Lockhart. The pudgy, incompetent moron from the Trouble books.

RJ always claimed the name was merely a coincidence, a placeholder that he forgot about until the books became too popular to change it. Bullshit.

He glanced around. Where was that slick son of a bitch? Lilah never liked him. Said he didn't smile with his eyes. Women notice those things. In a better world, they'd be the police. In a better world…

Gottfried Leibniz, the guy who invented calculus, said humans were living in the best of all possible worlds. Fuck that German prick.

He found RJ's better half schmoozing with some Silicon Valley guys by the bar.

"What gives, Valerie?" he asked. "Your husband too good for his own parties?"

They hugged, exchanging perfunctory kisses on the cheek, and Val grimaced behind her masquerade ball mask.

"Just shoot me, Blake," said Val. "He has been such a handful lately. Will you try him?"

Lockhart didn't think he held much sway with RJ—they barely talked these days—but he'd take any excuse to ditch the gala for a minute or thirty. He ducked out of the Fairmont ballroom, took off his stupid mask, and tapped the contact for **Dipshit Writer** on his phone.

"You know I hate it when you call me," said RJ, in place of a proper greeting. "Always makes me think something bad's happened."

"It hasn't," said Lockhart. "Why aren't you at your gala? You really want to leave your wife alone with Fede Lombardo?"

"I'm working on something," RJ said. His voice sounded distant, and Lockhart could hear papers shuffling. "As a matter of fact, I've been meaning to talk to you about it. Can you get away?"

"You know I can't, Villanova would shit a brick. Get your ass over here. The shrimp's not half bad this year—shit, hang on." He glanced at his phone. Alicia was calling. "Hey, I gotta take this."

"Sure, talk later?" said RJ. "Tell Fede to have Val home by midnight. And for god's sake, wrap it up. I don't want the cl—"

Lockhart disconnected and switched over to Alicia. "What's up?"

"Can you come over? To the place where I had my accident?" Alicia asked. Her voice was pitched higher than usual. She was scared. "I need your help."

IT WAS 8:10 PM WHEN HE REACHED THE TURNOFF, JUST BEFORE ALKALI Estates. He remembered, because it was the exact minute the sun set and when his phone switched to night mode. He parked at the end of the frontage road and walked into the tall grass, to the spot where he'd found Alicia three years ago. She was upright this time, thank god. She was also holding a big kitchen knife.

A train whistled in the distance.

Two yards away, Alexander Aaron stared her down. Her dad was empty-handed, but seeing the way his hands were opening and closing into fists, Lockhart judged he might go for the knife anyway.

"That's close enough," Lockhart said, unholstering his service pistol. "You've got three seconds to back away from the girl."

"It's okay," Alicia said, raising her hand to Lockhart like she had this under control. "I've got this."

"Oh, sure. Why'd you call me, then?" Lockhart asked, not lowering his weapon.

"He tried it again," Alicia said quietly.

"Don't listen to her, man!" said Alexander. "She's fucking crazy! And a liar!"

The train whistled again, closer.

"Tried what?" Lockhart asked. "With your mom?"

Alicia flinched. She wouldn't look over at Lockhart, only shook her head.

"With you?"

Ever so slightly, she nodded. Lockhart switched off the safety on his pistol.

"This is bullshit! You can't believe her! She and her mom have been trying to get rid of me for years! Think they don't need me. Who puts food on the table?!"

"Mom has a job!" Alicia shrieked. Alexander's eyes widened in surprise. Lockhart got the sense the man had never heard this tone from his daughter before. "She'd have a better one if you only let her!"

"The man of the family provides," he said. "She needs to know her place."

"You don't know your place, you piece of shit!" Alicia screamed.

"Look, Lockhart, I was just trying to wake her up! She's always assuming the worst of me!"

The earth rumbled with the approaching train. They were only a stone's throw from the tracks.

"Alicia, I want you to put the knife down, and go back to the trailer with your mother," Lockhart said.

The knife was shaking in Alicia's hands. She stole a frantic glance at Lockhart and frowned.

"Mr. Lockhart, would you please take two paces to the left?!" she yelled.

"Huh?"

"Please! Now! Not you!" She brandished the knife at her father when he tried to back away.

Lockhart found himself pacing to the left. In the distance, the oncoming train came around a bend, its big front headlight shining right in Lockhart's face. In Alicia's face—

"Alicia! Look out!" Lockhart shouted.

The train whistle blared.

Shadows danced across his burned retinas.

He thought he saw Alicia fall into the tall grass.

A loud metallic ping! *sounded over the roar of the locomotive. Then a wet impact.*

Lockhart felt a gust of wind as something unseen flew past him, inches from his right cheek. The blinding light was gone; the train thundered past them.

"Alicia?!" he called out, blinking his eyes, gripping his pistol white-knuckled.

"I'm okay," she said, from somewhere below, when the train had gone by and he could hear again. Dimly, he could make out her blurred form rising from the grass. "Oh. Sorry."

"For what?" Lockhart asked.

He glanced down and found his sports jacket misted with red droplets. Alexander Aaron collapsed at his feet. His head was missing.

"What the fuck? What happened!?"

"Railroad spike," said Alicia. She spat on her father's corpse. "I didn't miss this time, asshole!"

RAIN PATTERED ON THE SOLAR PANELS ATOP DREW's Masturbatorium. Lockhart stopped talking and let out a bone-rattling sigh. Mirai's cat hopped into his lap. Drew held a bottle of Gatorade to his lips for a sip he'd been distracted from taking for the past two minutes. Jenny leaned against the sectional, too antsy to sit, and absentmindedly played with Drew's center punch, making it go *squeak squeak* as she pushed on the tension spring, just short of triggering a punch.

"That's fucking metal," said Jenny. "So she'd been trying to off her dad with that railroad spike the whole time?"

Was that why she laughed at the suicide allegation? Cunt.

"She and I spent half the night cleaning up the scene and disposing of that son of a bitch," Lockhart said. "That's why I wasn't on the scene at your dad's place after Jack found him. Officially: 'The bastard ran out. He was always talking about going back east.' Near as I can tell, not a soul in town misses him, and Alice and Alicia have been unbothered ever since."

"Then there's no way Alicia could have been involved in RJ's death," said Drew. "Or you, for that matter."

"So he says," said Jenny. "How very convenient for two suspects to provide each other's alibi. And wasn't a railroad spike the exact murder weapon you suggested at the will reading for my father? I suppose you'll tell me now it was just on your mind at the time?"

Lockhart shrugged and stroked the cat's back. "What do you want me to tell you? I wasn't there, Jennifer. If I'm lying, then where's Alexander Aaron?"

"Can you take me to the body?" Jenny asked.

"We fed it to some pigs," said Lockhart.

"That's pretty smart, actually," said Drew.

"Your approval means *so much* to me, Porter."

Jenny looked at Drew. "Is that it, then? Wanted to show me what a good Boy Detective you've been on your own?"

"I wanted you to know that you can leave Alicia alone," Drew said, glaring. "I say this out of concern, Jenny, but you've been a righteous fucking cunt to the poor girl, and you owe her an apology!"

Fresh rage bloomed in Jenny's ribcage. How dare he?

"You can't say that to a girl, Drew," Lockhart said. "Even if it's true."

"Alicia wouldn't need an apology if she'd just given it to me straight," Jenny said. "If she's so innocent, why did she sell me a duped heirloom?"

"It doesn't matter," Drew said.

"All this white knighting isn't gonna win her back, Drew," Jenny snapped. "You get that, right? She's with Jack now."

"And I'm with Kazu now, so suck it," said Drew. "I'm not trying to score points, I'm trying to get your head back in the game. Ever since you started going to that arcade you've become completely obsessed with Alicia. She's a red herring. The game is the Stranger, not her."

An icy fist gripped Jenny's heart.

"What do you mean, you're 'with Kazu'?" Jenny said.

"Okay, well we're not—we have a date tomorrow," said Drew. "But nothing's official yet. I'm just taking her to Mel's. She wanted to try our local cuisine."

Now she's stealing my sidekick. The only friend I had left.

"I see," Jenny said. "You were just waiting to drop that one on me, huh?"

"It's not like that," said Drew. "I didn't want to jinx it."

"Yes yes, everyone likes Kazumi more than Trouble, why should you be any different?" said Jenny. "Don't let me distract you from worshipping her. Thank you for the thrilling yarn, Lockhart. I might even believe half of it. Now if you'll excuse me, I'll show myself out."

Chapter Twenty-One

Rails

THE BACK OF LOCKHART'S POLICE SUV WAS JUST AS UNCOMFORTABLE as Jenny remembered.

"You didn't have to handcuff me," Jenny said as he slammed the car door shut on her. "Ignoring Shelly's texts isn't a crime."

Lockhart climbed into the cab and switched on his radio.

"No, but burning down private property is," he said.

He glanced up to give her a hard stare through the rearview mirror. Jenny shrugged.

"Don't know what you're talking about, chief."

"Really? How about the vandalism on George May's car? Or shoplifting a bottle of tequila from Andy's Liquor? Or breaking all the windows on that Tesla?"

"Couldn't be me, I was with my friend Ash at the arcade last night," said Jenny. "You can even check the video."

Provided Jenny could get a message to Asha about doctoring it first…

Lockhart glared harder and turned the key in the ignition. But before he could pull away, there was a tap on his window.

"Great, what now Drew?" said Jenny.

Lockhart rolled down the window. It wasn't Drew; it was his mother, Mirai Porter.

"Do I need to worry?" Mirai asked.

"Everything's fine, Mirai, just picking this one up to bring her home," Lockhart said, pointing his thumb at the back seat. "She's not under arrest, she just likes sitting back there."

Jenny felt her whole face burning with shame. She couldn't even bear to look at Drew's mom. In the awkward silence, she could imagine Mirai's disapproval radiating off of her in waves of loathing.

"How've you been?" Lockhart asked.

"Work helps," said Mirai. "I don't know what I'll do when Drew goes to college. The house already feels so empty. How did you handle it with Mason?"

"A lot of dark nights of the soul. I got lucky, though." He glanced at Jenny in the rearview mirror. "It helps to have someone to share them with."

"Who's gonna want to date an old widow like me?" said Mirai.

"As if you don't get three marriage proposals a week from rich tech guys who can't take their eyes off you," Lockhart said, and they laughed at some shared joke.

"Rob Haines *is* still single," said Mirai.

"No!" Jenny shouted, but immediately regretted it. "Sorry, he's just… you deserve better."

Mirai's eyebrow twitched.

Oh god, just shut the fuck up, Jenny.

"'Deserve' is a dangerous word, but thank you for saying so," said Mirai. She patted the SUV door and stepped back. "Take care, Jenny."

Jenny spent most of the ride home with Mrs. Porter's words echoing in her head. *Take care, Jenny.* There'd been an edge in her voice, hadn't there? An admonishment. An accusation. She must see Jenny as the worst person on the planet.

The SUV slowed and pulled over to the curb. Jenny finally looked up to find they were still down the street from Jiji and Baba's house.

"Heard you had a chat with the mayor this morning," said Lockhart.

"Can't say he earned my vote."

"Don't underestimate him," said Lockhart. "He holds grudges like a motherfucker, and he'll be all too happy to take revenge once you're

18. If I were you, I'd be doing everything I could to make him forget my name."

"Kinda hard, when my name is—"

"Yeah yeah. Can I trust you to walk from here?" Lockhart asked.

"Why don't you just drive me to the door?"

"It'll look better if Shelly doesn't know I drove you home," said Lockhart.

"For me, or for you?"

"For you, idiot."

JENNY SLIPPED OFF HER SHOES IN THE FOYER AND BRACED HERSELF. From Lockhart's warning, she was expecting an inquisition. Instead, she found Aunt Shelly sitting cross-legged on the couch, working on her laptop, with HGTV on the television. Jenny paused and waited for the inevitable eruption. It didn't come.

"Hey," Jenny said.

Shelly ignored her, staring at the computer screen. She was shopping on The RealReal.

"Oh, right. I get it. The silent treatment," said Jenny. "Baba did this to you and Mom a lot, didn't she?"

Shelly yawned and turned her way. "I don't know what you want me to say, Jennifer," said Shelly. "Nothing I've tried has worked so far. I'm glad you're home. You look like you could use a bath."

She went back to her online shopping.

"Is that it?"

"25 days," said Shelly. "In 25 days, you'll be 18. After that, when you go on one of your manic, self-destructive episodes, Blake won't be driving you home with a stern warning. I hope it was fun."

It was!

Jenny knew exactly what Shelly was doing. This was some kind of reverse psychology to make Jenny feel even worse. Well, it wasn't going to work!

"Better enjoy it while I can, then," said Jenny.

She spun on her heel and stomped up the stairs. Eliza's door was cracked, and when she looked in the room, she found her twin engrossed in the very important business of picking out an outfit to wear for her date. Eliza paused on an elegant white dress, holding it up to her chin.

"Not that one, he's just taking you to Mel's," said Jenny.

"I shall wear what I please," said Eliza. She held up a blouse to her chest, one with a deep neckline.

"Too much cleavage."

"That's the idea."

"But it's *Drew!*" said Jenny. "I can't have him seeing our body like that, it's gross."

"It's *my* body, not ours, and if Drew plays his cards right, he'll be seeing a lot more of it," said Eliza.

Jenny gagged. No, this was so wrong!

"This is a terrible idea, Lizzy, you know that," Jenny said.

"I don't go hassling you about that weird nerdy girl you're dating!"

"We're not *dating*, we're… I don't know what we are," said Jenny. "But Drew is different! Charlie already knew the secret. How are you going to date Drew and keep that quiet?"

"You didn't have a problem telling Jack. *When I specifically asked you not to!!*"

"Girls! No yelling!" their grandfather yelled from his study downstairs.

"I had no choice!" Jenny said. "But the more people we tell, the more likely it gets out and everyone knows. This is for your safety, remember? Not mine."

"So you're saying me dating Drew would be… *dangerous?*" Eliza asked with a sneer.

"That's not what I meant!"

"Honestly, Jenny, the fact that you disapprove only makes me want to date him more," said Eliza. "After the shit you pulled yesterday with Alicia? I've never been more ashamed to be related to you. So please, keep telling me how to live my life, and I'll make sure to do the reverse. Now get the hell out of my room."

She would have argued the point further, but Eliza's words cut deeper than she was prepared to admit. Better to stomp off before Eliza noticed how hurt Jenny was.

She didn't mean it, did she?

Finding out she had a sister was legit the best day of Jenny's life. And now that sister was ashamed it ever happened. Shelly didn't care about Jenny anymore. Drew had a new distraction. Jack would probably never speak to her again. And Dinah? She jumped ship a long time ago.

Fuck it. If they didn't want her, Jenny knew someone who did. She retreated to her room, threw a change of clothes into her backpack, and hurried down the stairs—only for an unexpected obstacle to block her way.

Her grandfather was standing between the stairway and the front door, holding her Doc Martens in his hand. "Where to, Jennifer?" he asked.

"Pixeldrome," Jenny said. "You know, the place where Mom learned how to think for herself."

Jiji's wispy eyebrows shot up, and Jenny regretted her insolence immediately.

"I'm sorry, sir."

His lips pulled into a grim smile. "Laura could think for herself long before she ever took a summer job at that arcade," he said. "And I'd watch that tone when your grandmother is around, or she'll make you drink ipecac syrup until the filth is purged."

"Yes, sir."

Jenny was expecting more, but he surprised her by stepping aside and holding out her shoes.

"Right. Bye then," she said.

As she walked past, Jiji couldn't resist slipping in a mini-lecture.

"I'll tell you what I told your mother," her grandfather said. "Be careful you're not letting someone else think for you. That, and don't get into a car with anyone who's been drinking."

"Yes, sir," Jenny said and walked out into the cold rain.

After a miserable, wet walk to the south side, Jenny spent the rest of her Saturday half-heartedly playing *Final Fight* until Asha's shift was over. Last night's shenanigans had impressed Rob enough to boost her to level 36. Which felt close to 50, but by Jenny's rough estimate, it was only about halfway there in terms of XP. Unless she and Asha robbed a bank, she'd be at this another month, minimum.

25 days…

Fuck. Was she still going to be burning through quarters on the *Simpsons* video game when she was 18?

"Why the long face?" asked Rob.

"Everything sucks," said Jenny.

"You're not wrong, but there are a few exceptions."

"Yeah, like what?"

A glint sparkled in his beady eyes.

"Rick Astley, cocaine, and impromptu dance parties!"

He hopped behind the counter, hit a few buttons, and a new song started playing on the P.A. system.

"The rickroll song?" Jenny asked.

"Fuck that, this is a classic!"

Rob cranked up the volume to ear-bleeding levels and wiped off a space on the counter in front of him. Onto it, he poured out some white powder from a baggie.

Holy shit, you weren't kidding about the cocaine!

"Don't worry!" Rob shouted as he used his Pixeldrome membership card to shape the mound of coke into lines. "I already tested it for fent!"

Jenny watched in fascination as he rolled up a dollar bill and used it to snort a line.

"Goddamn!!!" Rob screamed and wiped his nose.

He gestured to Asha with the rolled-up dollar straw. Asha made a "pbbbt!" noise and waved him off.

"Pussy!" he shouted. "What about you, Trouble?!"

He held out the straw to her. All of Jenny's worst instincts were screaming *do it!* But what was the catch?

"How much XP do I get for it?!" she yelled.

"XP? Fuck you! This shit ain't free!"

"Enjoy your coke, boomer!" Jenny yelled back.

"I'm Gen X!" He seemed so wounded. "Fine! Do a bump and I'll bump you to level 37!"

"Fuck it, then!"

Jenny grabbed the dollar bill, lined herself up for a rail, and snorted hard.

Holy shit! It was like taking 20 pills of Adderall, bottling up the next eight hours of manic focus, and injecting it into her brainstem to experience all at once. The coke burned down the back of her throat. Such a horrible aftertaste. The kind where you had to keep doing more to get rid of it.

"You missed like half the rail!" Rob said, laughing at her and pointing to the line she'd attempted to snort.

"Go easy on her, she's a beginner!" Asha yelled and pulled Jenny away. "Let's dance!"

Suddenly, dancing seemed like the best idea ever. Watch and learn, Lizzy! She jerked and gyrated around Asha, feeling the old '80s song buzz down her nerve endings. No wonder Dad never let Trouble grow up. She'd be solving mysteries in two minutes like this!

Ohhhh!!! That's how Jimmy did it! Duh!

Jenny glanced around. There was Rob, finishing off the coke and jumping up on the counter to perform what must have counted as dancing a million years ago. Nathaniel was doing a bunch of awful thrusting and hand gestures, and that little piece of shit Jimmy Figg was attempting the robot. Jenny shimmied over to him, taking her sweet time to move in step to the beat. The coke high was wearing off, but the invincibility remained.

"Hey, Jimmy!"

Jimmy grinned. Jenny dropped to her knees and punched him in his little dick.

"Thanh Trân says hello!"

Jimmy let out a lusty groan and folded over.

Nathaniel burst out laughing. "Ahahahaha! Suck it, Jimmy!"

"Hey hey hey, don't harsh the vibe!" Rob yelled at them.

He waved her over for another rail. Before Jenny could oblige, Asha pulled her close from behind for a sensual embrace and whispered. "I want you. Now."

Sex on coke? Absolutely!

"Food run!" Asha yelled suddenly, pushing Jenny away. "What'd do y'all want?"

Jenny grinned as Asha took orders she had no intention of picking up, and then hustled her out back.

It's just a date, Eliza had to keep reminding herself. Who knew, maybe the vibes with Drew would be off once they gave it a shot? "Don't overthink this and build it up in your head!" she told her reflection in the mirror. She needed a distraction.

Aunt Shelly was downstairs, working on her laptop. Baba was watching a cooking show on TV, shaking her head at the host's inability to properly temper milk chocolate. Shelly had been acting surprisingly casual about the whole Jenny situation. Too casual. Eliza cautiously took a seat next to her on the couch.

"Whatcha doing?"

"Lesson plans," said Shelly. She banged one of the keys several times. "Motherfucker! Is the WiFi down?"

"See, I told you, Kiki! It worked fine until you messed with it while we were in Okinawa!" said her grandmother.

"Mother!" Shelly turned to Eliza. "Can you go reset the router? It's in Jiji's study, on the bookshelf."

"Why do I have to get up?" asked Eliza.

"Don't start with me, Lizzy!" Shelly snapped. "I'm at my limit right now. My absolute limit!"

Eliza grumbled and got up. As usual, it fell to her to deal with the fallout from her sister's bad behavior.

Her grandfather's study was empty. Eliza found the WiFi router, tucked behind a shelf of old *Ellery Queen Mystery Magazine* issues. The AC adapter had come unplugged, so she plugged it back in and waited for the lights to go green. One of the *Ellery Queen* issues had a faded movie ticket stub tucked into it, like a bookmark. Eliza pulled the magazine out to check the movie. It was 1997's *The Game.* Not one she was familiar with. The bookmarked article was for a short story called *Last Will and Testament* by Patricia Hall.

The hair on the back of her neck perked up at the pairing. A coincidence?

"If you're going to read that, make sure you put it back in order," said her grandfather from the doorway.

"Oh! Sorry, am I messing your collection up?" Eliza asked, wincing.

"Not my collection," he said. "Your mother's."

"My...? These were *Mom's!?*" Eliza asked. "I didn't know she was into mystery stuff. Seemed like more of an RJ thing."

Her grandfather scoffed. "Where do you think he got it from?" he said, a bitter tang creeping into his voice. "When they met, Johnny was trying to write the next, ah, what's that Brad Pitt movie where he's not real and punches people?"

"*Fight Club?*"

"Yes, that one," said her grandfather, snapping his finger. "He wanted to write like that. Every agent rejected him, so he got Valerie to pay to self-publish his book. Total flop, hah! Johnny wanted to be a *rock star* writer. Until he met Laura."

His hands clenched when he said "rock star," like he could still strangle the bastard. Eliza thought about Dad's diaries that they'd found at Schloss Schwarzwald. She could see it: the edgier tone, the wannabe gonzo style.

"What was his book called?" she asked.

"*The Strangler in Sausalito,* or something stupid like that," he said. Eliza's eyes widened. "He needed Laura to introduce him to the concept of a cozy mystery. People don't want to read all that ugliness and degeneracy. They want to spend time with their fictional friend, solving a murder that won't make them feel bad." He sighed. "I suppose you could say Johnny was honoring your mother, in his way, writing all those books about your sister."

"You don't sound convinced," said Eliza.

"I was very sorry to hear about his passing," said her grandfather.

"I always thought I'd give him a real piece of my mind one day, and then it was too late."

He gave Eliza a hard stare and ran a hand through his thinning wisps of hair.

"You need to heal the rift between you and your sister, Elizabeth," he said.

Eliza frowned. "Why should I? She's been a monster to me all year. If I let that slide, she'll never stop walking all over me."

"Sometimes, we must show grace," he said, and when his voice shook, Eliza's vision blurred. "I chose pride over grace 18 years ago, and I've been living with an empty seat at the dinner table ever since. Don't tell your Baba I said so, she still argues with Michelle about it. But Michelle was right. We didn't have to lose Laura then, and we can't lose Jennifer now. I don't think she'll listen to an old man like me, but you're her twin. She has to listen to you."

He took the *Ellery Queen* issue back from Eliza and carefully replaced it on the shelf.

"You unplugged the WiFi router, didn't you? So I'd come in here," Eliza said. "That's very Jenny of you."

Her grandfather smiled. "The Onishis pride ourselves on clever solutions."

"All right," Eliza said. "I'll try."

Kazumi:	Drew, you're going to hate me
Drewboo:	What for?
Kazumi:	I'm so sorry, but I need a raincheck on our date
Kazumi:	Some family stuff has come up that I have to deal with
Drewboo:	Damn
Kazumi:	I'm not blowing you off, I promise! I really wanted to go!
Drewboo:	I'll hold you to that!
Kazumi:	Please do! I was so looking forward to it. Bloody hell, this sucks

Drewboo: I'll forgive you if you send me a pic of the outfit you were gonna wear

Kazumi: Absolutely not! You're going to have to wait, mister!

Kazumi: But I might send you something else… 😳

Drewboo: *afraid to say anything*

Kazumi: Stay tuned. Thanks for understanding.

Drewboo: I'm an understanding guy

Kazumi: XOXO see you Monday

Eliza flopped back on her bed and sighed. Jenny had better appreciate this! Now she was kinda craving Mel's, though. She heaved another sigh and opened her message thread with her sister.

D: We should talk. Can you meet me at the Mel's in Santa Rosa tomorrow night?

It took several minutes for Jenny to reply.

T: What time?

D: 7

T: See you then

Chapter Twenty-Two

We Used to Be Friends

Like everything else Jenny had looked forward to before her senior year, cocaine sex ended up being a total letdown. Maybe it was because by the time they found a sufficiently private alley to park in, the buzz had completely worn off, and Jenny felt like the last half-inch of warm tequila and backwash at the end of a party. Maybe it was because Asha was annoyed at Jenny for doing coke with Rob, so her spirit wasn't in it. After 10 minutes of lackluster effort, she gave her quasi-girlfriend a tap on the shoulder, and they agreed to get dinner instead.

Asha's roommate was watching TV in the living room when they got back to her apartment, so they retreated to her bedroom and ate on the floor. Jenny's watch vibrated with a text from Eliza.

Ugh, what now, bitch?

She read the message twice, not really understanding it.

> **D:** We should talk. Can you meet me at the Mel's in
> Santa Rosa tomorrow night?

Wasn't her date with Drew at Mel's? Jenny dismissed the alert and winced at the monster headache she was getting.

"Are you okay, babe?" Asha asked. "You haven't touched your Chick-fil-A?"

They'd been watching a trippy anime called *Serial Experiments Lain*, and Jenny's chicken sandwich was getting cold on the greasy fast food wrapper in her lap.

"It's just my bitch of a—er, cousin," Jenny said. "She's trying to date my only friend at BSA. They're going to dinner tomorrow…"

She wants me there so she can tell Drew the secret.

Jenny took a bite of her cold sandwich, choking on the dry chicken.

"So?" said Asha. "Fuck 'em both."

"Yeah, but this… I can't let them date, it fucks a lot of shit up for me. It's like worlds colliding, you know?"

"Their dinner needs to be a total bust, then," said Asha. "What would ruin the date for your cousin?"

Eliza had been thirsting after Drew for over a year. He'd have to do something heinous, like insult *Harry Potter*, or act way too aggressive and pushy, but Drew wouldn't do that.

"I don't know," said Jenny. "The way my cousin talks about this guy, I feel like all he has to do is literally not puke all over himself and they'll hook up."

"There you go, slip something into his drink," said Asha. "Make him hurl."

"Hmm. What even does that?" Jenny got her phone out. "Let's see: 'what drug makes you vomit?' … Fuck you Google! I don't have an eating disorder!"

"For real?" Asha asked. "More woke bullshit."

"Isn't there, like, some syrup they used to give you if you accidentally drank bleach?" asked Jenny.

"Ipecac?" said Asha.

"Right, yes! My grandmother has some! Perfect!"

Except she wouldn't put the syrup in Drew's drink. She'd put it in Eliza's. That ought to teach her.

"See, where would you be without me? Probably some pathetic sex crime victim." She scowled at Jenny. "Doing coke with Rob!? Jesus Christ, Jenny! Slow the fuck down!"

"Jealous much? I wouldn't touch Rob, he's like 50, and gross, and a dude."

"Do you honestly think he cares about any of that?" Asha asked. "That's what the coke is for."

"I had it under control," Jenny said.

"Sure you did," said Asha. "I don't want to be dating no crack ho."

Jenny tried to roll her eyes, but the remark stung. She'd thought she was being fun and spontaneous and based, and now Asha was punishing her for it. Wasn't Jenny the one stooping to date her?

"You're not, relax," Jenny said.

She dropped her bland chicken sandwich and texted Eliza back. 7:00 PM tomorrow night. It was a date.

Mel's Drive-In wasn't actually a drive-in. It was one of those retro '50s diners with sparkly red vinyl booths, jukeboxes, and a bunch of old-timey rockabilly memorabilia. Jenny had to take a Lyft over, burning another hefty chunk of her ever-dwindling funds, and even though she arrived 20 minutes early, Eliza was already there, waiting alone in a booth and sipping on a Dr Pepper. Now, how to slip the ipecac syrup into her drink?

Wait a minute, Eliza wasn't wearing her Kazumi makeup.

Her sister had her hair pulled up in a bun, and Jenny's black shirt with three-quarter-length sleeves on. If Jenny wasn't rocking a mohawk and Mom's old jacket, they'd be twins again.

Not knowing what her plan was, Jenny found herself walking inside and taking a seat across from Eliza. "Hey," she said.

"Hey," Eliza replied and forced a smile.

A waiter approached, carrying a basket of french fries and a butterscotch sundae.

"Can I get you anything else?" the waiter asked.

Eliza gave Jenny a questioning eyebrow. Jenny ordered a Dr Pepper too, then waited for the server to leave.

"Is this for Drew?" Jenny asked, pointing to the sundae.

"No, it's for you," Eliza said.

She pushed the sundae over to Jenny's side and moved her fries to the middle of the table where they could share. *Why is she being so nice?* Jenny tried to keep her head on a swivel, ready for a trap, but she found herself overcome with the strangest fascination as she watched Eliza dip her fries in ranch dressing.

"What?" Eliza said, chewing on her fry.

"Something's weird," Jenny said. "I can't put my finger on it." She reached for the ketchup, in a daze.

"Oh, I think I know," said Eliza. She smiled for real this time and wiped the salt from her lips. "We've never done this before." She gestured vaguely to the diner surroundings. "We were always too paranoid, back when we first met."

"We ate at the Oxbow Market that one time, last Thanksgiving," said Jenny.

"We ordered at Oxbow, we ate in the park," said Eliza. She settled into her seat and let out a sigh of contentment. "This is nice."

"You eat your fries with ranch?" Jenny asked.

"Yeah, it's delicious."

Jenny was dubious. Still, she bypassed her ketchup to try a fry with ranch. Maybe she was just hungry, but it was the best fry she'd ever tasted. The perfect crispness, the salt, the tang of the ranch... How had they never shared this? A whirlwind of memories overwhelmed her. *Getting that Ace of Clubs tattoo to match Lizzy's. Huddling under a blanket for warmth in the treehouse, sharing their favorite YouTube clips. Ordering two sets of ridiculous outfits and playing dress-up in the mansion while Shelly was out of town.* How much else would they miss?

What the fuck am I doing?

Hot tears welled in her eyes. "I've missed you, Lizzy."

"Oh hey, what's wrong?" Eliza said, touching her hand.

"I just—I just realized," said Jenny, fighting back sobs. "I was going to do something bad, but I-I won't. It's not you I hate, it's me. But I love you more."

"Jenny, no," Eliza sniffled. "Great, now you've got me crying!"

"Twins!" Jenny said and laughed through her sobs. "Drew is going to think we're both insane when he sees us."

"He's not coming, dummy," said Eliza. "I canceled our date."

"What? Why?"

"Because this was more important. Jiji said I can't lose you to that stupid arcade the way he lost Mom."

"You won't. You won't," said Jenny. It was like a dam had broken inside her, and half a year's buried emotions came gushing out. "I just… I thought being back, you know, senior year? It was going to be so good. But it's been so hard, Lizzy. It really sucked. And I'm such a shit sister. I was going to sabotage your date with ipecac syrup, and I told myself it was to keep our secret intact, but really I was just jealous. Because if you had Drew, I'd have no one left in the whole world."

"You've got that Asha girl, don't you?" Eliza asked.

"She's awful!"

"I mean, I wasn't gonna say it, but… ipecac, seriously? Like to make me puke?"

"I know, I suck. I'm so sorry. For everything. The only one who deserves to be puking tonight is me."

Jenny pulled out the bottle of ipecac syrup from her purse and unscrewed the cap. She was about to drink it when Eliza yanked it out of her hand.

"You're not drinking that, you crazy bitch!" Eliza said. "Eat your sundae before it melts! And this isn't even ipecac, this is where Shelly hides her Delta-9 THC oil."

"For real?"

"Don't tell Jiji and Baba," said Eliza. "She says it helps her sleep."

"I can't even picture Shelly high," said Jenny, cracking a smile. "Fucking Lockhart, I'll bet this is his influence."

Eliza laughed. "Look at what regular sex does to Clan Onishi! Mom got preggers, blackmailed Val, and died. I turned into a vapid mean girl. You became a total fucking degenerate. And now that Shelly's getting that big Lockhart D, she's a stoner who goes blonde and wears shorter skirts than I do!"

"Please never say 'big Lockhart D' ever again," said Jenny.

"Come on, you know he's packing."

"I might throw up for real." Jenny plugged her ears and retched. "Shelly getting high. No shot. I guess we all have our secrets."

"Since we're sharing again, how the hell did you rig the Homecoming ballots?" Eliza asked.

Jenny tried to grin, but thinking about Homecoming made her sad now. "I should have rigged the vote for you," Jenny said. "That was selfish of me. And I ruined things between you and Jack. I'll talk to him. He can hate me, but not you. And I'll make Drew take you someplace nicer on your real date."

"You need to talk to Alicia," Eliza said.

"Oh god, she'll murder me if I try," Jenny said, grimacing. "By the way, talk about secrets. I should tell you some things Drew found out about Alicia and your big hero Lockhart. Shit... Drew. He must hate me now too."

"I doubt that."

"You can tell him about us," Jenny said. "It's okay."

"No, you were right, the fewer people who know the better," said Eliza. "I can still date him as Kazu." She ate another fry drowning in ranch. "Ipecac syrup. That's beneath you, Jenny. That's like a prank Mason would pull. Or like when Jimmy crapped his pants at Jack's Christmas party? Wait—was that you?"

"No, I wish," Jenny said, laughing and dabbing her eyes with a napkin. "Actually..."

The neurons in her brain exploded with crosstalk, linking together so many random events from the past year. Obvious connections she should have made sooner, if she'd been paying attention instead of wallowing in misery at Pixeldrome. Thanh's hair. Homecoming. Jimmy at Christmas...

"They were all for XP," she said to herself. "He's been after you all year."

"Huh?" asked Eliza. "Who?"

"Jimmy. Jeez, where to begin?" said Jenny. Everything about the arcade seemed so stupid now when she tried to explain it to Eliza. "Don't judge, but I kinda did coke last night. I know, it was so retarded of me, and I'll never do it again. Shit, I have to stop saying that word. I've been spending too much time around Nathaniel. But when I blew a rail, I suddenly realized how Jimmy Figg shaved Thanh's hair and got away with it: he got Rob or Asha to alter the video timestamps at

Pixeldrome to give him an alibi."

Eliza tilted her head, concerned, but interested. "Are those people just psychotic at that place?"

"Yes, but it's also part of Rob's RAM philosophy," said Jenny. She briefly explained the concept of random acts of misanthropy and Pixeldrome's XP system between spoonfuls of butterscotch sundae. "The owner, Rob, gives extra points if you do something mean or misanthropic. It's all part of his twisted Peter Pan syndrome, I think. Jimmy hated you for rejecting him and would have been trying to earn more XP by shaving your head, but he fucked it up and got Thanh by mistake because she had your hoodie on."

"Okay, that follows. But what do you mean he's been after me all year?" asked Eliza.

"Remember the pigs at Homecoming? And the Stranger mannequin? That had to be Jimmy, too. Probably with help from his loser friend Nathaniel. Targeting you *and* me, because I accused him and embarrassed him at lunch. There's been other stuff, too. Remember the stink bomb at Career Day?"

"Oh, Charlie mentioned that," Eliza said. "I'd actually been thinking of checking out the photography booth—oh wow!" Her eyes lit up, making a connection of her own. "I told Charlie I was going to that booth. And Jimmy was nearby! He probably overheard us. But I changed my mind and left instead."

"And his accident at the Christmas party," said Jenny.

"When he tried to corner me under the mistletoe, I thought I saw his hand near my drink, so I took his. Hah! In your fucking face, Jimmy!" Eliza's eyes lit up. "Wait! That fire in the trash can at lunch! He tried to give me a valentine, but I put it on Meghan's tray to throw away. There must have been something nasty waiting for me if I'd opened it."

"I never mentioned it, but when I went to see Jack at the Crow's Nest, posing as Kazumi, someone tried to shoot me with a paintball gun," said Jenny. "Those were all XP missions. Must have been. And Asha never said a word to me about them. That fucking bitch."

She paused. There was something else about that paintball incident that nagged at her.

"We need to put an end to this," said Eliza. "And not in some 'oh, we've turned the tables, the semen ended up in your clam chowder, not mine!' way. We need to shut their whole stupid club down. This is what Trouble and Danger were put on this earth for. We solve mysteries and we right wrongs."

Jenny beamed, and her heart felt full to bursting. It didn't seem fair that she could be so horrible to her sister yet get this much love in return.

"You're being too nice. I deserve worse."

"You do," said Eliza. "But I'll let you in on one more secret." She leaned closer and stole a bite of Jenny's sundae. "I've missed you too."

THEY TALKED FOR HOURS, CATCHING UP ON EVERYTHING THEY'D missed in each other's lives. Jenny wanted to know all about what happened with Charlie, and Eliza had so many questions about this Asha girl and Jenny becoming a dirtbag gamer. And of course, there was all the hot gossip about the Unfridgeables—

"Except we don't call ourselves that anymore, after Nilay." Eliza grimaced.

"Oof. For real."

Jenny told Eliza how Alicia lost her leg (*What a little firecracker!*), and how Blake helped her dispose of her shithead father (*So hot!*). Something had unlocked inside of her sister. Eliza had been prepared to bite her tongue and suffer through Jenny's crabby attitude, but her mood was lighter than air. Eliza hadn't seen her like this since they met on the roof of the psych ward that night in LA. A chill shot down her spine at the realization: she might have saved Jenny's life again tonight. Eliza would happily trade all her lingering resentments to get her sister back.

When she told her about RJ being the author of *The Stranger of Sausalito*, Jenny was giddy with excitement, though not sure what to do with the info. Eliza was just as shocked to learn the grisly details of Mr. Webb's demise, and everything about the secret heirloom clue,

Pixeldrome, and its creep of an owner.

"I seriously thought you were just obsessed with that arcade because of Asha," Eliza said. "A game token? What a weird clue."

"I can't say Asha hasn't been a bonus," said Jenny. "She's not—I shouldn't talk shit. I think, deep down, she's just as miserable as me. I told myself I was a good influence on her, but maybe we're worse for each other."

"What are you going to do about that?" Eliza asked.

"If she goes along with the plan tomorrow? Well, I guess things will work themselves out."

They decided that the best way to deal with Rob Haines would be to pit him against another enemy of theirs: Valerie Valentine. Eliza was about to quiz Jenny on the details when a group of noisy college kids walked into the restaurant.

"Oh no," she said.

"What?"

Jenny turned around to look. The college kids were boisterous and full of energy, joking with each other and feeding on all the sudden attention they were receiving. And there in the back, laughing along with them, was a tall blonde with purple streaks framing her heart-shaped face. Dinah Black.

As if feeling their stares, Dinah glanced their way and did a double take, mildly surprised. She said something to the girl next to her and walked over. "Careful, girls, you never know when someone from Blackbird Springs might come in and recognize you," she said.

Eliza watched Jenny's brain furiously calculating the body language between Dinah and the girl she'd spoken to by the entrance.

"What are you doing here?" Eliza asked.

"Some of the peeps in my college class invited me to an escape room," said Dinah. "It's like an anti-Valentine's Day get-together for all the single folks. What are you two doing here?"

Since Jenny seemed incapable of speech at the moment, Eliza answered. "Turning over a new leaf, and plotting revenge on our enemies."

"Plus ça change, plus c'est la même chose," said Dinah.

Jenny's concentration broke, and she smiled. "You're not one of them, Dinah. An enemy, that is."

"I should hope not, I'm the best thing that ever happened to you."

Eliza took a sip of her soda to hide her grin as Jenny's face warmed.

"All single folks, huh?" Jenny asked, nodding to the college kids.

"You know how it is," said Dinah. "Nobody's *really* looking to stay single."

One of the college boys called out to Dinah and waved for her to rejoin them.

"Case in point," Dinah added, rolling her eyes. "I better not keep them waiting. Wouldn't want one of them seeing past this thing and noticing you're twins." She reached out and ruffled Jenny's wavy mohawk. "Happy Valentine's Day, Jenny Valentine."

Dinah walked back to her college friends. Eliza studiously scrolled Instagram on her phone until Jenny had collected herself.

"Do you think…?"

"One thing at a time, Trouble," said Eliza. "We've got an aging Gen X loser to destroy."

Chapter Twenty-Three
The Medic's Tale

THERE WAS NO SCHOOL FOR JENNY IN THE MORNING BECAUSE she was suspended. Shelly surprised her by taking the day off to personally tutor her on all the lessons she was missing. Jenny didn't know what Eliza had told Shelly, but her aunt was in her magnanimous era, never mentioning how cunty Jenny had been for months. Jenny returned the favor by being a good student and earnestly following Shelly's teaching. By lunchtime, she'd plowed through all her lessons and homework for the whole week.

"Imagine where you could have gone to college if you applied yourself like this from the start," said Shelly. They were in the kitchen, making a salad for lunch. "Maybe we can still get you into Calistoga."

"I don't want to go there," said Jenny.

"It's February, Jennifer, and you haven't even applied anywhere," said Shelly. "Your options are dwindling."

Jenny paused chopping vegetables.

"I want to do something special for Jiji and Baba," she said. "Their anniversary is soon, isn't it?"

"It is," said Shelly warily. "What'd you have in mind?"

"Maybe a little trip out of town? Something fun? I have a little extra money." Jenny wiped the last slice of cucumber off the end of her chef's knife. "Also, I need to go to Pixeldrome this afternoon."

"And there it is. What makes you think you're not grounded till you're 25?" asked Shelly.

"I only need to go a couple more times."

"I'd rather you didn't go at all."

"My investigation is almost done."

"Is that what you've been doing there this whole time? Investigating?"

"I haven't *not* been investigating," said Jenny. "I've learned a lot about the owner, that Rob guy. I think he and Mom—well, I'm not sure exactly what went down, but I can't shake the feeling that he took advantage of her."

"It wouldn't surprise me," said Shelly. "Laura always resented how strict your Baba was. She worried about not fitting in when she went to college. I think she wanted to 'catch up' beforehand."

"And that piece of shit would have been eager to help," said Jenny. "Even if nothing ever happened between them, he's not a good guy, and people need to know."

"I don't want you doing anything that could get you arrested," said Shelly.

"I won't!" said Jenny. "In fact, I was thinking we could do a movie night on Sunday. You can even invite Lockhart, so he can keep an eye on me."

Shelly narrowed her eyes. "What are you planning?"

Jenny smiled innocently.

"Did you ever do that?" Jenny asked. "'Catch up,' like Mom?"

The flush of red in Shelly's cheeks answered the question for her.

"Eventually," said Shelly, with a far less innocent smile in return.

WITH ACTUAL PERMISSION FROM AUNT SHELLY THIS TIME, JENNY rode her bike down to Pixeldrome. The usual suspects were all there, crowded around a fancy new video game machine that Rob had moved into the spot previously occupied by the foosball table. It was a fighter jet game called *Afterburner*, and the player sat in the "cockpit," rocking up and down while they "flew" the plane.

"Check it out, it's the same one John Connor plays in *T2*," said

Rob.

If he felt any shame or awkwardness over trying to get an underage girl blitzed on coke a few days before, he didn't show it.

"I don't know what that means, but congratulations to you," said Jenny. "Is Asha here?"

He jerked his thumb to the back office. "I got her doing the books," said Rob. "Careful, I think she's on the rag."

How charming. Nathaniel yanked Jimmy Figg out of the *Afterburner* cockpit so he could have a turn. He plopped his bulk into the pilot seat and sniffed. "Dude, did you queef in here? It smells like dirty taint," said Nathaniel.

"Smells like your mom!" said Jimmy.

Jenny was going to savor ruining these guys' lives like a tall glass of *Ressort Rouge*. She walked to the back office and peeked her head in. Asha was messing with spreadsheets on the computer, and when she spotted Jenny, she hardly shrugged a greeting her way.

"Rob tells me you're on the rag," Jenny said. "Must be cool to have a boss who's so attentive to your cycles."

"Your phone broken or something?" asked Asha sourly.

"Sorry, my aunt took it," said Jenny. "I could barely get out this afternoon, and I can't stay long. I'm kinda grounded all week."

"Because of your cousin?" Asha perked up. "Did you make her date puke all over?"

"Didn't get a chance," Jenny said, trying to act bummed out over it. "Shelly dropped the hammer on me before I could. It's because of the Alicia thing. I'm in the penalty box until my suspension is over, I guess. On the bright side, she made Kazu cancel her date too."

"Lame. You're not getting any XP for that."

"I've got a better idea for XP." Jenny took a seat in the chair next to Asha, seeing her quasi-girlfriend with new—but not unfeeling— eyes. "It's risky, though. If it went south, and you couldn't work here anymore, what would you do?"

"What, like if Pixeldrome burned down or something?" Asha yawned. "Probably beg Rob to keep me on payroll as his personal assistant or something. I'll be the Ghislane to his Epstein if it keeps me in ducats and DoorDash."

Jenny's heart sank. "Dude, that's vile."

"I'm joking! Don't be lame."

"Okay, but you'd still want to work with Rob? Not somewhere else? You're pretty smart, I'll bet you could be doing better."

"In this job market? In Blackbird Springs? Fucking please," said Asha. "I'd be lucky to earn minimum wage. You've probably never noticed because you still live at home, but this is an expensive fucking town to live in, and Rob pays me well."

"Oh," said Jenny. "I didn't realize."

"Besides, I like working for Rob. I mean, sure, he's a horny creep, but he leaves me alone, and he never lectures me on my attitude or customer service or any of that shit. I can be myself here, ya know? That's why you like it here, isn't it?"

"I guess it is," said Jenny. "All right, let's go pitch my new mission to Rob. But just in case, switch the cameras off."

"For real?"

"Like I said, it's risky," said Jenny.

Asha futzed with the security cameras, then they rejoined the others out in the game room. Rob was in the *Afterburner* cockpit now, and he had some cheesy '80s song blasting on the P.A. system.

"Trouble! Bubby!! Wanna take a ride on the Danger Zone?" Rob shouted and gestured to his lap.

I'd rather die.

"Fuck your stupid kiddie ride," said Jenny. "I've got a random act of misanthropy so good you're gonna want in on it."

"Do you now?" his eyes sparkled. "Let's hear it."

She waved Jimmy and Nathaniel closer and unfolded her scheme. They were going to break into the Valentine Foundation offices and tamper with their spring mailer. Jenny's pitch was to stuff a bunch of envelopes with a replacement newsletter full of offensive words and images. It would crater Valerie and the Foundation's reputation in Blackbird Springs.

Rob loved the idea of sending out a nastygram to all the rich local donors who looked down on him, and sticking it to Val was icing on the cake.

Then Nathaniel had an idea he liked even more.

"What if we do it more subtle?" Nathaniel suggested. "You know, like the graphic design just happens to look like a dick or something. A little more plausible deniability?"

"Gay," said Jimmy.

"Let me finish, shitbird!" Nathaniel cracked his knuckles and grinned. "And then at the bottom, we leave a QR code for people to scan and donate. Except it's not going to the Valentine Foundation, it's going to us."

"The Human Fund!" said Rob.

"Seems like they'd eventually trace that back to you," said Asha.

Of the four of them, she was the only one who seemed wary of Jenny's plan.

"Can you use crypto?" asked Jenny.

"Bitcoin is ass now," said Jimmy. "Ever since the Satoshi crash last year."

Heheheheh go Nari!

"Doesn't matter, we'd only be using it to wash the money," said Rob. He bit his lip, thinking. "Yeah, I think I could set that up."

"Do it, then," said Jenny. "I'm grounded all week, but I should be free this Sunday night. Can you have it ready by then?"

Rob nodded. "You planning to break in on your own? They've probably got a security system."

"I can beat it, but I'll need help on this one." Jenny looked at the others. "You guys have the balls to back me up?"

Jimmy and Nathaniel were in, but Asha waffled.

"Someone should probably stay at Pixeldrome," she said. "I can be your alibi, in case Trouble's plan goes tits up."

Does she suspect, or is her bark bigger than her bite?

"Makes sense!" Jenny said, faking a smile. She turned to Rob. "If I pull this off, I'm level 50, right?"

"You pull this off, and I'll give you a personal tour of the VIP room," said Rob. "Same one I gave your mom."

Gross.

They hashed out the details and agreed to meet up that Sunday, an hour before closing. Honestly, it was a pretty good scam. Jenny was almost bummed she'd have to ruin it. Then Jimmy suggested they use the stolen money to order "the works" at an Asian massage parlor, and Jenny was reminded all over again why she and Eliza needed to crush these assholes.

IF KAZUMI'S REPUTATION HAD BEEN SHAKY BEFORE, RETURNING to school after her cousin sent Alicia Aaron fleeing in tears was doing it no favors. Alicia was nowhere to be seen, and the rest of the Unfridgeables wore veiled looks of scorn for poor, innocent Kazu. Eliza intercepted Jack after school and found her brother distraught, furious with Jenny and Eliza both.

"Alicia broke up with me over text and she won't return my calls," he revealed. "She says she never wants to see me or anyone else from school ever again. I'm worried about her, and it's all your fault!"

"I'm Eliza, not Jenny."

"You know what I mean! You're both toxic as fuck. Honestly, you might be the worst thing that ever happened to me."

"We're going to make it better," said Eliza, wincing at how hollow it sounded. "Believe it or not, Jenny feels worse about this than anyone. She's going through a really hard time."

"Oh, I'll bet, let's not lose sight of who the real victim here is!" Jack fumed. "Everyone be sure to pity Jenny fucking Valentine!"

"I'm not saying what she did wasn't horrible," said Eliza. "I'm just asking for a little grace. She wasn't in her right mind."

"See, now I'm wondering if you actually are Jenny—wait, you know what? I don't care. Fuck you both. Leave me alone."

He stomped off just as Drew was walking up. His grin for Kazumi morphed into a frown of concern when he passed Jack. "What was that about?" Drew asked.

"He's very cross with my cousin, and therefore me too," said Eliza, switching back to her posh accent.

"You didn't have anything to do with that."

"That never seems to matter around here, innit?" said Eliza. "I did hear you tried to stage a, uh, what do you call it over here? An intervention of some sort with Jenny? That was kind of you."

"For all the good it did," said Drew.

"Don't be so hasty, it may yet have an impact. One can hope."

"So not to be pushy, but how are you feeling about that raincheck?" Drew asked. "Can you do dinner this Sunday?"

"Oooh, not that day, bollocks." Eliza grimaced. "Family thing again, Sundays are rubbish for me. Perhaps Saturday? We could do an activity? Go somewhere fun?"

"What, like an arcade?"

"No!" Eliza shouted, a bit too forcefully. "Something outdoors. A hike, maybe?"

"It's a date," said Drew. "Let's just hope it doesn't rain."

BEFORE SHE WENT HOME, JENNY AND ASHA FOOLED AROUND IN Asha's car on her break. It felt weird, doing this when she was actively plotting against Asha. She didn't want to tip her off that anything was amiss, though. After some perfunctory heavy petting, Jenny lied and said she needed to go. She wouldn't be able to see Asha again till Sunday night. As she rode her bike home, her girlfriend's lip gloss still on her tongue, she knew with certainty that she would never taste Asha's bubblegum lips again.

This was new. Jenny had never been the one to end things. It didn't feel good. Was this what Dinah was going through last year? Or the girl who shall not be named, back in Glendale?

She was getting dangerously close to forgiving that bitch a tiny bit when Shelly texted.

ShellsBells: Can you pick up some tampons?

Jenny: At least we know you're not pregnant

ShellsBells: Jennifer.

There was a Nugget Market a few blocks over, so Jenny changed course to buy Shelly's tampons and a wedge of Vella high-moisture

Monterey Jack. As she walked out of the store, she sensed someone in the corner of her vision. They'd been heading her way, but stopped and turned around. Someone wearing a uniform, walking back to their ambulance. A paramedic!

"Hey!" Jenny called out and ran after him. "Are you stalking me?"

He stopped, and his shoulders tensed. When he turned, it was just as she suspected. He was that paramedic with the soul patch. The one who'd been staring at her after Mr. Webb was murdered. The one Eliza said was mean-mugging her in the Crow's Nest penthouse after Nilay was killed.

"I don't want any trouble," he said.

"Well you've got her!" said Jenny. "Where do I know you from? Not the park, or the Crow's Nest. I've seen you somewhere else before."

The paramedic (his name tag read: **Dalton**) clenched his jaw in frustration.

"I was one of the medics you called to Valentine Manor, the year before last," he said. "When Mr. Carnegie suffered a stroke."

That was where she'd seen him!

"You know, they call you the Angel of Death at the hospital."

"Very original," said Jenny. She studied him with maximum Trouble-scrutiny. He was still wound up. "But that's not what you wanted to talk to me about, is it?"

Dalton smiled meekly at her deduction, and his whole body seemed to deflate. "It's not," he said. "That… that wasn't the first time I'd been to Valentine Manor. I was there a few months before."

Jenny's heart froze to the core.

"Me and my partner were first on the scene when RJ Valentine… you know." Dalton glanced over his shoulder and moved closer. "I know I shouldn't be saying this, but I feel like I owe you an apology. If we'd acted faster, maybe he would have made it."

"What are you saying?"

"When we found him, RJ was unconscious, but his vitals were okay. No tachycardia, respiration was steady. His condition was concerning, sure, but not something we'd do ALS for. Advanced life support. If we'd known the head injury was that bad, we might have had him in the ambulance twice as fast."

"I see," Jenny said calmly, as her mind reeled. What if they'd moved RJ faster? What if RJ had recovered from his coma? What if she could have hunted the Stranger with his help, just like in the books?

Dalton's face was rigid, pleading. He wanted absolution. He wanted Jenny to say there was nothing he could have done.

"Did he ever wake up, in the ambulance? Even for a second?"

He shook his head. "I was driving. I guess his condition deteriorated later. Head injuries are… tricky."

Jenny tried counting to 10 in her head. There was nothing to be done about it now. *What ifs* at this point were little more than fantasies at best, and maybe closer to self-harm. She glanced at the wedge of Vella cheese in her hand and couldn't imagine wanting to eat anything less just then.

"Do you like cheese, Dalton?" she asked.

"Uh, sure. Vella?"

"It's yours." Jenny pressed the wedge of cheese into Dalton's hand and plucked the Certified Paramedic pin from his lapel. "I'm taking this as a marker. Someday I might need your help, and then we'll call it even. Sound fair?"

"Absolutely," said Dalton.

As Jenny rode home, her excitement about taking revenge on the Pixeldrome gang faded to an obligation. She would deal with these people, as any good Girl Detective would, and then it was time to get back to the important business: RJ's dangerous game, and the identity of his Stranger.

Chapter Twenty-Four
Movie Night

ELIZA SPENT THE WHOLE WEEK PRETENDING TO BE CHILL FRIENDS with Drew at lunch, avoiding any mention of Alicia, who had yet to return to class, and counting down the days to her hiking date. So of course it rained on Saturday.

"My luck is absolute shite!" said Eliza.

"It's just me, you can stop talking like that," said Jenny.

Her sister was pinning Eliza's hair up to hide it under a ski cap.

"I rather like it though, luv," said Eliza. "I think you're a wee bit jealous that your accent wasn't up to scratch, and Jack clocked you after one go."

"Whatevs. So you just watched a movie with Drew in his masturbatorium?"

"I suggested *Crazy, Stupid, Love*, but then he found out I'd never seen *Scott Pilgrim* and insisted we watch it," said Eliza. "And so I sat there for two hours, waiting for him to make a move, and he never did, so I hugged him, and kissed him on the cheek, and I left. The end."

"That's just how he is," said Jenny. "You're gonna have to make the first move. I seem to recall him saying that Alicia basically rested her boobs on his shoulder before he worked up the nerve to kiss her."

"I'm not doing that!" said Eliza. "You need to talk to him."

"Me?! For all I know he hates me now."

"You know he doesn't. He's your number one fan." Eliza stood up and pulled on a black beanie. "Now if you'll excuse me, I must go bamboozle some incels."

"Not Nathaniel, his pederast aunt punched his V-card," said Jenny.

"Excuse me!?"

"That's how they act around each other, okay. So if you're ever not sure how to respond, just say the most vile thing imaginable. And maybe toss in a few ethnic slurs."

Eliza wanted to gag. Then a stray thought struck her.

"What if this is all just a troll job by Dad?" she asked. "What if he left the game token to the Stranger to keep him occupied playing video games with those losers for months?"

"Like a honeypot?" asked Jenny. "Huh, maybe. If so, the joke was on me."

She walked Eliza to the window in her bedroom and gave her a hand as she slipped out and dropped into the backyard. Eliza collected herself on the grass and looked back. Jenny tossed her down a box of Pocky.

"In case you get hungry," Jenny said, winking.

Eliza smirked and hurried off into the night. How long had it been since they'd worked together as a team? Sand between her toes and daredevil feats weren't all a girl needed to function. She needed her twin, too. The Valentine girls' sister act was back, and who better to shake the rust off against than those Pixeldrome bozos.

THE LAST OF JENNY'S TEN GRAND FROM DREW HAD GONE TO FUND a week-long trip for Jiji and Baba to Seattle. They had old friends up north from their college days. It was the least Jenny could do after being such a miserable granddaughter all year. Fortunately, with Eliza back on her side, they could share all the money Jenny had funneled to Kazumi's bank account, so she wasn't totally broke anymore.

Kazumi, meanwhile, was supposed to be hanging with the Bitchy Brigade, which meant Jenny had Shelly and Lockhart all to herself for movie night.

"All right, you two. What are we watching?" Jenny asked as she came downstairs.

Then she witnessed a harrowing sight in the kitchen and screamed.

"What is it?" Shelly asked, closing the fridge in alarm.

Jenny pointed in horror at Lockhart, who was in the middle of preparing some guacamole. He'd just plopped a massive spoonful of whipped cream cheese into the bowl of mashed avocados.

"That is a hate crime!" she yelled.

"I had to carve off a bunch of brown spots," said the sheriff. "The cream cheese will give it volume."

"That is the most gringo shit I've ever seen!" Jenny said. "I'm telling Drew!"

"You're not even Mexican, but if you don't want any, then good," Lockhart said, grinning. "More for me and Shells."

"Make yourself useful and queue up a movie," said Shelly.

"We each picked one of our favorites that the other hasn't seen," said Lockhart.

Shelly handed Jenny two Blu-ray discs and lowered her voice. "You should see how he makes ramen."

"Why do you put up with this?" Jenny whispered.

"Because there's a lot more to relationships," Shelly whispered back. "He makes me happy."

Jenny scowled. How awful.

"Fine. Let's see, what are we feeling first?" She looked at the Blu-rays. "*The Parent Trap*, or *The Fugitive*. Rather on the nose."

Shelly winked at her and shoved a guac-laden tortilla chip in Jenny's mouth. Jenny forced herself to chew and swallow, vowing she'd go to her grave before ever admitting to Lockhart that it tasted all right.

Eliza met up with Jimmy Figg and Nathaniel at Pixeldrome, and the three rode back north on their bikes. Like Eliza, they'd dressed all in black and wore ski masks—which Eliza made them take off for the bike ride so they wouldn't look stupidly suspicious coming up Broadway.

The Valentine Foundation offices were right off Town Square, making a frontal approach a no-go. Instead, they parked their bikes in an alley a block away. It was the same alley, Eliza noted, that the Stranger had attacked Jenny and Drew in, resulting in Eliza accidentally hitting poor Drew in the back with a throwing knife. She hoped this wasn't an omen.

Nathaniel dug into his backpack and pulled out a can of spray paint. Before she could stop him, he shook it. The *clack! clack!* of the can sounded thunderously loud in the narrow alley.

"Quiet!" Eliza hissed.

"It's for the cameras," Nathaniel whispered.

"Jenny, can we put our ski masks on now?" Jimmy asked.

"Yes. And no more names from here on out."

They donned their ski masks, and Eliza led them to the rear of the building she knew to be the headquarters of Val's charity. It had once been a Craftsman house, converted long ago for business use. Rather than a typical residential door with a deadbolt on the rear entrance, there was a commercial-use steel door with a grade-1 lock. That might have seemed like a deterrent, but it was the key to their plan—Jenny and Eliza's plan, that was.

She sent Nathaniel to the back door first, and he used his height to reach the security camera mounted above the door and fill the lens with paint. Once he finished, Eliza and Jimmy hurried to the door to join him. Eliza unslung Jenny's Coach mini backpack and retrieved a pair of black latex gloves.

"Damn, yours are way cooler," said Jimmy, frowning at his white gloves. "We look like cucks, now."

"You have to have a wife to get cucked, Jimmy," she said. "I need a light."

"I got you," said Jimmy.

He pulled out a glowstick and cracked it. Nathaniel snorted as soft magenta light bloomed in Jimmy's hand.

"Where'd you get that, homo? The Rainbow Cattle Club?" Nathaniel said.

"These are, like, tactical Israeli chemical lights!" Jimmy hissed. "The color is so it doesn't mess up your night vision. You're the homo for even knowing about the Cattle Club."

Eliza rubbed her temples. A few minutes with these dipshits and she already wanted to run into traffic. No wonder Jenny had been so miserable. She got to work on the grade-1 lock with her lockpick kit. According to her sister, turning the key only halfway on this kind of lock would allow the door to open, but it would stay locked—even from the inside—when it closed. Once she felt the last tumbler move, she snapped at the two idiots to get their attention.

"All right, we're in," she said. "Remember, Nathaniel goes first to do all the cameras. Jimmy, you go straight to the printer once Nathaniel gives you the signal. I'll hang back to fix the alarm. You've got your laptop, right?"

Jimmy pulled his backpack open to show her said laptop. On it was the modified newsletter they'd be printing on Valentine Foundation stationery. Eliza pretended to check on the computer—and dropped a wireless microphone into the bottom of Jimmy's pack.

"Ready?" she asked.

"Rock and roll!" said Nathaniel.

Eliza turned the tension bar halfway and pulled the door open.

Nathaniel rushed in to spray paint any cameras he could find. After 10 long seconds, he called out, "Clear!"

In went Jimmy, jogging to the printer. Eliza leaned inside and located the alarm panel. If she didn't enter the correct code in 15 seconds, the silent alarm would trigger. That was fine and all, but she wanted to scare these boys. She opened the little plastic latch to the keypad and pressed the **Cancel (X)** button over and over until the non-silent alarm went off.

WHOOOPWHOOOPWHOOOPWHOOP!

The siren was so loud even Eliza jumped at it.

"So long, suckers!" she shouted over the din and retreated back outside, shutting the door and locking them in.

Back at the Onishi household, Jenny slouched on one side of the couch, side-eyeing Shelly and Lockhart snuggling together on the other. Either her aunt was humoring him, or she was actually enjoying *The Fugitive*. It wasn't terrible. Jenny had picked up a few tips, at least.

Her watch tapped her on the wrist: a message from Eliza.

> **D**:   Trapped like rats in a cage.

She got her phone out to reply and Lockhart loudly cleared his throat. Jenny looked up to see that he'd paused the movie.

"This is an important part," he said.

"Okay, hold on, dude."

> **T**:   Good. Get clear.
>
> **T**:   Can't talk now. Lockhart won't let me text during
> the movie.
>
> **D**:   Hahaha. You're missing out, that Nathaniel guy is
> losing his shit! 🕊

Jenny put her phone away, smiling at the thought, and let Lockhart start the movie again.

Eliza crouched on the roof of a building in the nearby alley. She had her AirPods in, listening to the chaos ensue inside the Valentine Foundation offices over the wireless mic she'd planted in Jimmy's bag. She could hear pounding and cursing as the idiots tried and failed to force their way out.

"Where the fuck did she go!?!" Nathaniel shouted.

"You idiot!" screamed Jimmy. "Don't you get it?! This whole job was a setup. She fucked us. She fucking rammed it in with no lube and broke it off!"

Graphic, but I'll allow it.

Down below, she could see a police car converging on the building. The station was just around the corner.

"I can't go to jail!" whined Nathaniel. "Oh fuck oh fuck oh fuck."

"AHAHAHA!" Jimmy was cackling now. Had he snapped?

"Shut up!!" Nathaniel roared.

"You peed your pants! You peed your pants!!" Jimmy shrieked over and over until Eliza heard a loud crash and some grunts. "You peed yo—oww! Fuck you, dick!"

More groans and smashing. Jimmy began chanting "Retard strength!" until the police kicked the door in and arrested them. Officers Peña and Mack, from the sound of it. Mack tried to read them their Miranda rights, but Jimmy wouldn't shut up.

"Jenny Valentine set us up!" he insisted. "It's her you want, not us. She trapped us!!"

That little weasel! No honor among thieves. She'd bet Jenny he wouldn't crack until they got to the police station. Now her sister would get to pick out their next tattoo.

"What is that smell?" Mack asked.

"He peed his pants!" Jimmy gleefully informed them.

Nathaniel groaned.

"Oh Jesus, he's doing it again," said Mack.

"You're saying Jenny Valentine is part of this?" Peña asked, dubious.

"It was all her idea!" said Jimmy. "She tricked us into coming here, and set us up to get in trouble."

"Jenny? Trouble? You don't say," said Officer Peña.

"What do you think?" asked Mack.

"I'd like to plead the fifth and incriminate Rob Haines in exchange for diplomatic immunity," said Nathaniel.

"Shut up," said Officer Peña.

"Isn't the boss literally at Jenny Valentine's place right now?" asked Mack.

"He said to only call in an emergency," said Peña.

A pause passed between the cops.

"I'm blaming you if he gets pissed," said Peña.

Lockhart's phone buzzed on the coffee table, inching closer to the edge with each burst of vibration. The sheriff grumbled and grabbed the remote to pause the movie again.

"Sorry," he said. "They wouldn't be calling if it wasn't important."

Jenny tucked her legs underneath her, delighted. She knew exactly who was calling.

Shelly must have noticed her grin and narrowed her eyes.

Jenny shot her a wink. "I'm really enjoying movie night, Shells! We should do this more often!"

Lockhart answered his phone. "We're right at the St. Patrick's Day parade chase, and Dr. Richard Kimble is about to drop his jacket and nobody notices. This had better be good, Darcy." He listened to Officer Peña on the other end of the line. "Great, book 'em. What's the issue?" he asked.

Her reply caused Lockhart to cock his head at Jenny.

"That would be rather impressive, considering that she's been sitting right next to me for the past hour and a half," he said.

Yes!

"Miss Valentine, the streets are saying you just helped Jimmy Figg and Nathaniel Davis break into the Valentine Foundation offices," said Lockhart. "And that Rob Haines was behind it all, trying to steal money from the Foundation's donors. Is that true?"

Shelly's eyebrows shot to the ceiling. Jenny leaned over and grabbed the phone from Lockhart.

"Okay, those guys have been messing with me and Kazu all year!" said Jenny. "I told you! Jimmy was the one who attacked Thanh, and I'll bet he was behind the wild hogs at Homecoming, too! And Rob's been covering for them! They're trying to frame me because they knew I'd been sniffing around their operation. Suck it, assholes!"

She handed the phone back to Lockhart.

"Get all that?" he asked. "No worries. Call their parents, but let the kids stew overnight. Teach them a lesson. We can talk to Rob tomorrow. Lockhart out."

"Finally, you caught those guys," said Jenny. "They're a menace."

Lockhart nodded, already bored of the topic and reaching for the remote. Shelly stared at Jenny, shaking her head in rueful disbelief. Jenny shrugged, and her aunt winked back.

"Rewind it a little, I missed the last part," Jenny said.

"Jenny, have you heard from your cousin?" Shelly asked. "It is a school night."

"She texted earlier," said Jenny. "She'll be home soon."

THE SCHOOL NIGHT GAVE WAY TO A BRIGHT MONDAY MORNING. Jenny's suspension was over and she was due back in class—at least until her expulsion hearing. She and Eliza stopped by the Basque cafe first to enjoy a quiet breakfast before she had to face her peers again.

It was as awkward as expected. Before, Trouble was a pariah. Now, she was radioactive! The way classmates scrambled out of her way wherever she walked, lest she ruin their lives too, was breathtaking. Two weeks ago, this kind of treatment would have thrown her deeper into despair. With Eliza back on her side, and the rift between them finally healing, it was water off Mr. Duck's back.

There was no sign of Jimmy Figg, nor any rumors of his arrest. Jenny would have happily spread them, but no one wanted to talk to her. She tried calling Asha during first break to see if she'd heard, then texting when she didn't answer, but so far it was radio silence from her soon-to-be-ex.

At lunch, after another failed attempt, she marched right over to sit with Drew at the Unfridgeables table.

"Hey," she said to him, ignoring the stares and grumbling around her. "I didn't thank you, for what you did the weekend before last. I hope you know that I appreciated it, after I had some time to process, and I'm elated to know you still cared enough to help because I certainly didn't deserve it."

Eliza shot her a sly grin, back in her Kazumi disguise.

"Oh, uh, no problem, Jenny," said Drew. He blinked rapidly, covering it with a smile. "I'm sorry I called you a cunt."

Penny gasped next to him. "Drew!"

"I'm sorry for being one," said Jenny.

Next to Drew, Jack was turning red in the face. "If you think—"

"Don't ruin the moment, Junior," she said. "I know I've got a lot of work to do. I'll talk to Alicia."

"Please don't," said Jack.

There was a tap on her shoulder. Jenny turned to find Vice Principal Carter looming over her.

"Miss Valentine, we've scheduled your disciplinary hearing for next Tuesday," he said. "The entire school board, your juvenile corrections officer, and the mayor will all be in attendance. I would heavily advise you *not* to contact Miss Aaron before then."

"I'll take that under advisement," Jenny said. "Now if you'll excuse me, I need to go dump my toxic FWB. That's right, ladies, Trouble's back on the market. Ciao!"

She got up and left them to finish their lunch in peace.

"What an absolute, bloody, raving nutter!" she heard Eliza say behind her.

I love you too, Lizzy.

When school let out, Jenny tried Asha's phone one more time. Still no answer. She'd have to go to the arcade in person. But before she could leave campus, she found Tori Valentine waiting for her between the sycamore trees out front.

"What were you trying to steal?!" Tori demanded.

She didn't look so hot. Her face was stuck in a scowl behind dark sunglasses, and her perfect chestnut hair was tied up in a messy ponytail. She was clutching a latte from the Basque like a lifeline.

"Rough night?" Jenny asked.

"Bite me!"

"Just asking, jeez."

Tori grumbled. "I don't sleep well when Darcy works the late shift. You didn't answer my question."

"Uh, I heard from Lockhart that there was a break-in at your mom's foundation," said Jenny. "But I didn't have anything to do with it. Ask him, I was with him the whole evening. Shelly had him over for movie night. We watched *The Fugitive* and *The Parent Trap*."

"You're explaining too much, and I know that you know that I know what that means," said Tori.

Jenny shrugged innocently. "It is sketchy that somebody broke into the Foundation offices, right? I heard someone burned down the treehouse recently, too."

Tori narrowed her eyes. "I was *sure* that someone was you, Jennifer, but according to Darcy, those jackoffs who broke in last night may have done it. They found a gas can in the big guy's locker."

"Tsk tsk. Sloppy," said Jenny. "What do you think they were looking for at the office? Something in your files?"

"The only thing they'd find is a bunch of boring old charity receipts and business records," said Tori. "And before you get any fresh ideas, I'll be moving all the hard copies to the archive at the mansion for safekeeping."

"The mansion? It's almost like you and Val are still acting like you own the place, even though it's supposed to be waiting in escrow until I win it again," said Jenny.

"If," said Tori. "And yes, that's called the perks of being the executor, and Daddy's favorite."

Jenny bit her cheek, resisting the urge to take the bait. "Are you ready to tell me what you left out at the park yet?" she asked. "The rest of your conversation about the game with my dad?"

It was Tori's turn to steel herself. "Why don't you focus on the clues you do have, Jenny. You're running out of time."

Chapter Twenty-Five
Mystery Girl

WHEN JENNY ARRIVED AT PIXELDROME ON HER BIKE, SHE FOUND, to her mild surprise, that the neon sign was turned off, and the entrance was barred with a padlock and chain. A sign was taped to the door:

Pixeldrome will be closed indefinitely
Thanks for the memories

Well, well. Was Rob lying low, or had the cops shut the place down? Only one way to find out. Jenny rode back to Town Square and parked her bike in front of the police station. She entered through the slick glass doors and walked up to the modern wood and aluminum front desk.

"Hi, I'm here for my Genius Bar appointment," she said to Deputy Calderon.

The deputy cleared his throat and pointed to the bulletin board on his right. Someone had printed out a picture of Jenny with a big red circle and slash over her face. Below, it read:

Shoot On Sight

"That's not funny. I could sue you for that."

"Qualified immunity, chica," said Calderon.

"Whatever, is Lockhart here?"

Calderon leaned back and called behind him. "Boss, are you here?"

"Who's asking?" It was Lockhart's voice.

"Trouble," said Jenny.

Lockhart came strolling out of his office, eating, of all things, a chocolate donut.

"What do you want?" he asked.

"Did you arrest Rob Haines?" Jenny asked. "Or did he close down Pixeldrome on his own?"

"As a general rule, Blackbird Springs PD does not share details of ongoing investigations with the public," said Lockhart. "Especially you."

"You forget that I have leverage over you now," said Jenny. She turned to Calderon. "Did you know he puts cream cheese in his guacamole?"

Calderon gave her a knowing grimace. Lockhart smirked and reached under the counter. A loud *BZZZ!* sounded, and the glass door next to the front desk opened. Blake ushered her back to his office and pointed her to the guest chair. Of course, she took his own instead. Jenny was tickled to see the sheriff had battered paperback copies of all 12 *Trouble* books on his bookshelf.

"Seriously, did the cops shut down the arcade?" Jenny asked. "I need to get in there."

"The city has yet to file any formal charges against Rob Haines," said Lockhart. "Keeping Pixeldrome open to the public or not is his own business, but he could be looking at obstruction for giving us doctored video of Jimmy Figg, the night he attacked Thanh Trân. And then there's the break-in last night. Those kids had a lot to say about Rob's involvement, and what goes on at that arcade. They had a lot to say about you, too."

"They've wanted revenge on me all year after I almost busted Jimmy for shaving Thanh's head," said Jenny. "Obviously you can't believe anything they say about me."

"Obviously," said Lockhart. "Jimmy and Nathaniel confessed to a lot, including the wild hogs at the dance. However, both of them have alibis for August 10th, 2019. Real ones, not the kind that Rob could fake with video timestamps. Neither of them killed RJ."

"They were never on my suspect list," said Jenny.

"Sure. And as you already know, Rob has an alibi for that night, too," said Lockhart.

"So it seems."

"Then my question for you, Trouble, is this," said Lockhart. "What the hell have you been doing hanging out with these people for four months? And why do you still need to get inside that arcade?"

"You know why: the token heirloom," said Jenny. "To say more would be tipping my hand. We are, after all, still rival contestants in the game."

The sheriff took a seat in one of the guest chairs and stretched his long arms behind his head, sizing Jenny up.

"Okay, fine, there's this."

Jenny dug the **High Score** card out of her pocket and explained how it came into her possession. When she was finished, Lockhart chewed thoughtfully on the last of his donut and swallowed.

"My guess: it's a honeypot," he said. "The token doesn't mean anything. RJ's just trying to lure the Stranger to that arcade, figuring he'd be obsessed with that *Trouble* game."

"You're not the only one with that theory," said Jenny. "If you're right, then RJ's tempting the Stranger to search for some deeper mystery behind the game that doesn't exist. Which is why I need to get down to that stupid VIP room and check the high score."

"Hey, boss."

Calderon leaned into the room and handed Lockhart a note. He read it and scowled, then tried to cover his reaction with a fake cough.

"Thanks, Miggy," he said and passed the note back.

"Bad news?"

"Maybe there was never a killer," said Lockhart. "Maybe RJ slipped and fell after drinking too much. And then his wayward bastard daughter saw an opportunity to step into the role he'd written for her. But she couldn't be Trouble unless there was a Stranger to oppose her. And if none existed? Well, you're a clever girl. That's the mayor's favorite theory, you know?"

"Why Hector, I'm flattered," said Jenny. "But I'm five foot one. The Stranger's a big guy."

"Your buddy Drew Porter's a big guy, too," said Lockhart. "Maybe you're working together?"

"The Stranger literally stabbed Drew in the back," said Jenny. Technically, it was Eliza's knife that struck home, but same difference. "I saw it with my own eyes."

"So you say. How many times has the Stranger attacked, with you as the only witness?"

"I don't know, ask Nilay Nagra. Or Valerie Valentine. And before you say it, Drew was at Arizona State for a college trip when that happened."

"Your brother Jack?"

"Vegas. Of course, there's always Mason. Where did *he* go, Thanksgiving night? And hell, in a big black coat and mask, it could be anyone with some height. Tori, Penny, Yvonne, even Dinah. Do you know what *projection* is, Sheriff Lockhart? It's when I point out that you and Alicia could be acting as the Stranger together, and then you turn around and accuse me of the same."

Lockhart grinned. "You're seeing all the angles, then. Good." He grabbed his keys from a desk drawer. "Okay. Let's go."

"Where?"

"Pixeldrome. You need into that VIP room, right?"

"Um, yeah, definitely," said Jenny.

She hopped to her feet, afraid to say anything that would change his suddenly cooperative mood.

ROB HAINES WAS WAITING FOR THEM AT THE ENTRANCE TO Pixeldrome. Surprisingly, so was the damn mayor, his slicked-back hair immune to the windy weather. The bags under Rob's eyes were darker than usual, and he was squinting, even though it was overcast. This was the first time she'd seen him outside the arcade, Jenny realized. How sad.

"What are they doing here?" Jenny asked.

"Shit rolls downhill, kiddo," said Lockhart. "If I'm about to eat some of it, we might as well get our money's worth."

Jenny hopped out of the police cruiser, suddenly wary. Was this a trap? At the sight of her, Rob stared down Jenny with a look of pure loathing.

"And here I thought you were fun, like your mother," he said.

"I'm getting the feeling that Mom was never as much fun as you wanted her to be," said Jenny.

Rob sneered and turned to the sheriff. "Do you have a warrant?"

"Like I said," the mayor interjected, "It's better for everyone if we keep this one off the books."

"Stuff gets broken so easily during an official search," said Lockhart.

He put an edge into his voice for Rob.

The mayor spread his hands in an "aw, shucks" gesture. "We're just here for a chat, aren't we?" said the mayor, throwing an arm around Rob's shoulder. "Rob here has always been a loyal supporter of Blackbird Springs, and from what I hear about that Figg kid's confession, this one"—he jerked his thumb at Jenny—"was the instigator in all this."

"I'd love to make that case, Hector, but I literally had eyes on her all night," said Lockhart.

"I'd hoped for more… creative crime prevention from my sheriff," said the mayor. "But I understand, Blake. You have your own entanglements to manage."

"The long and the short of it is this: we've got a real shit sandwich on our hands," said Lockhart. "Rob, the sooner you let her in that damn basement, the sooner we get her out of your hair, and I can wrap this thing up with way less paperwork."

"You're not going to arrest him?!" Jenny screeched.

"Shut up, Jenny," said Lockhart.

The mayor smiled at her, all white teeth and dead eyes. She could see Rob weighing the options in his mind and arriving at the path of least resistance.

"Fine, come on," he said.

Rob unlocked the door and led them inside. The mayor declined to follow, pulling Lockhart back for a word.

"My patience, Blake," she overheard the mayor say as he jingled his car keys. "It's growing thin."

Lockhart grunted a reply and joined them inside.

Though the ceiling fluorescents were on, the strobing neon lights were off, and there was no hyper synth-wave music blasting on the P.A. In the harsh light of day, Pixeldrome was a pitiful warehouse full of faded video game cabinets and stale air, choked with rancid sweat and grease.

"Whoa, isn't that the one from *T2*?" Lockhart asked, nodding to the *Afterburner* machine. "Nice."

"I see you're a man of culture," said Rob.

Fucking men.

At the stairway, Rob unhooked the velvet rope and let them pass. The door to the VIP room remained closed at the bottom of the stairs. Rob took out his Pixeldrome membership card and swiped across the spot where a doorknob would usually be. Something beeped and a mechanical latch shifted. Rob pushed on the door and it swung open.

Unlike the sorry state above, the VIP room was full of pulsating blue and orange lighting, and an '80s song was playing softly on the stereo. There were rows of old arcade cabinets, some couches, a stocked bar, and a giant flat-panel television that was currently showing a *Star Wars* movie. Behind the bar, a custom-made neon sign spelled out **Club Pixeldrome** like a beer logo, next to a bunch of plaques and photos of Little League teams that the arcade had sponsored over the years.

Jenny could feel her face warming with anger. Four months of misery for this bullshit!

"That's it!?"

"What were you expecting?" asked Rob.

"I don't know, something cool?"

"That's the original, de-specialized version of *Episode 4!*" Rob replied, pointing at the TV.

Jenny made a jerk-off motion with her hand.

"You lack culture," said Rob. He waved to the video games. "Most of these are ROM hacks. When someone makes it all the way to level 99, they get the right to re-skin any classic 8- or 16-bit game into whatever they want. The one Miss Valentine will be interested in is over here."

He led Jenny to a game at the end of a row. Lockhart ignored them, examining one of the Little League photos. On the side of the cabinet, someone had painted the silhouette of a dastardly villain in a dark trench coat and black hat. It looked a lot like…

"Behold, your *Trouble* game," said Rob. "Technically, it's a *Final Fight* cabinet that I ROM-hacked." He inserted a game token and pressed the **Player One** button. "Give it a shot."

Jenny watched in fascination as rudimentary, pixelated cut scenes unfolded. Scenes of the mayor's prized golden retriever being kidnapped. Of a Japanese Girl Detective in a purple trench coat and a red fedora being hired to track the puppy down. The gameplay was just like *Final Fight*, moving around and beating up bad guys, but instead of a muscle-bound dude, Jenny played as, well, herself. Maybe it was just her imagination, but the mini-boss sure looked a lot like Rob.

After beating the level, Jenny looked up at the cabinet marquee. The title was in kanji.

**ミステリー
ガール**

"*Mystery Girl*," Jenny said aloud, translating. "Why not 'Trouble'?"

"Because RJ Valentine's attorneys didn't want us trading on the *Trouble* name, even though we were first," said Rob.

"What are you talking about?" she asked. "First what?"

Rob laughed bitterly.

"This is gonna rock your world," he said.

From under the bar, he pulled out a Polaroid photo and held it up. *No fucking way.*

The photo was faded and wrinkled, with half the colors bleeding to brown. In it, an 18-year-old Laura Onishi was posing next to the *Mystery Girl* arcade cabinet, holding a paintbrush. The silhouette of the Stranger on the side was only half-painted.

"What the fuck?"

Rob laughed and handed her the photo.

"This has to be photoshopped," Jenny said.

"It's not," said Rob. "She did all the artwork herself, back when she worked here that summer. Where do you think RJ got the idea? *Allegedly*, mind you. I get a tiny chunk of revenue sharing every three months to keep my mouth shut about this."

"I need to sit down," Jenny said, and did.

She'd always known their mother named them "Trouble" and "Danger." It had never occurred to her that Laura Onishi envisioned much more than mischievous names for her daughters. But what did this all mean? When RJ made his secret heirloom the game token, he had to have known Jenny would end up here eventually, right? Which meant he wanted her to find this. He wanted her to know her mother's role in *Trouble*. The books weren't just for Jenny. They were a tribute to Laura, too.

"You don't need to cry about it," Rob said.

"Shut the fuck up, Rob." She wiped her eyes. "Did you mail RJ the game token?"

"What token?"

"The one—never mind." Jenny ground her teeth. The Stranger must have learned about this *Mystery Girl* game. And he sent Dad the game token to taunt him about it. "How do I see the top score?"

"Just let the game end."

Jenny let her character die. The **High Score** screen appeared.

```
2,796,386 — ROB
2,223,945 — ASH
1,956,220 — NIN
```

Rob and Asha were at the top. Typical. Could Asha, somehow, be a suspect?

"Who's NIN?" Jenny asked.

"That's that Nilay kid," said Rob. "RIP to that dude."

"Wait! Nilay? How? I never even saw him here!"

"You wouldn't have," said Rob, laughing. "He came here last October and used an exploit on *Paperboy* to run up crazy XP. Hit level 99 in a week. Normally, I'd have zeroed him out for cheating, but it was an old-school hack, and the dude was cool. What can I say, I liked him. Poor guy."

A puzzle piece clicked into place.

"Would he have gotten one of those 99+ pins?"

"Yep."

So that's where the pin came from—the one Eliza found in the Crow's Nest penthouse chair cushions. Fucking Nilay. Jenny had to admit it: he wasn't that bad a Boy Detective after all.

"Well," said Lockhart, coming up beside her. "Anyone turn up in the honeypot?"

"No one who wasn't already on my radar, or dead," said Jenny. "Maybe my dad wanted to me to know that my mom played a part in creating me."

"That's usually how nature works," said Lockhart.

"I meant the character," said Jenny. If their honeypot theory was correct, then the Stranger must have been smart enough to stay away—might have even known about it, given he knew the token was an heirloom in the first place. Meaning the game token was just another red herring. Figured. There were always one or two of those in every *Trouble* book. "I guess we're done. I gotta talk to Rob real quick, then I'll meet you upstairs."

Lockhart raised a cautionary eyebrow at Jenny, then Rob, and nodded. As he left, Jenny spied a blank space on the wall where a Little League photo had just been hanging.

"That was real clever," Rob said. "Tricking the boys into that break-in. Did you warn Asha? Is that why she didn't want to help?"

"She didn't have a clue," said Jenny.

"So you say, but guess what? My kung fu is a lot better than yours, Trouble," said Rob. "As soon as I heard the dispatch on the police scanner last night, I nuked anything that could tie you guys to me. Including your membership. You're zeroed out and 86ed. No more VIP room. Hope it was worth it."

"Hate to break it to you, Rob, but I never planned on making a hobby out of this," said Jenny. "And neither, I suspect, did my mother. To put it in your lingo, you were just another mini-boss we both had to get past. Answer a few questions for me, and I promise I'll stay out of your rapidly thinning hair."

"I'll pass," he said.

"Shall I go get the sheriff?"

"Fine. Shoot."

"You get a big deposit in your bank account every three months," said Jenny. "That's for the *Mystery Girl* game, right?"

He nodded.

"You never thought to share it with my grandparents?"

"They disowned her," he said. "Fuck them."

"Me, then?"

"Well, I didn't even know you existed for a long time," said Rob. "And I think you cost me plenty last night. I'd say we're even."

"What about the nine grand you deposited last fall, right after Hamilton Webb was killed?"

Rob hesitated. "That's… confidential. It's not what you think"

"No one paid you for VIP access? Or any info about the game?"

"Nope."

Jenny bit her lip. All right, now for the tough questions.

"Did you kill my father?" she asked.

"No."

"Did you kill my mother?" she asked.

"No, of course not."

"When's the last time you saw RJ Valentine alive?"

Rob had to think about that one. "I don't remember the exact date," he said after a while. "Probably a few days before the gala. He came into the arcade and uh, bought some stuff off me."

"What kind of stuff?" Jenny asked.

Rob's face soured. "We keeping this between you and me, and not your cop buddy?"

Jenny nodded.

"I sold him some drugs. Sedatives. People need 'em, sometimes, and I can get 'em."

"What did RJ need sedatives for?"

"He didn't tell, and I didn't ask," said Rob. "Maybe he was having trouble sleeping. He looked a little worn out."

What the hell, Dad?

Jenny bit her lip. She didn't know what to do with this information, but as far as she could tell, Rob wasn't lying.

"And my mother?" Jenny asked. "Tell me when you last saw her."

This one he didn't need to think about at all. "March 9th, 2003," said Rob. "Laurie came by Pixeldrome that afternoon, extremely pregnant, begging me for money."

Why would Mom need money if Val had written her a check for fifty grand?

"And you said what?"

"I—I wasn't able to help her," said Rob.

"Lies. What did you really say?"

"I told her she was a bad investment," he said, his lip curling into a cruel smile. "Damaged goods. Post-pregnancy chicks, that's like throwing a hot dog down a hallway."

Jenny was biting her tongue so hard she tasted blood. "Pig. She must have turned you down bad, back when she worked here."

His face curdled with envy. "All that bullshit simping I did for her attention, and it turned out she was screwing some dirtbag who worked at the record store across the street the whole time," said Rob. "Just another teasing bitch. You know the difference between a bitch and a slut, Trouble? A slut will fuck anyone. A bitch will fuck anyone but you."

"Oh, you poor baby," said Jenny. "Did you forget the rules of this place? In here, it's still the '80s, man. The geek never gets the girl."

"He did in *Sixteen Candles*," said Rob, smiling wistfully.

"That was sexual assault."

He laughed.

"That's funny?" Jenny asked, focusing very hard on not punching him in the balls.

"You haven't gotten a single '80s reference I've made in four months, and yet somehow you know that movie?" said Rob.

"It has a notorious racist Asian caricature in it," said Jenny. "So yeah, I know it, whether I wanted to or not."

"It was just the time."

"What a great fucking time. Scary to be gay, lots of dog whistle racism, everyone had bad hair…"

"Everyone had bad hair, and it fucking ruled, because we weren't all so irony-pilled that we were afraid to live a little!" said Rob. "I'm not saying it was perfect, but it was real! We had personalities, you've got identities. We had culture, you've got content. Laurie got that, at least. Why do you think RJ set the *Trouble* books in the quasi-80s? Because he got it too."

A thousand retorts tickled the tip of her tongue, each of them more inadequate than the one before. Asha was still in her head, telling her how lame and naive she was to even care.

"That may be true," said Jenny. "But Trouble grew up, whether RJ wanted her to or not. And she's not gonna end up a has-been ghoul like you. Do you know the difference between a simp and a cuck, Rob? A simp always thinks he's got a shot. A cuck knows he doesn't, but he's too big of a coward to move on."

She spit in his face and left Pixeldrome before he could reply. With any luck, she'd never be back here again.

Chapter Twenty-Six

Stratford Photography

SHERIFF LOCKHART WAS WAITING IN THE DRIVER'S SEAT OF HIS police SUV, staring out into space. He didn't notice Jenny's return until she knocked on the window and pointed to the back seat. He leaned over and unlocked the passenger door, for once letting her sit up front.

"So, uh, what'd you steal from in there?" Jenny asked once they were on the road.

Lockhart frowned, trying to play dumb.

"There was a photo missing from the wall. You took it," said Jenny.

"Maybe I did," he said.

"Can I see it?"

He hesitated a moment, grumbled under his breath, and pulled out a photo plaque from the side compartment on his door. As Jenny predicted, it was a team photo of a bunch of little leaguers from 2014. Jack and Mason were in the back row, flashing toothy smiles and wearing hats that were too large for their heads. They'd have been around 11. The perfect age… That wasn't why Lockhart had stolen the photo, though. Two coaches stood on each side of the kids. A younger, almost baby-faced Blake Lockhart on the left, and on the right, a beautiful woman, still full of life. Her hair, the color of a nice Blackthorn merlot, was tucked under a baseball cap.

"She's so pretty," Jenny said.

"Yeah," Lockhart said, his voice thick. "She was. Homecoming Queen. A real one, not like you."

"Rude."

Jenny stared at the photo. Oh! There was pre-teen Drew in the front row! She hadn't even clocked him because of a smudge on the photo that obscured part of his face. He looked so tiny! Must not have hit his growth spurt yet. She tried wiping the smudge off, but it was part of the photo itself. There were some squiggly scratches near it, distorting another boy's jersey—

"Holy shit."

"What?" Lockhart frowned, glancing over.

"Do you mind if I get a copy of this?" Jenny asked. "Also, do you remember who the photographer was?"

"No idea on the second question, yes to the first, if you want," said Lockhart. "To what end?"

"I'm trying to solve a murder here, chief."

"I sincerely doubt that team portrait connects to your dad's killer."

Jenny worked the photo free of the little corner flaps and turned it over. On the back, it was stamped by the portrait company.

Stratford Photography

Excitement rippled down Jenny's spine, washing away Lockhart's bad, sad, dad vibes. She smiled at him.

"Not Dad's. Mom's."

THAT NIGHT, AFTER AN HOUR-LONG PHONE CALL WITH DREW THAT meandered and went nowhere interesting, Eliza let Jenny into her room so they could discuss Jenny's new clue. Her sister laid the heirloom photo on her bedspread, next to the blackmail photo Eliza found in Dad's briefcase inside his vacant hotel room at the Crow's Nest. Beside them both, Jenny set her phone, showing the photo she'd taken of Blake's Little League team portrait.

"It's close," Eliza said, after studying the team portrait.

"Oh, come on! It's exact!" said Jenny.

"It's not exact. Look, see how the scratches seem longer here? And the spot a little further away?"

"That's just… but they can't not be the same lens," said Jenny. "That's way too insane a coincidence. Maybe… maybe it was the same printer?"

She got her magnifying glass out and studied the heirloom photo up close. Eliza hid a smile. It was always a bit surreal to see her sister mirror her fictional counterpart so precisely.

"Damn, this is a chemical print," Jenny said, her magnified eye an inch from the picture. "You can tell from the grain pattern. See?"

She handed Eliza the magnifying glass and color printout to show the difference. The printout was of Valerie Valentine's face; Drew had printed it a million years ago for the first Big Board.

"Drew! That's who we should ask," said Eliza. "He takes photos for the school paper. Or he used to, anyway. Before Mr. White was killed."

Jenny bit her lip and picked up the heirloom photo. "I don't know. I like keeping this one a secret."

"But he's already seen it. The day you met, right?"

"Yeah, but he's nosy. He's always asking why we don't investigate this one, and I have to tell him I solved it, and it doesn't mean anything. If we show it to him again, he might finally figure out that's not a peace sign Mom's making."

In the heirloom photo, Laura Onishi was holding up two fingers to tell a grinning RJ her bulging belly held not one, but two amazing daughters within.

"Oh no, then I'd actually have something to talk about with him on the phone, besides movies and gossip," said Eliza.

"Don't blame me for that. He's got to step up his game."

"It's not him, it's Kazumi!" Eliza flopped back on her bed. "I never realized, but she's so boring when she's solo. My move has always been to lurk in group convos and throw out a well-timed bon mot. I don't know what to say to him when it's just us, other than randy innuendo. And, like, he hasn't earned that yet."

"This is why you should date girls," said Jenny. "Less talking, more kissing."

"You didn't talk to Asha because every other word out of her mouth was repellent."

Jenny slapped a hand to her forehead. "I still need to dump her. Balls!"

"I'm asking Drew," Eliza said, using her phone to snap a picture of the heirloom photo. "We'll crop it so he just sees the blemishes and nothing else."

"Very well," said Jenny. "You do that, I'll make myself single again."

Jenny grabbed her own phone while Eliza cropped the photo. Now, how to phrase the question to Drew…

"Wait, shit, I can't send this, I'm Kazu."

"Jesus. Yes, obviously. Let me."

After the text was sent, Jenny remained on Eliza's bed, calling Asha.

"Did you want some privacy?" Eliza asked.

"Nah." Jenny shook her head. "You'll probably have to do this someday. Watch and learn."

Her sister put the phone on speaker as it rang.

"She probably won't even answer," Jenny said, just as the line picked up.

"Wrong again, Trouble," said Asha.

"Oh, hey there," said Jenny.

"Hey."

"I tried calling you, and you weren't answering," said Jenny.

"Wasn't sure I could trust you," said Asha. "Still not sure. Why are we on speaker? Are you recording this or something?"

"No. Um," Jenny grabbed the phone and took it off speaker. "Sorry, I know I should be doing this face to face." She paused, listening. "It's not like that, but yes, I don't think we should see each other anymore." Another pause. "'Okay'? That's it?"

She paced, still listening.

"Of course it meant *something*. Everything means something." Jenny glanced back at Eliza and grimaced. "See, this is the thing, Ash. You always expect the worst, but that doesn't protect you from being hurt, it just makes you miserable all the time. You don't even know how to enjoy being happy." Jenny rolled her eyes. "No, it's not from a self-help book, it's from me. … Fine, you want it to hurt, how's this: I didn't like myself when I was with you, and I missed the girl I was before we met!"

Yikes! Eliza bit her fist. *Goddamn, Jenny.*

"I'm *what?*"

Jenny held the phone away from her ear. Eliza could hear inaudible shouting coming out of the tinny ear speaker.

"Cool. Fuck you forever, hope I never see you again—wait! Did you kill my dad? … Okay, fuck you, bye."

She ended the call and stuck her hands on her hips, so much like their aunt.

"Sounds like it went well," said Eliza.

"Did I use her?" Jenny asked.

"No more than she used you. How do you feel?"

"Now? Fantastic, honestly."

Jenny came back over and flopped on the bed beside her. Eliza squeezed her hand. It had been far, far too long since they'd spent an evening together like this. Did she still have lingering resentments for all the strife Jenny had caused? Sure. But if Jenny didn't like who she was with that Asha girl, Eliza didn't like who she was without Jenny.

Through their clasped hands, she felt Jenny's watch vibrate.

"It's Drew," said Jenny, checking her watch. "Aha! He says it's probably a zoom lens, which, quote: would distort any blemishes in wider focal lengths. Yes, of course. And he wants to know why I'm asking. I'll tell him I told Lockhart I'd try to hunt down more photos from that day. See if there are more of Lilah. He says he can't remember who the photographer was, but he remembers taking a solo portrait for his baseball card."

"Does he still have the card?" Eliza asked.

Jenny texted back. "That's it, Lizzy! A baseball game!" Jenny grinned. "Have him take you to an A's game and get on the kiss cam, then he'll have to plant one on ya!"

"There's got to be easier ways to get to first base," said Eliza.

"Not for the A's, they suck this year. I'm telling him to take you to a game." Jenny started texting again.

"Don't!"

"Too late."

"Bloody hell," Eliza groaned and held her head. "Opening Day isn't for like a month."

"Then you've got that long to make it happen your way," said Jenny. "Or don't make it happen. Maybe you're all wrong for each other, and you can date someone who isn't my best friend. Drew says the baseball card is in storage. Whatevs. But I was right. Same camera lens."

"Same photographer," said Eliza. "Works for Stratford Photography. Maybe exactly the kind of person you hire if your family owns a portrait studio, and you need someone to spy on your husband, but you don't trust hiring a P.I. A job like that wouldn't be on the books, but taking Little League photos? There should be records of that somewhere, right?

"Sounds like another second-story job for Danger," said Jenny. "Crap, but Tori said she's moving their business records to the mansion because of the break-in. We're gonna need to figure out a way past Tori's security goons. Or get back in Jack's good graces so he'll let us in."

"There's no way in hell Jack's forgiving us any time soon," said Eliza. "Alicia dumped him after you... did what you did. And he blames us for that, too."

Her sister's face fell. *Yeah, you screwed that one up, Jenny. Can't help you there.* Eliza lay back on her pillow and pondered a solution. Maybe Jenny could cause a big commotion at the Valentine Manor gate, and Eliza could slip onto the property from the west and make a run for the conservatory...

"Maybe it's not Jack's good graces we need to be in," said Jenny. "Have you heard anything from Alicia?"

Eliza laughed. "She might be the only person in town who hates you more than Jack."

"I know," said Jenny. "Which means we've only got one move."

It was the smell that did it. The lobby carpet in this apartment complex got steam-cleaned weekly by a housekeeping service that used lavender-scented shampoo. The sense memory put Eliza on autopilot—and her new romance with Drew far out of mind.

"It's the second floor, Lizzy," said Jenny.

Eliza blinked. She'd hit the button for Charlie's floor without even thinking. "Right, sorry."

They spent the rest of the short elevator ride in silence. When the elevator chimed, Eliza turned to her sister.

"If this doesn't work, she could seriously fuck us over," she said.

"Nothing ventured, nothing gained," said Jenny.

They halted at the door with a sign for **The Aarons** next to it.

"Don't forget we've got leverage of our own," said Jenny "Worst case scenario, it's a Mexican standoff."

She knocked on the door. Within moments, they could hear footsteps on the other side, then someone affixing the chain lock on the door.

Alice Aaron opened the door wide enough to reveal her stern face. "Leave now, or I'm calling the police."

"Do it, and I'll them all about how Alicia killed your husband and covered it up," said Jenny.

Eliza grimaced.

Well, this is starting out well.

Alice stiffened, her eyes darting around in a panic. "What do you want?"

"She wants to talk to Alicia, mum. To apologize," said Eliza. "I'm here to make sure she does. Tell Alicia that Kazumi personally guarantees Jenny will be on her best behavior."

Alice Aaron shut the door to deliver the message. A minute passed. Then another.

"Shit, maybe she really is calling the cops," said Jenny.

Just then, the chain lock clattered, and the door swung open. Alice stood aside and waved them in.

The loft apartment was much bigger than Charlie's little studio; this was the biggest floor plan available in the building. The Aaron girls had decorated it in cozy earth tones, full of antique mahogany furniture, tufted gingham seat covers, and dozens of little knick-knacks strewn about. One whole wall was lined with bookshelves, bursting with careworn paperbacks and hardcovers, many of them Eliza's favorites. Alicia Aaron sat on a comfy couch, an orange tabby cat in her lap. She had on a Gryffindor pajama top and boy shorts, and she'd removed her prosthetic leg, letting her bare stump breathe. Eliza forced herself not to stare at it.

"Are you sure you're okay, honey?" Alice asked her daughter.

Alicia regarded the Valentine girls with impressive scorn. "It's fine, go to your bible study." Her voice had a slight lisp; she had her retainer in. "I'll call if I need you."

"You have a lovely house, Mrs. Aaron," Eliza said.

Alice scoffed at her and walked out, leaving Alicia alone with them.

The little redhead crossed her arms and pointed to mismatched armchairs facing the couch. "Well, let's hear it."

They took their seats.

Jenny inhaled a deep breath and did her best. "Alicia, I did a horrible thing to you, and I am so, so sorry." She even made her voice quiver a little. Impressive. "I'm going to regret it for the rest of my life, and I will do anything I can to make it better."

"Great. You're not forgiven," said Alicia.

"That's not the point of an apology," said Jenny.

"I don't want you to do anything for me," said Alicia. "I can't even imagine what that would be, but I'll be damned if I want to find out. You've said your piece. I hope it makes you feel better. Wait—no, I don't. You should feel miserable for the rest of your cursed existence. You can go now."

"You've every right to be upset, Alicia," said Eliza. "I wouldn't expect you to forgive Jenny so easily. But I came here about Jack. Believe it or not, he's pretty distraught about you. By all means, hate Jenny, but he doesn't deserve this any more than you did."

"If he's so hurt, why don't you go back to dating him yourself,

Kazumi?" Alicia asked.

Jenny coughed next to her. She was probably dying to make an incest joke right now, but Alicia was *not* the audience for that!

Eliza stood. "We'd like to bring you in on a little secret, Alicia. One that puts us at your mercy. If you still hate us after we tell you, well, that's understandable. But maybe you might find it in your heart to allow for a little redemption."

Alicia remained dubious.

"Also, Jenny would like to graciously offer you her share of the media rights for *Hands of Adamant*," Eliza added.

"As, like, an olive branch," said Jenny, holding out an envelope.

"May I use your bathroom?" Eliza asked.

Alicia's eyes narrowed, but she pointed Eliza to a doorway off the living room. Before Eliza closed the bathroom door, she glanced back, hoping Jenny and Alicia remained civil until she returned. Then she took a Neutrogena towelette from her purse and went to work.

A minute later, she exited the bathroom with a freshly scrubbed face, just in time to witness Alicia's tabby cat jumping up into Jenny's lap.

"See, she doesn't think I'm so bad," said Jenny.

"It's a he," said Alicia. "And he's the dumbest cat who ever lived, so don't think that means anything."

"Aww, you're not dumb, are you?" asked Jenny.

The cat tried to eat Jenny's phone. He did look sort of cross-eyed.

"What's his name?" Eliza asked, without the accent.

Alicia glanced over. "General Hux—what the hell?" She tried to scramble to her feet, but couldn't very well on one leg.

Eliza held up her hands in surrender and took her seat. "You don't need to worry about me and Jack," said Eliza. "He's my brother."

THEY DIDN'T TELL ALICIA EVERYTHING (CERTAINLY NOT ABOUT THE time Jenny hid under Drew's bed at Schloss Schwarzwald while Alicia gave him an HJ), but they told her enough to get the idea that Eliza, the secret twin, had been in and out of Alicia's life far more than she knew. Jenny had been sure that this information would buy Alicia's cooperation. Eliza remained skeptical, but damned if Trouble didn't know how to read people.

Alicia was so tickled by the whole twin thing that she even forgot that she hated Jenny for a few seconds. "There were always some days when I liked you, and some days when I didn't." Alicia looked at Eliza. "Danger! That's so cool! You're the one who smokes, aren't you?"

Eliza chuckled and tossed Alicia a pack of cloves from her purse. They both lit up a dart and blew smoke in Jenny's face.

"And the one who loves Harry Potter," Eliza said. "She only reads our dad's books."

"And lesbian space necromancer fiction," said Jenny.

"Oh, I know that author!" said Alicia. "We're OOMFs. She might blurb *Hands of Adamant*."

This information left her sister nonplussed. "How nice for you," said Jenny. "Well now you know our big secret, and if it gets out, the Stranger will 100 percent try to murder Lizzy. He's a stickler for canon. I know I don't deserve it from you, but for her sake, can you please keep this between us?"

Alicia crossed her arms, remembering again how awful Jenny had been to her. "Who else knows?" she asked.

"Jack found out at his Christmas party, and now he hates us both," said Eliza. "Let's see. Mason knows."

"Mason?"

"First one to figure it out, believe it or not," said Jenny. "He's not as dumb as he looks. And of course our aunt. And Dinah Black."

"And Charlie," said Eliza.

"Fine, I won't tell," said Alicia. "With that many people in the loop, it will probably come out on its own soon, anyway. But I still don't forgive you, and we are not friends, Jenny Valentine!"

"That's tough," said Eliza. "Because we need your help, Alicia."

"Hah! Even if I wanted to, how would I help you?"

"We need you to talk to Jack, and get him to let us into the mansion," said Jenny.

Alicia's face fell. "I can never be in the same room with him again.

Not after what you did."

"Of course you can," said Jenny. She removed a folded-up piece of paper from her Coach mini and handed it to Alicia. "I double-checked your DNA and it turns out I was wrong. It's one of your ancestors who married a cousin. According to that, you're practically Irish royalty, Your Grace."

Oh, well played, Jenny.

"Is this real?" Alicia asked, studying the paper.

"As real as you want it to be," said Jenny. "As I understand it from Lockhart, the guy you called 'Dad' was a real piece of shit. Fuck him. Write your own backstory."

A sly smile spread across Alicia's lips.

"Jack told me he's secretly a duke in Austria," she said.

"Hah!" said Jenny.

"Legally speaking, he sort of is?" said Eliza. "I can put the word out to the Bitchy Brigade that Jenny was wrong, and I helped you test your DNA to prove it."

"If you really want to sell it, you can come to my expulsion hearing, and I'll tell everyone how wrong and sorry I am," said Jenny. "And then you can graciously forgive me and tell Vice Principal Carter how the real injustice would be expelling me without giving me a chance to make amends or some bullshit."

"You're not going to do anything to screw Jack over if he lets you into his mansion, are you?" Alicia asked.

"Of course not, he's our baby brother," said Jenny. "But one request: if you talk to him, can you *not* tell him we asked you to get us in there?"

"Why not?"

"I haven't had a chance to apologize to him yet," said Jenny. "I don't want him thinking it's just transactional."

"Isn't it?" Alicia asked. "Isn't *this*?"

"No, it's not," Jenny said. "I'm being sincere, Alicia. I know it's no excuse, but I'm sure you're aware that I spent some time in a psychiatric facility. I was… in a bad place, mental health-wise, when I did what I did. I'm not normally *that* much of a bitch. I really am truly sorry."

Alicia sighed, looking back and forth between them, still guarded and wary. "I make no promises. You may go now. Huxie!"

She patted her thigh, and the orange tabby leaped from Jenny's lap and scampered back to Alicia. He tried jumping up to her, slipped on the hardwood floor, and bonked into the side of the couch. Eliza bent down and lifted the kitty back onto the couch.

"What a luxurious coat," Eliza said, running a hand over General Hux's soft orange fur. "I'm surprised you didn't name him Crookshanks."

"I wanted to." Alicia smiled, pulling the cat into her lap. "But Crookshanks is clever, and paper bags defeat this guy."

The twins gathered their things to go, Eliza affixing a beanie and a surgical mask over her face.

"By the way, I liked your book," said Eliza.

"Thanks!" said Alicia. "Maybe I'll give my MC a secret twin in the sequel!"

Jenny snorted from the doorway.

"So long as you make her evil, and give her a British accent," said Jenny.

Eliza pinched her as they left. But she waited until they rode the elevator down, walked to the jeep, and were driving back home to ask the question on her mind.

"Why don't you *really* want Jack to know we asked Alicia for help?"

"He's a momma's boy," said Jenny. "Can't have him figuring out we're searching for evidence connecting Val to a murder. Besides, I was thinking about Thanksgiving night, when the Stranger attacked Nilay."

"Jack was in Vegas. He sent me a selfie."

"That's just it, Lizzy," said Jenny. "He could have sent that selfie from anywhere."

THE SCHOOL WAS ABUZZ THE NEXT DAY WITH NEWS OF JIMMY Figg's arrest, which had finally gone public. He'd copped not only to shaving Thanh's head but also to sending a bunch of wild hogs onto the Homecoming dance floor, with the help of some Harbor High kid. A greater betrayal, Blackbird Springs Academy had never known. Students began to murmur about how Jenny Valentine had tried to stop him before the dance. And maybe Jimmy rigged the Homecoming vote to discredit her. And wasn't Jimmy roommates with Lance Ashcroft on the senior trip when he died? That seemed sketchy! And maybe Jimmy drugged Jenny Valentine a couple of weeks ago, and that's why she went so hard on Alicia Aaron!

Those last two rumors, which Jenny had started herself, weren't exactly taking off, but at least they muddied the water. Eliza and the Bitchy Brigade let it be known that Alicia was in fact Irish nobility. And—for real, no cap—who *hadn't* tried to fuck their hot cousin?

With her reputation on the mend, Alicia was back in class and glued at the hip to Jack. At lunchtime, Jenny hesitantly joined them at the Unfridgeables table. Jack shot her a warning glare when she sat down, but he allowed it. After he and Alicia finished their lunch, Jack motioned to the other seniors to bring it in.

"Ladies. Gentleman. Trouble. Huddle up," he said. "In a few weeks, my mother is attending an overnight women's retreat in Santa Barbara. It so happens to fall within a week of my birthday. You know what that means."

"Hell yeah!" said Lai, dapping up Jack and the other boys.

"We're keeping this exclusive," Jack warned them. "If you're not listening to my voice right now, you're not invited, and my sister Tori will throw you out if you try to gate crash."

"Can I bring a chick?" JeRay asked.

"You don't have a chick!" said Penny.

"I could!"

"I'm allowing a plus-one, but no Harbor High kids," said Jack. "The date is March 9th. That's a school night, so make arrangements. No gifts, please. I only ask that you bring yourselves, a good attitude, and a better excuse to keep your parents from asking questions."

They all leaned back, snickering about the trouble they were going to get up to. Jenny waited until she caught Jack's attention and gave a questioning shrug. He appraised Jenny and her sister.

"Alicia seems to think you deserve a second chance," Jack said. "You've already burned that one. We're probably on chance eight or nine by now."

"Why not make it an even dozen?" said Eliza.

"A baker's dozen," said Jenny.

"You're not bringing that girl from the arcade," said Jack.

"Already dumped her ass," said Jenny.

Jack leaned back, shaking his head ruefully.

"Something tells me I'll live to regret this," he said. "Just remember, you'll turn 18 at midnight. Fuck up again, and I won't hesitate to tell the cops *everything* I know."

Meaning: if Jenny wasn't on her best behavior, he'd tell the whole world about Eliza.

Chapter Twenty-Seven
The Party

THE NEXT FEW WEEKS PASSED IN A BLUR OF HOMEWORK AND studying. The teachers all knew they'd lose the seniors' attention for good once Spring Break came, so they were determined to cram their students' heads with as much useless knowledge as they could while the days were still overcast. Jenny read several non-*Trouble* books and even enjoyed some of them. Especially *Never Let Me Go* (because she watched the Carey Mulligan movie instead). If she or Eliza ever needed a spare organ, they had each other covered.

Much to Vice Principal Carter's chagrin, Jenny escaped expulsion by the skin of her teeth. At her hearing, Alicia came through in the clutch with an endorsement, and Lockhart successfully argued that Jenny was a much greater threat to the town without high school to keep her occupied. That must have swayed Mayor Villanova to vote in her favor. "This is your last—I repeat—very last chance, Jenny Valentine!" the superintendent warned.

Whatever.

February rolled into March. Mom's retro clothes went back into a box in the garage. Jenny's favorite three-quarter-length sleeve top made a triumphant return to her wardrobe.

Eliza helped her ditch the mohawk, cutting her hair back down to pixie length. Then she cried the whole time when Jenny returned the favor. Sorry, sis, but they might need to revive their famous switcharoo act at the party, so it was wigs for Kazu from now on.

Without all the fast food and alcohol in her diet, Jenny found herself with boundless energy to burn. She and Aunt Shelly took up jogging at the ass crack of dawn again. Getting up that early was murder, but sometimes their route would take them near Dinah's neighborhood, and they would pass Dinah jogging the other way in her Lululemon workout gear. What a coincidence!

Heheheh.

When Jenny eyed herself in the mirror on the morning of March 9th, an older, leaner, lethal Trouble smiled back at her. Eliza appeared in the reflection next to her, still sans makeup, brushing her teeth, once more a perfect, identical twin.

"Girl, you'll be a woman soon," Jenny said.

She grabbed Lizzy's head and pulled it down to kiss her on the forehead. Eliza retaliated by spitting out her toothpaste in Jenny's cup of tea. The night before, she caught Eliza coming home from the drugstore with a box of condoms in her shopping bag.

"I thought you said you and Drew still hadn't kissed," Jenny had asked.

"We haven't!" Eliza snapped. "I'm just taking precautions for the party. That's what Trouble does, doesn't she? Prepares for all outcomes?"

"Trouble wouldn't be caught dead with one of these," Jenny said, shooing the latex away.

An hour later, with Eliza now in her Kazu disguise, they joined their grandparents, Shelly, and Lockhart for breakfast. They ate in silence until Jiji's tea finished steeping—the signal to the table that conversation could commence.

"I understand congratulations are in order," said Baba, practically beaming at Jenny.

Oh no, now what?

Jiji handed Jenny a heavy, bulky envelope. The logo for Stanford was printed on it. Jenny gawked.

"Open it!" said her grandmother.

Jenny tore the envelope open, and sure enough:

> Dear Jennifer,
>
> Congratulations! You have been admitted to the Stanford Class of 2025!

"I didn't even apply there," Jenny said.

"They think you're a legacy," said Jiji, laughing. "Johnny sent them a bunch of money for Tori. They're expecting you to do the same."

"That's so… bloody unfair!" Eliza said.

"Stanford is practically Ivy League!" said Baba. "It could open a lot of doors."

Dinah was going to an Ivy…

"This is… unexpected," said Jenny. "Thanks? I guess? Since you're in such a good mood, Kazu and I have a favor to ask."

"Oh god, what?" asked Shelly.

"Jack is throwing a birthday party at the mansion tonight," said Eliza. "He'd love it if we could attend, since it's almost, er, Jennifer's birthday too."

"Absolutely not," said Shelly. "It's a school night."

"Shelly, please," Jenny pleaded. "We'll do all our homework right after school, and Val will be there to keep an eye on us. Come on, I only turn 18 once."

Shelly glared at Eliza as if she should have put a stop to this.

"I'm sure it will be quite all right," said Eliza. "Jack tells me this is a posh affair. Black tie, only."

Her aunt's glare narrowed further. She looked at Lockhart for support and found no such backup.

"I was gonna say," he said. "Semisonic is playing at Cache Creek tonight."

"Relax, Shells, it's just a dinner party," said Jenny. "What's the worst that could happen?"

Drew splurged and picked them up that evening in a rented stretch limousine. He rang the doorbell in a nice dinner jacket that he had the good sense to get tailored, and just about passed out when he saw Eliza all dolled up in Shelly's black cocktail dress, a wig of silky straight hair, and five-inch stilettos.

"Wow! Y-you look amazing!" he stammered, before noticing Jenny standing there, too. "And Jenny! You, uh, you look like the Joker's waiter."

"Mine is not for the male gaze," Jenny said.

Tonight's outfit was slacks, her favorite black top, and a purple waistcoat. Simple, fashionable, and easy to get in and out of, should the need arise. Not super warm, though. Dark clouds were creeping on the horizon. She leaned back inside to grab her hoodie.

"Be good, you two!" Shelly warned them.

"Have fun at the concert, Shells!" Jenny called back. "Lockhart better drive safe! It looks like rain."

The limo driver held the rear door open, and Jenny found the passenger cabin already packed with Meghan May, Mason, and Penny. All looked spiffy in evening wear—especially Penny, whose braids were wrapped up in an intricate bun.

"What's with the backpacks, girls? You forget to do your homework?" Mason asked.

Jenny tucked her Coach mini under her feet. Eliza shrugged, patting her bag as if it were just a big purse.

"A Girl Detective's work is never finished," Jenny replied.

"Hey, none of that!" said Meghan. "Tonight is about drinking and partying. Good vibes only."

Jenny pulled her backpack to her knees and flipped open the top flap, revealing a bottle of Crown Royal Whiskey. "The vibes are on lock. I got you, Meghan."

Meghan didn't need to know that under the whiskey bottle in her pack was her lockpick kit, fingerprinting kit, plaster of paris, a flashlight, her collapsable riot baton, a taser, and her heirloom photo— just in case Jenny found more photos in Val's records and needed to compare them.

She looked at Mason. "No college for you?"

"You guys don't even know, man," said Mason. "The coolest thing about college is nobody cares if you take a day off. It whips ass!"

They spent the ride listening to Mason's college stories until the limo eased to a stop. Jenny reached for the door.

"Not yet," Drew said, stopping her. "Got one more to pick up."

"Who?"

In answer, the door opened, and Dinah Black slid into the last empty seat. She was dressed casually in skinny jeans, a leather jacket over a loose top, and Saint Laurent high-ankle booties. Damn. Even when she wasn't trying, the girl couldn't help looking otherworldly pretty.

The others were being rudely quiet, everyone watching Dinah until she looked up from fastening her seatbelt and noticed Jenny.

"Oh," said Dinah.

"I didn't think you were coming," said Jenny.

"I wasn't aware you were coming, either," said Dinah. A dubious smirk spread across her face as she turned to Drew. "Someone failed to mention it when they insisted—nay, begged and pleaded—that I attend, for Jack's sake."

"Sparkling cider?" Drew asked, offering Dinah a glass.

Attaboy, sidekick!

Jenny braced for a nasty look from Dinah. Something, anything to let her know not to get her hopes up. It never came. Dinah smiled at Jenny and raised her glass to toast.

"To the real birthday girl," she said. "Sorry, I didn't bring you a gift."

Eliza snickered next to her, and Jenny was sure her cheeks were glowing bright red right now. When they reached the mansion, raindrops had begun to pepper the roof of the limo. The driver produced a giant umbrella and ushered them in pairs to the front door. Jenny made sure to pair up with Dinah.

"This feels like the beginning of *Clue*," Dinah said as they hurried up the coral flagstone steps. "What, with you dressed like Wadsworth and all."

"Hey!"

"Kidding. You're closer to the Singing Telegram girl. Thank god you ditched that mohawk," said Dinah.

They waited under the eaves of the entrance while the others shuttled over.

"It was a phase," Jenny said. "I guess that makes you Yvette."

"That's Charlie, she speaks better French," said Dinah. "Spiritually, I'm more of a Mrs. White, though I suppose I'm dressed as the Motorist tonight."

"Sure, if the Motorist was fashionable and gorgeous," said Jenny.

Dinah gave Jenny an "aw, shucks" smile and accepted the compliment as Meghan and Mason joined them.

"Miss Scarlett and Colonel Mustard," Jenny whispered to Dinah, who giggled.

She had no idea what was happening. It was like Dinah had forgotten she hated Jenny, and they could just be friends again. It felt so good.

"I'm excited!" said Meghan. "This is the first time I've been here! Jack's never invited me over before, the punk!"

"Peacock, Mrs. White, and..." Jenny murmured, when Penny, Eliza, and Drew walked up to complete the party.

"Has anyone actually rang the doorbell?" Drew asked.

"Go for it, man," said Mason.

"Mr. Boddy," Dinah whispered back, her breath in Jenny's ear sending shivers down her spine.

The door swung open, and Jack greeted them with Alicia on his arm.

"Mr. Green!" Jenny and Dinah said to each other, giggling.

Jack frowned at them, nonplussed, and ushered them inside. His charcoal suit had a red tie and cufflinks, which complimented Alicia's crimson and black layered dress. It was the one she wore to Homecoming, Jenny realized, with the provocative high slit showing off her prosthetic leg.

"Jack insisted I wear it again," Alicia said, grinning as if she could read Jenny's mind.

"So would I," said Dinah.

"Hello hello, children," said a voice down the hall with an affected mid-Atlantic accent. Tori Valentine wore a simple linen dress and jeans under a long knit coat. "Refreshments and entertainment can be had in the game room. There are bathrooms across the hall. I'd appreciate it if you kept to that part of the mansion. Valentine Manor is rather larger than it appears, and I'd hate for one of you kids to get lost."

For that last sentence, she stared directly at Jenny. The group matriculated down the hall to the game room, with Tori bringing up the rear to keep them from wandering.

"No Officer Darcy to keep you company?" Jenny asked her.

"She's working," said Tori, frowning. "Night shift."

They found Lai, Thanh, and JeRay already mingling in the game room. There was a pool table, ping-pong, foosball, darts, and a whole cabinet of board games. At least there weren't any video games. Jack had lightly decorated the room with balloons and a hanging banner that read:

Happy Birthday, Valentines

Jenny smiled and drifted over to the refreshment table. Dinah joined her. The spread was mostly charcuterie and caviar, with a crystal punch bowl and an ice-filled chest full of La Croix, sparkling cider, and soda. Tori leaned past them to grab herself a Diet Coke.

"We have a veggie platter in the fridge," Tori said to Dinah. "I'll bring it out in a bit."

"We can go get it," Jenny offered.

"No, really, stay where you are," Tori said, giving her maximum stink-eye.

Jenny assembled a little mini sandwich out of the cured meats, Vella cheese, and pull-apart sourdough from the Basque. Dinah handed Jenny a limoncello La Croix—which happened to be Jenny's favorite—and helped herself to a Diet Coke. Drew got a game of Giant Jenga going, and Jack cranked up the stereo. Some of his favorite Canadian indie rock. Thank god it wasn't '80s music.

"Cheers," said Jenny, tapping cans with Dinah.

"So Drew and *Kazumi*, huh?" said Dinah. "Does he know?"

"He does not," said Jenny. "It's still early, he hasn't even worked up the nerve to kiss her yet."

"What are you going to do when he does?"

"I still say it's an if, not a when," said Jenny. "But as always, I will burn that bridge when I come to it. Jack knows now. I don't know if I'd told you that."

"You didn't, since other than that night at Mel's, we haven't spoken all year," said Dinah.

Jenny stuffed her mini sandwich into her mouth, not sure how to respond. They'd been so in tune with each other tonight, and now, a sour note in their tentative nocturne.

"My doing, I know," Dinah went on. "I could have handled that better."

"Hah!" Jenny said through a mouthful. She forced herself to chew and swallow. "Give me a break, D. You know I've done far worse to you."

"I know," said Dinah. She turned to fix Jenny with shining blue eyes. "I forgive you."

"Um. Why?"

Dinah swallowed and dabbed her lashes. "My mother has cancer."

"What! Oh no, I'm so sorry!"

"It's okay," Dinah said, squeezing the hand Jenny had unconsciously clutched her arm with. "They caught it very early, the prognosis is excellent. But it put things in perspective, you know? When I saw you with Eliza at Mel's, I realized it made me happy, not angry. I think you only ever let me know half of Jenny Valentine. You were hiding the best parts."

"Yeah, everyone loves Danger," said Jenny, glum.

"No, Jen, I'm talking about you." Dinah moved closer and lowered her voice. "The you who has a sister. It was so obvious. You can be your full self with her, and I think that's beautiful."

Jenny managed a wobbly laugh. Her free hand had become entwined in Dinah's, and she didn't want to let go.

"Damnit, D, you've got me all flustered now," said Jenny. "I'm still horrified for your mom. Is she really okay? Can I send her flowers or something?"

Tori approached, bearing a big platter of fresh fruit, deviled eggs, celery sticks, baby carrots, and a variety of dipping sauces and other finger veggies.

Dinah helped herself to a carrot. "She is, and you're welcome to but don't overdo it," said Dinah. "She's already getting annoyed at my dad for fussing, and Lancer follows her around everywhere. It's like he knows."

"Good dog," said Tori.

"Enough about that, we shan't be maudlin at a birthday party," Dinah said. She stared at Tori, who was lingering. "Bye, Tori."

Tori tossed her hair and went off to lecture Lai about using a coaster.

Once she was out of earshot, Dinah leaned closer and whispered, "I assume you'll require a distraction to sneak away soon?"

"What makes you think that?" Jenny replied.

"Because you're nothing but Trouble, Valentine," said Dinah. "Why else did you come to this party?"

A mischievous smile twitched at the corners of Jenny's mouth. Jack called Tori over and made her take a turn at Jenga.

"It *is* my birthday," Jenny said. She checked her watch. "But not for another four hours. There's no hurry."

With Tori focused on the Jenga tower, Jenny pulled the bottle of Crown Royal from her Coach mini and tipped it into the punch bowl. *Glug glug glug.* Dinah's eyes widened as Jenny poured the entire bottle in.

"Jesus," said Dinah. "I think that's more whiskey than punch, now. We're all gonna be shitfaced."

Jenny grinned and began ladling the spiked punch into red solo cups.

"That's the idea." She handed two cups to Dinah and picked up two of her own. "C'mon, let's go show these fools how to play Truth or Dare."

Chapter Twenty-Eight
Truth or Dare

SOME SMALL VOICE IN THE BACK OF ELIZA'S MIND WAS TELLING HER to be wary of this sudden rekindling between Jenny and Dinah. *Just like that, and they're holding hands again?* The rest of her brain was telling that voice to shut the fuck up because Drew looked dashing in his tailored sports coat.

Booze helped. Eliza knew she couldn't get too wasted, but the spiked punch Jenny and Dinah served was calming her nerves. With luck, it was loosening Drew's Boy Scout inhibitions, too.

Her sister caught Eliza's gaze and raised an eyebrow, tilting her head.

"Is it Trouble time?" she asked in Japanese.

"No, it's kissing time!" Jenny replied in kind. "No rush for Trouble, enjoy the party."

Eliza suspected that Jenny's relaxed timeline had a lot to do with Blondie sharing a loveseat with her, but she'd take it.

"What are they saying?" Mason asked, as though an interpreter were present.

"We were talking all about *you*, Mason!" said Jenny. "That's all we ever discuss in our own language. Particularly what we suspect to be your inadequacy as a lover, and how your breath smells."

"Sounds like you got some bad intel," Mason said and belched loudly.

"They're half-right," said Meghan, waving his burp away.

"How droll," said Eliza in her accent. "Forgive me, but I was telling my lovely, troubled cousin that this party was missing something."

"Strip poker?" asked Mason.

"Truth or dare," said Jenny.

"No dares that might break things!" Tori called from the corner, where she was reading a book. "And nothing too gross!"

"Better put your AirPods in, Tori," said Jack.

And so it began, with JeRay immediately getting dared to lick Alicia's stump. Alicia said only Jack was allowed to, so the challenge was amended to licking Penny's knee, which gave Penny a case of the giggles so severe she had to run to the ladies' room before she peed herself.

"Who knew she was so ticklish?" JeRay said with a grin.

"Okay, I think it's time we all had the truth outta *you*, Jenny Valentine!" said Mason.

"Not so fast, I might say dare," said Jenny.

"I'll dare you to send Jimmy Figg your nudes," he said.

"Truth!"

"Admit that you rigged the Homecoming vote, reveal how you did it, and tell us who would have won," said Mason.

"That's three truths, not one," said Jenny. "I will simply say that my contribution to the dance was much more exciting than Jack and Dinah winning again, which is what would have happened if I'd stayed home."

Everyone booed.

"Does the Bitchy Brigade crown mean nothing to you people!?" said Meghan.

"Yas queen!" said Drew.

Eliza frowned despite herself. She'd secretly harbored the hope that she was the real winner.

"I voted for you," Drew muttered in her ear.

Awww! Drewboo!

All the couples took turns earnestly swearing that they voted for their significant other.

"I voted for Jimmy," said Lai. "Just wanted to see fancy boy Jack lose at something for once."

Jack removed his arm from Alicia's waist to dap Lai up.

"If we're doing truths, I have a confession to make," said Meghan. She turned to Eliza. "Kazu, I told Jimmy he should ask you out to Homecoming, and that you'd say yes if he did a flashy proposal."

Everyone burst into laughter, and Eliza found herself torn between anger and appreciation for Meghan's little stunt.

"Why'd he have to come at me for that, and not you?!" Eliza asked, deciding on the latter and laughing along with them.

"I know, I kept expecting him to," said Meghan.

"He did," said Jenny. "Meghan, do you think it was a coincidence that your mom came home early and caught you and Mason before Homecoming?"

Meghan gasped at the realization. Mason shook his head, chagrined.

"Thank god we don't have to pretend to be nice to that little bitch anymore," said Thanh.

In the months since Jimmy's attack on her, Thanh's hair had regrown into a shaggy mop that Eliza thought looked quite fetching. Thanh hadn't brought him, but the rumor was she'd started dating a college boy.

"Oh, was I not supposed to invite Jimmy?" said Jack, faking surprise. "He's gonna be here any second."

Thanh was horrified until she realized he was just yanking her chain, and then they all took turns roundly abusing the little asshole.

"As if! He literally shit on my ballroom. Banned! For life! Jail!" said Jack.

"Guys like Jimmy don't last in prison," Mason said sagely.

"He's not going to prison, he's only 15," said Penny, just returning from the bathroom. "He'll plead all that down, get a ton of community service, and they'll expunge it from his record in three years."

"Okay, but wait! How *did* you rig Homecoming, Trouble?" Alicia asked, yanking Jack's arm back around her midsection.

"Who says I did?" Jenny smirked. "But if I wanted to, the real trick would have been getting everyone's write-in vote in their own handwriting. Heheh. Okay, my turn! I pick Kazu." She put on a terrible British accent. "Truth or dare, innit?"

Everyone groaned at the sad attempt.

"Was that supposed to be Kaz?" Jack asked, giving Jenny a knowing, nasty smile. "You sound like a drunk Irishman."

"No need to be redundant," said Drew.

"Easy there, friend, yer talkin' to a Countess of me homeland over here!" said Alicia, busting out a terrific Irish brogue.

"Oi, it's a cinch, really," said Meghan, in an impressive Liverpool variant. "All us birds 'ave an accent from the Isles in the back pocket of our trousers."

"All of us except for Trouble, bruv," said Penny. "Highly ironical, don't you think, considering she's keen to be the master of disguise?"

"Even Tori's got one," Dinah said in a British accent. "She did it so much, it got stuck that way."

"Mine's real!" Tori said from the corner, taking an AirPod out.

Jenny glared at them all, turning pink.

"Right, then," Eliza said, shaking with laughter. "I choose dare before my cousin tries her accent again."

Jenny stewed for a beat before a worrisome grin spread over her lips.

"Come here, Drew," Jenny said, walking to the refreshments table.

She grabbed an apple from the fruit basket and instructed Drew to stand about 10 paces away from Eliza. Then she placed the apple on Drew's head and whispered something into his ear that Eliza couldn't make out.

"You know what to do, Kazu," Jenny said, turning back to her.

A crack of thunder outside startled them all.

"I can't watch this," Tori said, rising and putting her book away.

"While you're up, can you get more punch from the kitchen?" Dinah asked.

Tori nodded and left the game room. Eliza smirked and reached into her purse for her kunai dagger. The others already knew she had it, from Homecoming, so what was the risk?

Other than missing, of course.

She flicked her wrist and sent the knife flying. It skewered the apple cleanly and knocked it off Drew's head.

"Fuck!" he shouted.

The other kids all oohed and awed.

"Goddamn, Kazu!" said JeRay. "I didn't realize I was going to school with a super ninja!"

Jenny retrieved the stuck apple and handed it to Eliza.

"Ah, point of order," said Jack. "That felt more like a dare for Drew, than Kazu."

The others agreed, dashing Eliza's plan to dare Drew to do something naughty to her.

Dammit, Trouble!

And then Drew surprised her.

"I pick myself, and I pick dare," he said, and walked over to Eliza, extending his hand.

Charmed and curious, she let him pull her to her feet.

"I dare myself to kiss you," he said.

Before Eliza had time to consider the request, he was leaning in and pressing his lips to hers. Fireworks exploded in her brain, and she lost all sense of herself and her surroundings. Drew wasn't an aggressive kisser; his ministrations were soft and gentle. She parted her lips to let his tongue in, and they explored each other, only dimly aware of the wolf-whistling and hollering around them.

This was a worthy first kiss, she told herself as they finally parted. Not that kissing Charlie on the floor of Schloss Schwarzwald, while covered in blood and recovering from a fentanyl overdose, didn't have a certain tragic grandeur to it. But this was a Hollywood movie kiss. A kiss to make the rest of them jealous and yearning.

When her brain started working again, Eliza spotted Jack and Alicia edging towards the door, trying to sneak off for some passion of their own. Unfortunately for them, they ran right into Tori returning with more punch.

"Where do you think you're going?" Tori asked.

"I thought I'd give Alicia a tour of the Manor," said Jack. "She's never really had an official one."

"Ooh! Can I come!?" Meghan asked.

"It's more of a private tour, Meghan," said Jack.

Mason whispered something in Meghan's ear. Who knew the Queen Bee of the Bitchy Brigade could blush?

"Eeeeegghhhhhhh," said Tori, or something to that effect.

Jack glared at his older half-sister.

"Why don't I go get the dessert platter ready," she said, backing out into the hall. "And then drink some bleach."

"We'll be back!" Jack said to the room before exiting with Alicia.

The leftover guests laughed, and Penny restarted the game by daring Lai and JeRay to kiss. After mutually declaring "no homo," they embraced so passionately that Eliza was feeling a little annoyed at being shown up by the time they parted.

"Damn, I think they win," said Penny.

"In your fucking face, Drew!" said JeRay.

"Owned your ass," said Lai.

They high-fived and took a seat, calling on Penny to go next. Eliza and Drew had stumbled back onto a sofa at some point. She whispered in his ear to meet her in the hallway in two minutes, grabbed her backpack, and announced she had to pee.

"Yeah, we're gonna need to get more booze," Dinah said, reloading the punch bowl.

At the door, Eliza glanced back to catch Jenny's subtle nod. Almost time to get to work. But first…

"I think they could tell I don't actually need to pee," Drew whispered to her in the hall outside the game room, exactly 120 seconds later.

"Good, it's better to go after," said Eliza.

"After what?"

She gave him her sultriest smile, took his hand, and led him upstairs. A flash of lightning through the window illuminated the second-story hallway. The Red Room—nicknamed for its distinctive red accent wall—was one of the few bedrooms in the east wing of Valentine Manor. It had its own bathroom and would afford them plenty of privacy. If Drew found it odd that Kazumi knew exactly where a free guest bedroom could be found, he wasn't about to complain about it.

Thunder rolled. Eliza pushed Drew onto the bed and locked the door.

"You're sure?" he asked.

"Honestly, I appreciate how little you've pressured me, Porter," Eliza said. "You've been a right proper gentleman, but I had to wait a month to get a snog from you, so I hope you won't think me a harlot if I say I'll be damned if I'm to wait another month before we can shag. Get your trousers off, mister!"

He didn't need to be told twice. She marveled at his ripped calf and thigh muscles, and the ease with which he pulled her cocktail dress over her head.

It was her first time with a guy. She didn't entirely know what she was doing down there, but certain skills she'd honed with Charlie transferred quite effectively to a male body—if Drew's reaction was anything to go by. He wasn't quite so experienced, but that was okay. There'd be plenty of time for practice. When they paused so she could retrieve the condom from her bag, Drew made a "What else you got in that bag?" joke.

"Just you wait," Eliza said.

Much fumbling and youthful exuberance followed. They never quite found the same rhythm, and then it was over, and Eliza was full and content.

"Now, you pee," she whispered and nibbled on his ear.

Thunder rumbled again in the distance. Drew got up to take care of things, and Eliza lay back, pondering the whole affair. After a year and a half of pining, invisible in her sister's skin, Eliza had finally done it! Sex with a man felt different than sex with a woman, and Eliza greedily enjoyed both flavors. She reached into her backpack to prepare her next steps before Drew returned and snuggled under the sheets next to her.

"Um, wow!" he said, a big dumb grin on his face. "That was… amazing. Do—do you want to go again?"

"I absolutely want to, Drewboo," Eliza said, lifting the soaked rag in her hand. "Just need to clean up a bit, first."

"Oh, sure," Drew said, and politely averted his eyes.

Oh, Drew.

He was so new to sex that he didn't recognize a chloroform rag when he saw one. Eliza rolled over to drape her arm around his bulging, muscular shoulder and pressed the rag over his face. He melted into the mattress in blissful contentment, never even resisting as Eliza sent him into a dreamless sleep.

She held him for a solid minute, pressing her ear to his chest to listen to the steady drumbeat of his heart. Then she sat up and pulled off her wig. Apart from the condom and the chloroform, her bag contained an exact duplicate of Jenny's party attire.

Another flash of lightning lit the room, followed by an ear-splitting roar of thunder. The game was afoot.

Chapter Twenty-Nine

No Mystery Is Complete Without It

BACK AT THE PARTY, ANOTHER KIND OF GAME WAS PETERING OUT. Thanh had called "truth" and was asked by Dinah to reveal the naughtiest sex act she'd ever performed. Of course, that made her think of her dead boyfriend, Lance, and she threatened to start boohooing.

Rain pattered on the windows and a growl of thunder rumbled in the distance. As Jack liked to say, the vibes were officially chalked.

Tori returned with a tray of cookies, cupcakes, and crème brûlées. Lai was quick to shove a pink macaroon into Thanh's mouth, lest the vibes deteriorate further. Jenny licked all the rainbow buttercream frosting off a cupcake, telling Dinah she needed the sugar boost while letting her eye contact send a different message. Lizzy sneaking off to get laid had made her a tad jealous. Okay, very jealous, and a little annoyed. Jenny would love nothing more than to do the same with Dinah, but she had Trouble business to attend to. And they were all out of booze, which had the group chat popping off right under Tori's nose.

Meghan:	Doesn't this place have a wine cellar?
Mason:	Yeah, but you'd need a safecracker to get inside. They keep the good shit down there and lock it down like Fort Knox.

Thanh: How rude of Jack to ditch without restocking! It's his fucking party!

Penny: Welcome to the Jack Valentine experience.

Lai: Alicia wasn't even drinking.

JeRay: What about the kitchen?

Jenny: Mrs. Rivas or the cook might be in there.

Thanh: Tori said she sent them all home.

Dinah: Come on, Trouble, you lived here. Don't let us down.

Jenny: I would never, babe. There's a minibar in the study. Might take a bit to pick the lock, but I can get in there.

JeRay: Huzzah!

Jenny: I'll require a distraction.

Mason called Tori over to help him release the balls for the pool table, pretending he just couldn't find the switch himself. As soon as Tori's back was turned, Jenny snuck away, hand in hand with Dinah. They hurried the short distance to the study and slipped inside. Jenny breathed in the familiar scents of the room and sublimated fully into her Trouble role.

A memory stirred: Tori's tale after Mr. Webb died, of the time this study had been filled with *unfamiliar* scents. Pine-Sol and cleaning chemicals.

"Okay, where to?" asked Dinah. "I assume we're not actually stealing booze, right?"

Jenny tried to focus on a detail from Tori's story… Damn. It was gone.

"Um. Right. Archive room," Jenny said. "Wherever that is. I'm guessing the storage lockers off the garage."

"Yes." Dinah nodded. "There's a whole file room down there. What are we looking for?"

"We?"

"I'm trying to appreciate the whole Jenny here," Dinah said. "Don't go shutting me out now."

Before Jenny could reply, a tremendous flash of lightning boomed outside the windows. In the split second of blinding light, her gaze was drawn to Dad's desk and the large calendar blotter atop it. Sure enough, as though she'd expected to find it there, a star had been drawn on tomorrow's date. Her birthday.

A loud *thunk!* sounded in the distance and the power went out.

"Great," said Dinah. "Did you bring a light?"

In the darkness, Dinah instinctively edged closer, but Jenny couldn't stop staring at the desk.

"Jenny?"

In her mind, she mapped the details Tori had shared all those months ago onto the desk. The old detective novel—written, as she and Eliza had learned, by RJ himself—was on top of the blotter when Tori arrived. Hadn't there been more?

"Hey!"

Alicia's skeleton key, and… Jack's yearbook? But that was later, when Tori returned from rehab in the fall. When Dad was plotting the game.

"Sorry, sleuthing," said Jenny. "Not shutting you out, but we do need to deliver on the booze run if only to keep the guests busy." She retrieved a tiny flashlight from her Coach bag and pointed it at the minibar, which was also locked up. "I'll get started on the minibar. Can you, um… can you search the bookshelves? I think Jack's yearbook might be in here."

Dinah shrugged, game to help. "Yeah, sure."

Jenny gave her the flashlight and went to work on the minibar lock with her backup penlight clenched between her teeth. The first two tumblers fell easy, but this third was being a bitch…

"What year am I looking for?" Dinah called.

"Uh… sophomore year, I think," said Jenny. "You know, I never had a chance to ask, but why were you in here, in the study, that one day for Jack's sweet 16?"

"Huh?"

"Tori said she came in here to meet with RJ, and you were reading on the couch. It was before Jack's birthday party, two years ago."

"Oh, jeez, I totally forgot about that," said Dinah. "Jack wanted an early birthday present from me, if you take my meaning. I didn't a hundred percent know I was gay yet, but I knew I didn't want to do *that*, so I told him to work on his homework first and maybe we could later. I was always sneaking in here when RJ wasn't around. It's such a great room for reading."

The tumbler clicked into place.

"Here we go, sophomore year," said Dinah.

Jenny turned the tension bar and the door to the minibar swung open.

"Voila," she said and shone her light inside. "What do you think? More whiskey?"

Dinah joined her, pressing her body against Jenny's as she leaned over her and appraised the liquor stock. Jenny pointed to a brown bottle of scotch whiskey.

"Jenny, that's a 25-year MacCutcheon," said Dinah.

"Is that bad?"

"That bottle probably cost a thousand dollars."

"Psh, rookie numbers next to *Ressort Rouge*," said Jenny. "What about some Everclear?"

Dinah snorted. "Babe, we want them buzzed, not on the floor."

She bypassed the bottle of 190-proof gasoline and grabbed a frosted glass carafe of vodka.

"Can't go wrong with Grey Goose," said Dinah. "Maybe some Malibu, too."

Good choices, but Jenny wanted a look at that yearbook first. While Dinah handled the liquor, Jenny returned to RJ's desk. She couldn't even say why. Call it Trouble intuition. There had to be a reason Dad had this book out while he was planning the game. She turned to the portrait section and was amused to find a young Jack Valentine with one of those broccoli haircuts so many boys sported that year.

"Color mugshots? Damn rich kids," said Jenny. "At our school, only the seniors got color. Everyone else was in black and white. I can't believe you dated Jack with that hair."

"He *is* very handsome," said Dinah. "Imagine my jubilation when I discovered he had a sister with those same cheekbones."

Those cheekbones were glowing pink right now.

"Okay, I gotta see it," Jenny said, and flipped a few pages back, looking for the Bs. "Dinah Eve Black. Hah!"

Younger Dinah had bangs and a fuck-ass bob.

"Gawd, I hated that hair!" said Dinah. "A few days after taking this, Meghan May told me I looked like the girl who gave the best blowjobs at Mormon summer camp. I cried all night and begged my mother to take me to a real stylist."

"Aww," said Jenny. "Go Mom."

Dinah set the bottles on the desk and leaned closer.

"So what are you looking for?"

Jenny flipped back another page and let out a quiet gasp. In the top left corner, next to the very first portrait, someone had drawn a little doodle in the margin in purple ink. A man in a hat, peeking over a wall. Next to it was a drawing of a globe.

"This," said Jenny. "I think I was looking for this."

The first portrait was of Alicia Aaron. Of course it was; the students were in alphabetical order. Alicia looked impossibly young, with her red hair brushed to one side and a sullen glower on her face.

"What is it?" Dinah asked.

"It's the Stranger's calling card," said Jenny. "But it came from Dad's books first."

"RJ always used purple pens," said Dinah. "This is probably one of his."

Jenny raised a curious eyebrow.

"If I caught him on a good day, I could get him to proofread my English essays," Dinah explained.

Why would RJ doodle a Killroy next to Alicia's photo? What did the globe mean?

Another tumbler clicked into place.

"Holy shit."

It was so dumb that it had to be the answer.

"I can't even," Jenny said. "Dad, you fucking dork, are you serious?!"

She was laughing now, which Dinah found none too amusing,

seeing as she wasn't in on the joke.

"'No mystery is complete without it,'" Jenny said. "That's what Dad said in his will when he left Alicia Aaron the skeleton key."

"Okay…" said Dinah.

"What's something every good mystery needs?"

"A surprise ending? A twist?" Dinah guessed.

"You're getting warmer," said Jenny. "What's that thing called in a mystery where the author makes you think one person is the killer, and then it turns out they're not?"

"Misdirection? Or, oh! A red herring!"

"A red herring!" Jenny shook her head. "Drew was more right than he even knew." She pointed to the photo of Alicia in the yearbook. "A red hair-ing. Get it? He wants to slip a bogus clue into the mix, just to spice things up. Who does he give it to? It can't be anyone connected to him, that defeats the whole purpose of it. So he cracks Jack's yearbook, turns to the mugshots, and the first person he sees is Alicia Double-A Aaron, with red hair, to boot! It's a goddamned pun! A dad joke from beyond the grave!"

Dinah's jaw hung slack as she considered the solution. "Then, the skeleton key…?"

"Doesn't mean anything," said Jenny.

They both stared at the yearbook, mulling over the implications.

"To think, you told the whole school Alicia was inbred over nothing," said Dinah.

"Yeah, that was real shitty of me," Jenny admitted. "I'm trying to be a better person. I did apologize—"

Jenny froze. Was she just imagining it, or was she hearing footsteps nearby? Dinah nodded to the bookshelves next the Dad's desk. They both tensed. Jenny grabbed the crystal bishop paperweight, in case she needed a weapon. Something behind the shelves clicked, and the last section along the outer wall swung open. A dark figure stepped out from the hidden passage. Jenny aimed her weak penlight at their new guest.

It was Eliza Valentine, dressed identically to Jenny, right down to the purple waistcoat.

Jenny checked her watch. "Took you long enough."

Eliza shrugged. "He wanted to cuddle. What'd I miss?"

Howling wind rattled the tall bay windows in RJ's study. With every passing minute, the storm outside was getting worse. Jenny quickly explained her red herring theory to Eliza. It certainly sounded like something RJ would do. The prick.

"What's the globe drawing mean?" she asked, pointing to the doodle next to Killroy in the yearbook.

"I don't know," said Jenny. "A good question, but not a pressing one. We need to get back to the party before we're missed."

"They'll just assume we're off somewhere hooking up," Dinah said.

She'd retreated to the minibar and was mixing herself a drink while the twins caught up. Eliza didn't like how easily Dinah had reinserted herself into Jenny's orbit. Were they both pretending the last year didn't happen?

"Don't tease, babe. We can't have Tori come looking for us," Jenny said.

"Send Dinah back with the booze, and we'll search the records," said Eliza. "Just say Jenny isn't feeling well."

Jenny shook her head. "You know it's gotta be you, Lizzy. Otherwise, Tori will ask questions."

"Okay, I'll go back with Dinah then," said Eliza. "Drew's passed out upstairs. People will assume Kazumi is with him."

"I'd better go with Jenny," Dinah said, returning to RJ's desk bearing three tumblers of liquor. "I know where the archives are, and two can search faster than one."

Eliza was keen to disagree, but it made logical sense. "Fine. How do we meet up again?"

"I'll text you," said Jenny.

"Have you looked at your phone recently?" Eliza asked. "I think a cell tower is down or something. I'm not getting a signal."

"That would explain why the Unfridgeables haven't been blowing up the group chat demanding their booze," said Dinah.

"Damn. Okay, uh… we'll find some pipes to bang on or something," said Jenny. "When you hear a commotion in the garage, that's your cue to get back upstairs and become Kazumi again."

Dinah held out a glass to each of them. An inch of brown liquor sloshed within. "That MacCutcheon was calling my name," Dinah said.

Eliza stared at the glass but didn't take it.

"We got off on the wrong foot, Elizabeth," she said. "I thought we could start over with a better sense memory."

How magnanimous of you, Blondie.

She could feel Jenny's glare, so Eliza reached out and took Dinah's glass instead of the one offered, just in case.

"Touché," said Dinah. She raised her glass. "To the Valentine Girls. Happy Birthday."

Jenny and Dinah downed theirs. Eliza settled for a sip. The scotch burned like liquid smoke in her throat.

"Showtime," said Jenny.

"She'll catch up," Eliza said to Jenny, gesturing for Dinah to stay. "Just wanna have a quick chat with Blondie."

"It's okay," Dinah said. "I'll meet you in the garage."

Her sister shot Eliza *be nice!* daggers and retreated to the secret passageway.

"She's in a more delicate place than she looks," Eliza said, once they were alone. "And the last time you dumped her, she ran away for half a year. If this isn't serious, please don't get her hopes up."

"I understand," Dinah said. "And I'm glad she has someone like you looking out for her. I don't even know what this is right now—if it's anything at all—but I'm not one to play with hearts."

"Thank you," said Eliza.

"Good luck," said Dinah.

The tall blonde headed into the passageway, and Eliza closed the concealed door behind her. A cacophony of laughter reverberated down the hall. Eliza checked in her bag. Perfect, she still had one last Adderall pill left. She popped it into her mouth and washed it down with another sip of scotch. Grabbing the booze, she made her way back in the dark. Flickering candlelight spilled out from underneath the game room door.

"Game on, Trouble," she whispered to herself and pushed the door open.

Jenny was strongly tempted to stay and eavesdrop on the conversation Dinah and Eliza were having, but that would be against the spirit of their renewed bond, wouldn't it? She just hoped Lizzy wasn't being mean. When she reached the end of the passage, she heard the glass conservatory roaring under the downpour outside. Maybe Jenny was just imagining the high-pitched squeals piercing through the din. Jack's bedroom was right upstairs...

"Everybody at this party is getting laid except for me," she grumbled.

The conservatory smelled different. More earthy, and full of sweet decay. Another lightning flash revealed why: it had been transformed since Jenny's last visit. No more cherry blossom trees and soft gravel. It was back to Val's stifling ferns, and her black and crimson roses. What a shame. Jenny peered through the glass door leading into the mansion. There should be a stairwell nearby that led to the garage and basement rooms.

"Shit."

A figure was moving down the hallway. In the dark, she couldn't make out who. Tori? Whomever it was, Jenny couldn't go this way, the roar of rain when she opened the door would surely draw their attention. She'd have to enter the garage from the outside, which meant a walk through the storm. Goddamnit.

Fortunately, the scotch she'd swallowed was working its way into her bloodstream, bringing with it that toasty sensation of invulnerability. It—plus her flimsy hoodie—would have to be enough to protect her from the elements. She spun around and ran out into the dark and stormy night.

Chapter Thirty

The Archives

W ITH NO ELECTRICITY, AND WITHOUT JACK AND HIS CAREFULLY curated playlists, the party had been forced to rely on Lai's phone for tunes. He was playing that Weeknd song from Homecoming. Thanh and Meghan made shadow puppets on the wall in the dim light of some candles they'd scrounged from the board game cabinet.

"Finally!" Meghan shouted when Eliza stepped through the door.

She bounded up to relieve Eliza of the booze. A glance around the game room revealed no trace of Tori.

"What took you so long?" asked JeRay.

"You know what took them so long," said Thanh. "Where's Dinah?"

"Freshening up," said Eliza. "Where's Tori?"

"She went to start the backup generator," said Meghan. "It was supposed to kick on, but it didn't for some reason. So hurry up with that!"

Meghan got to work mixing up some hunch punch with the Grey Goose and Malibu. As they ladled out cups, Eliza noticed the party roster had thinned further.

"Where's Mason?" she asked, looking around.

"Poopin'," said Lai.

"And Penny?"

"She had a headache, and went to lie down," said Thanh.

"Come on, *Homecoming Queen!*" said Meghan, shoving a red solo cup full of booze into Eliza's hand. "You're not legit until you complete the TikTok dance challenge! Show us what you got!"

Eliza smiled. She never did get to finish her routine…

MOST VISITORS TO VALENTINE MANOR ONLY SAW THE ROUNDABOUT driveway with the decorative wishing well in the middle. But off to either side, cleverly concealed by landscaping, offshoots of Cellar Drive plunged into the earth and ran right underneath the mansion. The garage could fit 12 automobiles comfortably and had separate entrances and exits, so one could drive right through below and come out on the other side. Jenny seldom came down here after her initial exploration of the mansion, since their driver would always meet them out front. Thus, she'd never given any thought to the lack of an eave over the service door, leaving it completely exposed to the weather.

"F-fucking Kwikset 908s!" Jenny growled. She was soaked to the bone, her teeth were chattering, and her fingers were starting to go numb. She tried the tension bar again. Nothing. "Fuck!!"

She pounded on the door in a rage. To her shock, it sprang open a few seconds later.

"Jenny! What are you… Get in here, you poor thing!" said Dinah.

She yanked Jenny inside and hustled her over to a workbench.

"Good lord, you look like a drowned rat!" Dinah said. She rummaged in the cabinets until she found an oil-stained drop cloth. "This will have to do."

Jenny allowed herself to be enveloped by the drop cloth, and to be warmed by Dinah's body pressing against her own. Her hands moved rapidly, creating friction. Maybe this would work better if Jenny got out of these soaked clothes…

"Th-thank you," Jenny said.

Their eyes found each other's. Such a pretty, piercing blue. Jenny felt herself leaning in by instinct, searching for Dinah's lips…

"Why didn't you use the stairs?" Dinah asked, turning away.

So close!

"There was somebody in the hallway, near the conservatory," Jenny said.

"Huh, must have just missed them," said Dinah.

"Did you and Lizzy have a good chat?"

Dinah glanced back, teasing with another demure smile. "We're all good. She's only looking out for her big sis. Come on, I think I found the room you want."

Jenny wrapped the drop cloth around her shoulders like a cloak, and Dinah led them deeper into the dark garage with her flashlight, past a storage room and some plumbing equipment, to a plain gray door in the wall marked:

Archives

Jenny reached forward and turned the door handle. It opened easily.

"Oh, thank god. If I had to try picking another Kwikset 908, I might cry."

Dinah scoffed. "As if you don't love it. Be honest, it's no fun when it's too easy."

"Not always, but every now and then, you know?" She grinned at Dinah. "I won't tell if you don't tell."

Dinah clicked her heel and held up her left palm. "Trouble's honor. You never told me what we're looking for."

From Dinah's flashlight, she could see rows of shelves lined with file boxes. In the back of the room, excess boxes were stacked haphazardly in a pile.

"Business records for Stratford Photography," said Jenny. "Circa 2014. I need to know who took the photos of the Little League team that year."

"I see," said Dinah. "Go on."

Jenny explained the photographic fingerprint on the surveillance photos of her mom and dad, and how they matched the Little League team photo. Find the photographer, and they might find the bastard who ran their mother off the road.

"You think they're the Stranger?" asked Dinah.

"Maybe," said Jenny. "If I can link them to Val, and put her away for Mom's murder, I'll consider it a start."

"All right," said Dinah, pulling a file box off the shelf. "You take the other side, and let's find out."

MAYBE IT WAS THE ADDERALL. MAYBE IT WAS THE AFTERGLOW FROM sex with Drew. Maybe it was inhabiting Jenny's identity again. Could be all three. Whatever the case, Eliza killed her dumb TikTok dance.

"Not gonna lie, I didn't think you had those moves in you, girl," said Lai.

"Hate to say it, but he's right, Jenny. That was much better than your cousin," said Thanh.

"Kazu's always been a bit phony, though, hasn't she?" said Meghan.

"Go easy on her," said Eliza, trying not to show her annoyance. "Kazumi's never had a normal high school experience before this year. She's just trying to fit in."

"She tries a little too hard," said Jack, behind her.

Eliza turned to see that he and Alicia had returned. They'd done an impressive job of smartening up their clothing and not looking disheveled, but they couldn't hide their dopey grins. Eliza was wearing the same one on her face.

"Welcome back, Birthday Boy!" Meghan whooped.

The others applauded, turning Alicia's cheeks as red as her hair.

"I'm not saying the power went out because of us," said Jack. "But I ain't saying it didn't, either."

"Jack!"

Alicia lightly slapped him on the shoulder as the others laughed and Lai and JeRay dapped him up. When Jack had finished greeting his bros, he peered at Eliza with suspicious eyes.

"Sister, there's something *different* about you," he said.

"Yeah, you're not being nearly as cunty as usual," said Meghan.

Anger bloomed within Eliza. If she of all people could forgive her sister, what right did they have to talk shit?

"Look, I'm sorry I've been so wretched, but it's been a really hard year, and none of you gave me any support!" Eliza said. "I thought you were my friends, but where were you when I needed you?! I've *killed* to protect you, and that fucks a girl up, ya know? I had nightmares about Campbell Batori for months. I still see Burke Brunner's face, every time I smell a wood fire. But you guys wanted to move on, so I kept it to myself. I would love to live a normal life, but I can't, because there's some deranged lunatic out there who won't let me. I just wish you hated the Stranger half as much as you hated Trouble!"

That got more personal than Eliza intended. Everyone stared at their shoes. Everyone, except for Thanh.

"It's just, sometimes it feels like it's all a game to you," said Thanh. "And real people get hurt."

"It's a game I've been trying to end from the moment it began," said Eliza.

"That's not strictly true," said Jack. "You could have refused to play."

"Do you really think the Stranger would have let me?"

Eliza wasn't sure if the bitterness in her voice was Jenny's or her own.

"I think we all need to take another drink," said JeRay.

"And a new song," said Meghan, since that same Weeknd song was looping again for the umpteenth time.

"All right, Trouble," said Alicia. "You've convinced me."

Eliza turned. Alicia was reaching into her cleavage to pull out a chain—and the skeleton key attached to it. She pulled the chain over her head and tossed it to Eliza.

"Do your thing," Alicia said.

Eliza caught the key and chuckled. Of all the heirloom clues to be freely given… But Alicia didn't know that, and it was a sweet gesture. What the hell, why not? She thought of the globe sketch in Jack's yearbook.

"No cap, I've always wanted to see you work," said Mason at the doorway, returning from the bathroom.

She stared at the skeleton key's engraved inscription along the barrel: *Before you use me, give the world a spin. Home and home and home again.*

A globe. Give the world a spin… Maybe Eliza could put on a proper Trouble show while her sister searched the archives.

"You guys want to solve a mystery?" she asked. "Grab the candles and booze, we're going to the Map Room."

"Found it!" called Dinah.

Jenny dropped her box of tax receipts and rushed over.

"Stratford Photography, 2014," said Dinah.

The box was full of manila folders, and Dinah had her finger on the one labeled **Freelance Invoices**.

"Let me see!" Jenny said.

Dinah pulled out the folder and handed it to her. Jenny flipped it open. There ought to be records of all the freelancers the portrait studio used—

"Fuck me."

Dinah frowned at the single page within the folder, and turned to Jenny, confused.

"What does it mean?"

On the page was a drawing of a little man in a hat, peeking over a fence. In black ink this time, not purple. Below the doodle was a simple message.

TOO HOT!

"It means I was on the right track," said Jenny. "And the Stranger got here first."

Six months of frustration exploded in her core. Jenny unleashed a howl of rage and kicked over a box of Valentine Foundation business records, startling Dinah.

"Ow!"

The box was heavier than she'd expected, and now her toe was throbbing.

"It's all right, Jenny," said Dinah.

"Except it's not!" Jenny cried. "He's always a step ahead! How am

I ever supposed to prove anything against Val if the Stranger won't let me?!"

She collapsed on another box and rubbed her poor toe.

"Don't give up," Dinah said. "You're getting closer, aren't you? There's got to be other records besides these somewhere. Maybe we can ask Tori if she has electronic copies."

"For all I know, Tori's the one hiding them," said Jenny. She wrapped her drop cloth tighter, fighting the shivers. Fighting despair. "Just when I think I'm getting somewhere, it's another dead end. By the time I solve this damn case, senior year will be over, and you'll be long gone at Brown, and I'll never see you again! You know, there was something Dad wrote once, in one of his journals, about knowing you're in the good times while you're in them. Well, these are supposed to be my good times! And I'm missing them! I'm fucking missing them, D! This was supposed to be my year!"

She felt the box she was sitting on shift as Dinah sat beside her. Warm fingers wrapped around her cold hand.

"The year isn't over yet, Jenny," Dinah said.

"Might as well be."

"Since when does anyone get a whole good year, anyway? Hey." Dinah turned Jenny's chin, forcing Jenny to face her ex in all her red-eyed melancholy. "I can't promise you a perfect year, or even a perfect day. But maybe, in this dingy basement, covered in dust and grime, and dripping from the rain, we can share one perfect moment."

She leaned forward and their lips met. Jenny's heart ached at the familiar touch of Dinah's soft tongue, the taste of her cinnamon lips. Like coming home to a warm and cozy chair by the fire after a year stuck out in the cold.

Jenny was just getting started when Dinah pulled away.

"Don't you dare start counting again!" she said, a fiery passion burning in her eyes.

"Count what?" Jenny asked. Then she devoured Dinah's mouth.

…1,351

She let the greasy drop cloth fall from her shoulders and tackled Dinah to the floor. Hard cement was possibly the worst place ever to do the deed, but Jenny didn't want to risk breaking the spell by relocating to a guest room.

Dinah co-signed her thinking by reaching down and pulling off Jenny's soaked shirt. This was new. Dinah wasn't normally so aggressive. It was just about the hottest thing that had ever happened to Jenny, and her whole body shivered with delight when Dinah caressed her naked torso. Jenny returned the favor, kissing down Dinah's neck and burying herself in her chest. The groan from Dinah's throat was all the encouragement Jenny needed to keep going.

"Jenny," Dinah whispered.

She looked up to see a beautiful, vulnerable girl with all her defenses down.

"I'm a virgin."

Oh. Really? What about Dryden Street?

"That's—that's okay," said Jenny. "Are you okay? We don't have to—"

"No, I want to," said Dinah. She blushed and looked away sweetly. "I just wanted you to know. I might not…"

Jenny climbed back up to hover over Dinah's adorable face and kissed her again.

"You're perfect, and I love you," she said.

"I missed you so much," Dinah said.

That was enough talking. Jenny got back to exploring the contours of Dinah's neck, and the trail of freckles down to her heaving—

Her stupid, traitorous eyes glanced away from Dinah's fantastic body for a single ill-conceived moment, only to find a pair of vacant eyes staring back at her from behind a pile of file boxes.

Jenny screamed.

"What's wrong!?"

Dinah clutched at her chest, covering up, as Jenny scrambled to her feet in shock.

"It's not you!" Jenny said and grabbed at the file boxes, tossing them aside.

Dinah screamed too, when she saw the body that had been hidden beneath the files. It was Tori Valentine.

Chapter Thirty-One
Plan A

OF ALL THE LAVISHLY FURNISHED ROOMS IN VALENTINE MANOR, none was quite so suited to a candlelight aesthetic as the Map Room. Great European tapestries hung from the high ceilings, accompanied by giant maps printed on supple, browning vellum. In the southwest corner, next to a leather club chair, was an antique globe full of pre-Enlightenment cartography and *Here There Be Dragons* fanciful accoutrements. It was the twin of a globe she'd seen in the Masters' Chambers at Schloss Schwarzwald. In all the chaos after their trip, Eliza had completely forgotten about that detail, until right this moment.

"This room is so cool!" Meghan announced, gawking at a massive tapestry of a French chateau. "I could just move in and live here forever."

"What are we looking for?" Alicia asked.

Eliza went straight to the antique globe. "A keyhole. Somewhere, on this globe, is the hole that fits this key."

"How do you figure?" Alicia asked. "Because of the 'give the world a spin' line?"

"That, and I've seen the teacher's edition of this quiz," said Eliza.

She gave it a spin, watching half-discovered landmasses pass by on the globe as it ticked rhythmically on its ball bearings.

"'Home and home and home again,'" said Alicia.

"Hello?" called a male voice out in the hall. One that had very recently been moaning in Eliza's ear.

"Drew!? We're in here!" she called out.

He appeared in the doorway, stumbling across the threshold, looking groggy and confused. Damn, she'd expected the chloroform to last longer.

Lai laughed. "My man had his brains sucked all the way—"

"Are you all right?" Jack asked, reaching out to steady Drew.

"I think I drank too much," Drew said, squinting around. "Has anyone seen Kazu?"

"Er, she said she needed some 'me time,'" said Eliza. Then, seeing Drew's frown, she added, "It's okay, she's like that sometimes. You're good."

"You got here just in time, Drew," said Meghan. "Jenny's about to solve us a mystery."

Eliza held up the skeleton key.

"Oh shit, the key!"

He shuffled over, tripped on the rug, and crashed into the antique globe. The boys scrambled to help him into a leather armchair, and Eliza held a hand to his forehead. She wanted so badly to mother him and kiss him and climb into his lap, but Jenny would never.

"No fever," she said, letting her hand linger a tad longer than strictly necessary. "He should eat something. Mason, can you go grab him a cookie?"

"I think he's already had his cookies if you know what I mean," said Mason.

Yeah, he did!

"Some charcuterie, then!" Eliza snapped.

"I think he's already had his prosciutto—okay, I'll stop!"

Mason scampered out of the room, cackling.

"Get me some too!" Meghan called. "Jenny, look!"

Meghan was bent over the antique globe that Drew had knocked on its side. She was fiddling with the heavy wooden base, a massive block of mahogany with a string of fleur-de-lis carved around it. On what was nominally the "front" of the globe, a fleur-de-lis larger than the rest appeared to have come partially detached from the base. Meghan was wiggling it back and forth.

"I think there's something behind this," she said.

Eliza crouched and helped her set the globe aright. Meghan was right. The fleur-de-lis looked as though it could be slid aside, but it was stuck.

"I'll bet it's covering the keyhole," Alicia said.

They all stared at the skeleton key, and Eliza's heart beat faster. It might not be a *real* clue, but RJ wouldn't have been able to resist making it lead to *something*, right?

"It's like it's stuck," said Meghan.

"Locked," said Drew.

"How do you unlock a lock, when you can't reach the keyhole?" asked Alicia.

Eliza studied the globe, searching for any clue. *Give the world a spin…* She reached out and spun it again, listening to it *tick tick tick* as it turned. One tick for every revolution…

"It's not just a keyhole lock," Eliza said. "It's a combination lock, too."

They pulled Tori's body out from behind the file boxes and placed her on Jenny's drop cloth. There was no blood that Jenny could see. A broken neck, then? Jenny reached out and wobbled Tori's skull.

"Baby, don't!" said Dinah.

"We need to know how," Jenny insisted. "What if she was poisoned?"

"Maybe an OD?" Dinah suggested. "But don't they usually foam at the—OH MY SHIT!"

Far from deceased, Tori had just started coughing and wheezing.

"Tori! You're alive!!" Jenny exclaimed. "We thought you were dead!"

"You say it like that and you sound guilty," said Dinah.

Tori retched out a thin stream of drool and Diet Coke.

"I think I saw a first aid kit in the workbench," Dinah said. "Be right back."

Jenny sniffed, grimacing at the vomit smell. There was something else there, too. Like fresh-cut grass from a lawn mower. Chloroform.

"Wh-what happened?" Tori asked, wiping her mouth. "Where am I?"

"The archive room," said Jenny. "Do you remember anything?"

Tori winced, holding a hand to her temple.

"I was coming down here to start the b-backup generator," she said. "It's supposed to k-kick on automatically, but it didn't. And then, I think… I think s-s-someone grabbed me from behind. That's all I-I remember."

Dinah returned with a compact first aid kit and emptied its contents on the floor next to them.

"Um, there's gauze and bandaids…" She looked at Tori. "Where does it hurt?"

"She was chloroformed," said Jenny. "Here."

Digging through the supplies, Jenny found a packet of Advil and handed it to Tori.

"What are you guys d-doing down here?" Tori asked. "Did you come looking for m-me?"

"Not exactly," said Jenny.

Tori froze, suddenly wary.

"It was you! Wasn't it?!" she cried.

"It wasn't, I swear!" said Jenny.

Tori rummaged in her jacket and produced a thin box cutter, which she brandished at them like a cornered, feral cat. "You better start telling me what's going on right this second, or I'm g-gonna scream!" Tori shouted.

Jenny held her hands up and let Dinah talk since she was better at this sort of thing.

"We don't want to hurt you, Tori," Dinah said. "We want to help. Jenny and I weren't even looking for you. We came down to the records room to look for something else and stumbled onto you."

Tori glared at them, still holding up her box cutter in defense.

"I'll bet you did." She nodded to Jenny. "Surely you of all p-people know there are half a dozen guest bedrooms in this house, if you were looking for p-privacy."

Jenny frowned and looked down. Oh, she was only wearing a bra up top. "What can I say. Sleuthing makes me horny."

Dinah snorted and handed Jenny her shirt.

If it wasn't for this damned mystery…

"What were you really doing down here?" Tori asked. "And who attacked me?"

"The answer to your second question, most likely, is the Stranger," said Jenny. "As to the first: I was searching for my mother's killer."

Tori's eyes narrowed. "I think you'd b-better start from the beginning."

Ugh, fine. Jenny did her best to give Tori a crash course on the murder of Laura Onishi. She recounted her mother's claim to the neonatal nurse that Valerie Valentine was trying to kill her. The heirloom and surveillance photos with matching lens scratches. The Little League team portrait with the same photographic fingerprint. Searching through Stratford Photography's records for the identity of the photographer, only to find the file missing and a note from the Stranger instead.

Tori stared at the drawing of Killroy left behind, grinding her teeth in deep concentration.

"This doesn't mean anything," she said at last. "He c-could be stringing you along."

"He's not," said Jenny. "He doesn't do that. Not even in the books. He likes to play and tease Trouble when he's ahead of her in the mystery. If that file didn't connect to my mom's killer—or the Stranger's identity—in some way, he wouldn't have taken it. Or if he did, the note would have said, 'You're getting colder.'"

"Val is still the only one without a real alibi, the night of the attack," Jenny went on. "Even if what you say is true, about you and RJ setting her up to go the conservatory to catch her cheating, that doesn't mean she couldn't have attacked him anyway."

Tori shook her head. "It wasn't her," she said, almost to herself. "It was just supposed to look like it was her, in c-case something went wrong. You were too clever, Daddy."

"Excuse me?" Jenny said.

"You were right, Jennifer," Tori said. "I didn't t-t-tell you guys everything, back at the park, after Mr. Webb was killed. When Dad explained the will and the g-game to me, he gave me further instructions, too."

I fucking knew it!

Jenny's heart pounded in her chest. She struggled to steady her voice and said, "Go on."

"The truth is…" Tori heaved a great sigh. "The truth is, the will and the game, the heirloom clues: that was only s-supposed to be Plan B."

DADDY GLANCED DOWN AT HIS HEIRLOOMS AND CHUCKLED BEFORE HE remembered he was trying to be serious.

"Anyone who plays this game is in danger. Maybe is danger. And I don't want that for you. All I need you to do is keep a low profile, and watch."

He held her captive in his piercing stare, daring Tori to look away. Never! Tori gritted her teeth and stared right back. She wouldn't fold so easily! Finally, his features softened, and that famous mischievous grin crept back into the corners of his mouth.

"But with any luck, you won't need to," RJ said.

"What do you mean?"

RJ slid open the top drawer at his left, pulling out a thin metal case. He set it on the desk and lifted the top. Inside, embedded in foam, was a small vial of clear fluid and a syringe.

"What is that?!" Tori asked, suddenly freaked out.

Daddy hadn't started doing drugs, had he?

"This, Tori, is Plan A," he said. "A mixture of barbiturates and sedatives. 20 ccs will slow my heart and render me unresponsive for about 90 minutes. Don't worry, I've tested it. I researched the whole thing back when I was writing Trouble in Paris.*"*

"I don't remember anything about a knockout drug in Trouble in Paris,*" Tori said.*

"I ended up cutting it," RJ said with a wave of his hand. "The editor didn't like the idea of someone using Rohypnol in a Trouble *book."*

"What the fuck, Dad?"

"It's not for that, it's for me," he said.

"You're worried someone's trying to kill you, and your plan is to roofie yourself??" Tori asked, exasperated.

Just when she thought he was serious about all this…

"Precisely!" said RJ. "What better way to throw my stalker off their game than to make them think someone else beat them to the punch?"

He put the medical case aside and laid out a whole new scheme. On the night of next week's gala, he'd refuse to go down to the Fairmont with Val, making sure he was all alone at home in the study. Then he'd stage a scene to make it look as though he'd been attacked. Mrs. Rivas would find him unconscious and call an ambulance. He'd be taken to the ER, hospitalized overnight, etc. And then, just when the whole world thought RJ Valentine was at his most vulnerable, he'd wake up, and get to work.

"Doing what!?" Tori asked.

"Catching my would-be killer," he said. "It's the perfect cover. Trying to hunt for clues as RJ Valentine, famed novelist, is impossible without half of Blackbird Springs knowing what I'm up to. But if I'm at the hospital in a coma, no one will blink twice at a bearded guy with an eyepatch and silver hair, lurking in the shadows."

"I don't know, I think they might find that weird, too, Daddy."

"I'll dose myself by day, and sneak out at night. The best investigation is the one your enemy doesn't even know is happening, isn't that right, Tori? With luck, I'll catch this bastard in a week, tops."

Tori rubbed her temples. "Okay. Okay. This is madness. Does Val know about this?" she asked.

"Of course not. Two's company, three's a crowd. This is just between me and you."

"You and I. What about your Signal buddy?" Tori asked, nodding to his phone.

He frowned and shook his head. "Just us. But speaking of Val…"

Dad had an additional scheme in mind: to trick Val into returning to the mansion the night of the gala, by having Tori send her an anonymous note threatening to expose her.

"If she comes, it means she's got something to hide," he said.

"Why does that even matter, at this point?" Tori asked. "You've both cheated before."

He shrugged. "It's a little game we play. She thinks she has the moral high ground, and I want it back."

"Wait, what if she's the stalker who wants you dead?" Tori asked, even though she couldn't see her mother doing something like that. "You could be playing right into her hands."

"She's not," said RJ. "I've been able to confirm that much, at least, in my investigations. But if something goes wrong, I love the idea of her being stuck without an alibi. That'd serve her right, heheh."

Tori leaned back in her chair and studied her adoptive father. He could laugh all he wanted, but she had no doubt there was real fear lurking beneath his rakish facade. If this was his Plan A, and Plan B was death, then he was just about at the end of his rope.

"For the record, I hate this plan," Tori said.

"Duly noted," RJ said. "Will you help your dad, sweetie? Please?"

It was stupid, and she should have said no. But there was something so intoxicating about RJ needing her help. The little girl who still lived inside her, the one who ceased aging the day Casey Klein went missing, was desperate to be Trouble for him again, after all these years.

"I will, Daddy. Of course I will."

AS THE STORY UNFOLDED, JENNY CLUTCHED DINAH'S HAND SO TIGHT that her own went numb. Tori wasn't wrong: RJ's plan was madness. But if he'd been able to pull it off? Legendary!

Feeling well enough to walk now, Tori led them back to the garage.

"I don't know wh-what happened," Tori said. "The medical case was still in his d-desk drawer when I searched it later that night. I couldn't tell if he'd used it or n-not!"

At the workbench, Tori opened the bottom drawer, stretched her hand deep inside, and pulled out a slender metal case. Jenny took the case, set it on the workbench, and flipped the top up. Just as Tori had described, it held an unlabeled vial of clear fluid and a syringe.

"Did he ever test it in front of you?" Jenny asked.

Tori shook her head. "But I know I was supposed to give him 20 ccs in the rear if I needed to re-dose him." She slammed her fist on the workbench and grimaced in anguish. "I should have been there. I should have been at his side, at his hospital bed, that whole night. But I was worried I'd mess up the plan, so I didn't arrive until the following morning. And I waited and waited and waited for him to wake up, and he never did."

She sniffled and began to weep.

Jenny's thoughts drifted to that medic she'd encountered last month, Dalton. What was it he'd said? *No tachycardia, respiration was steady.* RJ had seemed stable when the paramedics found him in the study, just unconscious. Strange vitals, if he'd been attacked—but if he'd only faked an injury and sedated himself?

Then the killing blow was never delivered in the study. It had come later. Which meant…

"If he did use the drug, then a lot of people's alibis suddenly have holes in them," said Jenny. "Including yours, Victoria."

Tori hissed, glaring through her tear-smudged eyeshadow.

"RJ is the only person in the world who never stopped believing in me."

"Sure, and then he sent you to rehab," said Jenny. "Did you want revenge? Nobody would be more perfectly placed than you to carry out the murder, as I'm sure you've always known."

Her stepsister's face crumpled into sobs.

"Jenny," said Dinah.

"How can I trust her? When she's been lying to me all this time?" Jenny asked.

"Because RJ trusted me!" Tori cried. "Who do you think slipped that note into your pocket at the park last fall?"

Jenny's retort died before it reached her lips. "'High score'? That was you? I thought that was Mr. Webb."

Tori shook her head. "Webb didn't know about it," she said. "That's how secret it was. I didn't want to, but Daddy insisted I give you a hint, if it came to that.

"It was supposed to be a trap for the killer. To draw them to Pixeldrome where they might stick out. I paid the owner off to keep an eye out for any new customers spending a bunch of time there. But so far it's just been you, those idiots who broke into the foundation offices, Alicia, and Nilay Nagra. RIP."

"And they all have alibis," said Jenny. "Except they might not now. Just like you."

"Let's not forget that your alibi is toast, too, *Trouble!*" said Tori.

"You know, if you two weren't always so busy resenting each other, I'd bet you'd find you had a lot in common," said Dinah.

Jenny's mind rebelled against the very idea. "I was in the psych ward in LA," she said. "We've been over this."

"Yes, but you got out the next morning. It's only a five-hour drive," said Tori.

"I wouldn't even know how to get up here. I didn't have a license… or a car."

"Bullshit!" Tori regained her composure, her eyes blazing. "You managed to find your way up here the first time, who's to say you didn't do it again?!"

"The first…? What are you talking about?"

"That's why it was so hilarious when you tried to pose as that southern girl at the Bad Egg," said Tori. "You thought I wouldn't recognize you, but I'd already seen you."

"Seen me when?" Jenny asked, baffled.

"At the mansion! Dad asked me to leave because he was meeting someone, but he refused to say who. And it was you!"

Jenny shook her head, frustrated, and shoved the metal case and her note from the Stranger into her Coach bag. "I think the chloroform is still messing with your head. I was in the hospital, like I said."

"Well they must have let you out for a day, then, so Daddy could meet with you," said Tori. "I wasn't supposed to know about it. It was the day before the gala. He sent me off on an errand—sent everyone off, so the mansion was empty—but I snuck back in through the secret passage to spy. And there you were."

"You're high, I never met him," said Jenny. "I wish I had."

"I think he heard me in the passage, so I couldn't stay to eavesdrop, but it was definitely you! For the longest time, I thought you were his secret friend on the Signal app," Tori said, ignoring how plainly impossible this was.

Dinah cleared her throat. "Maybe Tori did see you, Jenny," said Dinah. "Like those times at Schloss Schwarzwald. Sometimes you *forget*. Especially when you're *in danger*."

The realization hit Jenny like an electric shock. It couldn't be! Eliza would have said something. Wouldn't she?

Wait. Why wouldn't she??

Chapter Thirty-Two

Danger Zone

Jack had his ear pressed to the antique globe, concentrating as he slowly rotated it clockwise. Every few seconds, he'd stop, give the globe a big long spin, and start over. This went on for several minutes. Eliza and the others watched him until, finally, he nodded and pulled himself away, keeping one hand on the globe to hold it in place.

"There it is," he said. "If we use the supporting meridian as a guide, it's clicking on California. 'Home and home and home again,' right? So, we turn it to Blackbird Springs three times?"

He spun the globe clockwise, then counter-clockwise, then clockwise again, stopping it each time when the meridian approximately lined up with Blackbird Springs, California.

Nothing happened.

"It wouldn't be the same place three times," said Drew. "This is RJ, not my dad, here."

Eliza smiled at Drew. Jenny had told her about their efforts to unlock his dad's phone last Halloween, and how the code turned out to be **0•0•0•0•0•0**.

"Why don't we just get an axe and settle this real quick?" asked Mason.

"That's cheating," said Alicia. "We're supposed to figure it out, not brute force it."

"Dorks," said Mason.

"Where were RJ Valentine's three homes?" asked Thanh.

Eliza turned to Jack, raising an eyebrow. He shrugged.

"You don't know!?" asked Meghan. "You're his kids!"

"RJ played things close to the vest," said Eliza. "Also, I never actually met him."

Well, Jenny never did.

"Dad might have considered Schloss Schwarzwald a home," said Jack. "He liked it there. Briefly."

"In his diaries, he mentions the Packers, and playing hockey," said Eliza. "I kinda had the idea he might have grown up in the Midwest."

Bong! Bong! Ba-dong!

They all froze. From somewhere below them came a strange banging. It stopped as soon as it started.

"What the fuck was that?" asked Thanh.

"Maybe it's the generator coming back online," said Eliza.

It wasn't. It was Jenny's signal. She was coming back upstairs.

Dammit, Jenny! I'm not finished yet!

They paused a moment, but the lights didn't come back on. Jack grunted and spun the globe clockwise.

"Wisconsin first?" Jack said. "If we're going chronological."

He turned the globe to the Midwest, then back the other way to Europe, then back again to Blackbird Springs. Eliza tried twisting the fleur-de-lis sticking out from the base. It still barely budged.

"Try the other way," said Eliza. "Do Blackbird Springs first, that's where it was clicking. Hurry."

"All right, all right," Jack said.

He hastily spun the globe again, this time using Blackbird Springs — Schloss Schwarzwald — Wisconsin as the combination.

"What are you guys doing?" Penny asked from the doorway.

Her face was puffy, and a crease lined her cheek from sleeping on a pillow seam. She squinted in the dim light and yawned.

"We're solving a mystery!" said Meghan. "Get over here!"

"This is it, it's tightening up," Jack said.

Something within the globe's base clicked. Eliza noted the meridian's location. It looked closer to the Dakotas, if she had to guess, though the map was hardly accurate. She twisted the fleur-de-lis again, and this time it rotated to the side, revealing an old-fashioned keyhole.

"Yes!!" shouted Meghan.

"Holy shit!" said Drew. "Try the key!"

"Alicia should do the honors," said Eliza.

She handed the skeleton key to Alicia, who grinned and shoved it into the keyhole. It turned easily, unlocking another hidden clasp, and the whole front of the base slid out. It was hollow, like a drawer, and inside it…

"Is that a map?" asked Penny.

A small stack of parchment lay within the drawer. Eliza lifted the first page out. It wasn't a map, so much as a visual clue. Hand-drawn, in purple pen. There was a drawing of the globe, then footsteps leading up, down, left, and right, stopping at new artifacts or locations, with vague hints along the way.

20 paces east from the King's Feast
Walk along the garden, until you encounter the ladybug
The bottom drawer holds your prize.

Eliza flipped through the other pages of parchment and found that each had its own clues and drawings. Each led to a different destination, somewhere on the property. She couldn't help but imagine her father making all of these—counting the paces, drawing the maps, soaking the parchment in tea to age it further—all the while looking over his shoulder and fearing an attack from the shadows.

How artsy-craftsy of you, RJ.

"They're all different," she said. "They're like treasure maps, I think."

"What do they lead to?" asked JeRay.

"Buried treasure, dawg, you think?" said Lai.

"Hell yeah! We should follow one!" said Meghan. "Come on, Mace."

She snatched the page from Eliza's hands and ran off with Mason, singing giddily about riches and treasure.

"Let's go!" said JeRay, and grabbed another map.

He bounced too, with Penny in tow, followed shortly by Thanh and Lai. A strange mania had overtaken the party; everyone was scrambling to hunt down a treasure, Tori and the storm be damned.

"Wait! Guys! These are supposed to lead to a killer!" Drew shouted.

He still didn't know Alicia's heirloom was a decoy. The treasure maps probably all led to gag prizes like whoopee cushions or something. Still, splitting up the party would take eyes off Eliza, which may help with Jenny on her way back up.

"Let's all meet back here in 30 minutes! Okay?!" Eliza shouted, though half of them were already out of earshot.

She handed a map to Alicia, who departed for the hunt with Jack, hand in hand. And then the only two people left were Eliza and Drew.

"Shall we?" Eliza asked, holding up a piece of parchment.

"The game is afoot!" said Drew.

Their map showed a double staircase as the starting place and seemed to point them to the second floor. That should help her avoid running into Jenny. Eliza hurried them out of the Map Room to begin their hunt.

Exposed pipes ran past the utility closet in the garage. Jenny rapped on them sharply with her riot baton.

Bong! Bong! Ba-dong!

"What are you doing?" Tori asked.

"I need to get back upstairs," Jenny said, ignoring the question. "And we need to call the police. Whoever attacked you might still be in the mansion."

"I still can't get a signal," said Dinah.

"You're underground," said Tori. She narrowed her eyes at Jenny. "What's got you spooked? You weren't like this when you first found me."

No shit she wasn't. That was before she learned that Eliza had come to visit RJ before his death—and never told Jenny. There was a whole day back in Glendale, after Jenny got out of the psych ward, where they couldn't meet. They had to wait for Shelly to stop watching Jenny so closely. In theory, Eliza spent the day nearby, crashing at a hostel. Or did she?

Lizzy would never! her Jenny voice shouted in her head.

It's not like she hasn't killed before! her Trouble voice shouted back.

What had they talked about, Lizzy and Dad? Why did he meet with her? What special communication was so important that Lizzy would keep it a secret?

Why didn't he want to meet with me?

A green rage threatened to envelop her. Jenny dug her fingernails into her palms, trying to take measured breaths and not completely lose her shit. Dinah put a hand on her shoulder. She'd gone pale with fear herself, and Jenny's panic probably wasn't helping.

"That was before we found this," Jenny said through gritted teeth, arriving at a suitable half-truth.

"Are you able to fix it?" Dinah asked Tori.

It being the backup generator, which Tori was studying with a scowl. Diagnosing the problem was simple enough: someone had sliced through the fuel line and siphoned out all the gasoline in the tank.

"Maybe," said Tori. "If I can find some sealant tape."

"We can't wait," said Jenny. "I need to get back upstairs and warn the others."

"I'll come with you," said Dinah.

"No, I need you to call the cops," said Jenny. "Get to the surface and head to the highway until you get a cell signal."

It was clear Dinah disagreed with her assignment, but Jenny wasn't in the mood to argue. She handed her the riot baton.

"If you see anyone, you run," Jenny told her.

"Wait, she should use the passageway," Tori said. "Both of you should, in case they're watching the stairs."

"In the conservatory?" Jenny asked.

"No, the other one. You didn't know?" Tori smirked, delighted to know something about Valentine Manor that Jenny did not.

On the opposite side of the garage, a heavy metal door was installed between the parking spots for the town car and one of Valentine Vineyard's jeeps. Tori tried waving her watch past the door's lock, grimaced when she remembered the power was out, and dug into her coat for her keys.

"What's inside?" Jenny asked.

Tori turned her key with a heavy *clunk!* and pulled the door open.

"The safest and most valuable place in the building," said Tori. "The wine cellar."

Jenny stepped inside, waving her phone's flashlight around, and found herself amidst rows and rows of wine bottles. The air was dry, and would no doubt be perfectly climate-controlled if the power were still on. Eliza had tried to sneak into the Valentine Manor garage once, Jenny remembered now. Jack thought it was Jenny, and assumed she tried to break into the wine cellar to steal Val's bottle of *Ressort Rouge*. Maybe Eliza did, for all Jenny knew.

Tori led them to the end of an aisle of red blends and pulled on the bottle at the very top left of the shelf. Something *thunked* and that section of the shelf swung out, revealing a doorway behind it.

"It comes out through the wishing well in the roundabout," said Tori. "You two go on, I'll do what I can down here."

Jenny and Dinah pushed the door open and found themselves at the bottom of a narrow spiral staircase. It reminded her of Schloss Schwarzwald. Was that Dad's inspiration? The stairwell was dank and smelled of wet decay. Behind them, the door to the cellar closed and locked. It belatedly occurred to her that if Tori was the Stranger, the Stranger had just outsmarted her by locking her out of the mansion. Nothing to be done about that now.

"Let's go," said Dinah.

They climbed up the spiral steps, reached the top, and found a lever that slid aside the false bottom of the well. Rainwater splashed down, drenching Jenny again.

Dinah smiled and ran a hand through Jenny's soaked hair. "It's not your day, Valentine," she said.

Jenny's watch vibrated. A text from Eliza!? No, it was midnight.

"It is now," Jenny said, showing Dinah her birthday notification.

"Happy Birthday, Jenny," said Dinah.

They kissed again. A long one, just in case. Then they climbed up out of the wishing well, and into a howling rainstorm.

"Good luck!" Dinah shouted.

"Stay safe!" Jenny called back.

Dinah jogged along the driveway toward Cellar Drive, into the dark night. Jenny turned back to the mansion. It loomed silent and black, lit up in silhouette as a bolt of lightning flashed over the ridge behind it. Thunder cracked the sky asunder.

The Stranger had returned to Valentine Manor. Jenny hoped to god it wasn't Eliza this whole time.

"Damn! That sounded hella close!" said Drew, after a thunderclap reverberated through the walls and shook the windowpanes.

The treasure map had taken them to the Sunroom on the second story. Massive arched windows formed a semi-circle, looking south on the front lawn, and the grapevines running down the hill. Beneath the windows, cushions had been built into the walls at sitting level. Perfect for lounging on, whiling away lazy summer days, reading books—which Eliza had often done when Jenny was gone last year.

In the flash of lightning, she'd spotted someone on the grounds below. Two someones.

"What does this mean?" Drew asked, staring at their treasure map. "'Follow the epitaph to nourishment, but don't skimp on earthly sustenance.'"

Eliza pointed to a message carved into the mahogany framing below the bay windows.

A good book feeds the soul — RJ Valentine

"'Nourishment' means books," said Eliza. "So, the study, right? That's where RJ's library is."

"But what about 'earthly sustenance'? That's like *real* food," said Drew. "The kitchen? I think we're supposed to go there first."

"There's two kitchens," said Eliza. "Let's split up. You check the service kitchen and I'll check the main one."

Drew held up his hands, frowning. "I don't know where the service kitchen is."

"I'll take that one, then," said Eliza. "You know where the main kitchen is, right? Let's meet up outside the study in…" She checked her watch and noticed her birthday notification. Happy Birthday, Eliza. "15 minutes. Okay?"

Drew awkwardly held up his hand to bump fists, and Eliza was struck again by the mindfuck of this chaste interaction after the intimate sex he didn't realize they'd had, only an hour earlier.

Oh, the tangled webs Danger weaves, when Trouble business demands that she must deceive…

She bumped his fist and went east. Drew headed down the stairs. Out on the roundabout, Jenny had been running west. Where was she going?

THE DOOR TO THE CONSERVATORY WAS HANGING OPEN, RATTLING IN the wind. Jenny eased it shut and chanced a light, using her phone's flashlight to navigate the unfamiliar pathway of Val's rearranged garden. She was nearly to the doorway that led into the mansion when she turned a corner and collided with a small body.

"Eeep!" Alicia Aaron shrieked.

Jenny stumbled, grabbing Alicia tight, and somehow keeping them both on their feet. "Sorry! Are you okay?"

"You scared the shit out of me, Trouble!" said Alicia, steadying herself. Even in the darkness, Jenny could feel Alicia's suspicious glare. "It is Trouble, right?"

"Yes. What are you doing in here?" Jenny hissed.

"Check it out," Alicia said. She held up a book, her fear abandoned with Jenny present. "Our clues led to a first edition of *My Name is Trouble*, signed by RJ. Jack went back to get another map."

"Uh, great. Do you know where Eliza is?" Jenny asked.

Alicia shook her head. "We all split up. Oh, right, you weren't there. My key opened up the base of the globe in the Map Room, and we found all these treasure maps. I'm guessing we need to collect them all to see what's next. Maybe when we put them all together—"

"Forget about that," Jenny said and gripped Alicia's shoulders. "Alicia, the Stranger is here. Somewhere in the mansion. Dinah went to call the police, but we need to get everyone to safety."

Alicia's smile faded, the fear returning. "What about Jack?!"

"I'll find him," said Jenny. "Come here."

She pulled Alicia with her to the corner of the wall that abutted the mansion and triggered the release to open up the secret passageway.

"This leads to RJ's study," said Jenny. "Get in there, lock the doors, and don't open up for anyone, okay? Not till the police get here."

"Jenny… What if…?"

Alicia's eyes were wide with fright. Jenny clutched at her shaking hands, trying to calm her. Never before had tiny Jenny Valentine felt so tall next to her peer.

"Here, trade me," Jenny said, passing her Coach bag to Alicia and taking her purse. "There's a taser in there. I'm sure you won't need it, but just in case."

"What about you?" Alicia asked.

"I've got my wits and my plot armor, Red." She kissed Alicia on the forehead and pushed her into the secret passage. "Wait!"

She'd just remembered the metal case with Dad's knockout drug inside. Jenny pulled it out of her Coach bag, loaded up a syringe with a dose, and pushed the case back into Alicia's hands.

"Better than nothing," Jenny said. "Get going. And remember: don't open for anyone. Not even me!"

Once Alicia was inside, Jenny closed the hidden doorway behind her. Then she let her own hands shake uncontrollably.

You can't have a panic attack. Not now!

She willed herself to act, and crossed to the mansion entrance, fighting off deja vu. Hadn't she just been here? This time, there was no shadowy figure in the hallway to scare her away.

"Lizzy?" she whispered into the dark.

No one answered. Jenny killed the light on her phone, gripped her syringe tighter, and stepped into the dark mansion.

Eliza made it all the way to the service kitchen before her brain kicked in.

"What the fuck are you doing, Elizabeth?" she asked herself.

So much for being the Smart One. There was no point in keeping up the charade with these treasure maps. Not when she knew the heirloom was a fugazi. Not with Jenny going off script. Had she found the records room, then? Drew could follow the map if he wanted the thrill of the hunt, Eliza needed to get back into costume.

She turned to leave the kitchen when a soft *thud* sounded behind her. She whipped around, her hand darting to the dagger in her waistband. Her startled eyes frantically searched for the source of the noise.

The service kitchen was silent. The rain roared outside.

Thud. Thud.

There! It was the pantry door, softly knocking against the cabinet as it inched open before swinging closed again. Like the wind was moving it.

Eliza crossed to the door and yanked it open. Shelves stacked with dry goods ran on either side of the walk-in pantry. At the far end, where the back row of shelves would normally be, the wall was missing. She crept closer. The shelves and wall had been pushed aside, and darkness lay beyond.

Another secret passage.

Someone had used it. Recently. And forgotten to close it—or didn't care to. Eliza unsheathed her kunai dagger and ventured into the abyss.

When Jenny reached the main foyer, she found the front door to the mansion hanging open to the storm. Curtains flapped in the breeze, and errant drops of rain spattered on the marble floor just inside. She shivered, the wind stabbing like icy knives through her wet clothes.

That door hadn't been open when she and Dinah left the wishing well. She was sure of it.

She hurried under the double staircase into the east wing hall. In the distance, she could just make out a soft, flickering orange glow on the left. Jenny tiptoed closer, holding her syringe out like a knife.

The glow came from the Map Room, where candles still burned low in their holders. Jenny peeked inside.

"Lizzy?" she whispered.

Lightning flashed again, and for a split second, the whole room was lit up like noon on a summer day. It was empty. A few pages of parchment lay scattered on the floor next to an antique globe.

Thunder rumbled, and a great gust of wind blew past, sending fresh shivers down her spine. All the candles blew out, and in the distance, she heard the front door slam shut.

Fuck. Someone must have just opened another door to the outside, somewhere in the mansion. Or closed it.

"*Aaiiiieeeehh—*"

A scream rang out, and just as quickly cut off. It sounded like Alicia Aaron.

Jenny jogged to the study. The door was locked. Damn! Alicia had her lockpick kit!

"Alicia!?" she called.

On the other side of the wall, something crashed. Glass breaking.

She sprinted full tilt back the way she'd come, trusting her memory of the mansion's layout in the pitch-black darkness.

When she made it to the conservatory, she heard the first whine of sirens in the distance. Coming from the south, heading up Cellar Drive. They'd be here soon, but not soon enough! Jenny triggered the disguised latch, yanked the hidden door open, and hurried into the secret passage.

When she reached the other end, the door to the study was already open. She stepped inside and tripped, tumbling to the carpet.

Somehow, she managed to twist in time, landing with a grunt on her side, the syringe miraculously unbroken in her hand. Jenny collected herself and glanced back at what had caused her to stumble.

Alicia Aaron was slumped on the floor, not moving. A dark stain pooled around her on the carpet.

Jenny scrambled to her feet in dismay—and beheld the grisly scene on RJ's desk.

Meghan May lay sprawled atop Dad's calendar blotter. Her throat was slit. A great wash of blood, inky black in the dimness, cascaded from her neck down the side of the wooden desk. Her lifeless eyes stared back at Jenny, frozen in surprise.

Unable to look away, Jenny's gaze traveled from Meghan's corpse to the boy in RJ's chair. Mason Lockhart sat peacefully, his arms resting at his sides. In the center of his chest, the hilt of a knife stuck out where it wasn't supposed to, surrounded by a growing bloodstain.

The hilt looked familiar. It was the kind of knife Eliza used. A kunai.

Suddenly Mason coughed and looked up at Jenny.

"I don't get it," he said.

"Wait! Get what?! Who did this!?"

Jenny rushed around to his side, but the confusion on his face was already draining away to a placid nothingness. His body slumped forward, head resting in Meghan's lap, and Mason was gone.

Sharp voices shouted in the distance. The police were here. Too late.

"It wasn't me," a ragged voice whispered.

Jenny leaped out of her skin, brandishing her syringe in a panic, to find she wasn't alone in the study. Another lightning flash lit up the room. Eliza stood by the broken bay window, staring in horror at the carnage. An identical kunai dagger hung limply in her right hand.

"What happened?!" Jenny whispered back. "Lizzy, what the fuck!?"

Her twin's mouth hung open, struggling to form words. There was shouting right outside the study door.

"Jenny?! Are you in there?!" called Sheriff Lockhart.

Oh god, Blake. Your son.

She wiped her eyes and grabbed her sister, pushing Eliza back into the secret passage.

"They can't find us both!" Jenny whispered. "Gimme your bag."

Jenny tore off her shoes and stripped, yanking Shelly's black dress from Eliza's bag and throwing it over her head. There was no time to zip up. She grabbed the wig, pulled it over her pixie cut, and shoved her clothes into Eliza's bag.

"Phone," said Jenny.

Eliza handed her iPhone over. Jenny smashed it against the cement wall of the passage and gave Eliza her own phone.

"Go. Run. Now. I'll find you when I can."

Eliza swallowed and nodded, retreating into the dark. Jenny closed the bookshelf door behind her. With luck, Eliza would make it to the conservatory. With more luck, she would make it to the property line and keep on running. But what about Jenny?

"Break it down!" she heard Blake shout on the other side of the wall.

Jenny frantically searched the room for something—anything that could help. Her eyes fell on Mason and Meghan. The broken window. Alicia's purse, where Jenny dropped it when she fell. Jenny's Coach mini backpack—

The Coach bag had been dumped out next to Alicia's body. There was her lockpick kit, her fingerprinting kit—dust spilled and blowing all over—her plaster of paris, the metal syringe case, the note from the Stranger. Alicia's hand still clutched the taser, for all the good it did her. Everything was accounted for—except for Jenny's heirloom photo.

It might have blown away in the wind, but Jenny knew better. The Stranger had it now. She stared at the syringe in her hand, and a new plan took shape in her mind. Not her plan—RJ's.

There was banging on the study door now. She had to act fast.

After a brief scramble, she pressed the syringe plunger, spraying out excess sedative. 10 ccs ought to be enough for her—who knew how fast this stuff worked? With a last, heavy breath, Jenny pulled her dress up and jabbed the syringe into her left butt cheek, depressing the plunger all the way.

The effect was almost immediate. A fuzzy haze rushed into her head and her limbs went slack. She fell to her knees and rolled the empty syringe under a gap between Dad's desk and the carpet. With her last strength, she pressed her hands into the pool of Meghan's blood and smeared it all over her face.

Then she lay back, unable to move further. A sudden panic struck her. What if she'd given herself too much? What if she was dying? What if she never solved the mystery? What a terrible ending!

With a crash, the study door flew open.

In her last moment of consciousness, a feral howl of rage and grief seared into her soul.

The world went black, and she knew no more.

Chapter Thirty-Three

The Marker

Jenny awoke with a splitting headache. That howl of rage was still sounding, somehow, as her body shook and jostled in a tight, enclosed space. Something yanked hard at her left wrist. As her consciousness rapidly returned, the howl shifted higher, taking on shape and texture. Not a howl, a siren. She was in the back of an ambulance.

Her eyes flew open, wincing in the glare. She was alone. She tried to sit up, but a sudden force pulled her back down. Jenny blinked away tears of pain and glanced at her left arm. They'd handcuffed her to the stretcher.

Smart. But not smart enough to do her other hand, too.

With her free right hand, she dug in her underwear for the few lockpick tools she'd stuffed in there, right before she drugged herself. Unlocking the handcuff was child's play. Grunting, she pulled herself upright and stepped on unsteady feet to the front of the ambulance. Through the small window, she could see into the cab.

Thank god. Her gamble had paid off. Dalton the paramedic was driving.

"Hey Dalton!" she cried.

He yelped and the ambulance swerved, sending her crashing into a cabinet of medical gear.

"What the fuck?!" Dalton shouted.

"It's me! Jenny Valentine!"

He did a double take, his eyes finally seeing past the crusted blood caked all over her face."

"I thought you were—how did you get up? You were handcuffed?!"

Dalton glanced back at the road, gritting his teeth as he straightened them out. Through his rearview mirror, he glared at Jenny. She held up her free left wrist.

"I'm calling in that marker, Dalton."

"What!?"

"You owe me. Time to pay up!" she said. "We're not going to the hospital."

His gaunt eyes darted back and forth between the road ahead and Jenny in the rearview.

"What am I supposed to tell 'em?" he asked.

"Say you got to the hospital, and when you opened up the back, I was gone," Jenny said.

He kept driving. Through the windshield, Jenny could see the hospital not far ahead.

"Are you gonna help me or what?!"

"Okay, okay," Dalton said.

He reached forward and killed the siren. They cruised past the hospital and continued down Second Street.

"Where to?" he asked.

The mansion was a crime scene. The treehouse was burned to ashes. Jenny couldn't go home; they'd be looking for her there. The Crow's Nest? Too public. There was only one safe place she could think of.

"Go left up here," Jenny said, and braced herself as Dalton took the ambulance on a sharp turn, heading south.

A POLICE SUV DROVE TO THE END OF CELLAR DRIVE AND STOPPED at the berm. Blake Lockhart got out, still dressed in the street clothes from his concert date with Shelly. He paced for a moment, then reached inside and pulled out a police baton.

With a primal scream of anguish, he attacked the hood of the SUV, smashing it over and over until the baton splintered into pieces. Then he started punching the metal hood with his bare fists.

"Blake! Stop!" Eliza shouted from her hiding place, just beyond the edge of the road.

In an instant, Blake spun, drawing his service pistol with the dexterity of an old west gunslinger and aiming it straight at her head. With his other hand, he lit Eliza up with his flashlight.

In the glare of the headlights, his wet eyes were puffy, and his mouth twisted up with grief. When he recognized Eliza, that grief shriveled and burned away, overtaken by feral rage. His breaths came in ragged gasps as he gripped his pistol, white-knuckled.

"Give me one good reason why I shouldn't put two in your head and one in my own?" Blake asked.

Eliza's heart broke for him all over again.

"You have a granddaughter!" she cried out.

Blake's wounded eyes opened wide in shock.

The neon lights of the Pixeldrome marquee were turned off; all the shops on the block had closed for the night. A few hundred paces away, Jenny stood on the sidewalk in front of Mystery Flavors, watching and waiting. The rain had stopped. It was after 1:00 AM on what was shaping up to be the worst birthday of her life. When Dalton's ambulance was out of sight, she shuffled down the street to the arcade.

Her muscles still felt like lead, but at least they functioned. Score one for Dad. Plan A might have worked, more or less, if something hadn't gone wrong. If the Stranger hadn't somehow gotten to him at the hospital, knowing he needed to finish the job.

Jenny circled to the back alley behind the arcade, the site of so many quickies in Asha's shitty Honda. The lock on the back door took some extra effort—Jenny didn't have all her lockpick tools, only some essentials—but she finally forced the last tumbler into place, and turned the lock with her tension bar. She slipped inside and searched for the alarm panel. She'd watched Asha enter the code plenty of times, never letting on that she was paying attention. With luck, it hadn't changed.

6·9·4·2·0

The panel chimed with success and the security system disarmed. Jenny closed the door and armed it again. The lights in the main arcade area were off. Jenny left them that way, navigating by feel to the stairwell next to the front counter. Down the steps she went, coming at last to the handle-less door of the VIP room. From her bra, she pulled out a membership card: Alicia's, taken from the doomed redhead's purse.

Jenny swiped the card across the doorway, and with a beep, the hidden latch unlocked. She pushed the door open and stepped inside.

The lights were all on in the VIP room, with '80s music thumping, and an old fantasy movie playing on the big screen TV—

Jenny's heart froze to the core.

There on the couch watching TV, his back to Jenny, was Rob Haines. Jenny's half-baked plan disintegrated before her eyes. She could outrun him, maybe, but there was no chance he wasn't calling the cops. They'd be hunting for her on the south side in no time. Her whole body tensed up, waiting for him to turn and shout.

Five seconds later, it occurred to her she was still waiting. Rob's head, with his thinning, dyed hair, was still pointed at the TV on the wall. Surely, he must have heard her. Was he asleep? Did she dare try sneaking away? She glanced back, making it two steps into the stairwell before her Trouble intuition took over.

You fucking know he's not sleeping, Jenny.

She gritted her teeth and turned away from the stairs. Abandoning stealth, she crossed the VIP room and moved around to the front of the couch to get a look at Rob.

His face was paper white. Someone had shoved fistfuls of golden game tokens into his mouth, choking him. More tokens spilled down his chest, and onto the couch around him. In a stab of mirthful whimsy, the Stranger had placed a coin, Pixeldrome logo up, over each eye.

Insert two credits for the boatman and press Start for your ticket to hell, Rob.

In the dead man's lap, under a smattering of stray tokens, was a thin stack of typed pages: a manuscript. *The* manuscript—or at least the first chapter of it—for *I Dream of Trouble.* On top of the pages was a little white card of the size and shape so preferred by the Stranger. Jenny picked the card up and read it.

He's getting colder
(haha)
You're welcome

Underneath, as always, was the little doodle of the man in a hat, peeking over a wall.

She let the card fall onto the manuscript in Rob's lap, and walked in a daze to her mother's arcade game, *Mystery Girl.* Just as she knew there would be, a new high score had supplanted Rob at the top of the list. Dad's trap had worked after all; the Stranger had merely been biding his time.

`2,801,789 — DEB`
`2,796,386 — ROB`
`2,223,945 — ASH`

Or her time.

Jenny stared at the top score. **DEB**. Even the World's Dumbest Girl Detective could have deciphered these initials. She'd just seen them a few hours ago, in Jack's yearbook.

"Dinah Eve Black," Jenny whispered to herself. "You tall, dark, and sexy menace! Beware?"

To be concluded…

ACKNOWLEDGEMENTS

Keen readers may have picked up on the somewhat episodic nature of this *Trouble* book, especially in the first half. That's because Marco and I originally planned book four out as a series of short stories. It would have been called *Dial T for Trouble, and other stories...* or something like that. There would even be stories told from perspectives other than Jenny's or Eliza's. We developed high-level concepts for seven or eight mini-mysteries and I began writing in January of 2023.

Three months later, the first three stories had bloated to 60K words and felt weirdly static. Jenny wasn't growing, she was just solving puzzles like a robot. Then I had to move twice in a few months (new home build) and was distracted from writing all summer. I started over again in the fall and wrote another 40K words.

I still wasn't feeling it. Perhaps I am simply bad at writing short stories.

Last Thanksgiving, I made the tough decision to throw out the short story structure and start from scratch. Pixeldrome was invented, and Jenny was given an arc about dealing with her depression. The words began to flow, and a completed draft was ready in less than four months. I hope you didn't mind the dark journey Jenny takes in this one. Marco and I always wanted her to be a character who contained multitudes and flaws. Her descent into a bitter, dirtbag funk felt like it was necessary to get her where she needed to be for the big finale in book five.

So a big thank you to Marco for being patient with me is in order.

And extra thanks to you, my readers, for sticking with Jenny while she figures her shit out. She does mean well!

Early in the process, I traded manuscripts with friend of the pod Kaitlin Reilly. This was a huge help, both in getting feedback from Kaitlin and letting my brain puzzle over someone else's story and gain perspective. Major thanks to Kaitlin for trying this experiment with me. I like to think we both got a lot out of it.

As with the previous book, my beta readers Ally and Kayla provided fantastic notes and feedback on the manuscript between revisions. Thank you so much for taking the time, and being such dedicated fans of Jenny and Eliza. Being able to gauge reactions from readers who don't miss a thing is invaluable to keeping the mystery properly tuned.

Our previous editor retired, so for this book, I went with a new copy editor, Lily Omidi of Ello Editorial. She was fantastic! Could not recommend her more highly! *Game On, Trouble* is without a doubt the most polished and readable *Trouble* book, and it is all due to Lily's excellent work. (Note, Lily didn't edit this part because I'm writing it later, so apologies for any poor grammar.)

My good friend Michael Manuel drew the cover art of retro '80s Jenny at Pixeldrome. Thank you so much, Mike! It's your best one, yet!

Thank you to our families for moral support. To Krystal for keeping me honest. To our podcast listeners for all the pre-orders. To my favorite Starbucks baristas Abby, Gabi, and Lexi for giving me free scones while I wrote. And finally, to the musicians of the 1980s for making such excellent music to write to, though I will need a long break before listening to any '80s pop again.

I've already written 19K words for book five, and it's incredibly exciting to get to scenes we've been thinking about for almost a decade. I promise the final *Trouble* book won't take two years this time!

ABOUT THE AUTHORS

JAMES TAYLOR is a writer and podcaster with many strong opinions, loosely held, about the proper way to fool your reader—without losing their trust or interest. When he's not writing mystery novels, he enjoys reading speculative fiction, haunting local coffee shops, traveling up and down the west coast, and playing with his cat Trudy Campbell. He has a film & digital media degree from the University of California, where he learned how to make playing video games part of the curriculum. He lives in the Golden State.

MARCO SPARKS is a writer living in California. He's suspiciously tall. His fiction and non-fiction can be found in various dark corners of the internet. He is the co-host of several podcasts, particularly focused on teen murder shows. Also, he has the kind of cats where, when he suddenly ends up dead, no matter how much it looks like it was an accident, they were behind it.